A DECENT DEATH

Stephen Eisenstein

ISBN – 13:978- 1722628949
ISBN – 10:1722628944

2018

Cover design: Stephen Eisenstein
Cover production: WPG Ltd, Welshpool, POWYS
www.wpg-group.com

Dedications

The dead
Eva Buka Fels – Auschwitz 1942
Ursula Sophie Käthe Fels
Martin Eisenstein

The living
Helen Theresa Rooney
Good friends and family who contributed more
than they can know.

The author is an aged retired orthopaedic surgeon who has been brooding for some years about the themes covered in this story. He does have a Holocaust family history but no family history of dementia, so far. He is happily married to Helen Rooney, a psychotherapist not in any way retired. The author owes her a significant debt for consistent encouragement.

This is a debut novel and it probably shows. It is published at the risk of causing huge embarrassment to his three children.

Apart from many professional research publications in peer reviewed journals, the author self-published 'Spinal Disorders for Beginners', also through CreateSpace/Amazon. Potential patients appreciate it for its demystification of a complex subject. It was written for Primary Care practitioners. They don't want to be bothered.

2046 somewhere in England, I expect.

I am lost. Again. I am lost in a neighbourhood I know perfectly well, a blighted urban landscape of decaying multistorey car parks and shopping malls. I can't remember what I came to get. Not mission impossible so much as mission forgotten. My predicament is compounded by the fact that I am stark naked. I have covered my genitals with my left hand, leaving my right hand free to open doors, where necessary. At every near-familiar turn, my surroundings quickly become unfamiliar. I know that all will be revealed through the next door. And then nothing is revealed. For the moment no-one seems to notice my lack of covering, but then the knowing smiles and giggles and pointings of passersby cause me unendurable embarrassment. What happened to my clothes? Where can I get emergency replacements? Answer comes there not. All I want is the sanctuary of home. I absolutely cannot figure how to get there and in my nakedness I have no repository for money. So I can't even get a taxi or a driverless.

Eventually, through another door I find myself in the centre of an auctioneer's cattle pit but furnished like a High Court room with oppressive but expensive wood panelling. On a dais, the Queen of Hearts, dressed in a mixture of Town Criers' and Law Lords' flamboyant robes is screaming in concert with an enraged mob all around me: "Too old, too old! Zieh aus, Zieh aus! Undress, undress!" I take my left hand away from my crotch to show that I am already undressed. Amid raucous laughter from the mob, the Queen points a craggy finger at me and screams: "Out, out! Put him away, away, away!"

A sweaty bull-necked servant dressed only in a skimpy leather apron frogmarches me away from that cacophony and towards a furnace. I can see the flames and hear the roaring through the gap where the doors don't quite meet. The doors spring open and the heat blasts towards me. As I am pushed towards the flames, everything turns grey and I wake. Not shouting and shooting bolt upright and sweat-soaked panting like in the movies. Just quietly shattered. Again. It always takes me many seconds to convince myself that none of that was true or real. Just real in my head, and that is real enough for anyone. Really. Too much childhood Alice and Looking Glass and Wonderland and too many Holocaust stories? Now I occupy a wonderland of my own.

Another old man, another bearded Jew, from long ago and far away said that dreams were the unfinished business of the day. I suppose I must have a lot of unfinished business from the past thousand days and more. In this place my dreams and nightmares are the only movies available to me.

. . . .

Ho Hum. Piggy's Bum. Where to begin? Can it matter? Treason carries the death penalty, unless the court elects for a life sentence through some sort of mitigation. Such as my End Day, only four years away. Meaning, why execute me when with a little patience the state will feel obliged to execute me anyway because I will have turned 70? In any event I suspect I will be here for a good while yet, whatever form of execution awaits. So I can begin anywhere. I am not allowed any kind of computer or word processor, but after repeated begging, at last I have pens and paper. Mad. I could stab one of my teasing keepers in the eye with an ancient pencil – quickest way to the brain – but couldn't harm a fly with a computer and no internet. Perhaps they want to start punishing me before sentence is passed, on the grounds that execution would be too good for me.

Do I deserve this punishment? There are so many punishable acts & thoughts in one lifetime, but my so-called treason is the least of them. Here is a list of some sins then, to make a start: naivety, infidelity, sarcasm, arrogance, and once in a rage asking a group of prominent and respectable religious whether they thought God had fucked my mother. So add anger and blasphemy. Also vanity, abandonment, and jealousy. Maybe I deserve this punishment but certainly not for treason.

I must write or I shall go mad myself. I have nothing else. No papers, books, TV, radio. Certainly no ComCam. No view of the outside world. Good

3

old-fashioned solitary confinement. But I do hear countryside sounds occasionally. Sheep. And rain. Seemingly endless rain. Bleating sheep. Black sheep, like me? Who knows, or cares? But this is England so the chances are, in sheep democracy, they will be white.

What I don't hear is the sound of any other prisoner in this place. Surely all this: house, guards, food, heating, ventilation, cannot be for me alone. Even if I am not alone, there cannot be many other prisoners here: too quiet. I must be terribly important, That thought gives me some satisfaction.

But I feel a need to explain myself to myself. I can do this best by writing things down. Who else will read this? Nobody. So I might as well get on with it.

Baa baa black sheep, Have you any wool?
Yes sir yes sir, Three bags full
One for the master, One for the dame
And one for the little boy
Who lives down the lane

Ho Hum. Piggy's Bum. From whence came that? Fruits of an expensive prep school education a life ago.

And Apophis the Snake draws near. Who knows or cares? Too few, it seems.

. . . .

LIFO. Last In, First Out. One of the acronyms of warehousing of non-perishable goods, for best benefit of the balance sheet. Also a cruel rule of very perishable memory, it seems, memory being some of the merchandise of the brain. I can't remember what I did yesterday, living my life in solitary and in my failing head; Last In, First Out. And yet I can remember rhymes and scenes from my childhood with near perfection. And that article on warehousing, probably found in a barber-shop magazine half a lifetime ago. Last In, First Out. Not much benefit to the balance sheet of my mind. I have a dreadful fear that I may be turning into my father. *Tick tock.* Time will tell.

Solitary. I presume the intention is to prevent contamination of other prisoners with my treasonous notions. And rhymes are my prayers. Their nonsense gives me the comfort others derive from prayers to a deity. I have no deity.

Sally go round the stars
Sally go round the moon
Sally go round the chimney pot
On a Saturday afternoon

I love this one best of all. It takes me back to my childhood and a holiday at a guest farm. Sally was an older girl and I was smitten. A wild, laughing, urchin girl of the farm, dancing barefoot through the summer dust. Even as a child, I think I must have

5

been charmed by the rhyme's steadily diminishing astral ambition, from stars to moon to chimney pot. A much older boy was hoping to tease her by dancing around her while singing out this rhyme. He was Jackie Kilgardie, my handsome hero and then a suicide in the farm pond. I was told by my parents years later, after sexual knowledge had crashed into my consciousness, that he had discovered he was gay and couldn't accept it. Sally was impervious to teasing. Happy child. I never saw her again after that holiday. All gone, inevitably, with the passing of childhood. That makes me sad but what sustains me is the memory of that glowing sunshine time. And the fact that my guards and keepers just cannot get a handle on the rhyme. They can't find it in any lexicon of nursery rhymes. Neither could I when I still had access to computers and libraries and ComCam. I suspect Jackie made it up. But the occasion was so intense that I never forgot it. I just cannot for the life of me remember the name of the farm. I know that I know it. Just not connecting right now. It will come to me. What makes me smile inside is the suspicion that I may have heard incorrectly. Jackie may have sung "chamber pot", naughty for those days and somewhat less flattering even than the 'chimney pot' return to earth from the stars. The guards have not the faintest notion what a chamber pot is. I have difficulty understanding how different our lives must be for that to be the case. I am indeed so much older than any of these people around me in the prison. Irony: Jackie

Kilgardie would be an honoured and valued member of society today. Homosexual men don't make babies. Much.

And just for the record: from the clarity of my memory of that ancient time, I have no memory of the slightest impropriety on his part.

. . . .

Recalling 2016.

I will revisit as accurately as possible the scenes and dialogues which are pertinent to this account, accepting the fallibility inherent in the passage of over 30 years. I have no ComCam for verifications. There is little else to occupy my time and brain in my present accommodation. *Tick tock.*

That day. That was the day when all of life changed for me; the start of all of this nonsense, leading quite possibly to something less than a decent death. Dad had breakfast egg still in the corners of his mouth. And the usual care home stubble. All that for £1000 a week in 2016 money. I would 'phone ahead when I could and the nurses would make valiant hurried efforts to have Dad as presentable as possible for visitors. Cleanish and not too smelly. I was always his only visitor. On that day I didn't have time to call ahead.

"Hi Dad. How are things?" Maybe there was some surviving ancient voice recognition because my question was graced with a brief smile, followed by the usual blank stare into the far distance. Maybe that was merely a grimace rather than a smile? Like infants who grimace when they get ready to fart and doting parents rejoice in the precociousness of their treasure. Grimacing, folks, not smiling.

I spoke intermittently, reporting recent family news and doings, looking all the while for some hint of understanding. Nothing. Never anything. Not for the previous two wearying years. Then suddenly a wide-eyed terror took over his whole body. Mouth gaping and drooling. Hands gripping the arms of the chair in a failed attempt to rise. Arms and legs shaking with agitation. He started roaring, shouting, screaming. Orderlies came running to help him up, to help him totter away on scarecrow legs, trying to calm him with soothing voices.

Jack and Jill went up the hill to fetch a pail of water
Jack fell down and broke his crown
And Jill came tumbling after
Up Jack got and home did trot as fast as he could caper
He went to bed to mend his head
With vinegar and brown paper

"We'll have him back for you when he has settled!" one orderly called back to me. Devastation. This was not something my father had ever done. This was new. What could have triggered that dreadful fright and fear which raged through his threadbare mind? The other visitors soon stopped looking at my father and then studied me briefly before politely turning away, possibly now nursing their own dread.

I fled. I was not going to wait for Dad to "settle". Disbelief, shame, embarrassment, and fear washed through me in waves sufficient to make me dizzy. The vertigo of demeaning reality. Aghast at the human car-crash taking place before me. A surgeon renowned internationally, past president of half a dozen specialty associations, author, musician, loving father and husband, now long-term human shell, had become a raving animal bereft even of any animal intelligence. Only just enough mind left to perceive some nameless horror. Dad was 'Jack' with the broken crown. 'Jill' was Mum, 'tumbled' into cancer years ago and blessed by death from having to witness that day's episode overtake 'Jack'. Vinegar and brown paper was then as effective as any other treatment for dementia.

I sat in the car and wept. Out loud. I had not done that in my adult life, and have not since. Once I had got myself 'settled', I felt an additional shame. For thousands of families around the country and millions around the world, this could be their daily experience of their demented unlovable loved ones. And so many families must be nursing the demented at home. Care homes were the privilege of the well-to-do families in well-to-do nations. Self pity was not acceptable, but what was to be done? The world was being swamped by the demented. Confirmation came daily through press and radio and TV. Facts, figures, memoirs, and fiction relevant to dementia were pervasive. I should have known. And did know. As all the world seems now to know. I am (was) a health economist and this was my bread and butter. But no quantity of gee whiz statistics or stories of 'the lives of others' prepared me for the fright of that day and the evident suffering of my poor mindless shell of a father. Those were the days of the Alzheimer's Society and their impressive website. Long dissolved by almost vanishing need, thanks in part to the excesses which followed my efforts and my days of glory. Dementia cost Britain £25 billion in 2015; £30,000 per patient per annum; nearly one million diagnosed patients. Worldwide: 36 million cases. Dementia was the single most expensive disease then, double the cost of cancer, the next most expensive. Half the annual cost in Britain was borne by unpaid carers (Alzheimer's Society). You know what that means: families, lives, changed forever by having these unpredictable physiological preparations, zombies, living with them. It was my job to know these things.

Treatment! Oh, the expectations of treatment in those days. Aricept and others like it were moderately expensive, best for early dementia, and at best slowed the decline. In some patients. For a while. Then came the magic 'mabs', so good for arthritis but eventually not much good for waxed up brains. And then nothing, despite frenetic research. You can imagine the bonanza anticipated by the pharmaceutical companies, with the demographic time-bomb of increasing longevity. And the annual growth of dementia costs at 6% per annum in western nations. But nothing. Of course not! How can any fantasy medication replace dead brain cells. Or stop them dying, turning to wax. Can't remember for the moment what that wax is called. No brain cells, no acetylcholine (brain petrol). We were all living longer and longer, but not our brains. Lingering, not living, and lingering seemingly endlessly.

Humpty Dumpty sat on a wall
Humpty Dumpty had a great fall
All the king's horses
And all the king's men
Couldn't put Humpty together again

My dad was my Humpty. He was 78 not long before That Day. He was beyond help by 76 and pretty well without any useful memory after 74. I remember distinctly having to help him with the

11

names of people, places and things from about age 72 onwards. He would smile in embarrassment at his 'senior moments' but carry off these occasions with his usual jovial charm. The senior moments gradually became the norm. The charm was displaced by distress, before the final descent into the darkness.

I consoled myself in those days that my father had at least enjoyed his Biblical 'threescore years and ten' (Psalm 90:10, as every health economist should know). What a pity for him that he should live long enough to fulfill the prophecy that ends that verse:
"... and if by reason of strength they be fourscore years, yet is their strength labour and sorrow; for it is soon cut off, and we fly away." How could I remember that by heart? I hadn't. Thank the dusty prison Bible, King James version. Who would believe that was still lying around? But there is the nub: not cut off soon enough; not flying away soon enough. Not soon enough for him, for his residual family (me) and for society (here speaketh the health economist). At least he was saved the unpleasantness of our mother's fate. He was already far gone by the time she developed abdominal pain diagnosed as 'gall bladder', and was dead within 6 weeks from ovarian cancer. She was 72 then, a victim of the pathology of her gender. So many. How many men die of testicular cancer? Damn few, but she was transformed from robust good health to a khaki-coloured wraith within days. I was bereft of the only companion I had

12

when visiting Dad. (I refused to impose visiting duties on my wife). When Mum was dying, I remembered the booming recommendation made by our professor of gynaecology at medical school:

"Every caring husband should give his wife the gift of a total hysterectomy for her 50th birthday!" That was shocking to us as medical students then, but his point was that these organs were both useless and dangerous beyond 50. Ovaries are tiny time-bombs hiding in a cavernous pelvis, well able to create widespread cancerous havoc before anybody knows of it. *Tick tock.*

Now here was Dad, useless for all, especially himself, soon after 70, and dangerous only in the health economy sense of being very expensive. As I drove away from the care home, the biblical restriction of 'three-score years and ten' began to hammer away in my head. The miracle of modern medicine and social improvement had doubled life expectancy of the body in 5,000 years, but not of the brain. Forty was a good age when the Psalms were written. By 2015 we expected nothing less than 80 years for most of us. Mum was an unfortunate exception, going quickish. Or fortunate? Not the best way to go but better for all (including the Treasury) than the protracted drip drip of dementia.

The next thought was unavoidable, especially to a distraught adult child and health economist: if both could have somehow quietly and painlessly slipped away at 70 or soon thereafter, they and I and all their surviving friends would have been spared so much unpleasantness and pain.

Amyloid! There it is. The wax. Just come back to me. Beta amyloid. The wax into which so many of our brains turn in old age, and too often not very old for that matter. Tangles and plaques of misbehaving protein chains. The chief feature of Alzheimer's, the single major dementia type.
How come the name escaped me earlier?

Goosey goosey gander
Where shall I wander?
Upstairs, downstairs
And in my lady's chamber
There I met an old man
Who wouldn't say his prayers
I took him by the left leg and threw him down the stairs

....

2046

Peter, Peter pumpkin eater
Had a wife and couldn't keep her

Put her in a pumpkin shell
and there he kept her very well

I am Peter's wife. The Department of Population Control has not successfully kept me quiet. I am the ultimate turncoat, traitor, treasoner. So here I am in one of their better prisons (or pumpkin shells), in a room of my own in what appears to be a country house very much in the countryside somewhere, awaiting trial, and helping to pass the time by rendering my own account of all that has transpired, in longhand, on real paper. Computers are forbidden to prisoners like me just in case I find a way of getting online sufficiently well to poison the minds of more innocents. My ComCam is long gone, by my own hand. The authorities have found ancient ballpoint pens and some pencils. Amazing but exceedingly generous. Such museum materials are not easily available these days.

Many would not recognise this as a prison. I have a large bedroom with high ceilings and noisy air conditioning (because the windows are sealed and opaquely painted over) and a cot with a mattress and bedding; a table for eating at and writing on; and an *en suite* bathroom. This must have been a substantial country house. There are two chairs – there is obviously no anticipation that I will ever have more than one visitor at a time. There is nothing here to resemble the hellish prisons of the last one hundred years (three thousand years?) of almost anywhere. I must be very important to justify such comfort or is it merely the fact that we British are so civilized, even for our traitors? Our progress from the days of Bedlam? Or is it that my crimes are so great that I could not be expected to remain in occupation for long – 'might as well let him have last comforts', so to speak.

There are pictures on the walls of country scenes of no great merit, my only views of the world outside, perhaps to act as substitutes for windows. Strange, that blocking of light and sight by painting over the windows. Even if I was capable of identifying my location, what use could I make of that information? Semaphore signals to some potential rescuers? "Hey! I'm here! Come and get me!" Fact is, I do know semaphore. Did know semaphore. Bristol Boy Scouts. It is unlikely that the exclusion of the exterior is intended just for little me. There would not have been time for window painting once my captors discovered I was on my way back. Who has been incarcerated here before me? What was their crime? What was their fate? Fact is, little flakes of paint have peeled away and I can see enough through the gaps to know that I am indeed deep in the countryside. Have never seen another soul in the visible bits of field.

I have paced out my room: about 27 feet by 21 feet. More bedroom than I have ever enjoyed previously. And just as well because pacing this room is all the pacing I get apart from running on the spot. I have established a set of exercises for myself. I must keep fit enough to justify a good execution, a decent death. *Tick tock.*

My jolly keepers won't answer my repeated question about the possible presence of other prisoners. I have done the thing you see in the movies, tapping on my bedroom walls. I used to know the Morse Code; Bristol Boy Scouts again, but all forgotten now except for SOS, of course. Have not had any response to date. Again, like in the movies, looking for intergalactic civilisations and hearing only silence.

My keepers had warned me to expect a visit shortly from The Inspector. Inspector No Name it seems. I have at least four keepers, two at a time doing twelve hour shifts. So that hasn't changed. The impossibly long shifts, I mean. I have named my keepers Matthew, Mark, Luke, and John because I am not to know their real names. My keepers appeared to have derived some pleasure in anticipation of the arrival of this Inspector, and my level of apprehension rose proportionately. That may have been their jolly intention. The residual half of my lunch of sausage and mash was still on the table, appetite having fled.

"So!" he said, before any conventional greeting. I suppose he saw that any 'good' in a "Good morning" or "Good afternoon" represented an unacceptable hypocrisy. The Inspector introduced himself as my impartial guide and comforter, and the link between my transgressions and The Prosecutor, The Judge, and The Court generally. The charge was treason, as well I should know by this stage, and as was usual with such a charge, the proceedings would not be complicated by interference from that antiquated institution of Defense Counsel. The Prosecutor would be happy to submit any exculpations and excuses I wished to record in my own defense, provided he considered such interventions appropriate to the process.

Average height, late middle-aged (like me), scrawny, round-shouldered, sharp-nosed, starey-eyed, dark-complexioned, balding, shiny suited, scruffy shoe'd. And a barely perceptible limp. My Inspector. Neutral unplaceable accent in a scratchy voice. The whole presentation was menacing but without intent, I'm sure. Unmistakable lapel ComCam, and pale chip scar visible above his right ear.

"So! Any regrets, Sir Professor? Or Professor Sir? Whichever way round I am supposed to address you when I'm feeling polite."

"Yes. And no."

"Don't fuck with me. I am your only hope of salvation." Quaint. What presumption! I had absolutely no inclination whatsoever towards engaging in any sexual activity with this repellant individual of brief acquaintance.

"It is your choice, with the power you have, to address me according to your preference, surely? My only regret is the Treaty, and anything I may have said or done that helped inadvertently to bring it about."

"How do you like your accommodation?"

"There are worse prisons. We both know that. I haven't heard any torture screams, even at night, real or recorded. That is a blessing."

"All right then – how do you like your prison?"

I shrugged. "It's a prison."

Or words to that effect. Thus my salvationer; not quite my saviour, I suspect.

Matthew Mark Luke and John
Bless the bed that I sleep on
If this night I come to die
Bear my soul with Christ to lie

(An uncommon version of a prayer learned at childhood sleepovers in the homes of Christian friends. Cheerful early introduction to the concept of mortality.)

"So. I will visit when I choose. I am directed to achieve your story in writing for the court's benefit. I see you have made an early start. If it was up to me, I wouldn't have bothered, considering the enormity of your crime. Considering the generosity of the court, I would expect your full co-operation. It is up to you to decide what to reveal. You need to be wary of submitting statements which do not match objective evidence in our possession. That would go badly for you. You are invited to write things for the benefit of the court, over and above what I may record from our conversations. You should expect that all your writings will be confiscated at the end. The guards will have counted every page given, so that there will be no opportunity for hiding any writing. On the other hand, there are strict instructions against any misbehaviour by the guards in respect of your goodself. You are welcome to leave messages for me in respect of needs and or complaints. We will begin at my next visit. Interesting though; the presiding lady judge made a special application to hear your case. I suppose that you are some sort of criminal celebrity. If I were you I would fear the worst. Vengeful women! Bad news."

'A lady judge'? Was this some sort of Queen of Hearts of my recent repeated bad dreams? He could have been reading from a prepared script. Goes with the job, he might have said. Chilling, professional, he knew exactly where all this was meant to go and would go. "… confiscated at the end" – he means at the end of me. Nice touch. And at home he is probably a nice man just doing his slightly unpleasant work but grateful for the steady job.

I said: "Surely the judge must recuse herself if she has personal issues with me or my crimes?"

He said: "No proof, is there? Just looks like it, doesn't it?"

So. How does one explain the habit in many, of starting every new discussion with "So!", just like the Inspector? As if what follows is essentially and portentously consequent on what has just passed, even if nothing has just passed. As if the speaker believed that all actions and words had a consequence occurring in strict linear order. As if 'so' was a substitute for 'therefore' or 'thus' but is really nothing more than a linguistic disgrace.

"Where is my wife? What have your PADDAs done with her? When can she visit?"

"She is perfectly safe and comfortable and in our custody. Under Surveillance, of course. Her old Department. She may even be amongst friends. So she can't visit. At all."

"Where am I? Where is this place?" I was blessed with a silent crooked smile of self satisfaction. Pointing to my cold lunch with half a sausage unconsumed, he asked:

"How is the sausage?" I had to take some time here, half suspecting a catch. Eventually, playing safe, I said with a shrug:

"It's a sausage."

It was almost certainly a pork sausage. I would have no problem with that, normally, because I do eat pork if it is quality. And if I have an appetite. Yum yum, piggy's bum.

"When will I see my defense counsel?" I felt I had to push against the margins because I had nothing to lose.

"There is no such thing as defense counsel in Treaty treason cases. You should know. Perhaps you have been abroad too long. The Prosecutor will present whatever mitigations he or she may consider relevant."

"At what stage will I be called to give evidence? It looks like I will have to conduct my own defense."

"Not at any stage. You will not appear in court. Not necessary. We have masses of evidence in the form of witnesses from your various meetings, public and private. Hours of ComCam evidence. Undeniable. I do wonder why the Justice Department even bothers with a trial in your case. Waste of time and money. You're only four years away from your End Day. They should just take you away now and get it over with." Ending on a preposition! And I suspected I knew well enough why the Justice Department would bother with a show trial: to concentrate the minds of others.

There was a crooked man who walked a crooked mile
He found a crooked sixpence upon a crooked stile
He bought a crooked cat who caught a crooked mouse
And they all lived together in a little crooked house

So. I have two reasons to write: passing the time; and as of this day, if I am to believe my Inspector, perhaps serving some plea in mitigation of my crimes.

....

Recalling 2016

I drove back to work from the care home, not concentrating very well on the job in hand of driving safely. Fortunately no incident or accident. Thinking back later, I had no memory of how I got to my parking place in the university. I had to check my face in the rearview mirror for traces of my recent distress. The afternoon's timetable did not include any lectures. Only one tutorial. I had time to look up some references relevant to dementia and its financial cost. There it was, as well I knew: the most expensive disease in the first world was also the least funded proportional to numbers of sufferers. What then would be the expense if it was 'adequately' funded? Several papers offered information on peak age incidence. I knew these figures too but on that day I felt compelled to see them again: after 70 the incidence of dementia increases logarithmically, algebraically; exponentially; wonderfully rhythmic words resonating like a rocket launch.

Three second-year students came into my office. I got the coffee going. I had scones on offer, the constant supply from my versatile Spywife. I suspect that it was the coffee and scones rather than my own scintillation that explained the high attendance at my tutorials. Three students represented two more for a tutorial than would have been the case at Oxford, of my own fond student memory, but numbers dictate the need, as always. There were malicious rumours about, that even the wonderful Oxbridge one-to-one tutorials were by then historical.

I believe I was able to disguise all signs of my lunchtime experience. I hoped that my students would have been sufficiently preoccupied with their own performances to notice much beyond their own anxiety. I rushed them through their respective presentations and offered token questions to indicate interest. I reassured them that they had all done well enough. There was time left over to chat, to help elevate my mood, to share my burden without giving too much away. Two lads and a girl. 'Girl' ? No 'girl', but a young lady in the full bloom of womanhood. What could have brought them to the dreariness of health economics? Perhaps the subject was the only one left that could be accommodated by the timetable after more serious choices. The young lady was Sara, not her real name. I was to remember her easily by what was to follow, the strength of her character, and the fact that she reminded me so much of the Sally of childhood acquaintance. One of the young men was (who I now know) to be Lenny Cohen, thanks to recent coincidences. I cannot recall the name of the other.

"Do we live too long?" I asked.

"No. Everybody wants to live forever." One of the boys.

Sara: "So why are there suicides?" Shy Sara, unexpectedly animated.

Young Man: "OK. Nearly everybody. What would you expect from a representative population poll?" Good health-economics speak! "Who do you imagine is going to say we live too long? Only the very sad and the very sick."

Sara: "Public polling doesn't answer the question. There has to be a qualification. How long is too long? Too long for what? Too long for other people? Too long for one's own good? Too long for the nation's good, whatever that may be? Too long for the earth's resources? Dr Stern here needs to provide the specifics otherwise we will be here all night." South Wales Sara. Seemed to have found her Welsh voice at last, with some vehemence, enhanced by dark red hair. Excellent.

"OK: here is what we'll do. My question is indeed the subject for your next essay and tutorial. 'Do we live too long?'". I gave one of the 'boys' the specific topic of the opinion of society; and the burden on world resources to the other. I allocated our own personal good and that of our carers to Sara.

"Remember!" I called after them as they filed out, "in this department, utilitarianism rules, and appropriate references will help you to a good pass. And Sara. Apart from a good life, consider what might be meant by a good death, and how many of us are likely to get so lucky. Consider the proposition that we need to die better. A decent death. Does that mean we need to die younger? Think on. Provide whatever evidence you can."

At home that evening, there was little opportunity for introspection and the problem of lives ending badly. There was a call waiting: my Spywife working late. No surprise then, with the Russians behaving badly. There were the expected tensions, manoeuverings, and increased requirements for surveillance of diplomats in the run-up to the war with Russia. I was on the point of consoling myself with a double whisky when a normally cheerful neighbour, diminutive Denise, arrived at our front door. Tears and hand-wringing distress. Harry had fallen again and she had no hope of being able to get him up. A second Humpty Dumpty in one day. We went across to their house and between us we managed to get Harry up on his trembly legs and eventually into bed. He was 90, had been on dialysis three times weekly for years and conversing with rambling incoherence for many recent months. As we were leaving him he asked in agitation if I had come for lunch and please to expect him downstairs in a minute. Denise was in her middle eighties, sharp and feisty and funny. Both of them charming and long-retired GPs. He had been an almost life-long amateur astronomer of high calibre, a member of several respectable astronomical societies, and in possession of a powerful telescope which he perched on a stand to poke through a ceiling light on the top floor. I had regular invitations to see this or that planet and its moons, but these invitations had died off in the last year. Now I knew why. In any event, I was seldom able to see what he could see and ashamed that I had to fake some enthusiasm. There was simply too much light pollution for my unpractised eye. His main interest was in the asteroid belt, and his telescope was irrelevant to that. He belonged to a band of selected groupies around the Sentinel space telescope, launched earlier that year with only asteroids in mind. He would chuckle invariably whenever I was about to depart, that one of them would get us one day.

"My lovely rock garden" he would call them.

Mary Mary quite contrary
How does your garden grow?
With silver bells and cockle shells
And pretty maids all in a row

Harry, the asteroid amateur, certainly did hold beliefs contrary to the professionals. He told me so. But he was convinced that one of those pretty maids would not stay obediently in its row.

Denise forced a whisky on me, so I had my whisky after all. That gave her the opportunity, after shaking her head in silence, eventually to say that Harry was no good for himself; that in his lucid moments and fed up with the rigmarole of dialysis, he wished himself gone from this world. We said nothing to each other about what we both knew was happening to his brain. She also wanted time with me to share in the good news. Their first great grandchild was born two days previously. All well.

It struck me only as I returned across the road in the dark and the rain but warmed by the whisky: here in the same family, one born in hope and one dying in despair. Who said that? "We are born in hope and die in despair". Perhaps TS Eliot. I would look it up. For the first time ever, I felt that sense, supposed to be the prerogative of contemplative older folk, of the pointless uselessness of life. Why rejoice on the occasion of new human life? This is not a miracle. This is a tragedy, many millions of times over every day around the world. Pathetic and ridiculous learned behaviour on the part of goo-gooing adults who know perfectly well how it is all going to end but who are universally in denial. Amazing – we just fuck for the most part without a grand plan, fuck and forget, and then hullo! There's a new human. No bad thing really if you can make a living out of it, as you could back then when the state would pay you to be a single parent. Now there is no money because there are too many of us, living too long, not working.

All because of too much fucking without thinking and mainly without contraception, even though it is free at the point of delivery.

At the door, on my leaving, came the feared question from Denise.

"What did you make of Harry's notebook that he gave you last year? Could you make any sense of it? He was so insistent that you should have it. He said you were the only one sufficiently distanced from his stuff and with enough brain to take on its secrets. He has dozens of them. Notebooks, I mean. That one was the only one he regarded as important." Ashamed again to be lying to this couple who deserved better, I made noises about it being very complicated and that I would have to go through it again more carefully. In fact I remember that I had flicked through it, finding only pages and pages of abstruse calculations and diagrams quite beyond my understanding. I would have to have another go, if only to salve my bruised conscience.

....

Reinforcement. That is what it was. In one day, my failing father, then failing Harry and the first great grandchild, destined to live how long? Probably too long. I am or rather was a professional health economist lecturing worldwide and advising governments on policies to maximise the good life.

My efforts were being sabotaged by the relatively recent stretch in life expectancy, at least in the developed economies. There was just too much life left in all of us, of poor quality for too many of us. Medical and surgical advances just short of miraculous were keeping us alive but not letting us have much fun. I was taking this personally. Why not? The demographic catastrophe of longevity was making a mockery of my job and profession. I had been dimly aware of all this for years but pushed these dark thoughts into the background to justify my chosen role in the life I had.

Spywife arrived home flattened by the day's exertions in attempting to keep the nation safe. Because she could not tell me of her day, I was free to tell her of mine. She was irritable and tired and unsympathetic and not obviously grateful for the whisky I dispensed.

"You know all of that, surely, or you should, in your job. Of course we live too long. So what? There are worse things in life. The planet is burning up, whatever the cause, and your problem will be solved when this blue dot returns to being a black cinder. Ashes to ashes on a planetary scale. Long life is not the problem so much as that there are too many of us using up too much of everything. Meantime Vlad The Impaler Putin is testing all of us, possibly into war. I am sorry for your dad and all the others but right now I don't give a shit. I am deep in compassion fatigue. What can be done about it anyway? Knock off all those docs, dieticians and researchers who are responsible for helping us live too long? Your great Rev Bobby Malthus got it wrong twice! What happened to war, famine, and disease – those great checks to population? Not sufficiently catastrophic! Not good enough! Even Malthus couldn't dream up the China one-child thing. What has that achieved apart from abortions on an industrial scale? All just little delays along the way to the inevitable. Living too long is not the only problem. We fuck too much". Pause, during which I was about to applaud, but then... "And then sometimes not enough. Sorry. I'm tired and becoming ridiculous. It is hard work trying to avoid World War III. I'm off to bed. Thanks for the drink. Let us hope that the Russians get fed up with Putin and chuck him. Fat chance – the Russians love a warlord. For imperialists through history, annexation has been an addiction that beats crack cocaine, and Vladimir has a really bad dose of annexationitis."

It wasn't whatshisname. It was Charles Dickens in Dombey & Son. I mean that business of live/born in hope and die in despair etc. TS Eliot. Why did I think it was his quote? Maybe because of: "I grow old; I grow old. I shall go with my trousers rolled". My father had a recording on vinyl of the man reciting his own words in that old raspy voice. Unforgettable for a teenager. *Tick tock.*

31

I went to bed and didn't sleep.   Wordplay banged endlessly around inside my head: dementia, dim-entia, dumb-entia, damn-entia, damnation.   I would make allowances for my gently snoring Spywife, obviously, if only because of the stresses associated with the merger of the two intelligence agencies, 5 and 6. Made sense I thought, but decades of carefully guarded turf and traditions would not allow the merger to take place without ill feeling and mutual suspicion. The government spy bosses were clear: chronic   institutionalised   jealousy   and reluctance to share intelligence would be sufficient justification   for   merger,   but   more   important, globalisation had made a nonsense of the concept of borders.   So why continue with MI5 and MI6 separated by a concept of home and abroad when no one was certain any longer where the boundary lay between the two? Mixing and matching people and departments in several different buildings had taken some staff to the edge, and some beyond, because of inevitable cost saving redundancies.

Spywife escaped the worst but along the way some of those she loved and trusted had taken a hit.

....

"Every life ends in failure! Everybody dies!" I would announce with something between a bark and a bray in my introductory lecture to first year students.

"'*Golden lads and girls all must,*
As chimney-sweepers, come to dust'.   Cymbeline, anybody?   Shakespeare having a private joke at the expense of chimney sweeps? Never mind."

Trite but dramatic, and we need tricks to capture the attention of noisy students who have landed themselves with Health Economics 1 as a compromise rather than a worthy choice. It is not the case that young college students lack the intellectual capacity to accept the inevitability of mortality. It is that they are young, and mortality is simply impossible.

"And every death is another problem solved. We no longer have to fret about how that person can be helped to live a good life at the least possible expense.   That is the point and study of health economics: the best life you can have for the money, meaning just a little money. That may include drugs but may also include rock and roll, and sex. (Cue cynical catcalls). And you have only one life on this planet irrespective of what beliefs you may entertain of the afterlife. (Trite again but I know that teenagers are seldom ready for the 'one life' restriction). You will be required to embark on a review of a fascinating mix of the humanities and sciences as they apply to the well-lived life; medicine, law, mathematics, statistics, ethics, ethnics, culture, and philosophy. You will be dismayed by two things: Health Economics One is not a soft option despite rumours to the contrary. And you will need to look deep into your own souls when confronted by the too frequent dark unpleasantness of the end of life. You have time left to abandon HE if you feel you have not the commitment for this journey. On the other hand you could find yourselves buoyed up by a happy confrontation with concepts new to your young minds, and the realisation that you have a fine mind indeed, each one of you, according to Admissions. (Something to take away). A gentle warning before we part today: one of your major confrontations will be with the concepts of what is good, what is right, what is moral, and most important, who pays. You need to know from the start that in Health Economics, 'humanity' is spelt (I write on the board) 'hu-money-ty'. Be prepared to have your current convictions, assuming you have any, turned upside down and inside out. But remember also to have fun along the way. Before your next appearance in this department, you should have a working knowledge of the following life quality questionnaires: QALYs, ICERs, EuroQuol, IQOLA, SF-36, NHP, ODI; and biographies of the great utilitarians from Hutcheson to Gay to Hume to Paley to Bentham to Mill, but especially Bentham. Child prodigy, polymath, genius, modern even by today's standards, and extremely courageous. This is Bentham country. You will surely have seen him enthroned behind glass on these premises. Read all you can about and by Bentham inside of the next two weeks. You will find your further progress otherwise severely compromised".

Or words to that effect. I may be making this up to some extent but my Inspector will get the drift. In its generalities, this account remains true.
Thus endeth the first lesson, read by the Senior Lecturer in Health Economics.

....

Recalling 2016
Longevity Tutorial, second year BA/BSc.

YoungMan1 was obviously dejected from the start. He simply could not find any population survey which posed the simple question: do we live too long? And which would have supported his intuitive expectation that there would be a massive rejection of that notion. The best he could find was the Gifford and Tinker paper of 2012. Good lad! I was a reviewer for that paper. Major publication. I was startled as he went on to rubbish it. The simple direct question was never asked: do we live too long? And he questioned the sample size: was 1000 enough to extrapolate to a population of 64 million? And then.

The whole drift of the conclusion was that we do *not* believe we live too long. Bring on more old folk! Altogether unsatisfactory; and inadequate in satisfying his tutorial task, he regretted. I was careful not to boast of my role in helping that paper achieve publication.

He could not resist the temptation to refer to that cliché of the 'demographic timebomb': the average age at death in the UK in 1964 was 65; in 2011 it was 80.

"Dr Stern, even if there is no consensus about how long is too long, we are living longer at one hell of a rate". Several other papers, all predicted varying increases in Western, Asian and Oriental aged populations – so what's new? And nothing really relevant to the greatest good of utilitarianism. He perked up when I congratulated him on his presentation and critical analysis. Good handle on the problem of sampling in population surveys. I reassured him that he had not missed anything. In the meantime he might want to apprentice himself in HE research by undertaking a survey of our own student population (thousands!). It could make a little paper suitable for internal publication. Big smile with cocked head and slow nodding. Health Economics may have a recruit! I asked if he had heard Prof Sikora (cancer specialist) being interviewed on the radio recently. No! (probably happened too early in the morning for him, poor lad). Sikora let slip that most cancers come on after 40. I added that Early

Man skeletal remains in Africa failed to show evidence of life beyond 40. Nice fit? Our cunning and ingenuity with everything over the millennia have given us a life expectancy doubled up to 80! The question remained: is that good? Or at least, is that better than 40? Deep! Nods all round.

YoungMan2 (Lenny Cohen). The burden of longevity on world resources. Happy lad. Had mined somewhat more information, deeply concerning, but which left him perversely cheerful. Recent trends in longevity in the developed world will bankrupt us all if these trends are maintained. To answer the question I had posed for them, he said, just adopt the American aphorism to 'follow the money'. The algebraic rise in pension and health care costs will not be sustainable. And making folk work a couple of years more before pension age, has achieved nothing but to keep youngsters out of the job market. Massive unemployment and its dole expenses will be the doleful consequence.

"And and and!" (so no one could interrupt his enthusiasm) "Remember the Accident and Emergency crisis of last winter? Mainly sick elderly with complex comorbidities?" He obviously loved that phrase and repeated it for effect and for its inherent poetry.

He was able to compile a list of the most expensive age-related diseases, from various sources. In order of merit: 1. dementia; 2. heart disease;

3. (together) cancer, diabetes, Parkinsons; 4. stroke; 5. Multiple Sclerosis and allied neurological horrors. Dementia top of the pops, beating cancer? Bit of a surprise for him. I had to swallow to hide my private recognition.

He presented figures for world costs, as best I can remember them: mental health $142 billion (mainly dementia); heart disease $123 billion; trauma $100 billion; cancer $99 billion; respiratory $64 billion; and so on, in diminishing billions down to kidney disease and diabetes. All expenses expected to increase by 5% to 10% annually.

How do I remember all that? All those figures? They are embedded because of what followed, I suppose. Our publication and what flowed from that. And because those memories are part of the one of the other acronyms of memory warehousing: FILO. First In, Last Out.

"Yes, and ..? Startling perhaps, but what has all this to do with longevity?" I asked, knowing the answer but needing to keep focus.

"I was just getting there, Dr Stern!" Offended by my interruption. "This is the crunch. Apart from trauma and a few cancers, the great bulk of expense in all other categories arises after the age of 70. The graphs go to the sky." He held up his computer in triumph, for all to see. "If we all lived short of 70, the world could so much better afford to look after us! The money tells the story. We are living too long for our own good and the good of nations. Modern nations." Grin with a giggle. "Apocalypse awaits". Such a happy young man. There was quiet for a while after that.

Little Jack Horner sat in a corner
Eating his Christmas pie
He put in his thumb and pulled out a plum
And said "What a good boy am I!"

Sara's turn. To tell us about the perceptions of the elderly regarding their elderliness, and how well they are affording to live well, if they are living well. Leaning forward to reveal a bouyancy of freckled breasts sufficient to make a viewing man gasp internally, she confessed she had nothing! That is, nothing found to assist her with her assigned task. There were no discoverable published statistics or surveys to answer that specific question. No one had gone out to visit old folk and ask them how well they were living, or not, as part of any study. Pubmed, the online list of medical publications in reputable journals, had articles relevant only to specific diseases in the elderly, and search engines had only adverts for retirement homes. No single survey looking for elements of poverty, pain, distress, depression, chronic illness, in any one population of the elderly. And on the other hand, no single survey revealing bliss in old age. Amazing. Certainly caused her some distress, voiced in the melodious accents of south Wales.

"BUT… a lot of stuff to do with dying and death kept appearing in my search engine lists, so that was useful for that bit of the question: what is a good death and how many of us get lucky enough to have one? Kubler-Ross was everywhere. All about grief and coming to terms with the diagnosis of terminal disease. Lots of Steinhauser and Emanuel and many others. Lots of ethics and philosophy but no numbers."

"Oh Dear! So we will never know our chances of departing happy?"

"Not unless we do the work ourselves" she suggested.

"So what is a good death?" I prompted.

"Interesting. All these clever people start off their papers or book chapters by saying they don't know and it all depends on which population, country, cultural context, ethnicity etcetera one is referring to. And then they all come to the same conclusion after telling how they interviewed terminal patients, their families, carers, nurses, from Japan to the USA to Papua New Guinea and for all I know, to Timbuktu. Dying folk everywhere want to be free of pain, free of distress, surrounded by family, and dignified. And at home. We have to presume that by dignified they mean not too much vomit, sputum, piss and shit in the bed." My eyebrows went up at the unexpected Rabelaisian terminology emerging from Sara. Then I remembered: this is Spirited Sara. She continued.

"The surprise finding was the absence of 'quick'. I would want 'quick'. Wouldn't you guys?" turning to each of us. "Apparently none of the dying want 'quick' because they need time to make peace with one god or another or some spirits or ancestors. So there we are: painless, family present, dignified, at home, and not too quick."

We three men thought that was good enough, but she hadn't finished.

"What is it with these academic sociologists of death? All over the place are 'domains' and 'scripts', 'domains' and 'scripts'. Why can't they just write English? I am damn sure they don't speak that stuff in the Senior Common Room after work!" I had to point out as gently as possible that poncy language of a certain kind seems in some circles to lend lustre to academic credentials.

She had still more. There was no discoverable evidence of a particular economic cost or saving in a good death versus a bad death. I reassured our dear Sara that she was perfectly correct and no penalties were at issue regarding the worth of her essay. But she added that the 'good death' literature included the whole palaver about assisted dying for those who wanted it. For the second time that session I had to swallow to hide a reaction. Served me right for imposing my own family concerns on my students and their researches. My dad had said a number of times, because he couldn't remember that he had said it so

41

many times previously, that he should be going to Zurich and let Dignitas help him be done with his failing brain.

Sara told us all about a membership survey carried out by the Royal College of Physicians in 2014 on the matter of assisted dying for the terminally ill. Someone in the RCP must have been wanting to test the appetite of top doctors for a Dignitas type service in the UK. The majority were against! I knew of the RCP survey; I helped design it. I kept that to myself. I asked Sara if she had any thoughts on the power of the 2014 survey. She said things about "majority opinion counts". I pointed out that I was thinking of statistical power, meaning validity, and happened to know that only 31% of the membership of the RCP responded. She appeared dejected. I did my best to reassure her. Obviously 69% of the RCP members were too busy or too lazy or too dismayed to respond. Perhaps too incensed to have anything to do with what they may have considered outright legalised euthanasia. Not for doctors to pronounce; that must stay with our political rulers! Thin edge of the Holocaust wedge. Who would want to be seen as a British Himmler? However, John Stuart Mill would have approved of the sentiments behind the survey. Other august British medical institutions were vociferously against. Yet Oregon, Washington and Montana had assisted dying legislation, without detectable fuss or having the sky fall in. Oregon for

19 years! The Netherlands for 43 years!! Also Luxembourg and Belgium, and of course Switzerland.

I complimented Redhead Sara on her broad interest in these matters, but assisted dying was somewhat peripheral to the questions I posed. I could not then reveal that assisted dying was very much occupying my thoughts: I was
already in discussion with Lord Sparrow's group trying to get his Assisted Dying bill through parliament. My poor dad would not have travelled to Zurich really, and there was nothing available here. I could not resist however, telling how it was when I was a medical student, a time I think when there was more wisdom and less oppressive oversight, and certainly no National Institute for Health and Care Excellence. NICE.

"We knew what to do back then, or at least our consultant bosses did. A terminal patient would have to be kept pain free, whatever it took. That was the order that went out to the nursing staff and heroic doses of morphine would be prescribed. Eventually the patient died quietly of respiratory failure and that was the end of the matter. A decent death. Nice. The medical profession has been conducting assisted dying for generations as an expression of common humanity and because we could. Nobody boasted or even discussed what was going on. Was that what Shipman was doing? No. His victims were not terminal in hospital. Now, if it got out, we would all go to jail."

Quiet again. Were these kids shocked? Time to move on.

I remember finding myself in Sara's full gaze. I remember because of what followed later; never to be forgotten. She must have caught me glancing repeatedly at her half-exposed breasts. I remember she dropped her gaze halfway to the notes in her lap, with my crutch in her line of sight. Could she see the uncontrolled and uncomfortable bulge? Oh Deah! She added a knowing smile briefly, letting me know where the power lay. With her. Tit for tat. I had to end these dangerous few seconds quickly.

"In what premises are you most likely to have a good death?" They all knew that had to be at home. "Anyone listen to last year's Reith lectures? No? Atul Gawande? No? The pre-operative checklist? No? He is a cancer surgeon in the US. He said: patients have priorities other than merely living longer. A physician in the audience said: all my patients are terminally ill but do not fear death – they fear returning to hospital for more tests. Yes, 'east/west, home is best'."

"Now that we have our own working definition of good and bad in the dying business, what is more expensive, budding health economists? A good death or a bad death? Sara?" Shrugs in demurral again.

"No good studies that I know of," I agreed, "but at a guess I would say that 'lingering' in a bad death would end up more expensive, especially with those diseases which require expensive medications to extend life. That's intuitive, but not evidence. Finally, which is more common? 'Good' or 'Bad'? I can tell you straight off – nobody knows. I don't think anyone thought to ask. I have an idea, short of an expensive national poll. Go look at the death notices in the newspapers. I used to do that as a youngster, for reasons I cannot now fathom. What sticks in my mind is the semi-universal phrase '...after a long illness bravely borne'. Horror. Go count those, against the ones that say '...suddenly taken from us'. In other words, see how many in the paper 'die in despair'. A decent death is not for most of us, I'm afraid."

Or words to that effect. As they filed out satisfied – all had passed – "Lots of academic opportunity here folks, if you have an interest." Attempts at recruitment must never stop. Sara's bouncing breasts passed close to me at the door, as she greeted me on departure. It did occur to me then that the right tits and the right voice could get a man's ship to drag its anchor. Well, this man's ship and anchor.

That is roughly how I remember that tutorial, with some license regarding the dialogue. I remember it because it stirred all sorts of ideas in my head at a time when personal circumstances caused me some emotional upheaval. So much dying and so much living in one day. And no real opportunity to share.

....

45

2046

An Inspector calls

"So! One of the tasks set me by the Department of Population Control is to have me discover how the population control 'master of the universe' (crooking the index fingers of both hands) became a population control traitor and on the point of stoking insurrection. I suggest we go back to 2017, 2018. To help you remember, those were the years of the War with Russia. You had just published the paper which caused such a stir in academic circles, and the media made a great meal of it too, in spite of the distraction of the war, according to my investigations. I have a copy here."

Half-frame spectacles extracted from their case and positioned with a degree of theatricality. " 'Longevity: its implications for modern economies' in Health Economics Review". He dips his head to look at me over his half lenses. People with half lenses – do they ever look *through* them? "I see that you dragged some of your students into this as co-authors. Never mind. That is by the way. But what you reveal here are the impressively verified costs to the developed world of too many people living too long. You conclude with a warning that modern economies will not be able sustain these costs and yet remain viable. You recommend that nations attempting some sort of population control policy should therefore justify further study. So take us from there on this weird journey of yours."

He waited. I expect he wanted some affirmation of the obvious from me. I must confess that his nasal sneering arrogance got to me. I stayed quiet. Theatrical sigh from the Inspector. Equally theatrical removal of the spectacles, retained in his hand as a kind of admonishing weapon.

"There is something you need to understand. You have no counsel. That is the rule in treason cases. I should not have to remind you. So I remain your only route to engaging the court in some degree of sympathy for your declared position. So you need to engage with me. I will get us both some coffee while you consider your predicament."

Prison coffee is not something I would await with any joyful anticipation. I understood the need for some diversion. I decided I had nothing to lose by giving my version of events, resigned to the strong possibility of misinterpretation for the purposes of propaganda. All was lost anyway. And the legs of his chair were evidently and randomly of unequal lengths. He seemed to take particular pleasure of shifting his weight constantly to create distant gunshots of sound. *Crack crack. Tick tock.*

"That paper was perfectly innocent. All that was intended was to set out the reality of the situation confronting the developed world. Anyone could have done it. The paper stated nothing that was not available to anyone else in our business. But no one else had, up to that point, put it all together. My students were invited to join me as co-authors because they deserved that on the basis of work they had done and because publications are important for any aspiring academic's credibility. You need to understand that a good paper concludes with some suggestion for 'the next step'. Either more research or some other action. I was confronting readers with the implied question: 'what can be done about it?' China had had its one-child policy for many years by then. China decided to deal with the problem on a 'whole-life' basis. One child. Don't think for a moment that lots of other lives were not being created in China. It just meant that the abortion industry became industrial. And then, if your culture values boys, there will be many female foetuses 'not wanted on voyage'. So China was left with a new problem. A massive distortion of the social fabric: far too many young men unable to find partners of the opposite sex. Even you must be old enough to remember the Chinese epidemic of male-on-male assassinations of the 2020s in the competition for women? And certainly the abortion industry on that scale would never have been acceptable in the west with all the persisting religious constraints."

I couldn't drink the coffee. The Inspector had finished his without any hint of disapproval. Some civil servants, it would appear, were happy to abrogate all sense of discrimination for the sake of a free cup of prison coffee. He had by now abandoned his spectacles on the table and was far more relaxed, with arms folded, showing a semblance of rapt attention.

"So? Go on. Take us from there to national and international legislation as we now have it. You know, our End Day policy etcetera." *Tick tock crack crack.*

"That paper made no mention of any policy or any kind of wishful thinking. I see you have it right there in front of you. Perfectly innocent. You need to be corrected: the paper drew no attention from colleagues and others in health economics, probably because it revealed nothing but the obvious. I was very disappointed. Then weeks later I was confronted by the BBC at a conference. They have researchers going through all the top scientific journals looking for an item which might serve as a filler on a quiet-news day, in spite of the war. One of these folk apparently happened upon our dull article. The BBC must have been desperate. A nice BBC lady caught me out and that interview was the start of a roller coaster entirely out of my control. A classical media ambush. Entrapment. I had no perception of that at the time. Surely you have seen that tape or disc or whatever? I think the bad stuff started with her question: if the China solution is unacceptable, what is the alternative? As a tease, more than anything else, I replied something to the effect that if you weren't going to deal with the problem at the beginning of life then you would have consider dealing with it at the expensive end of life, but the BBC doesn't do irony, it would seem. I did try to say that my own interest was in a universal acceptance and promotion of assisted dying, at will, anytime but especially after the age of 70, when health care and social care costs became prohibitive. I was cut short and the BBC people ran off. Uproar and a kind of chaotic media frenzy broke out on the day of broadcast. Everything that followed was focused entirely on the previous bit about knocking off everybody over the age 70. Colleagues around the world took a ride on the roller coaster. In letters to our professional journals and in all sorts of electronic systems, I was condemned as the new Himmler, a promoter of the genocide of the elderly instead of the Jews, and much more. It was extremely unpleasant. Now there's an irony for you. You know that. I am sure your brilliant research can confirm all that. All history now."

I allowed myself a little sarcasm, knowing that he conducted none of his own research. He had an office full of dogs to do that for him. ('Why have a dog and bark yourself?'). He affected alarm at the passage of time, fussed with his watch and papers and spectacles. We would meet again? As if I had the option. Obsequious bastard.

....

Recalling 2016, maybe 2017
Health Care tutorial. Second or Third year BA/BSc

The remit for the three, YoungMan1 and Lenny and Sara, was 'Health Care in Britain: Past, Present, and Future.' Each one dealt with one of the three sections. YoungMan1 dealt with health care before and after 1948 well enough to get a pass. The Beveridge and Bevan miracle of the National Health Service achieved everything intended.   All the childhood killer diseases disappeared, or nearly, over the next 20 years: diphtheria, whooping cough, mumps, rheumatic fever, scarlet fever, tuberculosis, polio, but also malnutrition, rickets, and more. I took some slight pleasure in informing the trio that the Beveridge and Bevan miracle of the NHS was 100% overspent at the end of its first year of operation. Not a lot of people know that. But if the NHS was so successful, should it not have put itself out of business? What happened to transform the miracle into an unaffordable problem for all governments? Longevity, YM1 offered. Yes, and? I asked. No further offers from anyone.

"How about the man on the moon?" Puzzlement all round. "That is the shorthand I use to summarise the explosion in technology relevant to space travel. New but very expensive materials and imaging techniques quite suddenly made possible all sorts of treatments which would have been regarded as science fiction in 1948. Modern orthopaedics alone could bankrupt any NHS. I'll put money on it that all three of you have family who have had a joint replacement. Putting a man on the moon is only a slightly perverse way of describing how the wonderful vision of 1948 has become a nightmare. That other miracle, space travel, and its technological spinoffs, has done for the NHS. Longevity is the 'cherry on top' to make sure of that. Some irony here folks: the increase in longevity may be thanks to 60 plus years of the NHS, helping to make the NHS a victim of its own success. Who could have predicted?"

Lenny dealt with the present; the degradation of the NHS: no more money but many more performance targets coinciding with the increasing burden of the elderly ill; the fragmentation of the NHS from National to Provincial to Parochial to satisfy the demands of devolution; the mirage of private contracting out where costs hid the reality of reduced service. Private has to make a profit, so you get less work for more money; the disconnect between NHS and Social Services so you cannot get out of hospital those patients you take in; hence the chaos in A&E, and so on. Private health care covers 12% of the British population, and falling. In spite of all the negatives, the NHS had a 65% approval rating nationwide. The nation was in love with an ugly duckling. And finally, that so many countries without some kind of NHS wanted what we have.

I congratulated him on the 'less for more' and offered to quote him in future discussions and writing. Pass! What did he think of targets? Shrugs shoulders. I suggested that he consider the possibility that targets produce lies and oppression rather than action. 'Turkeys do not vote for Christmas' etcetera. I must have warned him that Americans can understand this very British observation if you change it to '… do not vote for Thanksgiving'. Did he know what percentage of the population over 70 had private health insurance? No, hadn't thought to look. Did he know anything about 'Obamacare'? Not really, except that it was as close as the US could get to having a national health service. Did he have a view on bedblockers? Those poor devils who could not be moved out of their hospital beds, causing the logjam all the way back to A&E and into the ambulances stacked up outside? Who are they? And if they could arrange to arrive in hospital, why can't they arrange to depart? The lad was stumped. Time to move on.

Sara had to do a bit of crystal gazing. What will happen to health care in Britain? How could the NHS become affordable? What can be done? It was her turn to reveal some dejection.

"It's all in my essay. But OK…. what can be done? The situation is impossible. The government demands annual 'savings' at all levels, from a service faced with increasing demand from an increasing population with multiple comorbidities but increasingly expensive treatments. More demand for less provision. More for less. Rather than less for more." I asked her to tell us about NICE, the National Institute for Health and Care Excellence. Did she think NICE was a cunning cover to employ doctors to keep costs down by refusing to approve expensive treatments?

"Well, it does look like that, doesn't it? But there are recorded instances where a NICE committee has advised in favour of an expensive treatment. Anyway, NICE by itself will never be able to save the NHS from collapse. What they save by blocking certain treatments is peanuts."

"What about going American and getting more people onto private health insurance, say, by persuading the Treasury to make insurance premiums tax deductible? Why not most people, not just more people? What about restricting government health care to the indigent, the elderly, those suffering life-threatening diseases and emergencies, and those involved in accidents? Everybody insures their holidays, cars, homes, pets, etcetera – why not their health?"

"I'm ahead of you there, Dr Stern." Theatrical frown. "Two problems. The first one is political. Can you imagine how long a government would survive that puts that idea into a manifesto? Surely not 24 hours? The NHS as is, is sacred to the nation. The second is the money. The cost to the nation of covering that list of yours would remain massive. It would mean a few more people pay for their hernias

54

and cataracts and so on. Peanuts again. And people would say that at our level of taxation in Britain, the equivalent of a private health insurance premium is in that already. And then I have run out of ideas. I just hope I haven't missed something. It just seems like 'free at the point of delivery' somehow just cannot be sustained. I have done so much searching for this tutorial. Dr Stern?"

Or words to that effect. I reassured her that she was probably quite right; that I had been playing devil's advocate; that I had no more ideas myself. They pass. I needed to wrap up.

"Is it then fair to conclude on a slightly pessimistic but conciliatory note to the effect that each country has the health service it fancies it can afford rather than what that country needs? And in many countries, no health service at all!" Nods. I pass.

All three took further encouragement from my instruction to combine their work for a paper we would submit together for publication. Because the health costs of the elderly came up repeatedly as the single major burden, they should put all their evidence into the problem of longevity.

Nothing is for nothing
Nothing is for free
I'll look after you Jack
If you look after me   Mary Piercy 1960

55

Sara: "Dr Stern. You qualified as a doctor? I mean a proper doctor? We have been dying to ask. Please forgive, but why are you doing this and not practising medicine?"

"First of all, I am a proper Doctor because I have a PhD. And by the way, it is my expectation that the three of you will eventually become proper Doctors. Medical doctors have the title as a kind of gracious honorific conferred on them by the public. The basic qualification for a medical doctor consists of two bachelor degrees, one in medicine and one in surgery. No doctorate in the university sense. A proper doctor is someone who has a doctoral degree, like a PhD or MD. Secondly, by the time I finished my house jobs, you know, internship, and finally fully registered to practise, I took fright at the prospect of the huge responsibility required of medical practice. I continued all the way through to qualify as a physician. Special interest in geriatrics. No glamour there but anyway that is when I bottled out".

Georgy Porgy Pudding and Pie
Kissed the girls and made them cry
When the boys came out to play
Georgy Porgy ran away

"But I also genuinely believed I could do more good for more folk – Oh Deah! here we go – by influencing health policy. Health Economics was the way to go for me. The medical qualification gives me street cred in the HE councils. OK? In fact my father is, was, a surgeon. I really don't know how anyone can do that. Thank goodness there are people who can. OK? Time to go. When we meet again, when? in three weeks, I want to hear from you what can be done about bedblockers, why over 70s give up their private health insurance, and I want to hear how we can make the NHS affordable. You are health economists in the making, I hope. Like me, you may not have the responsibility of healing the sick but you cannot shirk the responsibility for shaping policy. And... I want to see a draft of the longevity paper!"

Or words to that effect.

....

Recalling 2015

"Putin desperately needs a war and it looks like he may get one." Spywife was late home and fretful. I dispensed whisky for both of us. "His instinct for time and place is immaculate. Brilliant. Russia is going down the economy pipe but hey! He has a little thing going in Ukraine to undo the major humiliation of the loss of Soviet era territory. It is all because of a conspiracy by the United States and its vassal states in the west, don't you know. And the citizens are lapping it up. Putin is in his pomp and well able to keep his stable of tame oligarchs quiet while his approval rating rockets. He just took back Crimea. Because he could. Nothing said. Nothing done. Because NATO is bust, demoralised, and exhausted by our two decades in medieval deserts. No appetite in the west to confront this unreconstructed KGB thug with the whole nation behind him. He poisons old buddies relocated to the UK. He sends bombers cruising all over our airspace. Because he can. Are you listening to me?" I had to jerk my head up and make staring-awake eyes. "This is important. I know you've heard it all on the radio this week. But I was asked to sit in at the screens when the Russian ambassador was called in to be shat on for the rape of our airspace, seeing as how you can't call in Putin and that is the way it's done anyway. What you can't hear on the radio is the way he sat there, smug as a bug, a little smiley toad, loving it. The low level devastation Putin has created in eastern Ukraine has finally provoked a humiliated US into contemplation of arms for western Ukraine. Where does it go from there? You know. The ambassador knows. Putin is likely to get his war, and that will be right on our doorstep."

"Why not just give eastern Ukraine back to Russia? It's full of Russians anyway, just like the Crimea, and that could settle the problem? Ukrainian soldiers are dying every day in a part of their own country hostile to them."

Spywife reacted with feigned disbelief, head cocked sideways and down. "Don't be ridiculous! You sound like some of those softheads from '5' I have to work with now. Most of Ukraine's industry is in the east. Imagine England after we have given away the Midlands. And do you expect for a moment that Putin would leave it at that? Remember the addictive power of annexation!

And Putin has tapped into the national psyche of post Soviet humiliation. Humiliation and poverty together need only a messiah to change history. For Germany that was Hitler. Russia has Putin. Annexation is crack cocaine for autocrats. Goes all the way back to Alexander and Genghis Khan. Maybe you are not aware of the concept of the sanctity of international borders. How can we let Putin trample all over them and get away with it? What a precedent! And by the way, we remain trapped in unresolved conflicts in those same deserts, but everybody knows that too. So far we are all onlookers. I just have a bad feeling about what is to come. So many things are crowding together in a bad way."

Or words to that effect.

I wanted to be helpful. Especially as I found her animation made her sexually attractive all over again; heaving breasts and legs apart for comfort.

"If it is all up to Putin why doesn't someone do for him? He was well able to do a radio-active zap on Litvinenko, one of his own, right here in London. Couldn't we return the favour to the Russians? Shouldn't be beyond the wit of the Service. Or even one of his oligarchs dissatisfied with what has happened to their economy and their foreign assets thanks to Lord Putin." Mistake. Huge sigh and headshaking disbelief by Spywife.

"First of all, we do not engage in nuclear warfare on individuals. Secondly, Putin is surrounded by hugely grateful and protective oligarchs, most of whom are involved in re-arming Russia at great profit. You can be sure that any oligarchs suspected of suffering under the latest developments will be closely watched for any slacking in Putin idolatry. And we just don't do political assassination." This was not the occasion on which to remind Spywife that one of our high official government bodies had recently betrayed one of our citizens to the caring custody of a brutal and amoral autocracy resulting in his kidnap and murder and body disposed of no-one knows where.

Thus endeth another lesson. I remember a deep feeling of gratitude that world peace was not one of my obligations. Georgy Porgy was not just me but the whole of the West, it seemed.

Whisky gone. Night half gone. Professional pre-occupation meant hopes for sex were gone too. Again. Some discreet and priestly masturbation would have to do.

....

Recalling Term end 2016
Tutorial: draft manuscript and difficult questions.

"You will see that I have been through your MS with reasonable diligence. I have to say, I am impressed. I know you all have more demanding majors. I have to assume that you are either superfast or just not sleeping much. Most of my revisions are minor and have to do with syntax and punctuation. I have in mind a relatively prestigious journal as an appropriate destination for publication. We must make a good impression if we are to achieve acceptance. Am I right in guessing that this would be a first publication for all of you? Right. I have two more issues and a compliment. One issue is with 'only'. Somewhere, I think in the 'Introduction', you say '... longevity is only a problem for modern economies ...' suggesting that 'only' qualifies 'a problem' but I know you really intend 'only' to qualify 'modern economies'. So that sentence should read '... longevity is a problem only for modern economies ...'. Agreed? Am I a pedant? Yes? Am I right to be a pedant? Absolutely. Am I a fan of Lynne Truss? You know – 'Eats, Shoots and Leaves'? You bet. Who is Lynne Truss? OK, go find. I won't tell you. This will be a tiny taste of the technique of education known as FOFO. And I will not explain that acronym to you. Task your senior compatriots. But some few of us have to preserve this beautiful language and its capability for precision of meaning. Don't fret. You are in good company, unfortunately. Just be aware of lonely 'only', stuck out in places devoid of meaning even by highly praised writers. The broadsheets are full of it, like a contagion. Even the Economist, God help us. Seek and ye shall find, and with a bit of luck you too can spend the rest of your reading lives in peevish discontent."

"OK. Next problem has to do with a very good intention. That's in the 'Conclusion'. Was that a combined effort or …. ''. Sara has her hand up without hesitation. I have to continue with a smile to keep faith. "You finish off with what all of us are thinking, namely, the unthinkable. This article, remember, says nothing not already known, but its virtue is the way it gathers together all the damning evidence, for the first time pointing the finger specifically at longevity beyond 70 years, approx. But then you go on to say that the logical resolution of the problem is somehow to eliminate those people if we are to survive. Yes, because the Malthusian checks to population have failed, and, staring us in the face – there is no other solution. *But that is not for us to say.* That logic may be incontrovertible but that is for politicians. Our job finishes once we have presented evidence of this or that. We cannot be seen to be advocating the genocide of the elderly. And the journal would simply reject our article by return. That last sentence to come out, please Sara. No offence. Nicely rounded off even so." My hand up in a kind of salute to signal a satisfactory end to that bit of discussion.

"Nobody is listening to me! We've done all the sums and all the looking. Between health and pension demands, the elderly are destroying modern economies. And we really need to go now, Dr Stern."

I said: "We can either do away with the elderly or head for the Africa option."

"The Africa option?" she asked.

"No health care. No pensions." I waved them off, calling out that we may have to come back to Africa. Just so that I could have the last word.

Or words to that effect.

....

I changed my Health Economics introductory lecture slightly, after that.

"Everybody dies. The trouble these days is that we take too long doing it. We take so long that we can't afford it. We take so long that all our modern economies are going bust and moreover, few of us can look forward to a decent death. It is not the case that we simply live longer than at any time in history, but that we are living longer very expensively and mostly very unpleasantly. And modern economies tend to be burdened by a perceived obligation to treat all those expensive illnesses which encroach on most of us over 70 years of age. High blood pressure, arthritis, diabetes, asthma, high cholesterol, cardiac ischaemia - look that up!-, renal failure, hernias, cataracts, many many cancers, but top of the pops for cost is brain rot. Dementia of one kind or another. Dementia is not expensive to treat because there is no successful treatment. It is the baby-sitting of the dementia victim which costs." And so on.

I changed my concluding remarks as well.

"So what is the solution? How will this all play out if we do nothing? If we do nothing we all go bust. We are faced with the prospect of living in a dark and cold wasteland peopled by roving gangs of marauders. Literally, survival of the fittest and most violent. A genocide of the defenceless elderly will be inevitable. If that prospect alarms you, understand how come Health Economics has become a top choice of study in our universities and how come there is barely an empty seat in this room today. If that prospect does not alarm you, nothing ever will. Consider yourselves fortunate. And deluded."

"Again, solutions? One possibility is simply to decide not to treat the elderly ill. Let them take their chances with their bad luck to live too long." (Usually some nervous laughter and talk at this point). "Another possibility is to encourage old folk to commit suicide round about 70, in the line of duty to the state and succeeding generations." (More laughter of disbelief, to hear these words from a dreary academic). "OK. Off you go. Think about these things. I will want your better solutions next lecture."

Simple Simon met a pieman, going to the fair
Said Simple Simon to the pieman "Let me taste your ware"
Said the pieman to Simple Simon "Show me first your penny!"
Said Simple Simon to the pieman "Indeed I have not any!"

....

Recalling 2016
Happy birthday

"He's been calling for somebody. Helen, or Heather. Couldn't quite make it out. And he was getting anxious about being in time for his ward round, I think. When I asked him to say that again, it had obviously slipped his mind and he was quiet. He's been altogether much more settled after doctor increased his sedation. We are getting snatches of old memories for the first time." Thus Little Sister, the antithesis of Ken Kesey's Big Sister. Remember Inspector? 'One Flew over the Cuckoo's Nest'? Petite, smiling, kind, helpful new broom.

"Heather is my mother. Was my mother. I am surprised he is coming out with anything. I haven't heard him say a coherent word in ages. You know of course that old memories are retained better than recent ones. And here he is, revealing some indelible anxieties of his profession. Doesn't help him much now, that he was a well known orthopaedic surgeon. And thanks for having him look so smart. Yes, he is 79 today. I have left some cake for the staff. I will sit with him for a bit if that's OK."

"Hi Dad. Happy birthday!" More as a convention than with any expectation of response. He continued to gaze away, apparently unseeing into some distance. Then he turned slowly to me.

"Where are your notes? I can't see you if you don't have your notes." Words with perfect clarity, not heard like that for months, once again the surgeon in an outpatient clinic.

"Dad, it's David, your son". His gaze turned away and I had lost him. I stayed on in the hope that there might be more from him, even if from long past. Here was all that was left of the bright and cheerful mind of the father who taught me nursery rhymes and read me fairy tales at bedtime then later on Homer all those magnificent adventures of Ulysses this was the product of a classical education and musical could play the piano so well and I never could despite two good goes to this day a key signature means no more to me than a mess created by a spider come out of an inkpot and a competent wood worker going back to a gap year apprenticeship before starting medical school taught me to ride a bicycle and drive a car and swim I lost him then for some years to the rigours of specialist training and orthopaedic practice and academic achievement and international travel sometimes with my mother when I was older and giving papers all over the world and not lasting even ten years of lucid enjoyable retirement to me he was a Ulysses but better because he was never away from home for long and my mother never had to knit and pull it all out at the end of the day to keep other men from bothering her obviously I wanted to be like him he was not encouraging when I said I wanted to do medicine he said it was very stressful and a long training and in the end he was right but he was proud enough of me I think when I started making waves as a health economist even if the York gang wouldn't have me I advise Commons select committees he never did I remember asking him why we weren't Jewish he said we were and had impeccable ancestry in the Holocaust and all that but he couldn't believe in God that was fairy tales and mythology and superstition and childish and bizarre that intelligent people could follow that and my mother just wasn't interested anyway and that is me too no epiphany needed no god can help him now no god helped my mother would a fatal heart attack stroke accident at 70 have done him a favour he would have said yes if he could recall those few years of knowing his mind was going and his distress until he got so far he didn't know his mind had gone. We live too long.

"Would you like a cup of tea Dr Stern, and some of your own cake?" Little Sister broke my reverie.

"He thought I was one of his patients but at least he spoke. No thanks Sister. Very kind but I must go."

....

Recalling early 2018
The Nearly World War 3

The war in eastern Europe was not going well for NATO. The Russians had burst out of ... grad (name gone for the moment but I know it's not Leningrad or Stalingrad) by land and sea, just as predicted, and taken all three Baltic states almost overnight. Estonia, Latvia, Lithuania. Much cheering in the streets in all states. At least that was all we were fed because I suspect that those many who would have been distressed by these catastrophic events would have been wise not to show off their dismay in public.

Kaliningrad. That's it. (My memory for names is definitely deteriorating. Privilege of advancing years). And NATO countries had seemed to be in a competition to cut defence spending despite agreed policies. The war had further impoverished all of us, with expected privations on everything else including health. As with all major wars in the last two centuries, we were re-arming late and poorly. Huge arguments were raging between committees internally and between NATO member countries over uniformity and reliability of equipment. Language was another problem, and as always, frontline radio communication was a disaster. Tower of Babel.

Spywife was calmer. Now that the war was actually on, there was not much for her to do apart from debriefing and interrogating a few captured Russian soldiers. She would have been perfect for the job. Russian-fluent, going all the way back to that postgrad 'holiday' in St Petersburg. Charming and treacherous by turns, whether at dinner parties or (I suspect) during interrogations. Entrapment with menaces was her specialty. Part nature. Part nurture, in the Service.

It was about that time that I noticed one day that she had taken the car. Very unusual. We lived near enough by Tube to the riverside buildings of her employment to render such usage unnecessary. Turns out she had to see someone at The Farm. Service humour terminology for the Pirbright Institute, where they study things which kill agricultural animals rather than nourish them. I had my mouth open to enquire further as to the need for a Russian-speaking British spy specialising in surveillance and interrogation to go agricultural. Her waving finger and fierce look shut me up. Taking a Service car to The Farm would be a potential giveaway, was all she would offer.

Remember the 2018 death of Putin, Inspector? Not long after the Skripal poisonings? In his political and physical prime, together with how many of his close circle? After an informal dinner apparently in his honour (4th term as President) and to celebrate success on the field of battle? The reports described how all the victims seemed to just pass out within minutes of each other soon after the dessert, and beyond resuscitation. Remember the Kremlin palace coup and the set-up of a new regime by oil and gas oligarchs? The end of the war and the return of sovereignty to the Baltic states and western Ukraine? And in the years that followed how Russia prospered as the oil price recovered? All that. So close to a larger devastating war. I once raised the question with Spywife as to what she thought had happened at that dinner. She insisted she had no idea. She was lying. And she was letting me know that through intonation and gesture. Very slowly, with emphasis and fixed gaze: "I.. don't.. know!" Letting me know too that we would never discuss this again. Had I been instrumental? Had the Service taken on my flippant suggestion to Spywife? But we don't do political assassinations.

I do remember my end-of-discussion thought then: Putin didn't live too long. Lucky Putin.

Who killed Cock Robin?
"I" said the Sparrow "with my bow and arrow"
"I killed Cock Robin".

....

Recalling 2018 Autumn
College canteen

"It will look good on your CVs but that's about it. Made no waves. Sorry about that but there is a lot to be said for a quiet life." I handed out authors' reprints of our article in Health Economics Review. "I know it's online but there is nothing like having a publisher's print in your hands. Especially if it is your first peer-reviewed publication. Thanks for taking the trouble to make our coffee date. Sara here has decided to apply for a Masters in HE and will very likely carry on with me, amongst others. Thanks for your contributions. Pleasure to teach. Cheers." Thus farewell to the Young Men.

....

South Wales Sara, now slightly summer-tanned and suddenly quite grown up, wanted to discuss topics for her Masters. Then I mentioned the WHO project to improve third world health care.

Brexit not yet complete, so Britain qualified for a European multinational committee of academics, physicians, surgeons, accountants, and third world charity high priests. We had been commissioned to produce a consensus report as to how better healthcare in the black hole of Africa could be achieved. To what extent, and how much it would cost. I had been invited to join the committee. We were allocated Africa for good historical reasons; all the previous African colonial powers were European. My invitation had come through the Department of Health so I knew that someone on one of the select committees must have engineered the invitation.

I asked Sara if she would like to be an assistant researcher part-time. There would very likely be stuff she could use for an essay or two. Delighted. Bright eyes. Big smile. So attractive! Suddenly so grown up over the summer break.

I knew that the project was heading for complete failure before it started but I was not going to spoil Sara's pleasure by passing on my cynicism to her just yet. Large committees and conflicting personal agendas. Recipe for never arriving, but the journey could be interesting with a bit of travel and maybe even a paper or two.

....

Recalling 2018
Regents Park

The Regent's Park, to be correct. The European Commission on Third World Healthcare had picked the Royal College of Physicians (RCP, Inspector) as the venue for the conference. Great location to show off to visiting delegates, opposite the Park. Appropriate facilities for 40 delegates around the table; excellent accommodation and some of the finest private dining in London. Expensive perhaps but it works to get the folks together and the third world will have cause to be grateful in the end. Perhaps. Home from home for me and just a walk up the road from work. The chairman for this session was one of our knighted RCP eminences, suitably grey and gravel-voiced, fussed over by a hovering flame-haired Pre-Raphaelite teenaged minder, not previously seen on the premises. On later enquiry, she turned out to be a recently employed RCP policy wonk and Oxford graduate. Sara sat next to me, handling a stack of relevant evidence papers. Looking round the vast table, it was evident that the demands of gender equality were correctly observed, at least in terms of numbers, but I could see only one delegate not white. Well, I suppose that was going to be inevitable if this was a conference of previously colonising Europeans. We introduced ourselves in turn. The chairman was nicely self-effacing. I introduced Sara as my assistant, to save her any anxiety with this daunting ritual. At coffee later she issued a rebuke, suggesting that she was perfectly capable of introducing herself. Quite right. My mistake. Well-intentioned protection of that kind was something she no longer required.

Some of our visiting delegates delivered an oral CV with their introductions. Not a bad idea really but certainly not British. The first agenda item was a statement of mission for us: to define those countries we would consider "third world" and to record the present state of healthcare in each. Later on and probably at later meetings in continental Europe, would come recommendations for improvements and likely costs. All to be voice-recorded for a report intended for the WHO, which we all suspected of struggling in penury.

There was early pandemonium and a descent into shouting acrimony in a variety of accents. Wonderful! Compilation of a list of third world countries was not going to happen without multilateral disquiet. What was the definition of a third world nation? I was delighted but careful not to show it. Expectations realised so early! Order was restored when our capable chairman decided that we would use the impeccable authority of the WHO list. It was obvious to those who were watching rather than shouting, that this resolution was probably the outcome from advice offered by the Pre-Raphaelite Burne-Jones minder girl, leaning into the chairman's left ear.

We moved on to detail the existing healthcare provision country by country. As expected, and the whole point of this conference: sporadic, inadequate, mainly charitable, aggravated by endemic everything. Oh Deah! Malnutrition, malaria and all the other persistent and returned tropical infestations; yellow fever, Ebola (gone but not forgotten), HIV (very present and unforgettable), poor communications of all kinds (code for dangerous roads and minimal internet), poor infrastructure (code for no safe water and no consistent electricity or sewerage), unstoppable wars, and most endemic of all – "lost investment" (code for 'kick-back' corruption in high places). Malthus' war, famine, and disease in brilliant combination in a whole continent, but affecting longevity rather than numbers of bodies. Who around the table didn't know this anyway? The UN's own figures showed the best African life expectancy (South Africa) at 52 years, as against 80 for the UK. Southern Africa came off best but even there the lights were going out.

Here, around this beautiful shiny table were Belgium, Holland, Portugal, Germany, France, Italy, Britain; all previous demon oppressors and previous owners of Africa. We actually achieved a degree of consensus by lunchtime as to the devastation wrought by Africanisation of our respective colonial healthcare provisions. The "A" word was never used, rather the euphemisms "over time", and "recent developments". Our chairman suggested that after lunch we should study why healthcare had been better previously (had it been? for whom?) and how that could be achieved again and indeed, improved. We would break for two hours: several delegates had requested extra time to check in with their consulates across town and across two continents.

Lunch was an impressive buffet of temptation. Few delegates could resist heaping riches upon riches and then returning for more. I was relieved: there would be no spectre of malnutrition visiting these shores. There was time enough for some diversion. I suggested to Sara a "walk in the Park" and noted her laughing recognition of the aphorism. The early autumn weather was kind – that I remember – something else to impress those delegates who found the time to emerge from the College building. We walked in silence for a while. Sara started by asking if I knew any of the delegates. Yes, vaguely; some from annual professional conferences, some by name on publications and not previously met, and some not at all. But many *prominentes* in HE. Regrettably, I do not now remember any names. Also present were reps from WHO, obviously; Oxfam; Save the Children; MSF; Red Cross; World Bank; World Council of Churches; Department for International Development; Overseas Development Institute; and the rest. All the Third World high priests.

" 'All human life is here'. We should consider ourselves blessed. We should also harbour grave doubts as to whether Africa would end up blessed."

"Did you see that woman from the BBC? No? She was sitting almost opposite us, writing furiously on a BBC pad and also tending to her little recorder from time to time. She tried occasionally to catch your eye."

I said: "They must be desperate. Is there nothing else going on in the world? Did she manage to stay awake all the way through to lunch?" We had kept up a good pace and reached the zoo. I said it was time to make our way back.

"That is where they used to meet," she said.

"Who, where?"

"Harriet Taylor and John Stuart Mill." Ah yes. Yes indeed, on a bench in the zoo.

"You really have done your homework. As always, I am impressed," I said, seeing also an opportunity to make up for doing her introduction uninvited.

She said: "I wonder if they charged an entrance fee then. Otherwise those would have been expensive meetings, sorting the world's problems between them. Entrance is quite a whack. I saw the prices on the board." We walked on in silence again. After a while: "Do you think they had it off together, Harriet and John? Would be nice if they had." Before I could respond with perfectly correct total ignorance of the answer, Sara: "Those life expectancy stats for Africa don't look good, do they? Are they true?"

"They are United Nations kosher stats, and true for South Africa, the best in Africa. I don't think there is a true figure for the rest of the continent because of the difficulties facing data collection in primitive circumstances. You can be sure that the longevity figures for Africa south of the Sahara and north of South Africa will look a good deal worse." I could not resist adding, "They don't live too long in Africa, do they? Lucky Africans? And when you look further, not many Africans enjoy a good death." I presumed that the further silence which followed was occupied by contemplation of what should have been obvious to a bright Health Economics student but may have been a revelation.

We were on the sidewalk opposite the College when Sara warned, "Look who's coming this way! That's the BBC woman, with TV trailing." Flouncy bouncy bubbly breathless BBC babe, so happy in her work, just ahead of a huge camera and a fluffy bunny on a stick, both hiding BBC men.

"Dr Stern? Dr Stern! We've been looking for you everywhere. This is such an important conference! We would be so grateful if you could answer a few questions." I made noises about the greater wisdom of consulting our revered chairman on these matters, but she would not be deterred. The chairman had disappeared and diligent enquiries had been fobbed off by his young minder, apparently.

"Everyone we asked said you were the one who could help us. Please!" Hands upturned in supplication and head tilted with winsome smile. She asked if we could all turn a little for better lighting. Relenting, with Sara carefully backing out of camera,

I offered some homilies about how we, the fortunate well and wealthy, must do our best for the untreated sick and dying on one of the world's largest land masses, meanwhile doing my best to restrain my inner cynicism. There should be no illusions but that the task was daunting and would be expensive but a start must be made etc etc. I was gratified to see the BBC eyes start to glaze over, but as I paused in the hope that I had said enough, she suddenly focused fiercely:

"Your most recent publication has fascinating implications, don't you agree." I started to protest that the article had nothing to do with third world problems but she cut in:

"That is the point, though, isn't it, that what you describe as modern economies are just as threatened as the third world but in an opposite way because too many people are living too long too expensively?"

Where and how had this poor woman come across our article on the esoterics of longevity? I made another attempt to respond. I started to say that the information was not new, merely a compilation, merely sending a warning about the implications.

"Yes, exactly that, the implications, as I said. You focus on age 70 as a kind of watershed age when everything starts to go wrong in all sorts of ways, especially regarding our health and our healthcare and our pensions. But you don't offer any solutions. If I pressed you for any thoughts on a solution ...?"

I must confess to unprofessional irritation of high degree at this point. I said solutions were for politicians, not academics.

"Viewers might regard that as a cop-out, Dr Stern. Surely you must have some notion how to help us out of this predicament!" My annoyance let in the memory of Sara's academic suggestion of eliminating the elderly. The naivety of precocious youth.

"Well, in a fantasy world I suppose one would propose the elimination of the population over 70. What else? That would be taking the implications to their logical conclusion, but obviously.......". Obviously unacceptable in a civilized society, if she would have let me finish. Heavily sarcastic in voice and gesture, my turn to have hands up and head cocked, as if to say: 'Really! You stupid woman; what do you want me to say?' Strangely, she seemed ecstatic. Not at all insulted. Big happy sigh and smile, hands prayerfully together in thanks as she bounced away and fled with her team to allow the two of us to rejoin the conference. The thought flashed through me that I may indeed have said exactly what she wanted me to say. And as we made our way up the College steps, I realised that the College would have been a backdrop on camera. Nothing to do with 'the light'. Sara came to rescue me from my brief misgivings as we entered the vast boardroom.

"You were fantastic! The cheek of the woman, doorstepping you like that. You gave her both barrels! I would have frozen. I hope I never have to do that.

You can't teach that stuff in lectures. Brilliant!" Still, I would have valued a few more BBC seconds to make the point that, on the other hand, I was strenuously in favour of having assisted dying introduced into British legislation, with appropriate safeguards. Obviously.

There was a little girl who had a little curl
Right in the middle of her forehead
When she was good she was very very good
But when she was bad she was horrid

(I have no memory of my doorstepping BBC lady's hairstyle).

We took our seats. As we settled I noticed the absence of the BBC. Not such an important conference after all! I noticed also a creeping somnolence overtaking some of our number. Probably the poor buggers who flew in from the Continent. Early rising, much good lunch and a little wine, were the ingredients for an afternoon nap, however much unintended.

Our chairman started by asking whether there were any questions concerning the morning's deliberations, before we started on the vexed matter of recapturing excellence in healthcare for Africa. Still in a bloody-minded frame from the lunchtime confrontation and partially fired by Sara's fulsome praise, and also because I suspected the worst, I begged to know how many delegates had personal experience of and in Africa. That got everyone sitting up, some with sighs of resignation. No more than half had hands up. All the aid agency high priests had been, certainly. Our chairman had spent half his professional life in the third world, including Africa. He must have anticipated some nasty fallout from my enquiry and tactfully suggested that we move on. He caught my wink of assent, point made.

Post-prandial afternoons are not conducive to inspired new ideas for African healthcare, it seems. The discussion was desultory. The European colonising nations recorded their pride in what had been achieved under difficult circumstances in the old times, driven by greed but covered with an icing of European morality, ethics, and missionary certainties, and the solemnity of the Hippocratic Oath. Where in Africa, or anywhere, do medical professionals still swear the Hippocratic oath on graduation? I stayed quiet. We all had our hearts of darkness. Best to leave the history in peace and see what original thinking could achieve for the future, in what was left of the afternoon. At some point some wag only half jokingly suggested recolonising Africa. The embarrassed laughter round the table hinted at the possibility that this had been precisely the wishful thinking of others, in their quieter moments.

"Too late!" I shouted above the merriment. "It's happened, and you know it, if you've been there recently!"

"Dr Stern?" queried the chairman. I accepted his intervention as an invitation.

"China has done it without waving any flags or annexing any territory. But everywhere is a new presidential palace and a sports stadium in the president's name. And new roads and railways but only for the carriage of raped metals and minerals to coastal ports. And no extra healthcare for the indigenous population. China imports its own workers. I presume they are adequately provided for." Silence. "Did I say something wrong? Something anybody doesn't know? Am I mistaken? Oh yes! China, and the rest." Silence. "And then if I am not mistaken, can anyone here recall if a word of protest has been raised in the UN and the Security Council? No? Of course not. China had provided bread and games. China has bought Africa wherever there is something of value in the ground, from Sierra Leone to Namibia. Not a shot fired. Putin was such a fool to resort to a shooting war." Or words to that effect.

Not a useful intervention for the conference mission, really, and our chairman probably concurred because he adjourned the meeting until next day. As we strolled out it became evident that some delegates were at pains to avoid eye contact with me. But a couple came up to thank me for stirring trouble, in the best possible way. Our chairman strolled past.

"Having fun, Stern? We must all hope you will be more helpful tomorrow!" I felt the afternoon had gone rather well for me, if not so well for the black hole that is Africa. We headed east back to Gower street. Lovely Sexy Buoyant Sara asked when had I been in Africa. As a child when my father spent a sabbatical year in South Africa, gaining experience in the surgery of TB and polio; and eventually for my own recent sabbatical, in various countries north and south of the equator. Some good publications came out of that trip. May have helped towards the senior lectureship. We had a coffee in my office, just to unwind.

I had time to ruminate on the fact that all the ages of man harbour cruelties particular to each age, and middle age only slightly less than other ages, perhaps. Sitting opposite was a demure, clever, pneumatic, enthusiastic, probably spoken for, charmingly Welsh-accented redheaded Sara, suddenly become an object of intense desire, forever forbidden for too many reasons. I stood *in loco parentis* while she was my student; and how could she be attracted to one so much older, spoken for, slightly paunchy and jowly, and probably quite boring outside of work? Goodness knows, maybe even at work! Heading home, I had to consider how I might contribute more constructively the next day, to the salvation of health in Africa. Interspersed with intrusive fantasies involving Sara.

"Someone from the RCP 'phoned, moments ago. Young lady. Sounded careful, tentative. Didn't have your mobile, apparently. I've only just got in."

Spywife was home first for a change. "Your caller was quite insistent that you call back. Message from Sir somebody. Number is at the old 'phone in the hall." Pointless. It was well after 6pm. "She said she would wait until you called."

That was the first intimation of impending catastrophe. I phoned. 'Young lady' answered before the second ring. Very apologetic but our kind conference chairman was kindly requesting that I kindly absent myself from the next day's proceedings. No reason offered. After a few speechless seconds I started to insist on an explanation. Fulsome repeated apologies from 'young lady'; not in her remit and so on. I asked to be given Sir 'Somebody's' contact details. Not possible, she was afraid. I asked whether she was the conference chairman's 'assistant' this day. Well, yes. The Burne-Jones Flame flickered briefly in memory. Then relenting – clever girl perceiving how childishly ridiculous this all must appear – she said something about a TV news item on the BBC, and Sir felt that general awareness of this item next day was very likely, and therefore very likely to serve as a distraction from the work in hand. What item? Not prepared to enlarge. Oh god. Sick feeling in abdomen and a temporary threat of faecal incontinence. Regents Park. Must be. But what news item could be made of that brief nonsense? Rage and fear mixed, but mainly rage. What could be so exceptional about my few seconds in the Park?

"I am in disgrace," I explained when Spywife caught sight of my treble whisky. "Banned from the RCP conference tomorrow. Something about me on TV." I told my confessor wife the relevant bit about the BBC confrontation during the lunch break.

"Well, we should have a look, don't you think?" suggested wife-become-schoolmistress, obviously anticipating the need for recriminations to come.

"A prominent London academic and medical doctor has recommended the elimination of all elderly people as the only means of saving the NHS and the nation," followed by that lunchtime ridiculous filming. There was the RCP building the background, as the newsreader went on to say that I was attending a conference there. The wretched implication was that this should be interpreted as me speaking for the RCP. Suddenly there appeared the President of the RCP, another knight no less, to insist 'when questioned' that my gratuitous remarks had nothing whatever to do with any proceedings or policy stance within the College, and so on.

"Silly boy!" was the only comfort provided by Spywife. "What on earth were you thinking when you let that hussy accost you? Why didn't you just tell her to fuck off!?"

"I didn't *let* her. She just accosted. And you've seen for yourself, innocent enough to start with!" Spywife saw me furiously working my mobile.

"Don't even think of contacting the BBC. You'll just be making their further story for them. Trust me in this. You can't undo it, but you can make it run and run against you. STOP! We know about these things. All in the training. Let the dust settle. After a while someone will come after you for your version of the story, your rebuttal, etcetera. Maybe even with money! Finish your drink while I tell you something from my day."

She told me about some of the arrangements for Putin's funeral. Not yet in the public domain. Very secret, please. Very elaborate. Next week. No, not combined with the other dinner casualties. Putin too important for that. Day of national mourning. Spywife was invited to attend as a low-level diplomat in the British delegation. So far, no news of what killed them all, nor who could be blamed, if anyone. The catering staff had been thoroughly interrogated without result. No, she didn't know if any had survived the interrogation. Lab tests on the food remnants had failed to reveal any toxins or unusual chemicals. Spywife very calm now, and so was I. She seemed unnaturally pleased with herself. As if in celebration of something, we made love noisily and thankfully satisfactory to all. That I remember, from so long ago. And what happened next day. How could I not?

"Don't go near the street windows!" Spywife shouted to me through the shower door. "We're being papped! The street is black with cameras. Great work. You've hit the big time, and this is something I really don't need." She would go out the back and take the car to work. She thought I should stay in, for the day at least. No, I was not going to stay in. I was going to walk to the university as I did every day. This storm was not of my making. I had nothing to hide. She warned me to look straight ahead and say absolutely nothing however provocative the inevitable shouted questions would be.

....

2047 Inspector 'Jack' and recalling winter 2017

My keepers were amused, laughing and joking about something incomprehensible, until I caught a snatch of chatter.

"Have you seen his wife? She's huge! What a pair!" Another voice, "Watch it. He's on his way here right now to see our naughty professor."

He wanted me to recount the events of my Day of Disgrace and beyond. I told him I was not prepared to start on this venture if he was going to dash away as in the recent past. He assured me he had no deadlines and all his attention was fixed on me. I proceeded.

The noise of the baying pack as I emerged from the front door took me by surprise in spite of Spywife's warning. The forest of microphones being pushed into my face was almost suffocating and the flashing cameras temporarily blinded me. Apparently this is what it was like to be famous. Or notorious. No difference really. "Dr Stern! Do you want to kill my grandparents?" "Five thousand marathon runners are in their seventies. You want to kill them?"

Obedient to recent wisdom, I walked on northwards saying nothing, not allowing any eye contact. They trotted after me for a block or two, shouting stuff about a new holocaust and how long had I been a Nazi, and so on. Very unpleasant. The last of them eventually drifted away and I was left in peace. Until I passed a newsagent. "Geriatric Genocide!" "Doctor wants our old folk to save the nation – they must die." Or words to that effect. Again and again. That was when I realised after all these years of walking to work, how many newsagents there were along the way. I got to my office door in the Department without further stimulus to the turmoil in my head, there to find I couldn't unlock it. Wrong code? Try again. Stumped.

The departmental secretary was thankfully already in her office, crestfallen. Apparently I was suspended and the Head of Department said I was not to be found on the premises at all and a letter was on its way setting out all the conditions there was to be a full enquiry into recent events hopefully to end in my complete exoneration and return to full duties she was so sorry she didn't know what to say showing me a funeral face as if I had already fallen off a cliff.

I asked if I could see the Head. Sorry, again. She was closeted with the Press Office people. I thanked her for kindness and discretion. She was not about to quiz me on how I fell from grace. I was beginning to feel lightheaded with anger. I could sense witch hunt, so early in the morning, in this university with all its claims to academic freedom and diversity and all that shit. I got to the Dean's office. No one about, all locked up, too early for the likes of them probably. I got across to the Vice Chancellor's building with legs rapidly turning to jelly. His PA was in position with a cup of coffee and a newspaper showing my face flinty eyed and lips pursed as when I was trying to finish my sentence to the BBC in the Park with the RCP building behind. 'Granny and Grandpa for the chop. Famous doctor: "They bankrupt the nation."' When the same face appeared at her door, the poor lass could not hide a moment of shock-look, then surreptitiously slowly turning the page to hide the picture. The Vice Chancellor was in China at a recruitment conference. Would I like to leave a message? He collects his emails every day. It would be late night in China right now, but he would get it next morning.

Dead man walking, and not walking very well. Our street was clear by the time I got home. There must have been other scandals to manufacture that day. For the first time ever in my life, I started drinking in the morning. Whisky for breakfast, waiting for the tumble–drier of mixed up questions and fantasies of revenge sloshing around in rage, to slow and stop.

I don't remember much detail of the days that followed. I stayed indoors, temporarily imprisoned, happy to notice that there were fewer media people out front each successive day. I ate little but made short work of several bottles of whiskey – yes, Irish; smoky and best value for the money. That would be keeping to the principles of Health Economics. I do remember making many calls to the various institutions which made up the sand castle of my professional life: the university, the RCP, the secretaries of the parliamentary committees I had advised, publishers, journals I served as reviewer, colleagues. It had not taken much time to become a non-person. The university was reviewing my circumstances but I should consider myself suspended on full pay and please to remain off the premises until further notice. I remember making more visits to my father because it helped to fill the day. Taxis made sure it didn't matter if I was not quite sober. I was a dead man visiting a dead man who persisted in continuing to breathe in and out and stare into nowhere. On every occasion I made the effort of trying to reconcile my memory of this brilliant man with the spectre before me, and failed. I wrote a maudlin review article on death in dementia, mostly under the benign influence of whiskey. The Observer magazine took it. It earned faint praise and lifted my mood a little.

The RCP conference ended as expected with some fine resolutions but no planned action. I had been allowed back for the last day with strenuous requests to maintain a small presence. Colleagues were mostly sympathetic but having to dash off sorry mate it will all get sorted out don't worry personally don't understand what all the fuss is about. One or two buddies in the HE business surprised me with a poor facility for hiding a gloating tone. Ah well.

I certainly felt a need for exoneration through explanation of my view of this mad affair. Pleading innocence, perfectly justified. I detected a fear of contamination by association. Even Spywife reported concerns expressed by one of her bosses as to the risk of contamination. A temporary transfer to the spies' 'doughnut' (GCHQ) at Cheltenham was being considered. Apart from one expression of annoyance to the effect that my very public notoriety was unwelcome, she was very supportive, probably still buoyed by recent successes in Moscow, I guessed. Sara remained loyal. Got my number from the department.

Called daily to report departmental gossip and make encouraging noises. Cunningly careful not to sound patronising, I noted, student to senior lecturer.

....

All change. How many days later? Can't remember but an old-fashioned letter arrived by courier, to be signed for, from a Treasury Permanent Under-Secretary asking if we could meet. Would send a car. I was to report a media 'all clear' outside, beforehand. Expressed regret about recent publicity but that publicity had brought to their notice certain possibilities etc etc. Vague as hell, but sounding warm and friendly. Somebody semi-important wanted me, god knows for what, but most of us want to be wanted, and I had reached a point where I was more than happy to be wanted, by anybody. I was at home to sign for the letter because that is where the whiskey was, with general home comforts.

It was wonderful, some days later, to sweep chauffeured into a Whitehall car park and be ushered into a commodious plush office as for someone who somehow mattered. Not easily forgotten, Inspector, even after all these years. Dark panelling bearing a variety of framed certificates, group photographs certain to commemorate presumed close acquaintance with many prominent and famous. There was a faintly familiar heraldic crest. Only later did I realise that this boasted Jesus College, my own!

The Permanent Under-Secretary (PUS) remained engrossed for some seconds in his very pressing labours at a too-large desk, before glancing up as if caught unawares, then rising very erect to an impressive height to perform an effusive welcome.

Tight-lipped smile, firm handshake out of a regulation three-piece pin-striped suit. Booming big voice out of a large jowly head, a mane of silver hair; a lion of the civil service. So pleased I could make the time to see him. He guided me to an alcove of leather armchairs. So much admired my work. Really? He was impressed that an academic had so well grasped the conundrum of how the benefit of long life turned out to pose a threat to the financial viability of the nation. And indeed, all modern economies, just as I had written. He had done his homework, he announced with evident pride. Well, we know that someone did it for him, but he felt that I was just the person to do a job of work for the government, and he was not alone in this judgment.

The only snag was that he couldn't tell me what the job was until we had completed the small matter of having me sign the Official Secrets Act. Would I like to have a coffee while he left me with his PA to go through the motions? I expressed a concern about not wanting to compromise my academic independence by being discovered to be working for the government.

"Oh nonsense, Doctor, everybody of worth does it, including your own Vice Chancellor! How can we progress otherwise? After all, what do you call your work advising various Select Committees?"

I started to say something about my real interest being the promotion of the assisted dying concept for Britain, but he heard none of that while ushering me into the care of his PA. The OSA form was a single page with Ministry of Defence references all over it, even numbered MOD 134. The PA saw my alarm and reassured me that the form applied to all government secrets. No one from the Army was going to hunt me down and shoot me, ha ha. Still, any breach would be a hanging offence ha ha. It took all of thirty seconds to sign, all done even before my coffee arrived.

I suddenly felt like Alice in Wonderland, and I was at a mad coffee party with a modern March Hare or a Mad Hatter. Or even a Jabberwock? This experience was taking on elements of the surreal. Of all departments, why was HM Treasury grooming me? In my disgrace? Why the Official Secrets Act? But I had a trump card for when the PUS returned, all bustling busyness and confidence: I had nowhere to work. So sorry, he forgot to mention, that had all been sorted out. I would be welcomed back to the university in the new year in glory, he was sure, and not merely as a prodigal. All changed. My department at the university had received a financial windfall. Smile and wink. Enough even for a funded PhD for a student of my choice. Did I like old movies? Follow the money. You know, the Deep Throat one. Can't remember the title. Now, that is exactly what he wanted me to do for Her Majesty's Treasury. As thoroughly as possible, over the next three to six months.

"How much money could the nation save in terms of health and pensions if there was no one alive over the age of say, 70? No no, my dear man don't look aghast this is a fantasy exercise entirely theoretical just playing games here but an important factor in policy discussions in HMT good lord you don't think we would really want to knock off the oldies they are my parents after all but you must have guessed by now that the nation is bust so is the whole of Europe and the US nearly so and no prospect of salvation in sight if we were a sole trader we would be declared bankrupt and not allowed to trade dry as a witch's tit total meltdown Greece is not the end only the beginning after all it was in your own paper that we found the hint for how things may have to go that BBC interview brought you to our attention we can't do this stuff 'in house' this place leaks like a vintage British motorcycle ha ha very sensitive stuff very sensitive." I asked whether I could have a few days to consider.

"Don't be daft; this is too important and too urgent. Don't be so ungrateful."

Old Mother Hubbard
Went to the cupboard
To get her poor dog a bone
When she got there
The cupboard was bare
So the poor little dog had none

I asked whether this was not properly within the ambit of the RCP?

"By the way, no-one else there knows, and officially they wouldn't touch it anyway. Too controversial don't you see. Too contaminating." Meaning, better to get a daft pliable academic on the job?

I asked whether HMT couldn't just raise taxes to cover the costs of the elderly and I could leave quietly and go home.

"Don't be childish naïve on me! We've been through that. The polls show the nation won't have it. Taxed to the eyeballs as it is. Politically toxic. Just like the nation says it loves the NHS but just bloodywell won't pay more for it."

It was becoming apparent that I was to be associated with a fear of contamination on various fronts. Still, the project carried elements of excitement and personal salvation too tempting to refuse. I made a final half- hearted attempt at escape.

"Global warming more important? Yesofcourse. But long after us old chap. Point is, at the present rate of financial fallout we'll all be dead aeons before the planet burns. Mad as a box of frogs, those warming folk. Greenham Common leftovers. Long life is going to fry us financially well before the sun does."

The Inspector looked as though my account carried sufficient authenticity to be believed. He encouraged me to continue. Was all this being recorded back to head office? I pointed at his ComCam. "Oh indeed. Does that matter? Could be interpreted in your favour, after all."

The Permanent Under Secretary had given me named single persons to contact in both departments, Health and Pensions, for stats and general advice. They had been warned to give me everything I wanted but they had no idea of the true nature of the task in hand. And by the way, no emails, no 'phone calls. Only handwritten requests and answers – my contacts were primed on that. Envelopes sealed with sticky tape. We can tell then if someone has had a go at them. Did I have a safe in my university office? Otherwise they would have one installed. All documentation related to this task was to be kept in the safe. No work to be done at home. If I needed an assistant, the choice would be left to me but that person would have to sign the OSA as well. Delicate business when it came to choosing. Even low grade security clearance procedures can be daunting. What about mine?

"All done behind your back, old chap. It did help that you're also Jesus." I was about to protest that I professed no such elevation when he added: "And a rower!" Ah. Oxford days half a lifetime ago. Can never escape. Final instruction:

"Not a word to that lovely clever Merton girl you shacked up with. By the time you get home she will know all she needs to know." And so on. Or words to that effect.

'Twas brillig, and the slithy toves
Did gyre and gimble in the wabe;
All mimsy were the borogoves,
And the mame raths outgrabe.

Twas brillig indeed. But was I supposed to look out for the jaws that bite and the claws that catch? And what a dreary child I must have been to learn all that by heart and love it so much. And remember it so well, when I can't remember what I did yesterday. Not very much happening in this place, in any event. However, back then I was a Lazarus resurrected. Nice irony. Not bad for a Jew. Was Lazarus Jewish? They were all Jewish in that gang, weren't they? Christianity started out as a sect of reformed Judaism. Really? Enough of that. The health bit would be easy. I had all the stats I needed, thanks mainly to my students. The pensions bit would come from that department. Job done. The work on the assisted dying bill would have to drop in priority for a while. I briefly nursed a paranoid suspicion that this whole mad enterprise was intended to get me away from the assisted dying thing.

A courier would come to my office fortnightly to collect updated information as it appeared.

....

2046/47

"You Jewish?" That was your question, Inspector. That came out of nowhere, devoid of relevance except for my entirely coincidental and private Lazarus thoughts while I was recounting my first meeting with the Permanent Under Secretary at the Treasury.

"Is that important?" was my appropriate response to your arrogant intrusion. You waited with bony fingers interlaced and for once making direct eye contact. And waited.

I said: "Yes and no." I could see no harm in humouring you.

"Don't fuck with me!" came back with disconcerting vehemence for the second time in our short acquaintance, emerging from a man blessed with absolutes. With restraint I explained that I represented an impeccable Jewish ancestry but that I did not profess any belief or faith. I was and remain an atheist. You seemed to take this information quite badly.

"Well, forgive me but my concern was actually directed at your temporal welfare, your predicament, shall we say. You can guess what sentence awaits you. I was hoping for your sake that you could derive some spiritual support from prayer. Forgiveness from our Lord, you know, and the expectation of something better in the next life, in the arms of Jesus." Oh Deah! Who would have guessed? I stared in disbelief at my Inspector; after a life in secrets, a man eking out an existence in a retirement job and in a shiny suit, and deluded. I reminded you that at 67 I didn't have far to go anyway.

You nodded and sighed with some sorrow, it seemed, as you announced that we would continue on the next occasion. You limped out. I heard the alternating cadence of your steps recede followed by a burst of guffaws from my keepers.

I heard: "How do you reckon those two shag, him and the fat wife?! Slap her thighs and ride in on the waves!" Ha ha ha. "Bit past it anyway, dontcherthink." Crude and cruel. Maybe goes with the job.

Jack Spratt could eat no fat
His wife could eat no lean
So betwixt them both you see
They licked the platter clean

I went to the movies again last night; more or less the same nightmare except that this time my Inspector took the place of the Queen of Hearts. He was screaming at me for being godless and condemned me to everlasting fire. Same nakedness, same fiery ending as before. So it goes.

....

Recalling 2019 (I think).

All changed indeed. I found the code for the new lock on my office door in a text to my 'phone, with congratulations conveyed from the same Head of Department who had suspended me with head-spinning alacrity after Regents Park. An urgent handwritten message from the Vice Chancellor in my office post. Would I be so kind as to visit for a chat at my convenience? He had apparently returned in triumph from the foetuscide Far East with many promises from candidate students to study (and pay) at our famous university. No more panicky faces in administration offices when I appeared. Charming hale Geoffrey G, my colleague and office neighbour, statistician and climate change bore, was letting himself into his office when I arrived. Socks and sandals vegetarian Geoffrey, goatee-bearded, in a green velvet waistcoat but no jacket. Incarnation of Lytton Strachey. Why not, so close as we are to the Bloomsbury that was? Cheerily welcoming; regretful about my spot of bother last term; these things normally sort themselves out in the end; meet for coffee sometime? I made assenting noises and got into my office with gratitude.

Things had sorted themselves out very well for Geoffrey G. Bitter memories from not far deep, resurfaced. That lucky smiler had benefited from two pieces of my own work some years previously, published with our Head of Department, in my absence on sabbatical in Africa, and to wide acclaim. I had made the mistake of leaving my not quite completed work in the care of our Head of Department, and Geoffrey G was blessed with the task of 'having a look at it' without any reference to its origins. It is possible that poor Geoffrey was suckered into this in ignorance, by our careless Head of Department. Other colleagues recommended I 'get over it – it happens all the time'.

I suppressed my temporary lapse into professional jealousy by starting a search for Sara, leaving messages everywhere. Lost, but soon found. We spent the lunch break wrapped up and walking Gordon Square park. Yes, she had had a lovely Christmas in South Wales, thank you, but worried about what was happening to me back in London. Hence the daily calls. Sweet child! She was happy to see me returned from disgrace. She was happy to be invited to collaborate on this mysterious new task. She was not so happy to sign the Official Secrets Act, without which I could not offer any more information anyway. She would need to discuss this with her parents. Absolutely not! This was a tough decision for a just post teenager but not a word to anyone even if she decided against. I reassured her that she would not be a named author under any circumstances. No pressure. I was asking her as 'first refuser'. The paid PhD was a sweetener in my gift. A few days later she accepted and we got to work. Our findings could quite sensibly form the basis for her PhD thesis.

"How so, if I am to sign the Official Secrets thing?"

"It is not so much the information that is secret, as for whom we provide the information."

"'For whom? For whom?'. You trying to avoid ending on a preposition again Dr Stern? Get a life." Lively lady.

As we walked back through the park, Sara appeared distracted as if looking for something missing. She wanted to know why there was a bust of a Bengali poet but nothing to honour the tragic General Gordon. I had the useless information for her to the effect that the square and park honoured Mrs Georgiana Russell, maiden name Gordon, daughter of the Duke of Gordon and second wife of the Duke of Bedford, Mr Russell. Nothing to do with that ridiculous affair in Khartoum. Hence also Russell Square nearby. Past glories. But poet Rabindrath Tagore had been a law student at our university, briefly.

We came to the bust memorial for Noor Inayat Khan. Sara said she had walked past Miss Khan many times – never got round to checking the relevance.

Was she a student here too? No, better than that. She was an Indian princess who became a spy with the SOE. Parachuted into France at night, caught by the Nazis, executed at Dachau. What I did not reveal was that her story was one of the inspirations for Spywife's career choice. Why is she here? Sara wanted to know. I showed her the inscription on the side. She lived near here and came frequently to find quiet here. See all her decorations. What is SOE, what is GC? she wanted to know. You are the one who hates acronyms, she said, and here they are carved into the column. I said the carving was not of my doing but that there are times, especially when it comes to marble or stone, when brevity rules. She would need to look up both acronyms herself for the information to stick. She pulled a face of infantile disappointment.

We left the park and walked past white houses occupied by university departments. I told Sara that this was where some members of the dauntingly talented Bloomsbury group lived, wrote, painted, and loved promiscuously. And about the sad end of Virginia Woolf. And that her 'Mrs Dalloway' was a favourite of Eng Lit courses. And maybe she should have a look at it if only to try to figure out why that should be the case. She pulled another face which said where am I supposed to find the time for such diversions? I said too much work stuff would damage her fine mind. I received a brief hug.

All changed at home. Spywife was caught on several occasions gazing at me, followed by confessions of admiration. All threats to her career from contamination by marital association had vanished, apparently. A British middle-aged professional couple were in bliss.

Sara and I worked on 'The Project' in my office, carefully locking away all Project documents and working papers in our recently installed safe at the end of each working session. I suggested that we split the work into two sections: one should be costs current and anticipated; and the other: potential savings current and projected, all related to populations in modern economies over 70 years of age, existing and then pretend not existing. We must decide which economies were 'modern'. Was that up to us in the first place or should we use some list issued by a world body such as the World Bank, the IMF, the UN, the WHO etc? (the 'WHO'?! ha ha. Sara was not old enough to remember those rock geniuses and was perplexed by my chuckle). Could any of those worthy institutions be trusted to have a list unaffected by politics and favouritisms?

Our discussions came down to the need to define 'modern economy'. What part of the definition should rely on wealth versus style of government versus human rights and freedoms? Would a massive economy such as China qualify in spite of a strange perception of what constitutes democracy and a questionable human rights record? What about Greece, a collapsed economy in the birthplace of democracy? And Russia - Oh Deah! – recently become somewhat 'modern' but suffering pervasive corruption even without Putin? Africa? No, but we may come back to consider South Africa, still wealthy but corrupt and a fast-failing infrastructure. Australia/New Zealand? Certainly. South America? Brazil, sure, corrupt or not. Not so sure about the rest. Colombia is wealthy ha ha! USA and Canada? Of course. And all of Scandinavia/ Finland/ Iceland. India? Why not? Pakistan? Probably not. The Middle East? In the end we stuck with the wealthy corrupt but abandoned the poor corrupt except for Israel and Jordan, being poor, not very corrupt, and modern by anybody's standards. The UK? Ha ha again, but being 'our own' beloved benign really democratic safe green and pleasant not wealthy land, must count for something. And so on. We decided to decide ourselves, but slightly influenced by our Treasury sponsor's recommendation to "follow the money". Interestingly, China was a better bet than Russia, in those terms.

Our list went off to HMT by courier, followed by a brief note of satisfaction by return. Good start! What fun! We had a licence to create our own world divided into modern and primitive economies as we defined. A mutually congratulatory hug ended with embarrassed giggles as we both became aware of my suddenly palpable erection. Where had that come

107

from? We separated in some confusion but giving me a clear view of the tops of well developed freckled breasts. It was clearly time to move on to the next task before the situation degenerated into something unseemly. Enough of that then from an intermittently sad man, indeed just old enough to be her parent, never mind in loco.

The next task was the laborious business of listing all those disabilities and illnesses afflicting the elderly because they are elderly, and their costs to the nations. We started with 'our' nation, hoping for an easy start because of accessibility to the required information. We ended with a list of nearly every human organ and its expensive failure: minds in meltdown; bodies broken and bent; dentures and hearing aids and walking aids and wheelchairs. Nearly all of modern orthopaedics (joint replacements and spinal decompressions) was directed at the elderly, and very expensively; likewise cardiology and vascular surgery; much of cancer anywhere, and so on. We pillaged statistics from the multitude of relevant charities and medical/surgical Colleges and government agencies that exist to deal with these diseases and failures of the elderly. Laborious perhaps, but more fun. Whoops of joy as another frightening figure emerged. We became children in a health economics sweet shop. We were academics dealing in billions of currency like some predatory oligarchs, all on paper.

The Malthusian checks to population: war, famine, and disease, had failed in the UK. Where was the viral bird 'flu pandemic, supposed to help us out of this? HIV might have done it, but hadn't. Why not? Here was a virus transmitted by the second-most driving urge after hunger, mutating just fast enough to evade effective immunisation, and setting up home and safe haven in the very cells meant to destroy it. A designer virus, meant for some medical disaster fiction, and still not good enough except in most of the countries off-list.

As we moved on to other 'modern economies' it became evident that the Malthusian checks to population had failed everywhere. Most of the wars and famines were taking place blessedly far away in mainly off-list failed states, and there was no hint of a re-run of the Spanish 'flu pandemic of 1918. Worse luck. Contraception? The Reverend Malthus said nothing about that possibility because there wasn't much then in 1793 except sheep gut condoms for the wealthy, and there might just as well be nothing now for all the difference it was making. Not making. Infant mortality was doing some of the job in his day. I did take the trouble of pointing out from time to time which bits of information would be good in a Sara PhD.

Then we tackled the pension costs and trends, assisted by our reliable confidential sources arranged by the jolly Permanent Under-Secretary. Joy turned to alarm as the money mounted up day by day, not for ours to spend but for us to pay as a nation. The Office for National Statistics (ONS) conveniently gave us current and projected UK populations. Over 65s made up 11 million back in 2013, 17% of the total population, and increasing by 300,000 annually. (The ONS didn't do over 70s as a group). Getting similar pension information from our other listed countries, current and projected, was surprisingly difficult. Cagey paranoia characterised the responses to our queries, however innocently dressed. Our friendly governments were far more protective of their pension information than of the health costs of their elderly. Strange. Were they ashamed? Paying too little? Paying too much? Questions sent to embassies were either ignored or sidestepped with irritable questions back to us as to the 'true' purpose for which this information was intended. Appeals back to HMT produced most of the figures or guesses we could use. 'Gov UK' letterhead still carries more clout than that of most university departments.

By the end of the permitted three months our work sessions had become grimly quiet, punctuated only by my muttered expletives and no more congratulatory hugs. The five-year and ten-year projections suggested costs of hundreds and then thousands of billions, whether in US dollars or in sterling. I cannot remember the precise figures. They are somewhere in the HMT archives, but it almost doesn't matter. We were staring at a financial armageddon because of old folk (like my dad). None of the economic prosperity anticipated by our cleverest economists had a hope in hell of coming anywhere near covering the costs. We would need a new kind of Black Death, certainly by 2047, nicely 700 hundred years after the previous Europe-wide devastation. A new kind of extinction. What kind of exclusive insight did our glib and apparently superficial Permanent Under-Secretary possess in anticipation of commissioning our work?

Virologists were reported to be dealing with a new bird 'flu virus in the Far East – H5NX – or something. Dreading the possibility of cross-over to humans. Why dreading? Could be our Malthusian salvation!

Ring-a-Ring o'Rosies
A pocketful of Posies
Atishoo! Atishoo!
We all fall down

The unfailing and unidentifiable helmeted courier departed with our final report, to our great relief. I would be able to get back to work on Lord Sparrow's Assisted Dying Bill and Sara would be able to start serious work on her PhD. As our courier's bootsteps faded down the corridor, we permitted ourselves a chaste congratulatory hug. Chaste didn't last long. It is all too long ago to remember or even understand who or how or what started what but within seconds we were kissing and clutching and feeling each other everywhere including my own undeniable erection. Further developments were frustrated by my premature ejaculation into my underwear. I confessed and she laughed, giving me an additional firm hug as if to reassure me that it was her pleasure too. Flattered, she seemed. Not offended. But certainly a line crossed. Messy messy messy mess!

....

Recalling later 2019 (definitely).

"Is that Dr Stern? I am sorry Dr Stern. Your father fell again this morning. We think he may have broken his hip. He has just been admitted to hospital. Doctor came round and gave him something for pain before the ambulance took him away." Or words to that effect, soon after Sara and I had signed off on our Project.

I had visited at least once a month while Sara and I were uncovering the likely end of our civilisation. He was certainly becoming increasingly frail. I would sit in his silent presence without any human transaction; sedation prevented any repeat of that previous unforgettable incident. Now here was a sad irony: the famous orthopaedic surgeon suffered a fractured neck of femur. Why not? No status or profession protected one from that possibility. Not even the Queen Mother all those decades ago. There was never a plausible prevention of osteoporosis, and now it doesn't matter. So few now break their hips before their End Day at seventy. Job done. That is – your job, Inspector, not mine.

The consultant orthopaedic surgeon looked like a wrung out schoolboy; dark baggy eyes in a young face, and so polite. What a privilege to have my dad as his patient, he said.

"Best for a fractured neck of femur in old folk was a THR. Sorry, total hip replacement. Gets 'em up and about in no time. Just getting him worked up for theatre. On the list for tomorrow. We expect some difficulty with mobilisation post op, you know, the dementia thing. Our physios are great. They'll sort it!"

I remember being amazed at seeing him sitting out of bed when I visited next evening, apparently free of pain and quite calm. The consultant had heard I was visiting and came round to greet when he should have been at home for some time. We got lucky, he could tell me now. My dad's prosthesis was the last allowed for that year according to the hospital budget, and all THRs for the rest of the financial year were cancelled. Pretty much the same in most orthopaedic units in the country. What would happen to the next hip fractures in old folk, sure to follow?

"Oh, we'll pin 'em like we used to do way back but they won't heal properly. Bit of a mess really. Needs must. But your dad looks good. We'll get him doing first steps tomorrow. By the way, not just orthopaedics, you know. Cataracts, hernias, cardiac stenting etcetera, all cancelled till further notice. So far, nobody seems to have noticed. Mostly stuff for the elderly. Bit strange. Good night!"

Or words to that effect. I sincerely hoped my young consultant would now return to the bosom of his family, if he had one. A family, that is, or at least a bosom, if not.

....

It was a helpful distraction to be able to renew contact with the groupies shepherding Lord Sparrow's Assisted Dying Bill through Parliament. This story was turning into a saga of never-ending blocking tactics introduced by a small gang of sanctimonious great and good peers during the second reading in the Lords. These good guys were way behind the public, according to repeated polling. I was pushing for something more. I was nursing pure self interest in the hope of adding an amendment which would allow a person with normal mental capacity and very likely in good health generally, to choose death once undeniably demented, or incurably ill in any other way and bereft of any quality of life, at some later stage. It was necessary to counter the spurious pro-life argument that those so seriously ill may somehow become well again and therefore pointlessly killed.

Nobody in history, for example, once truly demented, has somehow one day become undemented. Or those rendered widely cancer riddled become uncancered, stroke unstroked, heart attacked become unattacked, and all rendered incapable of the activities of daily living.

And contrary to the provisions of Sparrow's bill, the patient would not have to 'self-administer the life-ending medication'. When you are that far gone you cannot self-administer anything but a big shit into your bed. And would we not all want that amendment for ourselves, never mind our dearest? You know, something very close to a DNR order - DO NOT RESUSCITATE - frequently in force for certain hopeless cases in our geriatric wards but now to be ordered by the individual concerned via a contract. Like a pre-nup! If it works for marriage, why not something alike for illness? Based on the ancient injunction 'do not strive officiously to keep alive when all hope is lost'. Who said that? Or words to that effect.

The bill had made it to committee stage in the Lords three years previously, and debate still raged. It would eventually have to get through the Commons as well. 'Go away Stern. Come back in ten years. The country may be ready for you then.' Hah. Irony: the country was eventually made ready for something much worse. An unimaginable something back then in 2018, which later became a storm of killing, for which I was set up to be one of the architects. A childhood memory of a sing-song weather change requested by a group at play outdoors, crept into my head.

Rain, rain go away
Come again another day

....

I didn't have to go away. I was called away. Dad had a temperature and a foul chest. He was on oxygen and antibiotics. He was fighting off the physiotherapists with some violence but his doctors did not want to sedate him for fear of suppressing his breathing still further. When I arrived it was obvious that he was struggling, propped up, chest heaving, pulling constantly at his oxygen mask. From time to time great gouts of pus were coughed up; one old man's hell behind curtains. Brain long gone; body going fast. I went to the nurses' station and discovered the ward sister concentrating on her computer screen, aided by frowns and soft curses. I moved to and fro hoping to distract her focus, without success. I had to use a throat clearing request to be excused.

"Yes?" Eyebrows up but head remains down.

"Good evening, Sister. I would like to discuss the management of my father. Bed 17. I..."

"Sorry, can't do that now. I'm into handover and still haven't finished my report."

"Should I ask one of the other staff?"

"You won't have much luck. They're all in handover. Try the night staff when they come out of handover."

I did, and I had some luck with a staff nurse with tired eyes, on the point of starting his shift. After offering my credentials as the son of the human shell in Bed 17 while hiding any taint of my medical education, I asked whether a 'Do Not Resuscitate' notice could be attached to the file at the end of his bed. We would have to confirm that with the doctor on call, he said. He thought there was little chance of getting a DNR approval so soon after successful surgery. I asked if there was any way I could have a word with the consultant surgeon. He was still in theatre, he thought. He pointed out that the physicians had been called to my father during the day and prescribed the treatment regimen just as I had found. I explained that I did not see the point in any resuscitation. He replied with commendable patience that this was not resuscitation, just routine treatment for pneumonia. I thanked him and said I would wait for the doctor on call. He said that I might have a long wait. There was only one surgical junior doctor on call at night and tonight she was already dealing with a major problem in another ward. There was a form I could fill in and sign, witnessed by the staff nurse, who would then try to get the attention of the doctor on call to approve and sign. Staff nurse warned me not to expect too much. I hinted that all I expected was that, with good fortune, my father would die in the night. The tired eyes nodded. He understood.

Not in the night after all, but the next day. No need for the DNR. Already in medical school days, pneumonia was called the old man's friend. My Health Economist mind could not keep out a flashed thought that a precious last-funded total hip replacement has gone unused.

So many kind people were offering condolences and I had to affect gratitude while feeling immense relief. 'Blessed release' and clichés like that. My poor father had effectively died years ago. Non-brain, I realised a long time previously, renders one a non-person, if we are honest. If the country had had the 'Stern' amendment in place, his body could have followed soon after his mind. That would have saved him so much pointless torment and the nation so much pointless expense.

Spywife shrugged and gave me a valuable hug, saying nothing and earning my deep gratitude. A couple of days were taken up with the bureaucracy of death: identification of the corpse, getting the death certificate, without which nothing much else can happen; informing solicitors so that the expensive tediousness of probate can get under way; starting arrangements for burial. Dad was never a global warmist but discovered when still well that cremation was hugely carbon costly. And an elderly dead body almost qualified as fossil fuel ha ha. Insisted on a basket coffin and a conventional burial, absolutely no ceremony, and minimalist stone, all written down for me and his solicitors so that there could be no deviation. 'Feed the worms, not the ozone hole' he insisted frequently, taking wicked pleasure in the alarmed response of his audience.

I sent his tireless hip surgeon a case of wine. Can't remember his name now. He achieved some prominence in his career, which was gratifying for me. So many names have gone out of my head these days. Standard MCI (sorry, Mild Cognitive Impairment) I expect. Distinct from dementia, you need to know. When I returned to work, Sara came to pay respects. I stopped her from starting to say something. I put up my hand and intoned the clichéd "Blessed relief". Another valuable hug, but thankfully we left it at that.

I was grateful for a return to the normal academic timetable of lectures and tutorials and endless assessments. I was not looking for any particular excitements, not for a while at least. Sara would arrive from time to time as arranged so that I could supervise her plans for her PhD. All a little premature: she would graduate BA soon and would then have to apply for admission to do an MA or MSc. There should be no problem with that because I had been promised a funded PhD for the student of my choice. The presumption was that the Master's would soon be converted to a doctorate if the quality of work justified it.

All quiet in my little tower, interrupted only by Dad's burial, but no funeral. Nice people had wanted to attend and I had to put them off; Dad's wishes. He had insisted on Bristol, our home town and where he had been educated, and where Mum was buried anyway. Some of his specialist training was done there and that is where he was eventually appointed consultant: a 'favourite son' situation but a known quantity and a safe pair of hands. Logical and normal for those days perhaps but sure as hell not in accordance with modern guidelines, transparency, and the formal appointments process. I was a late only child but I had a wonderfully privileged middle class childhood in the suburbs of a city founded on slavery, tobacco, and aeronautical engineering.

I arranged for a plot in the Jewish section. As near to Mum's as possible. Why not? We are Jews and paid a heavy price for that, repeatedly over the centuries. Neither parent had stipulated which cemetery or where in it. About as secular as you can get, really, and still be Jewish. The cemetery folk certainly did not insist on any evidence of a degree of observance to qualify for a hole in the ground. Nothing in my father's specifications ruled out my decision. I had some early difficulty with a local rabbi but she came round after a chat and a short history lesson relevant to our ancestral family's jolly times in the Holocaust. She and I were the only ones present and I was happy for the company. Her name is gone, too, I'm afraid. We wished each other 'long life' in the Jewish tradition in the presence of a life lost. I considered soon after, that such a wish may have been relevant in a biblical era of short and nasty lives lived but ran counter to all that was needed now. We should change that to 'long life but please not too long'.

Spywife was not anxious to make the journey and I had no problem with that. She and Dad were certainly fond of each other until his brain absented him from the enjoyment of the company of all. Dad was buried at the far end of the cemetery, near the little chapel and in the company of other Jews he never knew. Jewish dust to Jewish dust. And all that.

You Jewish?
Yes and no.
Don't fuck with me!

(This is not a nursery rhyme).

....

Recalling 2016

I have no great difficulty remembering the year of the IN-OUT referendum. Nothing to do with a military club in Picadilly but everything to do with the Europe question. A thirty years-old memory, but what about remembering yesterday? The OUTs squeaked

121

in and as I write we remain out after all these years; and until my incarceration, I couldn't tell the difference. European research funding for health economics and conferences still came and went as before, thankfully. Transferring my body to the custody of Europe and the protections of the European Court of Human Rights would have helped not a jot; all European states are UNPOPCONT Treaty states. There is nothing I could have done better to avoid imprisonment in this secret dreary place except to have stayed away in Africa.

I can't remember even how I voted. All so long ago, and all the tense discussions and vigorously held opinions matter nothing now.

....

Recalling 2018 (or thereabout)

"Finished your coffee, young man? Good. Let's take a walk. We'll go down to the river. No!" (warning hand raised). "Talk outside".

I had not finished my coffee. Pity. Good coffee for the Civil Service. It may have been the personal choice and at the personal expense of HMT's Under-Secretary. It looked like the peace was over and chickens were coming home etc. I was convinced, after a year or more of quiet, that our work for HMT had died in the corridors of Whitehall and for which I would have been thankful.

A courier had come to the university with a message to make myself available within the hour for the car which would collect me. I had to cancel a thesis supervision session with Sara. I knew from what was not said as I made my excuses, that she understood something secret was going on, and likely in relation to our previous work. Lovely loyal sexy freckled Sara. Beloved object of my frequent sexual fantasies. I had made it easy for her by saying that I had been called to a building near the river.

The PUS opened. "Your figures. In that piece you did for us with that bimbo of yours. How confident are you that you got 'em right?" I raised an index finger to protest his offensive reference to Sara but he had hands raised in apology and I left off my protest. Best not to make too much of his habitual off-hand language. And he couldn't know how much I would have wanted her to be my bimbo.

"They were right at the time. We checked and checked again. Reputation depends on getting it right. Do remember, in many instances we were dependent on what we were given by the officials of failed states and dictatorships. But charities and quangos and IMF and WHO were consulted and gave us useful moderations where there was obvious gloss. It's all there, in the references."

"Gloss?"

"Exaggerations."

"Oh. You mean lies, propaganda?"

"OK. Yes." Blessed silence for at least thirty seconds. I began to wonder if the PUS retained lingering doubts about the worth of our findings.

I said: "We had no personal agendas, you know. Always a good idea to ask someone else to repeat the exercise …". He put one hand up, head shaking. I was on the wrong tack.

"Talk implications for a minute. We have been talking of little else in our department, and others, for the last many months. I want to have your take on your figures. Go."

"Well, we are all going to end up with a lot of old folk who are going to cost us a lot of money through debilitating illness, mainly dementia, and pensions emptied out. 'We' being the modern economies."

"Jesus, we know that! Is that the best you can do? You said all of that in the paper. Christ, not for nothing the ivory tower! What I meant was: what are the policy implications? What can be done to prevent financial armageddon? 2008 will look like a Sunday picnic. Or have you no imagination at least?"

"That is unfair, Sir." My vigorous protest but retaining a semblance of respect; he really was a knight. "We must pray for another 1347 Black Death or a 1918 'flu pandemic, but they just aren't coming. Perhaps the modern economies can prosper and make enough money to cope, after all. We have done that through the centuries."

"No we bloody haven't! Where is your history, man? Bloody medics. Academic medics must be the worst. So let me tell you straight off: short of discovering that the Thames is actually a river of gold, there is no way we or any other bloody 'modern economy' is ever going to be able to survive the costs of the geriatrics!"

"What do you want me to say? I've already had one bad experience from a jocular reference to geriatricide. And if all the cleverness of your Whitehall colleagues has paid our report the compliment of close examination, then what am I supposed to say that will be cleverer, more pertinent, or more likely to bring us closer to salvation? And by the way, I am no longer a medic, as you well know."

"There is no BBC in sight here, and I am not wearing a 'wire'. I invite you right here to give me a bloody good feel to satisfy yourself, but I will stop at stripping off on the Embankment in broad daylight, if you don't mind."

"The answer, Sir, speaks for itself out of our paper. If there were no people alive beyond the age of 70 or 75, we'd be fine! Simple!" Sarcasm again, my unavoidable reaction to a Whitehall bonehead who had impugned my intellectual integrity. I continued: "So what policy initiative does the collected wisdom of Whitehall have in mind to magic this problem away?" Another silence, seemingly endless this time. Up to me to break it and give hope! "By the way, are you aware of my work with the Assisted Dying bill?"

"We don't have time to change the subject now. Sparrow is a sanctimonious twit anyway. 'Dignity in Dying'. Please!"

"I may know him better than you do, Sir, and he is absolutely not sanctimonious. He is genuinely trying to save us all from expensive and potentially criminal journeys to Switzerland. And I have been a medic long enough to know that it is absolutely necessary that we should not have to make that journey outside of Britain. How come Oregon of all places can show us up as medieval? In fact five American states have approved assisted dying. Also Colombia, Canada, and South Africa!"

"Passionate eh? Wow! And where will this diversion take us? Better be quick about it. I've got to get back."

I described my unacceptable amendment as we crossed the gardens back to his office. Amazing, how much time I have spent talking shop in London gardens. I described my intention of legislation in favour of an ante-mortem Will, something like an ante-nuptial contract, why not? Duly notarised while in good health and which would allow family, friends, doctors, solicitors, judges etc to sanction euthanasia for an individual who eventually does NOT have mental capacity but who is suffering the agonies of advanced physical and/or mental decay.

"Jesus!" (again). "The actual 'e' word! Can see why that failed to find favour. 'Here we go again, only 80 years after Hitler'. That's what they'll all be thinking. Why do you think that would make a difference of the kind we need anyway?" This was not the time or the place to explain that 'euthanasia' being Greek, begins with a diphthong, not a single letter. Therefore the actual 'eu' word should have been his reference. Is a Classics degree no longer a requirement for the civil service?

"Our figures show again and again, irrespective of disease or mere condition, 70 to 75 is the average cut-off for the good life. But we live so many extra pointless years in various degrees of suffering, and in varying degrees of mindlessness, that many people would find an ante-mortem contract quite attractive. Who knows? With some promotion and publicity it could catch on to become normal. Maybe so normal that the numbers would make up what we need for rescuing the finances? I buried my father not long ago, after years of dementia. I know he would have signed himself off in anticipation, if he had been offered the opportunity when still well. This is not entirely original, by the way. Baroness Helen Wilson proposed something like this back in 2008. Our national treasure in moral philosophy."

I had become preachy and immediately regretted it. The PUS observed a blessed silence. He must surely have been thinking ahead to his next appointment.

Not at all. "Christ Stern! You Jewish? Your people will love you for that idea. And I know Helen Wilson. She took a lot of flak at the time. Talk about the 'slippery slope'! In any case, the numbers would never come up to the need. OK. Not the end of the road. We'll talk again. Jesus! (yet again). A Jew said that! If this gets out, your people will crucify you. I'll get the car to take you back if you hang on right here."

He bustled off and did not allow me the opportunity to make the point that I do not have 'people'. Those 'people' have me. And I had already suffered a media 'crucifixion'. I hoped I would not make a habit of it.

....

Recalling more of 2018

I fancy I had a hand in getting the Sparrow bill moving again through the second reading in the Lords. The last holdouts had been the bishops and the Chief Rabbi. Their apprehensions were based on a combination of 20th century history and ancient theology. Sparrow was confident that the numbers would work for the second reading but felt that the project would fail in the long term without the churches on board. I offered the Sparrow team that I would meet with these peers, if they would have me, to see what additional assurances would possibly change their minds. My Jewish credentials (secular or not) and Holocaust family history, should reassure them that we were not slippery-sloping to geriatricide.

Just offering choice. An opportunity not to 'die in despair'. The right to a decent death.

After their tentative agreement to meet someone they knew not at all, thanks to the gentle persistence of Lord Sparrow himself, I sought and achieved permission to include representatives of the various Royal Colleges. We were fearful that successful passage through the Lords would be followed by blockage in the Commons by a variety of lobby groups, most persuasive of which would be the physicians and surgeons. Several knights agreed to attend, including a couple of harrumphing old buddies from the Physicians, apparently not yet quite reconciled to my previous notoriety. I would have liked to circulate my Treasury 'Project' document. The PUS refused point blank but felt there would be no harm in issuing a summary on university letterhead for distribution to delegates. He would clear it with the Dean of Faculty and the Vice Chancellor. There must be no contamination of the Treasury.

We managed to book a Lords committee room, with lunch. I was encouraged by the good attendance; many purple and red vests with dangling crucifixes on men and women, a couple of attractive turbans, several white skull caps (Muslim and Catholic?) and a couple of black kippahs.

My aim was to complete before lunch. Any post prandial proceedings were likely to be drowned in snores. I began by recounting my very personal and heart-rending own paternal bereavement, as an example of the inhumanity of the moralistic enforcement of life bereft of quality. Very 'Health Economics'. How often was this scenario repeated throughout the nation every day, and where only the well-off can afford the Dignitas arrangements in Switzerland? A life without sense or meaning other than suffering. A national disgrace! Then I told the story of my great grandmother and her end in 1942 at Auschwitz. I made sure to have strong eye contact with the Chief Rabbi. Hey, how could I and the Sparrow team members be genocidal maniacs? After that, I passed around the paper summarising the prospect of financial meltdown which too long a life presented to the nation. Disbelief of the figures rose like a miasma from my assembled greats, but I had some fun defending them with a show of academic humility leavened with integrity.

At last I was blessed with a contemplative silence. My anticipation was that the silence would end in consent. Then it went on too long for comfort. In a mild panic I broke the silence. I reminded the boys and girls that a clause of the bill makes provision for a limited pilot trial, followed by an assessment of opinions and attitudes of all 'stakeholders'. Dear God. I do remember; I actually used that appalling designation, all the while seeing in my mind's eye some actor in a movie from childhood holding a wooden stake just freshly plunged into some vampire's heart (Dracula?) as he lay in a coffin; a real stakeholder. More silence but this time with some nods. Then a bishop looked up and in a commanding pulpit voice filled the silence.

"Job one twentyone!"

"Sorry?" I asked on behalf of those of us lost in ignorance of the Bible by numbers.

"The Lord giveth and the Lord taketh away. It is not for us mortals to take life which is God-given, whatever the circumstances! We are made in the image and likeness of God." The congregation nodded almost in unison, including some physicians and surgeons. One irrelevant quote by some sanctimonious vicar, and I had lost them. More contemplation, but this time with a background shuffle of bodies moving as if to rise for lunch. My dismay gave way too rapidly to rage. I simply had no control over my verbal excrescence.

"My Lords, Ladies and gentlemen. Good for Job, I say. But I would want to ask Job what knowledge he had of Genghis Khan, Richard the Lion Heart, Saladin, Savonarola, Hitler, Stalin, Mao Tse Tung, Pol Pot, and all sundry murderers of the likes of my great granny, and their power to 'take away'. Would Job have said that was God-given? Or God-blessed? We are planning acts of mercy here, not murder, requested by sane but dying individuals in distress." I was verbally hurtling, not much in control.

"By the way, talking of image and likeness and the Lord giving life. Take a good look at me. Do any of you for one moment see any evidence to suggest that God fucked my mother? Yes? No? Come on!"

Ah well.   Pandemonium.   Shouts:
"Blasphemy!" "Sacrilege!" "Who is this person?"
Arms raised.   Some with head in hands.   Some
backing up of chairs in preparation for storming out, I
presumed. I felt a stab of regret that I had ruined what
would have been a wonderful lunch, as only the
Houses can offer, never mind the rats. I pleaded for
calm, patience, and more contemplation before
departure. Please. Lunch awaited and some excellent
wine. I announced that I would be the one to leave.
Members should consider the whole package at
leisure, taking not less than a week to do so and to
submit written opinions, including complaints, to the
Sparrow group thereafter.   Please.   I apologised
several times for the offence I had given. I pleaded
passion for the matter in hand. Please. Thank you.

"By the way, one last thought. Nothing to do
with theology but everything to do with relevance. Or
your lack of it. You honourable ladies and gentlemen
are operating behind the curve. A few ordinary folk
are taking matters into their own hands, but in
increasing numbers, leaving you all in danger of
counting for nothing. In case you don't know it,
people are importing medication from Mexico,
probably secobarbital, and doing their own Dignitas at
home, careful not to have any friends or relatives
providing illegal assistance. DIY Dignitas in Britain.
Mostly folk with early dementia, refusing to fall into
the black hole. You didn't know? And the polls are

heavily in favour. That you surely do know. Please take time to consider your position. Excuse me."

Or words to that effect. I fled, but noticed that nobody else was leaving. Food was being heaped onto plates, glasses of wine gathered up, and a hum of conversation rose behind me.

I couldn't face the Tube and took the long walk back to the university, hoping that the changing sight of other souls along the way would distract me from my sense of utter personal failure. From my office I sent a message of confession to the Sparrow team. I think I spent much of the afternoon gazing into the middle distance. I was waiting for a knock on the door, revealing an enraged dean or Head of Department come to hurl me finally into the outer darkness. Nothing. I thought of seeking sympathy from Sara but quickly abandoned that idea. This was not her burden. It would certainly be a burden for Spywife. I headed home to confess over a stiff whisky and was grateful to find her there ahead of me. Still in a power pinstriped suit, she was unfazed.

"What did you or any of Sparrow's crowd realistically expect? Even with the utmost politeness? I can't believe your naivety! These people were only doing their job, in their view protecting God's children from mad social engineers like you. You have no monopoly over what constitutes the greatest good. Full marks for effort, though. It must have been quite fun, really. Get over it. You've had no lunch. Let's eat out."

I took a week's sick leave, waiting at home rather than at work for the expected final discharge in disgrace. Silence. Nothing from the Sparrow crowd either. I made a tentative return to work, and during that next week I began to receive messages of congratulation from the 'Sparrows' as indications of assent trickled in. The bishops and doctors had relented and were up for it, mostly, impressed by the evidence and the conviction with which it was presented, it seems.

Sara called in at the office to discover how things were going. Apparently delighted on my behalf, but she appeared to have some other pre-occupation.

"I took your advice and wasted a huge amount of time on that nonsense 'Mrs Dalloway'. What's it all about? A ditsy middle-aged posh and well-connected London lady is preparing a dinner party. Out of the blue she is visited in her bedroom, it seems, by a tiresome nervous boyfriend from a lifetime ago. There are all sorts of disconnected bits, or only slightly connected. The old suitor is rebuffed. He sits in a park and watches a poor raving war veteran. There is a pretty good description of this sad veteran having a full-on psychotic attack with paranoia and voices. How do I know it is a good description of schizophrenia? Don't ask, I know. No, not me! Get your face back together! But you have to wonder how it is that Virginia knew so well. There must have been more to her troubles than just depression. I'll bet she was schizophrenic. Or she knew one. Then comes the party, boring as hell. All the society big shots are there, including the prime minister and her sad old suitor. And that's it! So? What have I missed? Where's the story? At no stage did she get me interested in any of those sad people except possibly the war vet. I really could have done with using that time better. No more Eng Lit recommendations from you, please."

Very cross, for the first time in my presence. There was some unintelligible muttering of such emphasis that I took it to be cursing in Welsh. For a moment I felt she was taking some liberties with our acquaintance through her admonitions. But then, after all, we were now more than merely acquainted.

"I also have a problem with third person stories. I keep asking myself how can the author have the cheek to pretend that she knows what someone else thinks or feels. Her sentence construction is chaotic and her use of adjectives is so frequently totally misplaced. Now you tell me why I may be the only person in the world to think like that about 'Mrs Dalloway'."

Or words to that effect. I pleaded in mitigation that not all writing must necessarily contain a narrative – sorry, story. You might call this a vignette, you know, just a slice of observation. I said that it was probably regarded as daringly *avant garde* at the time precisely because it broke all the existing rules of 'correct' writing. But I said also that I thought she,

Sara, was very perceptive; that I had long wondered if there was a bit of the Emperor's New Clothes about that piece; that I thought she had 'got it in one'; and that maybe we were both equally short on literary intellect.

She said: "Have you really not done some Eng Lit course sometime? How do you know all this stuff you spout?"

I said: "I don't. Just flying. My wife says I have never let ignorance get in the way of an opinion on anything."

She said: "Still boring. Can do better. Avon God? Bollocks. Was Virginia ever in Bristol? Your wife must be very clever, I think."

I said: "*Avant Garde* has nothing to do with Bristol or God."

She said: "I know. I just felt your pomposity needed a puncture."
I earned a kiss on the cheek, and she was gone.

The Assisted Dying bill, as we all know and as I certainly can remember, became law later 2018. I still have somewhere a handwritten letter of thanks from Sparrow on his Lords letterhead. But all of that has been long forgotten, overtaken by 'further developments', of course.

As I gaze into the dying embers
These in the main are my regrets
When I was right, no one remembers
When I was wrong, no one forgets

This is a rhyme, but not a nursery rhyme. It was burnt into a plaque of wood hanging in a doctors' canteen in one of the hospitals I visited in South Africa on sabbatical. So apt, it was burnt into my memory.

....

Recalling 2019 (maybe)

It was a weekend day. It had to be because I was at home in the daytime and from my study window noticed some activity in the street opposite. There was an ambulance outside and someone on a trolley being rolled into the back. Then I saw Denise in attendance and assumed some bad news to do with Harry, my mentor in astronomy matters. I rushed out and stopped Denise just as she was climbing in to be next to Harry. She had not been able to rouse him that morning, she said; his breathing was stertorous; the dialysis had conferred no benefit in the last several weeks. Her face revealed red-eyed exhaustion and tears. I asked how she was going to get back from the hospital. She climbed in and shouted back something about a taxi. I said she was to call me when ready. No taxi!

But no call. I had stayed up late. A call came next day. I was at home, so must have been a Sunday. Denise's weary voice just audible. Harry had died in the night, peaceful and painless. I went to fetch her home. Spywife and I sat with her for a good while chatting about their past life and sharing a surprising amount of laughter. Release? I suggested she help herself to an adequate whisky and get some sleep. She suddenly remembered something and went off to fetch a box file full of correspondence between Harry and some 'B612' organisation (I think) which promoted the Sentinel space telescope. She pressed this file on me, saying that it was Harry's wish that I have it, should misfortune befall.

"What did you make of that diary he gave you?"

"I did have another look at it. I have to confess I could not make much of it. Harry probably made a mistake entrusting that to me. Broken reed when it comes to celestial trajectories, I'm afraid."

"You know that Harry calculated that an asteroid was on its way here? He kept going on about twentyfifty, twentyfifty. Personally I think his renal failure sent him a bit doolally. It's all in there. He does, sorry, did trust you on this. At least to believe this stuff even if there is nothing to be done."

I promised to go through the file sometime and report back my impressions.

Twinkle twinkle little star
How I wonder what you are
Up above the sky so high
Like a diamond in the sky

Recalling 2000 (certain of this date).
Millennium May Ball at Oxford.

Sing a song of sixpence, a pocket full of rye
Four and twenty blackbirds baked in a pie
When the pie was opened the birds began to sing
Wasn't that a dainty dish to set before a king?

Sixpence? The ticket for that ball was in three figures, pounds sterling. I have no hope of remembering the precise figure but I was granted generous parental assistance and managed to spend their money quickly before tickets sold out. My parents felt that I should be assisted to celebrate the anticipated successful halfway mark through my medical course. I did reflect briefly on the affordability of tickets for many of our less privileged colleagues attending under the new inclusiveness of the Oxbridge spires. I would not have brooded for very long because I had a major other concern. I had no partner lined up to join me. Concern became desperation and thoughts turned to a possible need to sell on my ticket.

Rowing saved the situation. I had been down at the Jesus clubhouse at six in the morning and managed a full session on the rowing machines without vomiting, for once. For once therefore, I took some pleasure in seeing the vapour rising from the river. Walking back up through the Meadows I caught up with Sam, another Jesus rower, in first year, and a friend, also walking back. Sam introduced me to her friend. It was only then that I got a good look at her friend and felt a sudden and momentary sense of faintness, as if my head and chest had emptied and refilled, with a roar.

Much later I tried to deal with that experience as a dispassionate seeker after medical/physiological truth, and gave up. I was transfixed by an unexpected vision of feminine beauty, a face of perceived perfection, a shy smile of vulnerability, then immediately contradicted by a confident deep voice. It was if all my previous life had conditioned me to have this uncontrollable reaction on that day, still winding down from the exertions of rowing madness, at that time of day, at that place in the avenue of trees, Meadows glowing in the sun just up. I had not been looking but had found my own Zuleika Dobson. I heard myself gabbling a variety of awkward nonsense in the hope of covering my discomfort.

When we got past Christ Church, my 'vision' stopped to make her farewells, and headed for Merton. At that moment I was sufficiently overcome that I was prepared to jump into the river for this Zuleika incarnation. As Sam and I continued to the Turl, I quizzed her about her friend, using an enforced air of restraint to resemble, as best I could, nothing more than polite curiosity. Her friend was doing PPE at Merton. Knew each other from school. Parents both lawyers, father a judge. Samantha, 'lawyer' herself, was not fooled. Said I looked ill. Yes, the bloody rowing machine. She nodded with a smile of greater wisdom. Looking away before collecting my bike from the Jesus shed, I asked Sam whether she knew if 'Vision' was 'spoken for' and if not, whether she was already booked for the ball at New College. She laughed at my old-fashioned circumspection. No. No present lover as far as she knew. She volunteered to enquire regarding availability for the ball. I rode off to last pre-exam lectures. I was suddenly somebody else. I felt as if my life had changed forever in some indefinable way. Then quickly – no, what clichéd rubbish! Reality would surely define: a pretty girl, exams coming up, and a ball ticket possibly heading for resale.

Four and twenty blackbirds? More like two hundred, from memory. Blackbirds in black tie, and their women, as I walked into the quad at New College in my pomp and a little tremble in my legs, emboldened nevertheless to hold the hand of my Merton queen, so as to demonstrate some element of possession. And I was king David. I remember immediate glasses of fake champagne (can't remember the name for it), many shouted greetings and congratulations for examination successes, all blackbirds looking to see who had brought whom, incessant photo flashes, tented stalls with millennium themes, a live band clashing with a deafening disco, some dancing, some food, and more and more singing as the pie opened and inebriation took hold.

We two made it through to the 'Survivors' photo in the early morning, by which time sufficient intimacy had taken place in the form of kisses and hugs to hint at mutual affection and exciting possible developments. I haven't revealed her name for good reason: my ball date became my lover and then my wife (another Oxbridge cliché), who became a spy (another Oxbridge cliché, *pace* Milicent Bagot), and then a 'retired' spy still very much alive today, I hope and believe, and a fellow Treaty prisoner somewhere.

So, Inspector! What point is there to this most recent addition to the narrative? None, beyond my own pleasure, the pleasure of evocation, while still possible, of an ancient time of innocence, aspiration, anticipation of a good life ahead, and terrors but brief and all soon overcome. And there are few enough pleasures in this place. That parcel of memory arrived back in my head quite unexpectedly in the early hours of this morning, together with the usual early morning clanging deliveries to the prison kitchen. I got up from my cot to write before I lost it, possibly forever?

Before writing I had to pee, for the second time this night, as always. One must be grateful for small mercies, not so Inspector? There was a time when I was sleeping little and rising at least six times every night to pee. Nocturia can spoil your night, every night. I was rescued from BPH by an excellent urologist (name gone). BPH? Benign Prostatic Hyperplasia – too much prostate but thankfully no cancer. I am remembering that well enough – one of the clichéd landmarks of a life too long lived. How many men, if any, suffered from too much nighttime pissing when forty years was our life's lot a million years ago? How many suffered the full humiliation of prostate cancer back then? Too much information, Inspector? I must assume that for you, there is no such thing.

I am bothered additionally this morning by another acronym. MCI. Have I mentioned this previously? Mild Cognitive Impairment, the fun term for humorous geriatric 'senior moments'. We all have those, sooner or later, but I seem to be having more, recently. Am I staring after my poor father, into the abyss of dementia? Someone once said that if you are fretting about dementia, you don't have it. Not true. Ronald Reagan fretted very publicly, and had it.

One of the terrors was meeting her parents for the first time. They were welcoming and gracious, and never asked whether I was Jewish. Just for the record, Inspector.

. . . .

Recalling later 2019 (or thereabout)

"There is a flap on. A couple of American billionaires are funding lab stuff to get us all to live forever. One genius is planning to have his brain digitised for posterity." Another summons from the Treasury's PUS to walk and talk along the Embankment. I thought I detected stress in him sufficient to exclude his customary jokiness.

"Guys from Google, Facebook, and loony hedgies, can you believe it! They have the money to play God. As if the old Encyclopaedia Britannica went into biotech just for the hell of it. Can't have that. Old news actually, going back five years or so, as you must remember, but we here all thought that was nothing more than yankee bluster. Too much money, too little brain. They are going to show at some upcoming Euro conference in Berlin in a couple of months. Ageing and population. That sort of thing. We want you there, Brexit or not. No need to get into any fights. Just present your stats as forcefully as you can. No need to feel tainted by politics. You will be representing your university, so you should apply to speak. I suspect you will find no difficulty in getting a slot". He had turned enough to catch the question on my face.

"I mean with your reputation and so on." Silence, perhaps for me to contemplate his request and agree, in spite of the obvious fixing that must have been accomplished already. I knew of the conference, of course, and had in fact thought of attending. Not necessarily to speak there. 'The European Commission on Ageing and Population Conference 2020'. Pompous mouthful perhaps but conferences are our academic meat and drink, sometimes too literally. Everyone invited to apply, European or not. The conference publicity emphasised the theme: figuring how to finance adequate care for the ravening hordes of Euro aged. Our stats would only feed the fire rather than suggest solutions. Now I could be committing myself to speak. No harm in that; builds the reputation and street cred.

My hesitation was the consequence of family history rather than any doubts about the potential usefulness of the information I had to share. I had visited most Euro countries for work or as a tourist, including Poland and its ex-German killing fields. And Germany once. Never again, I had promised myself. That was in a northeastern spa town. A session in a large covered pool complex was one of the entertainments for delegates to that conference. I had wandered unknowingly into the sauna area still dressed in speedo pants. A young man in company uniform seemed to spring out of nowhere, screaming at me: "Zieh aus! Zieh aus!" while gesturing at my offending clothing. I put my hands up and fled rather than strip to qualify for my continued presence there. I knew enough German to recognise what would have been the last words heard by millions of 'my people' including great grandmother, heading for gassing and burning all those years ago. So polite. It became fixed in my consciousness that 'the Germans hadn't changed'. A return to Germany could be avoided without great harm to my career. Perhaps. Then again, the Under-Secretary surely must have been acting as a shadowy background fixer of my recently improved fortune. Perhaps I should not disappoint. Perhaps my sensitivities could become a source of future regret.

Then, before either of us broke the silence, I saw an opportunity to do a little more than 'present statistics'. I could contribute a potential solution by advertising my unacceptable amendment to Sparrow's Assisted Dying bill. The Ante-mortem Contract. That would be my offering: to reduce the numbers of aged, with their prior agreement, rather than hope to find the funds to care for them in their expensive decrepitude. Why the Silicon Valley tech tycoons thought that this would be a suitable hearing for their ideas on creating everlasting life, remained a mystery. I broke my promise to myself and agreed to go but kept silent about my full intentions. The PUS grunted his satisfaction. He continued by saying something that makes even a serious academic believe this PUS was clairvoyant.

"Last time we spoke you were wittering on about your amendment to Sparrow's bill. Why don't you test it on your fellow delegates in Berlin? Who knows? The Swiss may like it as an add-on to Dignitas etcetera. Could be good for their business. The idea might catch on eventually in Europe and then come back here? Just be sure to be emphatic about all the checks to potential abuse, and so on. The Germans will be anti. Toxic history of course. If there are ethical types and godbotherers and medics present, they will all give you a hard time. Could be great fun." I reminded him again that I was an 'ex-medic' myself but he did not respond.

We were now close to the back entrance of HMT again.

"The university will fund all your expenses. You can drag your bimbo protégé along if you wish, for moral support in case too many delegates end up shouting at you. Book yourselves into the Kempinski on Fasanenstrasse. You will find it acceptable, I think. Very central. Berlin not your stamping ground according to my information. I will leave you to book your flights." His German pronunciation was native and his information better served than I would have liked. Perhaps there was more to this apparently bluff jokey bloke than I had guessed. Modern Languages rather than Classics?

"Ah, yes!" As if he had only just remembered. "Look out for a new job being advertised in your department. Professor of Death or something equally cheerful. You should think of applying. You must be in with a chance. Would be good to go to Berlin as a prof of something." Or words to that effect. And he was gone.

I will never know if my appointment was fair or 'fixed'. I had arranged a meeting with the Vice Chancellor, my 'new best friend', to achieve some notion as to my chances. He was even handed, as he would have needed to be, but indicated that my application was 'absolutely expected'. The department had come into some money. The Senate had voted in favour of a Chair of Thanatology. Macabre really, and not really my professional interest, but hey! – the chance of a professorship at a top institution before forty? And Health Economics is but an arm's length of relevance from death and dying. The Vice Chancellor chased me away to discuss details with the Dean of Faculty. I confessed my misgivings to the Dean in respect of my meager skills in forensics but he waved those away with the information that I was the only medically qualified candidate on the shortlist and would know more about forensics than the others.

Now, as I write, the events of that time are something of a blur. I do remember that the 'process' did impress me with its unexpected and almost unseemly haste. There was an interview, of course. I was asked what sort of lecture course I would construct. My ambition insisted that everything should be in there: the history, the science of bodily decay and preservation, psychology, art, commemoration, bereavement, ritual, and especially the economics of death and dying. And plagues and pandemics. And genocide through the ages from Genghis Khan to the present. I would engage the services of university staff where my own expertise was deficient. I would go further and work to influence current issues such as the wider implementation of Sparrow's Assisted Dying bill, now long since part of UK law, as we all know. I was careful to say nothing about my failed Ante-mortem Contract amendment.

I was required to make a presentation, of course. I picked on a piece of work that was currently occupying my attention and said something about the unacceptable carbon cost of cremation. Or words to that effect. Notions stolen from a dead man, my father. That seemed to go down a treat, judging by the extended nodding from the members of that inquisition. However, I remember also that the acoustics allowed me to catch a remark as I left, along the lines of: "Well he would say that anyway, wouldn't he, considering his probable origins? Jewish, isn't he?"

We three candidates were required to wait to learn the decision of the appointments committee, rather than go away, to be informed by mail of some kind weeks later. My competition consisted of my cheerful departmental neighbour, Geoffrey G, (remember him?), health economist, sociologist, climate changer, and statistician; and a nice historian lady known to me but faintly, a national treasure in the history and science of embalming. After a fretful and embarrassing hour of excruciatingly painful small talk, a door opened, the committee members exuded, and there was a lot of handshaking all round with muttered regrets to my competitors. I was the first incumbent of the new Chair of Thanatology in our university, possibly by an opaque process of regulated transparency.

....

Sara had booked an appointment to see me, days after my 'elevation'. Uncharacteristic and unnecessary formality, I thought. She said she wanted to discuss the Berlin trip without interruptions. She came in, pointing to the new title on the door, offering congratulations. I was about to reply with my concerns as to a possible fix, when she closed and locked the door behind her. That seemed an excessive liberty but within seconds her hug and a kiss had developed into a grope of extreme body-wide sensuality, very quickly and overwhelmingly mutual, I must confess. I had a fear of embarrassing myself again in a reprise of that previous occasion but clothing was being shed with some violence all over my office floor. She put a forefinger to her lips to command silence while she guided me to the armless guest chair, pushed me to sit and straddled my predictable erection. I have a vivid memory of a brilliantly red-haired pubes bouncing on my lap in time to the creaking of a chair under stress until my premature ejaculation ended it. I had to bury my face in her freckled breasts to stifle a shout. I caught some deep earth perfume. We remained embraced and quiet for a while. I kissed her to reassure her and to indicate my gratitude. I soon had intrusive thoughts of possible consequences - emotional, physical, social - interrupted by my flopping out of her. I grimaced in embarrassment; she giggled. In the office of the Professor of Death we had been in the act of creating life. Potentially, but I hoped not actually. Creating life, I mean. We cleaned up and dressed, still in silence. I started to make us coffee. She came to give me another hug and the first words: "Congratulations, Professor!"

Oh Deah! Now a very wide line crossed and another mess made, but I had the love of two good women. I considered myself blessed, living a sexual fantasy given to few men, yet hoping none of this would leave me cursed. We discussed arrangements for Berlin and she left. I remember some later puzzlement as to what Sara saw in me. Certainly not a pretty face and not a pretty body. And then apprehensions about what amounted to our own unofficial and guilty secret, but with no Official Secrets Act to sign this time. The enduring buzz of pleasure in my crotch finally swept these apprehensions aside. Was Anthony Burgess onto something in his conviction that Welsh women were particularly randy? Physiologically that is nonsense. But sex, like love, is somewhat more than mere physiology. Maybe. The armless chair now bore a new significance. Armless. Harmless? No. Charmless? Yes, except now charmed by association.

'Living beyond 70: Cost and Consequences for Modern Economies'. Professor David Stern PhD FRCP (and my three co-authors). I am pretty sure that was the title of my Berlin talk as it appeared in the conference programme booklet: 'The European Commission on Ageing and Population: Conference 2020, Berlin'. Impressive, in retrospect, but you get only ten minutes to get your message across, and five minutes for questions. Generous by today's standards. Also strange in recollection: delegates would actually travel, often half across the world to gather in conference halls, sometimes in their thousands. No-one does that now, really. You attend online and you can use your ComCam in front of any connected screen. I must say that I did later miss the stimulation of physical meeting and face-to-face confrontation of colleagues and ideas. My very young students (when last I had any) have never had that experience and insisted there was no difference, when I bothered them with my reminiscences. Physical presence is an outdated concept, apparently. Presence was very physical for me and Sara in 2020, and in a different sense with certain other delegates, as I intend to relate.

....

Recalling 2020

The ride from Brandenburg Airport into the city was dreary, neither threatening nor reassuring, simply commercial-industrial as for most city airport roads. Sara seemed to sense that I wanted quiet in order to gauge any perceived threat level and thankfully made no attempt at small talk. No threat. All smiles and perfect English at Kempinski check-in. No threat. We had adjoining rooms. I couldn't decide at the time whether that was going to be good or bad for us. I suggested a city bus tour for familiarisation; we would not have time any other day of the conference. We caught the last tour of the day. No threat. On the contrary, here in the fading light was funky arty alternative edgy graffiti-covered rebuilt Berlin and preserved Wall remnants, with a whole city square given over to the stark dark concrete blocks of the Holocaust memorial and museum. Police patrolling synagogues. Berlin at least, doing penance.

At dinner in the hotel, Sara was awed by the unaccustomed luxury of our surroundings, and our accommodation. She was probably remembering the customary damp malodorous bed and breakfast establishments she would have frequented when travelling to give papers relevant to her emerging PhD. She wanted to know if this luxury was usual for the conferences I attended. Indeed no. Was it because I was now a professor? Unlikely; probably just this occasion, co-incidentally. Was the university paying for us or had I to chip in? Yes, to the first, and no. Why this occasion? I didn't know really; these were the arrangements made for us. By the university? Well, not certain about that. After a pause sufficient to allow a carefully considered further response, I reminded her that the government was interested in our work. I confessed that I suspected that my rescue from the outer darkness after the Regent's Park BBC debacle, may have been engineered by the government, working through the university. And that included her funded PhD. It was just possible that the government had funded the university for all this. Just perhaps and maybe. I revealed nothing about my meetings with the Treasury.

She was quiet, apparently concentrating on her food. Then: why the Official Secrets thing? We are doing nothing more than gathering stuff which is out there anyway, and just putting it together. What is the secrecy all about when we're here telling everybody what they should know anyway? What is the agenda? Are we being bought for some government purpose? Was this a fix?

Clever child, articulating all my own suppressed misgivings. No, not a fix but an opportunity. We should celebrate the refreshing fact that the government for once was interested in anything emerging from academic health economics. Or words to that effect.

This last offer from me reassured me. It may have reassured Sara because it put an end to the interrogation. We drank to that. I excused myself after we had finished, to go over my talk for the last time. I suggested that Sara should hang around to network; I recognised some of the delegates also at dinner in the hotel. Just put any drinks on my room tab. She shook her head and followed me up to our rooms. We came to her room first. I waited for her to open her door before moving on to my own but she grabbed my arm as soon as she had her door open and pulled me into her room. I was too polite to initiate any major physical resistance. A sudden hug from her, an appealing look as if asking to excuse her persistent dinner questions, and then a rapid progression to kissing, grappling, wild disrobing. And love-making without inhibition, unconditional, life-affirming. Living the fantasy. Again. The professor of death and his acolyte. Eros within the confines of Thanatos. As we lay together in recovery, the chill pedant deep within impelled me to issue some warning to the effect that there should not be any expectation of any binding relationship between us. She turned to me and with a bewitching smile confirmed that it was our official secret, old man. Or words to that effect.

With that reassurance, I returned to my room to review my (our!) talk after all, interrupted only by wonder at the extent to which the sudden prospect of an orgasm can overtake one's life, excluding all else, ever so briefly. Well, I suppose I should confine that to *my* life. The flattery of seeming attractive to this magnificent creature of impressive sexual precocity, nearly half my age, added intensity to the pleasure, no doubt. A golden glow of pleasure decorated with a dark rim of guilt, but a very narrow rim, in retrospect.

Hey Diddle Diddle
The Cat and the Fiddle
The Cow jumped over the Moon
The little dog laughed to see such fun
And the Dish ran away with the Spoon

....

'The European Commission on Ageing and Population: Conference 2020, Berlin'

There were nearly five hundred delegates at this gathering, including whole retinues from each of the Silicon Valley oligarchs and celebrity geneticists, come to offer everlasting life, bugger the consequences or the cost. Just as predicted by the Permanent US at the Treasury. The Google gang was there, in the guise of their CalGo Foundation, and hedgie Soon Xun offering a Longevity Prize, and bio-wunderkind Venster, and tech genius Paul Pearl representing his Prize and Foundation, and tech genius Barry Bellis, and Abie De Groen, a biology druid looking like a bearded biker. What was all this longer-life money and expertise doing at a conference intending to deal with the problems of longevity rather

156

than its virtue? Looking for an audience wherever possible? I spotted Oxford and Bath buddies-in-academia, come to restore seriousness to the debate, I expected, together with little me. And then the rest of the world was there, it seemed, not just Europeans. Bath: so appropriate, where Malthus lived and died and was buried.

This was a big deal conference, in a big deal venue. We were on the site of the Imperial Schloss, become the impressive Humboldt Forum, Berlin's 'British Museum', newly restored eighty years after major bomb damage and subsequent serial annihilations. Grandeur inside and outside, sufficient to overwhelm. This would have been a first visit for most delegates, confirmed by so much comic head-turning and so many exclamations of appreciation.

Proceedings were opened by a short welcoming speech from the European Commissioner for Ageing and Population ('EuroAgePop'), a tall, elegant, greying lady speaking in fluent English of indeterminate European, probably Dutch origin. Headphones worn by some delegates indicated the simultaneous translation service.

The Californians got early speaking slots: tweaking genes and medications would get us living to 1000 years. All it took was money and science, and they had plenty of both. It was what the whole world wanted. And so on. Nothing said about world overcrowding, unemployment, bankrupt pension funds, bankrupt healthcare. They got repeated enthusiastic applause and a couple of standing ovations. They had hijacked the conference with the prospect of immortality; a biblical seduction of life without end and without the nuisance intervention of heaven, apparently deeply affecting clever people who should have known better. Californian tech priests were offering what most believers wanted from religion, the promise of immortality. At lunch there were queues of delegates hoping to chat to the Californians, keeping them and themselves from the excellent food.

I had the first slot after lunch. I remember a hall of slumber and the occasional snore. With heartsink I spent the first five minutes presenting our devastating predictions to the post-prandial sleepers. I emphasised the major cost culprit as dementia, repeatedly, and no prevention in prospect. I hit on age 70 as the statistical common tipping point between health and expensive illness across the range of age-related illnesses. I did see a few polite nods from the night watchmen, those who managed to remain conscious. I stopped for a moment to check whether the Californians were awake. Bless them, they were. I then offered a partial solution in the form of my proposed Ante-Mortem Contract and which I predicted would be taken up with enthusiasm sufficient to effect a major reduction in the population of the potentially and expensively ill. I saw night watchmen nudging neighbours awake as I spoke. I acknowledged Dame Helen Wilson as the spark of this idea. I announced the start of what I called the Kilgardie-Wilson Project, doing honour, as I explained, to my childhood friend Jackie Kilgardie and his tragic end, and to Helen Wilson. (Have I told about gay Jackie, *Sally go round the stars* and his drowning suicide?). I quoted Atul Gawande as an all-American antidote to the Californians. I remember some angry gesticulating, shaking heads, and the odd shout as I came to the end of my talk.

No one remained asleep by this time. The allowed five minutes of questions became ten. The applause was late, muted, and brief. Questions and comments were shared between castigation and compliment. The more polite questions were much as expected and had to do with matters of regulation against abuse, appropriate legislation, the role of the legal profession and the churches. Much use of the 'slippery slope' cliché. At least one reference to the Holocaust. And so on. I had ready answers of a provisional nature, not satisfying all, judging from the persistent undercurrent of muttering from the audience. The support from Bath and Oxford was encouraging; my Oxford colleague had been a protégé of Dame Helen and had known her well. There was still a forest of hands showing, when the session chairman called a halt and recommended finding me at the coffee break.

Some Californians were smiling and chuckling to each other. In the queue for coffee, at least one delegate leaned over to call my sanity into question in some strong eastern European accent. A passing Californian stopped to offer commiserations: life beats death anytime, anywhere, don'cha think buddy? Sara joined me in an act of furtive queue jumping. She was unhappy that I had sprung the Ante-Mortem Contract on her as if she was just another delegate; she was a co-author and had never been consulted. The fact that she thought it was a good idea, was beside the point. My apology included some ridiculous crack about this being personal, not just business; that I was really anxious to get the concept across to this audience and couldn't risk possible objections from her. I saw to it that she was served ahead of me.

As we walked away from the table, the Commissioner approached us in the company of a couple of minders. Could we meet, possibly before the gala dinner, for further discussion, if I would be so kind? There was much to consider in my proposal; say seven, in room 21 (whatever) on the first floor? There will be refreshments. Certainly, but I would insist on having my co-author join us. Indeed (she inspecting Sara briefly, possibly wanting to approve, or otherwise). Sara appeared mollified by my insistence on her inclusion in these arrangements. I felt a reassuring squeeze on my non-coffee hand, behind my back.

I suggested we play truant for what remained of that day's proceedings, to allow us to walk back to the hotel along Unter den Linden, past the tourists at the Brandenburg Gate, and through the Tiergarten.

Those two hours gave us an opportunity to inspect the day's revelations and to speculate on the surprise of the Commissioner's interest. Back at last at the Kempinski, I am sure we had a drink at the bar, and made love before dressing for the dinner, as a kind of celebration I suppose, of having stirred up a kind of storm, for good or ill. That bit is blurred now. There was so much sex, I can't be certain, but I remember the dark rim of guilt beginning to thicken up. Too much sex? Is that ever possible? Yes, if it makes babies who then live too long. And yes, if it comes with violence and without consent. The Rev Robert Malthus (version 1) and Spywife agreed that we fuck too much. Mostly. Sara the Beloved reassured me repeatedly that we wouldn't make any babies.

She was quiet for a good while. Then:

"What does 'SOE' stand for? You know, on that woman's bust in Gordon Square. I didn't get round to looking it up. I feel so stupid." We had just made love, and this is what took over in her mind. I loved her the more for it.

"Special Operations Executive. Trained very brave young men and women to parachute behind enemy lines at night during World War II. They could operate a secret radio and kill silently with equal facility. Many were caught and executed."

"And 'GC'?"

"George Cross. A sort of civilian Victoria Cross. You know what that is, surely?" Nods on the pillow. "Noor Khan was not actually a soldier and not

161

in uniform, so the GC was appropriate. She would never have known. She was awarded posthumously."

"When I asked you at her statue .. bust thing what these meant, you said something like GOGO or FOFO. What was that all about?"

"FOFO. Fuck Off and Find Out." I could feel her jerk as if offence was taken. "No. Not you. That's what FOFO stands for. A cop-out for lazy teachers."

She said: "We should get ready."

....

Recalling 2010 (or thereabout, a memory just come back to me)

I had 'phoned home. The weekly chore of a dutiful son. By arrangement I would do the 'phoning, to suit the demands of my busy-ness. Dad was nine years retired, busy with the garden, reading, music, friends, and a variety of intellectual improvement courses. Mum volunteered for everything going that could improve the lives of others in the area, except the Women's Institute because she refused to have anything to do with the mawkish singing of 'Jerusalem' and its words of violent ambition. She answered the 'phone, unhappy. Dad was having 'senior moments' for the names of people and things many times every day, laughing at his own difficulty, insisting that "it will come back to me in a minute".

"Mum, that is what we all have to some extent".

No. He was forgetting dinner dates and booked concerts almost from one hour to the next.

"Probably a bit of MCI".

"What's that??" suspiciously.

"Mild Cognitive Impairment. Just some memory loss with old age". Worse was his recent tendency to tell the same joke several times each day, and then become offended when reminded of this, sulking. And yet, yesterday when his gang of 'decommissioned docs' came round for drinks and whenever episodes in his early life and surgical training came up, she could hear the details recalled with faultless accuracy.

"Is this dementia setting in? Say it isn't, for god's sake!" The panic in her voice was obvious.

"No Mum, it isn't. Dementia is one of my specialties".

"But you're not even a proper doctor anymore! How can you be so sure?"

The pedantry then took over, and so that I would not appear a complete incompetent at some future date.

"Mum. I am a very proper doctor, twice over. And in any case it is far too soon to say that. If this goes on, he needs to be tested before making a diagnosis". Bad pedantry, just to cover my arse.

After a brief silence I could hear her sobbing, and then she put the 'phone down. Too clever Mum. And I knew too that this was the start of that bleak journey to nowhere.

....

Recalling 2020

A taxi returned us to the splendour of the Schloss, in full night illumination. Sara stunning in a once-again fashionable simple black evening dress. Ushers helped us find our meeting room. We were encouraged to state a preference for drinks. I felt it was time for a whiskey to settle my apprehensions for this unexpected encounter. Yes, they had Irish. The elegant Commissioner swept in with her minders, welcomed us with a brief smile, perched primly with some notes before her, and wasted no more time on niceties.

How sure were we of our figures? The Permanent Under-Secretry all over again. The Ante-Mortem Contract was intriguing. Britain had at last legislated for assisted dying, in spite of the antipathetic performance of the British parliament back in 2016; the polls suggested then that the population was way ahead of the members of parliament and their inflammatory speeches about legalising killing; would Britain have the stomach for this possible next step? Surely that would require a kind of referendum or at least some pretty rigorous population survey?

I answered: "Perhaps, and yes, and yes."

She said: "Your obvious enthusiasm for the something-Wilson Project, the ante-mortem thing, is not evidence that take-up would be widespread."

I said Britain could lead the way for the rest of Europe; a population survey was essential; my enthusiasm was indeed not evidence but intuitively did she not agree that the notion of a bespoke and benign contracted end of life must appeal to nearly everybody? She batted that away by asking whether I ('Dear Professor'!) would head up a working party to plan a survey. It would be funded by her department; we would have to get the churches on board (oh God, not again!); we could use the vacant Commission offices in Smith Square, 'Lon-don', for meetings; we would need a reputable polling organisation like Mori (the Latin for 'to die' – how apt!); she would like to see a draft of the Contract; she would leave me to clear all this with my employer; she was sure there would be no obstacles; the whole idea made absolute sense in the face of the unsustainable medical costs of dying expensively. I put my hands up and said no, actually the whole idea was to allow people to anticipate the circumstances under which they would want to end their lives, my father's uncomprehending blank face before me as I spoke.

"Yes, of course my dear professor and the by-product could be a huge saving for all signed-up nations if you are successful. A by-product; only a by-product; an intended consequence; a double win; a win-win? Your brilliant idea after all. Let me know when you have considered appropriate candidates for your working party, let's say no more than five. I will need to approve your list and then you can start meetings, yes?"

Or words to that effect. Said with tilted head, conspiratorial shining smile, and the meeting was over. I remember feeling a bit faint as we left. I had been frogmarched from ideas to action by charm and flattery, momentarily overwhelmed. I recovered quickly enough to be seen by many delegates, including some of my Californians, those gesticulators and shouters, now all in evening dress, as we walked to the pre-prandial drinks, the Commissioner on one side and Sara on the other. We three had created a bit of a buzz about the place. That was one up for the Brits and the Euros versus the Californians and the Anti-choicers, I thought at the time.

Pussy cat, Pussy cat, where have you been?
I've been to London to see the Queen
Pussy cat, Pussy cat, what did you there?
I frightened some mice from under her chair

Not London, but Berlin.   Not Queen but Commissioner. And much more than mice.

....

Recalling late 2010 (approximately)

I can't remember which of us made the call, but my mother was on the 'phone in some distress. Dad had been to an orthopaedic meeting in Bath the previous day. 'Keeping up with the Boneses' in spite of retirement, he was fond of quipping. He had called on his mobile to say he was lost, trying to get home. We both knew he could have driven to Bath and back 'with his eyes closed', day or night, as he had done weekly for much of his professional life. There was still plenty of daylight but he couldn't explain how he had gone wrong. He couldn't remember whether he had been diverted by roadworks. He was quite alright, parked on the hard shoulder. He couldn't recognise anything in his immediate surroundings. Clever Mum had told him to click on his Navigation app and leave his phone on; make sure it was plugged into the car charger; switch on the warning lights; and above all don't move from wherever he had stopped. She had then called the police and they had found him on the road to Reading. They (the police) had been so good

– they had even driven the car back. All safe and sound back in Bristol, and Dad seemed perfectly normal this morning.

"This is it, isn't it." Statement rather than question. "This is dementia. I don't care what you say."

"Mum. We have all gone wrong at some time and ended up lost. Have you never got lost yourself? Remember when you ended up in Chepstow because you missed the turnoff from the M4?"

"Of course I remember, but I was always able to make my way home without assistance. And I was never lost. I was daydreaming. That's how I missed my turn and you know it. Your father had no idea where he was; how he had got there; nor what to do about the situation. And there is something else. One of his old colleagues came round to visit last week. Your father got some idea into his head that we hadn't met. He was trying to introduce us but couldn't remember my name! For godsake! He ended up just silent and dithering. Our poor visitor made some lame excuse about not being able to stay and ran off. Now what do you say?"

I cancelled tutorials and went home to Bristol. I had a good idea about why Reading. Mum and Dad had lived there during some spell in his early orthopaedic training. He was heading 'back to base' as his reverted mind would have prescribed. He was perfectly composed and cheerful when I arrived, puzzled that there had been so much fuss about nothing really. I made a few 'phone calls. His GP needed to know what had transpired. Dad would need a memory test. I needed to speak to a psychiatrist buddy – a 'proper doctor' – to ask whether he would accept a referral for consultation. Then back to London. I left Mum in tears. She knew enough not to have to be told what was to come.

....

Recalling 2020

My worthy Inspector will certainly be critical of my lack of sequencing in this account but I feel compelled to record a fresh memory when it arrives unbidden while I am already recording another memory, and before I lose track of this refreshed fresh memory.

The conference dinner was a partial failure, and not because of the food. Mass catering is normally a recipe for cold and dreary offerings, but the Germans had it right this night. The problem was my poor performance as a jolly and engaging company for Sara and our other near neighbours at table. I had been quiet for so long that Sara's glances were becoming more frequent, and eventually accompanied by a frown. I murmured a confession to Sara as to the storm in my head.

We left early for the refuge afforded by the Kempinski bar. I needed to talk and so did she. I reassured her that she would be on the working party as my gofer. We were obliged to have the EU Ambassador to Britain or his/her deputy, now that we no longer had a British Commissioner; we needed a pollster; and we needed someone versed in the arcane skills of guiding a final proposal through parliament. One of Sparrow's team on the Assisted Dying campaign would be ideal. The Famous Five would be a good code name for us. No, we should not have anyone from the AgePop Commissioner's office; that would look to an interested outsider too much like arranging oversight by a Euro puppet master. A necessity prior to any meeting was to have some sort of pro forma contract to go with the polling package. Sara and I would do that and then present it to our AgePop Euro Commissioner, as promised, for her approval. I dried up then, tired and somewhat whiskey soaked. I desperately needed my bed. I made my apologies to Sara.

"I am not attending tomorrow morning, but you should go while you can or use the time to see the exhibits in the Schloss. There is something I must do. On my own. Family business you might say."

....

2047

My Inspector has concerns for my soul. My deity denial rankles with him. It seems that this was the sole focus of his visit today. He must be expecting some very bad outcome from the judicial proceedings regarding my case. My Inspector has taken on the role of My Expector, by stealth. He does not declare that I am facing execution. Instead:

"So. How can you not believe in God? How can you explain the Universe? Infinity? Eternity? How can you believe that there is no life after death?"

"Well. Indeed. It just happened. It was a brief acquaintance with astronomy that finished any little belief I had. I was a bored teenager at home for the school holidays. I was desperate for something to read. I pulled out the first volume of an encyclopaedia. 'Astronomy' looked interesting. On a long afternoon that summer I was overwhelmed by the certainty that no Intelligence could have the slightest bit of interest in this pathetic speck of dirt near the edge of just one of many billions of galaxies. And would certainly not have any interest in the doings of only one form of life on that speck and least of all the doings of little you and little me. Blame astronomy, but I can't undo the change in my head since that day."

My Expector was not satisfied. "Have you no concern for your soul?"

"What is that?"

"You know perfectly well and I know perfectly well that you are purposely trying to provoke me. Your soul is that part of you that belongs to God; the essence of who you are."

"There is no part of me that belongs anywhere, except in your Department at present, but all of me will end up back in the earth in one form or another, and the worms will have a feast."

"You really are an arrogant little shit, aren't you?"

"Quite a lot of shit, if you insist, because of a passing bout of constipation but the opposite of arrogant, I would insist. I feel on the contrary that it takes some bloody cheek or arrogance to believe that some imagined deity will ensure you everlasting life. Because that is what it is all about, isn't it? The impossibility of an acceptance of the fact of mortality? No surprise that we need some consolation as we get to our End Day. This soul stuff can present you with difficulties if you cling too hard. Do you have a dog? Does your dog have a soul? Does your dog give a damn about its soul? Do you give a damn about your dog's soul? Or who is it has the right to say that beings without self awareness cannot possess a soul? Your dog may indeed have some self awareness at times because it is a very clever dog, I'm sure, but what about your goldfish? Not much self awareness in a goldfish, but it is still God's creature, isn't it? Soul or no soul? Worth God's worry or not? Sorry sir, but the soul is a can of worms in the face of some basic analysis. Maybe my soul will end in up in the worms and then one might say with some justification that worms have a soul."

The Inspector looked like he was making moves to leave, beginning with some headshaking.

"I don't have a dog or a goldfish and this conversation just ended. It confirms my belief that there is no hope for you. I had considered putting to Judge some plea in mitigation for you but I don't see the point. Making fun of God will bring its own reward, or rather punishment. I wouldn't envy your chances on Judgment Day." He stood up.

Too many judges for my one poor soul, I thought. But solitary produces desperate needs in a prisoner and I was not ready to lose my Inspector's company just yet.

"Please. Stay a moment. I have no wish to offend but I have two things to put to you. One general and one more personal." There was some pursing of lips, sighing, and glancing at his ComCam, and he sat again, but half turned as if going to stand again quite soon; I should have no illusions but that I was trespassing on his generosity. I proceeded to trespass.

"I read once that if you made a movie of the whole 4.5 billion years of the history of the planet, lasting a full calendar year and running twentyfour hours a day, life on Earth of any kind would take up only the last twelve seconds. And the life of us, homo sapiens, would take up a lot less time than that. In another twelve seconds it could be gone, all life on Earth gone, for one reason or another, possibly forever, thanks perhaps to some celestial calamity. 'Forever and ever, Amen' and 'World without end' but gone in a flash. My question is, assuming that there is no other intelligent life in the universe, and if there is no one left on Earth to believe in God, can God exist? Like Bishop Berkeley said: if you can't see a table because you have left the room where you last saw it, how can you say with certainty that it is still there?"

"That notion, that question, just proves your arrogance. What kind of idiot is that Bishop fellow? God doesn't need us. We need God. God exists without us." Said with some finality in his voice.

"OK. Last thing. Was there ever a time in your life when you believed in Father Christmas?" I was surprised that he was sufficiently engaged to forget his imperative that he asks the questions.

"Yes, of course, like all kids." He was prepared to humour me, but with evident irritation and diminishing patience.

"Do you still believe in Father Christmas?"

"Don't be ridiculous."

"Is there anything I could say or do to persuade you to believe once again in Father Christmas?"

"Now you are wasting my time and insulting my intelligence." Moves again to leave.

"I was just trying to paint a picture for you about how it is for me. Substitute God for Father Christmas."

Or words to that effect. I saw no virtue in pointing out that Bishop Berkeley 'was', not 'is', by some 400 years. I saw no virtue in complaining that Jeremy Bentham, the icon who got me into all this trouble, strenuously campaigned against religion. I asked after Spywife. I was granted what I took to be a look of sympathy, briefly, and he left without answering but with his subtle limp.

I don't care if it rains or freezes
I'm in the arms of gentle Jesus
I am Jesus' little lamb
Yes by Jesus Christ I am

(this is not a nursery rhyme: school cadet corps marching song, unofficial)

....

Recalling AgePop Conference, Berlin 2020

I took the S-bahn to Grunewald station, west of the city, guided by helpful instructions from the Kempinski concierge. At breakfast, Sara had offered several times to accompany me to wherever I was going and whatever it was I was up to. (Ending on two prepositions! I am actually wearying of my own pedantry.) I stressed that this was family business of a kind to which she should not be subjected. I was looking for Gleis Siebzehn, Platform 17, the departure point most favoured by captured Berlin Jews a century ago. Our common family history accepted that Great Oma Sophie had started her last journey from Platform 17 at Grunewald, 29th November 1942. Impeccable Nazi records captured by the Soviets and released after the fall of the Wall, proved her presence on that transport to Auschwitz. She was 50 then but her own compulsory End Day was imminent. There was no way of knowing whether she arrived alive at Auschwitz after days without food or water in the freezing cold of an exceedingly well ventilated cattle truck. If she had arrived safely, ("Zieh aus! Zieh aus!") she would not have lasted more than two hours. We do it better now with secobarbital and orange juice, a huge advance on the agonies produced by Zyklon-B.

On the stairs leading up to the platform, a very discreet notice announced the generosity of Deutsche Bahn in creating the Gleis 17 memorial. They had allowed the poplar trees to sprout up between the sleepers (cross-ties?) and the rusting rails. The platform edges were lined with large metal castings announcing every transport, with date and destination and numbers on board. Again, Berlin had come to terms with its recent history. The platform was deserted. I was surprised but accepted that this was all so long ago that most folk these days have not even heard of the Holocaust. I found her transport casting without difficulty, by date. I spent a while trying to imagine the circumstances of her arrival here, herded aboard with shouts and lashings and dogs snarling. I failed, I think, but we do it better now anyway with our End Day Party among family and friends, music, prayers, and final recumbency after the final drink.

Job done. Respects paid. And I am incarcerated here in England (I think) because I protested the grotesque deformity of my Ante-Mortem Contract imposed by UNPOPCONT, a kind of new holocaust. But loved by everybody it seems, for the time being at least, as a bounden duty owed to all society. That is a difference to be celebrated, I suppose, but not quite what I intended.

Who killed Cock Robin?
'I' said the sparrow
'With my bow and arrow – I killed Cock Robin'

I have a feeling I have quoted this one before. No matter. A lot of killing going on anyway these days. I met up with Sara in the Kempinski bar by arrangement and reported briefly on my Grunewald mission. She had difficulty with the context, confessing that 'early' 20th century was not one of her strengths. She in turn reported that she had in fact attended most of that day's Conference talks. Some of the Californians had had second papers accepted, receiving wild applause again, manifesting a kind of anti-Conference mutiny, she thought. No, our AgePop Commissioner was not present at all. I suggested that this was an indication of our Commissioner's disdain for that lot. They were offering tangible 'immortality' through biology, and the everlasting but intangible life offered by God would never match the competition. The boring statistics I had painstakingly laid before the conference, of the devastation awaiting all of us from increasing longevity, had been wiped from the agenda of the AgePop Conference, Berlin 2020.

Last love-making, slow and subdued (as I remember) before our return to London next day. I murmured my appreciation as we cuddled afterwards, and then went on to murmur my anxiety that she may entertain unrealistic expectations from our relationship. She laughed softly. "I wouldn't want to marry anyone as old and as ugly as you." Or words to that effect. Distinctly reassuring.

Ich bin klein
Mein herz ist rein
Sol niemand drin wohnen
Als Gott alein. Amen.

A child's prayer at bedtime. All that is left in me that is German and Great Oma Sophie. And now:

heart not pure by any means; and no God lives in it. My Inspector fears for me on Judgment Day.

....

Recalling 2012

I have no doubt about this date. Do you remember the sad certainty of the world's conspiracy theorists that this was the year of the Mayan prediction of the end of the world? Too long ago perhaps? I remember it as the end of my father's world of good health. The decline was terrifying in its banal and predictable progression. He had indeed failed the memory test. I had joined Mum at the consultation with a very gentle neurologist. He mapped out the likely timetable of deterioration and distress to come, but politely including Dad in the discussion as if Dad had come with nothing more than a hangover. Meantime he was to go onto Aricept and then one of the new 'mabs' if that didn't work. He would very likely have a perfectly contented time at home for months or years to come.

None of the medication worked despite best hopes. The descent was devastatingly rapid. I would visit weekly depending on work commitments and could measure the deterioration on that time scale. His repetition of stories from early life was amusing for a while and then became mind-numbingly hateful for Mum. She had to give up finally when he reached the point of soiling the bed almost nightly and the physical tasks simply became too much for her. He had 'broken out' a few times, usually at night, and in spite of the attempted hiding of door keys. The police had to be involved invariably. Mum would run into the street in her dressing gown in a panic but desperately hoping not to attract the attention of the neighbours. If she couldn't see him nearby, she would hurry back inside and report another runaway episode. A particular embarrassment came from a policeman who recognised Dad from his time involved with trauma cases in the hospital. Having successfully retrieved Dad nearly naked on a freezing winter's night outside a house where we had lived previously, he expressed his regrets to Mum repeatedly till she broke and wept and waved him away. Dad had been found shouting abuse at the occupants of the house, for illegally having taken possession 'like cuckoos in our nest', on and on.

The demands of appropriate sedation and personal hygiene required the expertise of an institution. That was the start of our personal merry-go-round of finding an acceptable place and funding for Dad's care. This jolly hunting expedition was an experience familiar to all who had required such care for a family member, and for which there was no state funding until the patient's family had achieved financial destitution. And dementia was the most common diagnosis underlying these lovely adventures in those days. Nobody gets beyond 70 now with UNPOPCONT 2032; the care home industry has pretty well crashed (sorry guys; not directly my fault) but families have been able to keep their hard-earned homes and pass them on to those left behind, free of tax. Legislated timetabled death has saved us so much money that we could abolish inheritance tax for homes. Everybody loves UNPOPCONT. Except me, it seemed at the time.

....

Late 2020

I have no difficulty remembering this year, the year of the Great Gridlock. Sara and I were to meet in my office to start work on a draft Ante-Mortem Contract. It was just before the Christmas break. Sara had been driving back to London from some new near-northern university where she had been examining as an external. She had called in to cancel our meeting. Rain had flooded many roads again. Traffic heading for the M25 hadn't moved for two hours. In the dark of late afternoon, she had assumed that, as usual, there had been some accident in the wet, but police had walked up the row of cars and trucks telling those who could, to abandon their vehicles and start walking. They said there was no hope of moving 'within the near future'; southern England was locked with traffic from Watford to the south coast. Special rescue vehicles would attempt to collect mothers with children and the infirm and take them to emergency shelters being erected. Sara said the scene was apocalyptic, like some wartime stream of refugees fleeing destruction, as one would see in history documentaries. Most walkers were without umbrellas or rain jackets. She had to quit talking to preserve battery; she had yet to call her parents before starting her walk to Bethnal Green. I wished her well to reach home safely, with endearments appropriate to our relationship but entirely at a loss for ideas to be of help. I had been in the office all day to tidy up many pending matters before Christmas, grateful also for the central heating, but deprived of all knowledge of what was happening on the roads. A brief look out my office window confirmed vehicles abandoned all along the road past the university. That explained why there was such blessed quiet recently.

'Tangles'. The word crept into my head as I tried to imagine what had happened. Tangles of vehicles along the roads. Then: 'plaques' – that would be vehicles massed at roundabouts. Tangles and plaques: the brain of Alzheimer's under the microscope. Nerves in knots and clumps. Our road system was demented! I realised then that I had been in the office too long and it was time for me to get home too. The difference was that I could walk home in half an hour and keep moderately dry thanks to a plentiful supply of umbrellas in the office, but Sara would be fortunate to reach her apartment before first light, and long wet through. I felt the burden of care for two women, and powerless to serve that burden on behalf of one of them that evening, against the flooding rain and demented road system. Pathetic academic. Oh Deah!

There was another difference: the gridlock would be resolved sometime, even if only temporarily, but Alzheimer's, like a De Beers diamond, is forever. I 'phoned home. Spywife was settled in front of the TV watching it on the news. She said it was all my fault for shouting "gridlock!" in a mock road rage every time we were stuck in traffic, however briefly. The Fates had now taken their revenge against the whole country because of my powerless road rages. I complemented her on her good humour and set off in anticipation of home, hearth, and whiskey.

Now I see the irony in her jokiness on that occasion. The Fates, in the form of the nation's government, have taken their revenge on me after all. On trial for treason on the basis of a misunderstanding. Road rages long forgotten. All to do with my good intentions for dealing with the consequences of the tangles and plaques of dementia. And the rest. Which reminds me – there were a few fatalities that night of the Great Gridlock, mostly cold exposure in the elderly and Type 1 diabetics who had run out of insulin while waiting for rescue or on the long walk into London. And out of. And within.

Hence the new rules, you will remember, making compulsory the carrying of emergency packs in every vehicle. Insulin-dependent diabetics who drive have to retrieve their insulin from the fridge each day. Or night. The trick for Type 1 diabetics to keep car and truck keys in the fridge originated from that first Great Gridlock.

Sara had made safe landfall in her east London flat after negotiating the floods of the Great Gridlock on foot. On the phone I offered to visit. She refused. She was planning to spend two days in bed catching up on sleep and temperature. She had been of service to some frail gentleman who should never have left his car. With another walker they had got him to safety but she was left too weary to entertain visitors. I was guiltily grateful. Any evidence emerging of such a visit, however well intentioned, would very likely be misinterpreted. We never did get to meet to hammer out a draft Ante-Mortem Contract. Well, there was one meeting in my office shortly after the start of the New Year new term but very little discussion or conversation took place. I did say on that intimate occasion that I would make some points on my own and how was she getting on with the arrangements for our Famous Five meeting it would be just as well to have them all in on the creation of the draft to give everyone a perception of 'ownership' of the result she said she was hot on the trail of someone who would fit the lawyer slot no pollsters we can hire them surely. She said that I had to make only one point to keep her

happy. Her laugh of wickedness as we dressed, a
tonic.

....

Report post-Berlin to the Permanent Under-Secretary
early 2021

      I was not called in. I made the call and was
well received. The PUS seemed less interested in
what I had to tell him than in what he wanted to tell
me. I realised after a short while that I was not telling
him anything he didn't know. He must have sensed
my irritation. He offered another biscuit and
explained that the *grande dame* EuroAgePop
Commissioner had already reported all that mattered.
Great satisfaction all round with my concept of an
Ante-Mortem Contract. Both His Majesty's Treasury
and the EU Ambassador would be funding our
working party activities. Possible only because Brexit
still not completed. I would find the vacant British
Commission offices in Smith Square to my
satisfaction, kept clean and warm by the caretaker. I
was strongly recommended to time meetings so that I
could move seamlessly from meetings to music across
the road at St John's. Do you listen to music? Of
course you do young man how else to calm the savage
breast best lunch hour in London all for free did you
know I'm off to New York buggers have made me

Ambassador to the UN somebody has got at me should have been ambassador to USA can't do any good in that UN sinkhole of corruption and babble come and see me sometime to cheer me up put it on expenses as instructed by me hope you live long enough to see this project through so much more to it than Sparrow's AD Bill I will be seeing the PM to warn him the government should take it on not just leave it as a private member's whatnot for the sake of humanity but you and I know we have a chance of reducing the expensive end of the population you will be called the Devil Incarnate but it is really God's Work you are doing you don't have to be religious to understand that and Lord Sparrow has moved on to other things I wouldn't bother him.

I asked to whom I would be reporting when he was gone. He didn't know yet but whoever it was would be fully briefed to look after the project. In any event, the PUS would be looking on from a distance. Important work, really very important. And would I be so kind as to let him know who will end up in the working party of the K-something Wilson project. And did I know by the way that Dame Helen Wilson had been a regular church attender as an atheist? Remarkable woman. Good choice of a name for the project. She would have approved, he said.

Meantime, as a parting gift, he had arranged for me to be invested with a ComCam. A whole lot more useful than a gong, he said. I had earned it and should enjoy the privileges and perks that go with

ComCam. Report to MI5 down the road. They will be expecting you. Your wife will tell you how to get there, assuming you don't know perfectly well yourself. A painless brain scan, a tiny cut in your arm, a little flower or something to go in your lapel, and it's done. Have fun! Goodbye!

....

2021

Smith Square sometime 2021, more or less

This was to be the first meeting of the Famous Five. I remember that Sara was curious as to the apparent mild amusement afforded me by the use of this code for our group. Her childhood had not included these stories and I teased her. I explained briefly. She tackled me on my ignorance of the legends of Welsh mythology. She declared then that, on balance, I was the one who had suffered childhood deprivation. I defended the feeding of my childhood imagination by adding in Grimm's Fairy Tales and Hans Christian Andersen. And for good measure, Strüwel Peter and Max und Moritz, reinforcing evidence of my German ancestry. We agreed finally that children are naturally attracted to fecklessness, naughtiness, witchcraft, violence, and bloody revenge. And we laughed as we simultaneously declared that

187

we obviously don't change as we grow up. By and large.

I checked the time and suggested we get ready to meet the three recruits about to join us in our first meeting. One originated from the office of the EU Ambassador, a gift to our credibility. A buxom blousy lady, surprisingly young looking, and evidently not in good humour. Reminded me briefly and unpleasantly of that BBC reporter, Regents Park. I had caught some shouty fluent French coming from no one else while she was preparing to enter from the corridor. I understood enough to gather that she was conveying her dismay to someone out of sight at the waste of time represented by her obligation to this ridiculous meeting. A senator in her previous life and Euro country, reportedly of daunting talent and severity. She had been enlisted to satisfy the condition set by our 'sponsor', the Euro AgePop Commissioner. As she entered she displayed no hint of discomfort at the realisation that we may have heard and understood her perjoratives. Omen of a bad start perhaps.

Then there was a nice man of my choice from Lord Sparrow's successful Assisted Dying team ('Sparrowman') honoured with a CBE for his efforts there. Should a bit of that CBE have been mine? I remember being amused at his bird-like appearance, from first acquaintance. A beaky nose, round shoulders, and a tendency to nervous glancing here and there as if anticipating the next trouble to accost

188

him.   Sparrowman could have been a sparrow in another life.

I was stuck for ideas for a fifth member but Sara had suggested somebody from the Health Standards Bureau (HSB), our healthcare police and the terror of all healthcare institutions.   Sara had read something about dissatisfaction with care of the dying, expressed by the HSB in a press statement.   The HSB had highlighted the discovery of clinical extremes of pointless resuscitation at death's door on the one hand, and the supervised neglect by starvation on the other. In too many cases there was a scandalous lack of pain control.   Someone from the HSB should perfectly complement our team.   (No – 'should complement our team perfectly').   And there before us was Samantha, the Jesus rower, lawyer and curator of my union with Spywife some twenty years previously.   Eighty million people on mainland Britain and we two end up in the same room to do business after all this time!

I remember Sara attempting to introduce us but I said it was OK we know each other from way back would you excuse us a moment I'll explain later amazing coincidence.   I shepherded Sam outside for a kiss and a hug.   Spywife and I and Sam plus husband (colonial, Australian as I remember), had socialised on occasion since Oxford, usually at Summer Eights on the river, but diminishingly, and then not at all in the years to 2021.   I marveled aloud at the remarkable coincidence of the manner of our re-acquaintance.   It raised briefly in my head the old question of who rules

Britain.   In silence I realised that perhaps not that many.   And did that matter as long as we all worked for the greatest good? I shepherded Sam back into our meeting room with earnest but customary vague invitations to get in touch so we four could 'meet for dinner sometime'.   I thought I noticed a brief hesitation in her step as if she wanted to say something but changed her mind.

As chairman, I started in the regular manner by suggesting that the assembled Five introduce ourselves to each other. I said we were here to do important work, to create the machinery for legally assisted dying *on request*, under specified circumstances not necessarily pre-terminal.   I then immediately shifted blame by making the case that we were here at the behest of the EuroAgePop Commissioner because she had taken up my suggestion of some kind of Ante-Mortem contract as the logical follow-on to the Assisted Dying legislation now enabled across the Union (except Poland). I said the idea was that it should be possible to improve our Quality of Death after all these years of obsession with Quality of Life; that it should be possible for every individual so minded and still of sound mind, to set out a wish list of the expected terms and conditions of their death; and in anticipation of the possibility that they may not retain the capacity of sound mind closer to the end; that my colleague (nod to Sara) had done some excellent research into what the majority of Europeans would consider a good death; that her PhD thesis was available online, if required; that, in case they didn't know, we two had developed a EuroQuoD score ('D' for Death) to match the EuroQuoL score ('L' for Life) so beloved of health economists like me; that Germany already had a system somewhat along these lines; that the Contract should be bespoke-tailored for each individual; that it was perfectly legal, with minimal fuss, to have assistance in killing a foetus but we were not allowed to have assistance to kill ourselves; that the polls indicated that the nation was well ahead of parliament once again – you must have seen in the papers; that the EuroAgePop Commissioner was waiting for our draft Contract before any further action could be taken.

So could we start with suggestions for the draft please? I said nothing about our hopes for population reduction through the enactment of such a Contract. I said only that we were in a powerful position, having the support of the Treasury as well as the European Commission, underwriting our endeavours in spite of Britain's planned exodus. In retrospect, I suppose I was then and there complicit in all that was to come upon me. None of my compatriots questioned the involvement of the Treasury.

I remember that the senator had her hands raised and head shaking before I had finished. "This is so silly. We have Assisted Dying throughout Europe now and I should remind you that I was the one charged with European implementation. That was an exhausting business. What more do you want?"

191

Sparrowman was nodding vigorously in acknowledgement of her magnificent effort on behalf of AD, and then nodding to me:

"It was enough of a saga getting AD through Parliament here, as I am sure you will remember." Nod, shake, nod, shake. "You were involved, I think. More legislation will be necessary for whatever it is you have in mind now. I don't know that anyone has the stomach for it. Man, woman or nation." Nod, nod, shake, shake. I was 'involved' he thinks. Faint praise. Recognition at last!

"OK. OK. Perhaps it would help if I got to some specifics. Assisted Dying works only for folk who are of sound mind and full mental capacity however sick they may be, AND they have to be certified incurably and preferably terminally ill by their doctors. And with full agreement of their families. But we know from our research that very many people live in dread of our modern miraculous ability to maintain life even in those who would rather be dead but cannot say so, for whatever reason. It should be possible for anyone to set out, *while still well and however youthful,* (I with middle finger tapping slowly on the table to the measure of my words) 'that under circumstances of XYZ, I want to be put down, put out of my evident suffering or complete uselessness, say, if in a long term coma, or deeply demented, or crippled by stroke etcetera'. Situations like that, from which there is no road back but life could continue for many years. You all know perfectly well – an intolerable burden to patient or person and their carers." Thinking of you, Dad, and millions like.

The senator, possibly wanting to end the meeting and get on with the rest of her life: "That is simply euthanasia. You are crazy. Forget it! No one will let it happen." Three looking at me. Sara and I with eyes down. Silence.

Eventually I said: "Yes. And no." Silence. I said: "Yes, euthanasia. But when you use that word you can think only of the great murderous genociders of history. What we are proposing is something quite different. It is euthanasia by request of the very individual seeking a dignified and preferably painless end. Euthanasia requested ahead of a time anticipated when life perpetuated would be seen as pointless and insupportable by the individual making the request." Silence.

Senator: " 'Mercy killing by request'. That would look good in the press! That is what we have with AD anyway." Our formidable Senator was not getting it.

Sam to the rescue: "Why don't you give us an example, or some examples of what you have in mind."

I said: "OK. I don't mind using myself as an example because in one sense this is personal. I don't want to end up like my father, for five years till death an empty shell, the living dead, alternately roaring and silent, recognizing no one, incapable of speech and doubly incontinent. Sound familiar? I won't insult your intelligence by offering a diagnosis. I would want someone to help me end my life as soon as I was too demented to receive visitors and was starting to present a major problem of physical care. I would want responsible people with capability to recognise those conditions of incapability in me and which I would have set down as representing the justification to 'go straight to auction'. Just like the car salesman said when I traded in my high mileage runabout. My father would have wanted that, I know for certain, but he was too far gone to make that request when his condition became relevant. (Leaning forward making serial eye contact): *He never would have qualified for AD. That is my point in this example. No sound mind. Eventually no mind at all."* Or words to that effect with finger tapping the table.

I waited in the silence that followed. It was already nearly 'half time' and nothing achieved.

"I think we need to start again. I'll call for tea and coffee. May I suggest that when we gather, that each one of you offer at least one example of what would represent an unacceptably bad death and in anticipation of which you would want to have some kind and qualified person help you 'to that act of supreme dignity'? Who said: 'That which most I feared has come upon me'? That is what I want from you as you come to die – what kind of dying you fear most. Rats eating your face in the 'Room 101' of dying? Thank you."

Or words to that effect. It is a good while ago now, and I have recreated a scene that has remained vivid in my memory even if the details of dialogue cannot be dredged up with perfection. Where is the harm in all that, Inspector? Additional power to the people seeking Assisted Dying; an extension of the definition of what should be legally possible.

Sara, armed with coffee, whispered something about why hadn't I told her about my father. I said it was not her burden and at the time she was just another undergraduate. She wanted to know what was that nonsense about, that smart-arse quote about supreme dignity and why am I always doing that? I said go back to Gordon Square, Bloomsbury, and Virginia Woolf.

"Oh God, her again. Bollocks. I don't remember that one. You still sound like an Eng Lit undergraduate show-off but you don't know your Bible. Be grateful for my Welsh upbringing. Job! 'That which most I feared…'."

I didn't have the courage to correct her; she should have said 'Oh God, *she* again'.

"Thank you Sara, love, and thank you Job. Working for me now!" Sara had no idea of course that I was referencing my last encounter with quotes from Job; and I marveled at her bold presumption of our egality.

The Senator disappeared without a farewell and I did not really expect her to return.

Little Miss Muffet sat on a tuffet
Eating her curds and whey
Along came a spider
Who sat down beside her
And frightened Miss Muffet away

Aloud, I thanked Sam for her intervention. To Sparrowman I said I had no wish to burden him with more legislation nightmares; it was the wisdom of his traumatic experience we needed. He appeared placated, head-shaking quiet for a while. We all moved serially to pee and take our seats. And the Senator joined us! Much later I had the notion that she might have 'phoned Brussels in the tea/pee break and had a word with the EuroAgePop Commissioner. She manifested resignation rather than aggression and I took that to indicate progress in our relationship.

I have to stop here for a bit to allow my 'hard drive' (remember those days?) to catch up. Having a 'senior moment' now and can't remember exactly what happened next.

Little Bo Peep has lost her sheep
And doesn't know where to find them
Leave them alone and they will come home
Bringing their tails behind them
(for a little while I am Little BP; my memories are my sheep, obviously)

....

Recalling 2004/5

I will take refuge in some earlier memory while waiting and hoping that the further proceedings at Smith Square return to my increasingly unreliable head.

Oxford graduation attended. An incubator of a certain sense of entitlement. How not? Camelot days of grand and ancient spectacle, gaudy gown colours, happy smiles and laughter, sunshine (surely not every time?), and plentiful food and drink in one or other college marquee. And terror on the first occasion. Spywife graduated years before I did. She was already working in London somewhere, not telling me how occupied, and back living with her parents. She had managed to extract an extra ticket from the graduation organisers, over and above the standard two-tickets allowance. How not, with that deep voice promising sex, great beauty of face by any standard, and ultimately winning smile?

Apart from doing honour to my beloved, the intention was for me to be introduced to her dauntingly establishment parents. I found them, *sub fusc* daughter first and then obviously the parents, in the throng filling the Sheldonian courtyard. Both 'handsome' middle-aged distinguished-looking, sort of cliché respectable, judges both by this time. He in heavily pin-striped suit with a dusting of dandruff on his collar. Comfortable and confident and charming with the introductions, practised at putting the awkwards of the world at ease. I was increasingly won over as we slow-marched with the queue to enter the building. This was home from home for them, as he reminisced about his own graduation here, and joking about the great pity that his wife (formal nod in her direction) had chosen badly and gone to 'the other place', the Oxford code for Cambridge. The humour of the superior class, those who rule Britain, I thought, smiling appreciatively through it all.

'Vision' left us to join her graduating group and we three took our seats in the high galleries. Before we were subdued into silence by some master of ceremonies with a big stick (ceremonial mace), her parents had me confirm that I was indeed studying medicine how brave we could never do that stuff with dead bodies and then all the dreadful diseases and blood and gore and then when all done having to cope with the fraught politics of healthcare in Britain. I really was beginning to love them, while frantically looking for where 'Vision' was seated below. We found each other at about the same time, she having been searching in similar fashion. Much waving and smiling across the space by so many, including ourselves once I had directed the parents' attention to their daughter. Silence at last. Then lots of Latin, excruciatingly English-accented; two lots of marching in and out with bowing and doffing, the second time with the treasured fake rabbit fur fringing the hood. I was in love with all of it. Such a beautiful day. Such beautiful and clever people everywhere, and my beloved the most beautiful of all. In another three or four years (allowing a year for the standard delay in these ceremonies), this could be me. 'Poland to polo in three generations' goes the common self-referencing joke among us aspirational Jews. Much photography followed, and then the stroll to Merton and a meal in a posh tent. Sorry, marquee. More Latin, this time from the white-haired eminence of the Warden, saying an obligatory and blessedly brief grace. More solicitous questions and praise came from the Judges. I was flattered that they should concentrate so much of their attention on me, until I realised after the first glass of wine that all this interest may be hiding a sophisticated and well practised form of interrogation of an unknown who may have aspirations towards joining the family. 'Vision' had surely briefed them anyway. I played along. They had to hear about a Bristol upbringing and acceptably posh school; a surgeon father with experience of southern Africa; and a mother who was an artist and sculptor of merely local repute.

He said: "Ah, the example of the father then, in your career choice!" I replied that I wasn't sure I had the stomach for surgery but the medical influence was undoubted. I saw my opportunity to turn the conversation to our local heroine of the day, and said something light-hearted about parental influence not working very well on her. I asked 'Vision' to confess her present paid occupation to us all, pretending that I assumed her parents were also without that knowledge. I remember her embarrassed smile at her parents as if asking their permission for her to reveal some precious truth. After a shrug she looked away and murmured something drowned out by the happy buzz of talk and laughter. My turn to shrug.

Looking at me and leaning closer she said quite distinctly: "Foreign Office" and giggled. I was stunned. What a dreadful waste of a top PPE!

I said, laughing gently to take the edge off the criticism: "That's a bit of a waste of a PPE, isn't it? Do they need Politics, Philosophy and Economics to be able to tell folk where not to go on holiday?" Their turn, the three of them, to laugh, but uproariously this time, attracting some attention from our table mates. She said, tapping her steel dessert spoon on the table for emphasis: "We should leave it there. Let's talk about my holiday! Something I deserve after today, don't you agree?" And that was it. She was going to St Petersburg. No, alone. That's what she prefers, she said. Tough steely cookie indeed but I knew that by then. Foreign Office? Quaint.

So, Inspector So! 'What is the relevance of this most recent reminiscence and digression?' you should ask. 'None!' should be the reply, except for the sake of digression. And except for an account of an event at a time of anticipation of achievements and glories to come, thanks to the benefits of some of the best education available anywhere in the world. This is an account you should enjoy, contrasting as it does with the eventual outcome: my fall from grace, and the fall of Spywife as well. Such gratification is sufficient relevance for this bit, surely.

....

Smith Square (continued) 2021 approx.

Some of this has come back to me. I had asked the other 'four' to offer suggestions of circumstances for themselves under which they would not want to continue living even if they were no longer capable of taking their own lives. I probably reassured them of our mutual confidentiality obligations. I probably reminded them that we should refer to our deliberations as the Kilgardie-Wilson (or 'KW') project, partly to humour me and partly for security. I asked them to consider themselves bound by the Official Secrets Act even if they had not signed a piece of paper.

Two of our number offered the advanced stages of dementia, having had some direct or indirect experience of this. No surprise. Another offered Multiple Sclerosis. But Sara surprised me by offering untreatable schizophrenia. I thought there must be a family story there but didn't probe. I offered both dementia and incurable cancer, making plain that I had family experience of both. I expressed gratitude for these confessions, explaining that we could not progress with the project unless each of us had some personal investment in its success. I then asked for us to play devil's advocate and suggest why the project must fail.

Sam waited not a second. "You can't have a contract. Or, whatever you end up with, it can't be a contract. There is nothing in our law which could support such a deal. There is certainly a place for suspensive conditions in our contract law but that has to do with a sale or purchase of something, anything. Property, goods, rights. You are not buying or selling anything."

I said: "We are making it possible for an individual to buy reassurance that if they reach a certain point of no return beyond which they are not capable of ending their life, then someone else can do it for them." Sam laughed and shook her head. "OK. If you're buying, who is selling? And for how much?"

I said: "Well, there has to be a fee for services rendered I suppose, like buying a funeral in advance. That is a good analogy, isn't it? That is a suspensive contract. I buy a funeral but the contract comes into force only when I die. That brings back something from my time as a kid in South Africa. There was a burial society, just like we have here, with the acronym AVBOB. You paid a small amount monthly for years. Used mainly by Afrikaners, but they themselves joked about it. One of the Afrikaans kids in my class told me the letters stood for 'Almal Vrek Buig Of Bars'. It still makes me smile. A kind translation is 'everyone dies, bend or break'!" I was smiling at the memory but no one else was and the Senator was making a show of consulting her watch. Sara was shaking her head to indicate that I was guilty of an item in very poor taste.

Sam said: "You still haven't defined a seller, number one. Number two – your story nicely highlights a suspensive condition; death is pretty specific as a definable end point. If for instance we are talking dementia, where in the progression of dementia would you want the seller to pour the medication down your throat or give you the injection? Sorry. No, not finished with the legal problems! Number three – what if the seller, say, a doctor who is willing enough at the time of signing then changes his or her mind about the whole thing? No court will conceivably enforce the contract. Forget it. David, you can't have a contract."

What was Sam up to? It seemed she was taking some pleasure in blocking my proposals. Almost vengeful in some strange way. My Jesus rower! Recruited in good faith by the tireless Sara.

I had my mouth open to ask what I could have instead but our Senator had an interventionist finger raised and waving: "More points I'm afraid, probably beyond resolution. Never mind about ministering doctors possibly changing their minds, what about the supplicants who change their minds but are no longer capable of communicating that change, and you would never know? And who will be in charge of the whole thing, to be responsible for conduct, ethics, and the rest, you know, general oversight?"

Sparrowman to the rescue, head jerking in all directions with excitement: "The Assisted Dying programme uses a judge and two doctors fulltime to assess each application. Each assessment is exhaustive and meticulous, to cover all the bases. Something similar could work for this Kil-something Wilson project. In two years of operation the AD programme has not had a single objection raised or court case brought against the decisions made."

Senator: "Kill something? Sounds to me like kill a lot."

I said, ignoring the opportunistic barb: "That is encouraging. No? The big difference here is that people who are pretty fit and possibly in large numbers, are setting out conditions for their termination at some future date which cannot be specified. Perhaps we should suggest a commission, not just judge and doctors, created by statute; a whole lot of the 'Great and Good' to oversee proceedings?"

Looking at Sam: "Obviously, only those doctors in sympathy with the programme would apply for certification onto the programme, and just as obviously they could leave the programme at any time."

Looking at the Senator: "I have no answer to the problem of a subject changing their mind and having no means of letting us know. Ideas anyone? I suspect it must be something made plain in the contract – sorry – agreement, that there is no way back if a subject loses all communication capability? Must be a pretty rare situation, surely. Even that poor locked-in fellow who featured in the Assisted Dying controversy (nodding in sympathy to Sparrowman) was able to blink his messages or something. There cannot be any compulsion to sign up to the project but if you do, you would be signing up to no way back. Yes?"

Silence.

Then Sara: "Sorry - what is the 'Great and Good'?" Welcome light relief. I explained that it stood for the worthy and blameless *prominentes* of our society, acting as guardians against bad behaviour and immorality, nodding the while to the Senator. Wonders! She responded to the gesture with a shy smile. I had the sudden insight that we could have her commit if there was a hint of a future role for her in such a commission.

I said: "It would be my strong recommendation that the Senator should lead such a commission. I know we have only just started down this road but our Senator is just the person with the credentials and appropriate modicum of scepticism for this work." Slow nods of agreement from the other three. The Famous Five were holding together thanks to Sara's innocent question.

I said: "We need to think of a title for this commission. Suggestions for next meeting please, but before we part – last task of the day - we should start to compile a list of adverse circumstances to present to project applicants to help them decide which should apply to them. Then all they have to do is tick boxes. Or not. And there should be space for an applicant to add a circumstance not listed."

We did quite well, as I remember. The obvious conditions came quickly: coma (of any cause) beyond say three months, advanced cancer, stroke with significant disability for the activities of daily living, diabetes necessitating repeated amputations, any major organ failure, schizophrenia requiring long term incarceration, and of course dementia associated with incontinence and failure to recognise family or friends..

I said: "What if I just wanted to go at say 75, reasonably fit and well, merely in order to avoid the possibility of suffering any of those deeply unpleasant situations we have just listed? I would be perfectly capable of delaying the day when it came to it, if I wanted to."

Senator with a sharp edge: "How different is that from just wanting to commit suicide?"

I said: "No different. But why in my determination to die for whatever reason, should I be left to my own sad devices by hanging or carbon monoxide or gassing or jumping or shooting, when I could be helped by experts, dying in comfort and in good company without leaving a terrible mess? I have a specific example in mind, to paint the picture. A man of my close acquaintance, a farmer of a small hillside, late 60's, fit and well apart from a very disconcerting TIA, during which he lost a day but gained the news that another one of those could kill him – good; or leave him densely paralysed – bad. And he was recently widowered. He lived every day in terror at the prospect of being left dependent on the care and kindness of strangers. Being a farmer, he had access to the right stuff and did himself a favour alone in his cottage one night. He sent an email to the police to come and find him, reluctant to involve any friends in illegality. Is that not a ridiculous situation; nothing was going to stop him from doing the deed but he had to do it alone to protect those who could have kept him company to the end?"

The Senator cut in – this was going on a bit longer than expected and there was a general restiveness – "So these experts will simply put down anyone who came knocking at their door? How do you imagine you will ever get that past the churches and through Euro parliaments however much the polls may favour it!" Vigorous assenting nods from Sparrowman.

I said: "OK. I suppose there must be something more involved than simply knocking at a door. There would have to be a period of counselling and attempts at dissuasion until all dissuasion seen to fail, and so on. And there could be a form of documentation with signatures. In fact there could be a whole new branch of medicine where the experts would have to be consultant physicians and trained counsellors? There we go! Consultant clinical thanatologists! Doctors for death! How about that? Like me, they would have to be registered with the General Medical Council and work under the supervision of our Commission, whatever we choose to call it." I gestured toward our Senator.

I said: "A whole new faculty for the College could come out of this! It would have to be part of the whole package we put forward to the EuroAgePop Commissioner."

It all came to me just like that, just because of an appropriate expression of cynicism from our Senator. She liked it and said so, something like: "That sounds a bit better" or some such. The others followed. We were still the Famous Five, hanging in there. I expected that the Senator was now on side sufficient to end her shouty French references to our meetings as a pointless burden on her time.

Euphoria needed blunting, probably, and Sara came to the rescue. Looking at the others but pointing at me, the accused, she asked: "Am I the only one here who doesn't know what 'TIA' means? And who likes to lecture on the vile oppression of acronyms?" Still pointing at me. The Senator nodded agreement for a required explanation. I offered a suitably guilty apology.

"'Transient Ischaemic Attack' – a ministroke, a cerebral absence followed by a full recovery of faculties. Maybe some memory loss. Maybe temporary loss of speech. Not to be confused with a mere faint. A portent of more to come, unfortunately, possibly a full stroke with paralysis and dementia, who knows?"

As we walked out of our conference room, Sam said: "I'm not finished. We need to discuss the implications for life insurances and wills and pensions. Pension schemes will love this. But the life insurance industry will kill it. Be ready for that. Forget the big issues of ethics and philosophy. Insurance money doesn't pay for suicide. We will need to talk to industry actuaries. Do you commission me to do that homework in preparation for our next meeting? And how about dinner, the four of us, to catch up without having to rely on coincidences?" I said yes; and yes. I had a faint remembrance that her husband was a medic of some sort, not Oxford or England even. From somewhere 'colonial'. Yes, Australia. That would be a relief, not having to spend half an evening playing 'do you know XYZ?'.

Sara and I left Smith Square together, heading for the river and then north, skirting the dark gothic ice cream cake of the renovated Palace of Westminster. Her body language suggested deep discontent but she continued walking with me in silence. We had arrived alongside the Ministry of Defence garden, somewhat beyond where I should have turned for home but where she would be heading to her Tube station. She stopped and said:

"How strange is that? I find a lawyer and all the time she is one of your clever friends. Did you know about this all the time? Have you been working behind my back? What is going on here?" I did my best to reassure her that I was surprised to see her name on our list as we gathered, having failed to consult the list or do the necessary 'due diligence' homework beforehand, pleading pressure of my real job in the university, as she bloody well knew. Or words to that effect.

Sara was not much mollified. "So what was this meeting all about in the end? Not a word about population control. All that work I did. And you played that Senator for a sucker. Flattery got you everywhere, and the prospect of another big job for her. You are shameless!"

"Shameless? Hey, come on! Who is shameless here? But I would not want you to change, ever. And you know very well it is exactly all about controlling the population of the expensive elderly. But we should not hit on that too much at this stage. The humanitarian element is just as important, don't you agree?"

"You are a driven bastard, aren't you? You are not doing this for the Treasury or for that grand woman at EuroAgePop. You're doing this for you. Isn't that right? This is personal. This is your fight. I'm just not sure it can be mine. Those examples, as you call them; your dad's dementia; your farmer friend's suicide; they have burnt holes in your head, haven't they? You have issues and you've got us all swept up in them. I think you're dangerous. I have to worry about my credibility if this whole thing crashes. I am only starting out but everything professional that I have and do, is thanks to you. Tell me you won't crash ….." Tears coming. Shocking. I thought she was South Wales cast iron. Full sobbing, head against my chest. Too much death and sadness in one day for a young lady brought up in all likelihood on 'Bible and brains'. And aspiration. We were attracting furtive glances from passersby. She settled, withdrew, apologised repeatedly against my reassurances while dabbing her face with proffered tissue.

"You've got me dead wrong. Sorry, just wrong. Driven? Never. I would always rather read a novel than do this. I am the character always shamed for producing the school report "can do better". Those examples of mine are just what they are, the illustrations that help our listeners understand. It helps them go to our movie. And population control is not the issue which will get this going, so no need to harp on it. It will be the spin-off to wish for to save our economies." She nodded to agree that reassurance or perhaps from mere politeness.

I said: "We won't crash. This will probably take a long time, yes, but remember, the momentum comes from the people. We are here to help the nation drag the lawmakers along with them. And by the way.

If you're looking for General Gordon, he's over there, poor deluded bugger." Nodding, brief smile. She put her hand in my crotch, gave me a quick kiss on the cheek, and disappeared into the night.

I walked home to prolong the buzz of perceived achievement tempered by the nagging doubts inevitably raised up like Lazarus by my wonderful second love. Spywife must have caught my mood. If I remember correctly, that was another occasion of very satisfactory love-making. Unless she was happily faking it. Spies can do that. And most women everywhere, I suspect, especially when confronted by men afflicted with premature ejaculation. I reported back on finding old Jesus friend Sam on our secret committee, recruited by my assistant and working as a lawyer for the Health Standards Bureau. Remarkable coincidence. We should make a dinner date. Spywife frowned and shrugged.

"Working for the HSB? I would have thought she could do better than that. But yes, let's have them sometime." The 'sometime' pretty well killed that possibility. And what was wrong with a senior job in the HSB? I left it.

....

Later 2021

    I had some difficulty arranging a Treasury courier to collect a briefing paper from me for the new Permanent Under-Secretary. For a good while nobody at the Treasury's primary filter could figure out who I was. On the 'phone, I was shunted about 'from Billy to Jack' until I got the new PA to the new PUS. New PUS, new priorities. For the first time I felt a deep sympathy for those sad *prominentes* who feel impelled to ask of some faceless human impediment to their progress: "Do you know who I am?" Except that I was an academic nobody who had enjoyed a brief episode of notoriety. The K-W project was indeed remembered following guarded prompting from me. No, she said, there was no pressing reason to take up the PUS' time. Use the courier by all means. My report, as promised, merely listed the members of our 'Five', with abbreviated biographies and, briefly, what had been achieved in our early discussions, with more to come. I requested that the report, if approved, be posted on to the EuroAgePop Commissioner, who would be waiting for it. And to PUS' predecessor, now our Ambassador to the UN. By now, the tone had changed and I could detect a hint of deference.

              ....

It must have been at about this time that the wretched ComCam system came into more general use. Trials had been conducted for years and news would occasionally emerge of this great wonder. We all now know that the technology was based on a combination of massive computing power pioneered by the likes of the old Google and Facebook in the Previous Days, and the new mind-reading electronics. Neural discharges in the brain decoded into computer language so that thoughts could be recorded and commands given. The wearable hardware, for those who still don't know, consists of the little lapel camera (various attractive brooches for the ladies); and the implanted microchip containing all the wearer's identity information as well as all the neural interpretive stuff. What is not well known is who was invited (or compelled!) to benefit from this facility. Don't ask me how I know but it was certainly the security services to start with, followed by senior members of the armed forces, followed by some obscure determination of who constituted the Great and the Good.

My Inspector has an early model, when it was still considered necessary to have the chip implanted in your scalp. 'Nearer my brain to thee' sort of thinking. Further improvement meant it could be implanted subcutaneously anywhere one chose. The procedure itself was minimal and the residual scar, tiny. What took some hours was the EEG, that hairnet of scalp electrodes which tuned your chip to your brain. Very bespoke. Many knights and dames were offered, including little me, but serious criminals were compelled at the completion of their prison sentences and as a condition of their parole. A wonderful confluence of knights and knaves.

Spywife warned against: there would be no seclusion or real privacy except when one mentally ordered it to shut down. The periods of shutdown were monitored as well, for frequency and duration. Too much shutdown could raise alarm. Apparently much amusement was afforded the monitors in the early days when the shutdown habit before sex was not yet adequately cultivated, for example. Shoplifting, wife-beating, and severe alcoholic intemperance were revealed as commonplace among the ComCam privileged. On the other hand one could order a taxi, continue office work, do some shopping, or call a friend merely by thinking these things while strolling in the park or along the River. Vanity impelled me to accept the offer, particularly because I had nothing to hide and Sara was no longer part of my private life.

ComCam was the single major reason for the three-fold increase in the work of GCHQ at Cheltenham, although I cannot fathom what useful security information could have been gleaned from all that effort and expense. I thought to ask Spywife, then thought better of it. Perhaps that very thought is registered somewhere in the Cheltenham 'doughnuts'. British neuro-electronics at its best, and now international. Well, international in the sense of modern economies. Best all-time customer was North Korea before it blew itself up by mistake in 2035. Remember?

Nothing in this piece has anything to do with population control. I write it only as a reminder of what was considered life-changing technology, while I can still remember.

Recently promoted PUS had said I would be expected at MI5. I wasn't taking any chances on that. Following a brief recce beyond Lambeth Bridge, made when bunking off a meeting in Parliament, I couldn't even figure which door to use without creating an embarrassing fuss. Had to resort to Spywife. Now she couldn't figure what made PUS think I deserved a ComCam.

"You are so switched off. You are married into the Service and you don't know how to get into that old building. Just as well you didn't try. They've mixed us all up, as you do know, and the ComCam service is now in our building but still administered by the wetnurses in MI5. Are you free tomorrow? Well, get free and come to work with me. I'll call ahead to make sure they are expecting you." Or words to that somewhat humiliating effect. Making the point that I wasn't supposed to know how to enter these goddam buildings, failed to improve her mood. Strong women are not uniformly easy companions.

"Which arm do you want your ComCam chip in? I would suggest the arm opposite to your handedness. Right handed? OK, then left arm, just in case it goes septic. You can still write, wank off, and shoot. Haha. Not licensed to kill? Never mind, nobody here is licensed but the punters out there don't know that. Too many fantasy movies. OK. Just a little prick for the local. Little cut and your new life just slides in. Couple of skin tapes and Bob's your aunty." Jesus! Do people still say that? Cocky little male nurse licensed to cut my left forearm to bury the capsule-shaped chip. Little prick.

Spywife had ushered me along seemingly endless corridors. In a large bright white room I had subjected myself to a brain neuroscan. She had disappeared to work across the river. "Got your deepest darkest secrets now, Professor. Haha." Cocky gloating lady/female radiographer with halitosis. What is it with these people and their elevated sense of entitlement to be disrespectful? How was it for you, Inspector? Very respectful I suppose. These are your people after all.

Surgical male nurse: "OK. All taped up. Watch for any increasing redness, swelling, pus, bursting tapes. That would be infection. Highly unlikely. You will need to rush back to us. *Not* to your GP. Not on any account. Any idea what you have here? Think of it as a mobile phone at the command of your mind. You can call anyone in your contact list anywhere in the world just by thinking it. Your speech will be picked up by your lapel device, crystal clear irrespective of noise around you. You can shop, book restaurants and theatres, dictate office memos, research reference libraries – hey, good one there Prof - call for help from a variety of emergency services including the military and our own Service, and on and on. A lot of this stuff you can do by just thinking it. There is no book of instruction. Never know, you could lose it. You just have to test it to its limits. Once you've got the hang of it you'll wonder how you ever managed without it. Best of all, you can switch it off just by thinking it off. There are times, you know, when you may be doing things which are private, ahem, and so on. And you can pin the lapel device anywhere to suit you as well as hiding it if you don't want to show off. Here is a box of lapel badges for you to choose from according to your mood on the day. See here – flower, heart, Union Jack, Mickey Mouse, (remember?) and so on. They click into this little square behind your lapel, a very expensive piece of kit which communicates with the chip in your arm and then with the world. So look after it. 'Cam' stands for camera, but I'm sure you had that worked out and in any case the missus would have told you. The video runs all hours unless you order it off. Anybody comes at you with menaces? We got 'em."

So. In a celebratory frame of mind, I chose a bright yellow flower lapel badge for first wearing.

Nine petals. Cam lens in the centre. No trumpets sounded but I was thus inducted into a certain elite, strictly by recommendation. I was now the equal of my Spywife without being a spy or a Treasury official or Great or Good. Wow! No exams, no interview, no election, no competition from other applicants.

In the lobby I thought I might as well test this magic device. I left a thought message for Spywife; thanks and I'm off home to recuperate from major surgery. Does ComCam do humour? Then I thought I would treat myself to a taxi. A driverless appeared at the entrance within seconds, with my name flashing on its roof board. ComCam works! The taxi wouldn't accept any payment. A disembodied electronic voice informed me that ComCam users do not pay for short journeys. A whole new world of status and privilege lay before me.

....

Recalling early 2022

"I have just the word we have been looking for!" Sam, ending her announcement in a preposition, triumphant at our second meeting of the 'Five' at Europe House. "'Covenant'! Yes? I have been round the houses with this nonsense since last meeting. We can't have 'contract' as I explained last time. I have been through compact, convention, agreement, construction, promise, treaty, protocol, settlement, arrangement, understanding, pledge, bond, - even concordat and entente. 'Covenant' fits best because in practice it is a breakable promise. What we need is something approaching a promise, but a sort of flexible promise to allow the signatories to change their minds. There are covenants on properties which are broken every day by planning officials. And so on."

Perfect. Clever Jesus lawyer. Sara not happy. Again. She felt that the 'Covenant' concept was very biblical. Inflexible, absolute. God made covenants with Noah, Abraham, Moses, and probably many others. We would demean the sense of the word if we used it as Sam intended and in the process offend many of those we wished to recruit to this concept. Here was the Welsh biblical tradition fully exposed. Oh Deah. I had to intervene. I made the points gently: that the covenant with Noah, rainbow and all, was to preserve all living things but the biologists tell us that there are hundreds of species' extinctions every day; that we know the physics that make rainbows; and that the covenant with Abraham, for example, was actually a bribe to make him head of a new nation provided (here came a condition!) Abraham organized the circumcision of all males, now considered child abuse by many; that the covenant with Moses was to reach the Promised Land but that didn't happen till the next generation – too many conditions. Finally, in an increasingly secular society in 'western' nations, not many people in my estimation would give a damn about biblical covenants. I called for a vote. Unanimous, with Sara putting up her hand late, half heartedly and pouting in a sulk.

Sparrowman, so long silent, sprang to life. "We will need a quango-type Commission to supervise and administer these Covenants. A whole bureaucracy, I fear. If this catches on there would be an enormous amount of work generated, checking on each Covenant document, each application for termination and its procedure. And so on. This is a big deal."

I asked how we go about creating such a Commission. Do we need an act of Parliament? Can the Home Office minister magic it out of thin air? If it is going to go Europe-wide, will each country have to have its own Commission or could there be a single Euro Commission? Yes, (Sparrowman) we need an act of parliament. A powerful minister could get it through almost under the radar. He himself was not going go with it, thanks. I said no need; I had some ideas of my own. I knew privately that if the Treasury wanted this they could have it and once it was done we would have done our bit and the AgePop Commissioner for Europe could take it from there. Britain proudly led the way once again.

I asked our Senator as likely Head of Commission to create a list of the sort of folk who should be required to serve on the Commission. She was ready! She had obviously pondered in anticipation. She made a show of accessing a document on her laptop. Reading off the screen, as if it was to blame for all that followed, glancing up occasionally to ensure that the rest of us were still paying attention, she listed representatives all of the the great and good the country had to offer: lawyers (nodding at Sam), constitutional experts (nodding at Sparrowman), health economists (ahem), to check on how well our Covenants were reducing healthcare expenses because that is a factor in all of this after all, isn't it (nod to Sara), representatives of the mainstream religions, ethicists, a parliamentary officer for oversight, and a head doctor of some sort perhaps along the lines of a consultant thanatologist as suggested (nod to me, at last). And the admin would require a chief exec and all the usual departments for an operation of this magnitude: policy, communications, strategy, events, all with deputies, clerks, cooks, and bottle washers. Humour! Didn't realise till then that she was humour-capable. I suggested that we should keep her list secret for a good while. There was still much to arrange in terms of various approvals and we should not frighten the Treasury till much further down the line.

Sam wanted to know why individuals could not bear the burden of cost rather than the taxpayer. After all, people pay lawyers for their wills, lasting power of attorney, house purchase and sale. Point! But the seriously impecunious don't purchase those services and things, I said, and our service should be available to all, just like the NHS used to be. Means testing may be the way to go. Frown from Sara.

We still did not have a name, title, designation for this great work of economic survival.

Sam unhappy. "Here we are, creating this unbelievably cumbersome and expensive edifice and yet there is a simple mechanism in existence onto which we could tack this service. You all know what it is if you stop and think a minute." She could not help a glance at the Senator while she paused. "The Living Will. The legally binding instructions we can all issue at any point in our lives about how we want the end days of our lives to be conducted, and ultimately our disposal. Within reason of course. Many individuals already tack their Living Will onto their Lasting Power of Attorney they have with their solicitor. For the small extra cost, individuals should be happy to pay if this is so important to them. So! Paid for by those who want it, and conducted by their solicitors."

Now the Senator was agitated, body language unmistakable.

I said: "Sam Sam Sam. Solicitors can destroy us in all sorts of ways, yes, but do you know of any who would do the killing required, or even supervise it?"

She said: "Solicitors could supervise for an extra fee. We could even get my HSB on board to do it as part of their remit at no extra cost to the individual. Worth a try! We would still need some medical establishment to do the final deed."

I said: "If you start like that, you will end up with pretty well what we have just agreed. Don't you think?"

The Senator charged in: " 'Some medical establishment'? You mean like they have in the States for penal executions, getting the lethal injection dose wrong half the time?" weaving her shoulders up and down in perceived victory, in best Maggie Smith style.

Time to rescue Sam: "What did you get from the life insurance people and the pension providers?"

"The pension people, well, three national associations of providers, plus the NHS, and a number of big companies with their own schemes – yes I *have* been busy and there is more to come. To cut a long story – pretty uniform response. The idea of pre-planned termination is barmy and just plain mad, but if in a fantasy world it came to pass, they would love it. Obviously. Knocking off a whole lot of pensioners just when all pension funds are in crisis would get their support as long as they are not seen to be lobbying for this. They would in all likelihood furtively support someone trying to get this through Parliament." Furtive glance at poor Sparrowman.

"Now life insurance. Easy. Just went to the ABI. Got a very different reception."

Sara had her hand up. "Please, not more acronyms?"

Sam, with an unhidden sigh of impatience: "Association of British Insurers? Same response to the lunatic concept - their words, not mine, promise - but very antagonistic. Obviously. Planned terminations taking place at unplanned times would result in payouts way ahead of what their actuaries would anticipate based on normal demographics. It would turn their actuaries suicidal and would bankrupt the companies, also because a lot of old folk being terminated who would otherwise still be paying premiums. More than one officer said that if anything like our scheme became a reality, they would lobby parliament to declare these terminations suicide and they wouldn't have to pay a brass razoo. If the life insurance people were successful in this, who would want to sign up to a scheme tainted with the whiff of suicide? And they have a point when you think about it – you are planning your own death – it's just that someone else is doing the deed for you. Smells of suicide to me, I must confess. It's a bit like hiring an assassin to do you in so your family can collect the insurance. Remember, 'Assisted Dying' is known generically as assisted suicide (*looking for support from Sparrowman*). That's where the insurers are coming from. 'Houston, we have a you-know-what'. And by the way, I did threaten all the folk I spoke to with the Official Secrets thing. Nothing guaranteed of course but I hope I was menacing enough to make a lasting impression. I fancy that most were flattered."

Sam was taking some pleasure in this, my reward for not supporting her sufficiently against the bristling Senator.

I said: "The whole point of getting this concept kosher through parliament is to cleanse the process of any taint of suicide. That must be a given, in spite of the insurance industry. And I'll tell you something else. Those actuaries don't commit suicide. They earn megabucks after a very long and daunting study. They will certainly get out their calculators and factor these new circumstances into their formulae. It will be as if some additional new illness was discovered to kill a few extra old folk. All part of the mix, and life will go on, possibly even without the need to increase premiums. Sam, a big job of work needed from you, again, please. These guys know you now. Would you return to them, saying words to the effect that you would value an actuarial model based on the possibility that the Bill which emerges from parliament forbids the taint of suicide from this concept etcetera? Force them to pretend that the Bill will also forbid any increase in premiums, on the basis that the uptake is anticipated to number no more than one in a hundred of the general population. I would be surprised if that number was ever achieved, and many of the hundred will have no life insurance anyway. My bet is that they will end up reasonably fatalistic and accepting. Finally, remind them of the Mori polls on the subject. That we are about a great work of mercy. A great good for a small number. Not quite Jeremy Bentham but getting there. Anybody?"

Silence, some tentative nods. All tired now, but I was determined to complete one more task. "Name? For the Covenant I mean. Please. Last thing before we head off." Silence.

A barely audible sound from Sara. I asked her to repeat. Louder and without hiding her irritation: "The Rainbow Covenant." Silence while we pondered. Sparrowman, peck-pecking: "Sounds good, Doctor. I am sure you have an explanation for us – such a vivid image comes to mind."

Sara said: "The elephant in our room is also to be found in Noah's Ark. The other great good this scheme is aiming at is some effort towards population control, let's face it. David, sorry, Prof Stern, knows exactly what I am talking about but no-one here wants to go there in these discussions. The biblical fact of the covenant God made with Noah to save all of life from then on and promising no more floods, sealed with a rainbow, will resonate massively with the general public, religious or secular. (*Looking at me*) I know, I know, I know – millions of extinctions since and thousands of floods later etcetera. Ask me, I know about flooding. Remember the Gridlock? OK? And incidentally, Noah features in the Koran too, before you ask. Every financial crisis facing modern economies comes down to too many people living too long and too expensively. This scheme will not be enough to do the job of the flood, but it must help a bit towards saving us all?" Or words to that effect.

Brilliant. Rainbow Covenant. South Wales religion in a health economist and sex goddess. I stood up in admiration, arms open and then clapping my applause. Time for home.

As before, I walked with Sara north towards her Tube. My praise was fulsome. She had brought my day of fraught colleague relationships to a triumphant close.

She said: "Why are you wearing a fake flower all of a sudden?"

I said: "I just took a fancy to it. Don't you like it?"

She pulled a face which mixed disbelief with disapproval. She said: "What is a brass razoo?"

I said: "Brass farthing. But not real money. An expression. Razoo is Australian. Sam's husband."

She said: "What is a farthing?"

....

Recalling still later 2021 or early 2022, but winter in any event

"Well Stern? I hope you haven't come to make trouble. We're right in the middle of launching our policy on tobacco and minimum pricing for alcohol after years and years of dancing with the government and getting nowhere. The 'phones are red hot. The Treasury and the Revenue are accusing us of wanting to turn off the country's light and water. 'We need the revenue from these products. People aren't going to stop smoking and drinking. They'll just find the money somewhere. Maybe stop eating'. So they go on. But we, as the nation's leading doctors are the guardians of the nation's health, never mind the money. What do you think, Stern? Mr Health Economist?"

I said I thought the Royal College of Physicians, led by its august President, should let the smokers and drinkers smoke and drink themselves to oblivion and that would serve the Treasury and the Revenue perfectly right. And it would save the health service a lot of money. Early death does that, you know. That did not go down well, seeing that it was Sir Norman, the President himself, with whom I was conferring. I tendered a mild apology, pointing out that I had made the appointment to discuss something quite else; that I understood the stresses on his time; that I very much appreciated the time he made for me; and that we all know that most politicians and some civil servants are barbarians. He settled and took time to hear me out.

I said: "You are one of the first people outside our little committee to hear this and I must warn you that this information is covered by the Official Secrets Act. You don't have to be sworn but the implications of any indiscretion on your part would carry the appropriate consequences, I'm sorry." I looked glum to fit the circumstances, but I had his intrigued attention, dragged from a nation smoking and drinking itself not quite fast enough to death.

I said: "I chair a small committee under the auspices of the European Union Commission on Age and Population but funded by our Treasury and the EU Commission. Yes, I know we're heading out of the EU but this EU commission is aware of our expertise in the matter and they want us. We are looking at the possibility of a humanitarian attitude to people who wish to plan their end of life under certain anticipated circumstances, should they arise, in a sort of bespoke contract we call a covenant. The national polls are strongly in favour as you must surely be aware. We are looking to create a different Commission, arm's length from government, to oversee this whole project. In our discussions it soon became evident that we would need highly specialised physicians to counsel applicants, and see them and their families all the way through to termination in the most humane and dignified conditions. I am proposing the development of a specialty of Thanatology within the College, requiring a two-year Diploma from one of our top universities, available to RCP Membership graduates and encompassing all the subjects pertinent to the task of supervising and conducting terminations requested by individuals as per their bespoke covenant. This development would come free of cost to the College." I stopped to take breath.

I said: "The drive for this comes from the top in Brussels. The intention is to roll this out through Europe eventually, and then beyond, wherever the World Health Organization wants us to take it. Yes, it's that big. We, the British, have been asked to lead on this because of our hugely successful track record in pioneering the Assisted Dying legislation. You yourself were significantly influential in this project, as I understand it, Sir Norman."

I am a bastard, just like Sara said. Sir Norman was a major thorn in the flesh of poor Lord Sparrow and his team and single-handedly brought Sparrowman close to a total breakdown with his intransigence as the 'conscience of the nation'. Not a complete lie from this bastard; I did say 'influential' without specifying the direction. But the involvement of WHO at this stage was a complete figment on my part. Otherwise known as a lie.

He said: "Fascinating. Brilliant. On the face of it, this looks like a grand humanitarian project and the College must be involved in leading on it. I tell you what. Let's have a document from you. Short. Two sides of A4. No more. Strictest confidence. I need to pass this around the Council, various Officers, Specialty Presidents, the Board, and ultimately the whole Membership. And I nearly forgot. Congratulations *Professor*! You are the man to create the curriculum for this Diploma. An appropriate enlargement of the College's engagement with the nation. Fascinating! (*again*). For once Stern, you have brought some light into a dreary day!"

Dear god, what it takes to tempt vanity into goodness! A creative, driven (yes, Sara), manipulative, flattering, adulterous, lying, arse-creeping bastard. I should have gone into business to live well off these talents. Inspector?

....

Recalling 2022

Not difficult to remember this year. This was when the Royal College of Physicians established its specialty of Thanatology with a two-year part-time Diploma curriculum; I was specialty President. In the autumn, there was a small party for me in the College, richly catered as always, to welcome me into the higher echelons of the College as President of the new specialty. In his wry and blessedly short speech, Sir Norman, a renal physician in his day job, made the expected crack after asking forgiveness ahead of the eventual mild profanity, about preferring me in the tent pissing out, rather than the other way round. Great day. We had another stone in place for the K-W project. And another stone on the grave of my illustrious career. Do you see where this is going, Dear Inspector?

However, in the spring I was still mulling over the ideal curriculum and asked Sara to join me when she could, to vet my suggestions. I had included a bit of ethics, psychology, counselling, toxicology, diagnosis of death, religious observance in various faith systems, history (additional employment for our embalming expert and a rival for the Chair, remember?) – all to do with death and dying. Both of us had been too busy to see each other for some weeks. The sexual tension was overwhelming as she came through my office door and locked it. The armless chair took our combined weight once again, with only slight creaking in protest. We didn't take long and were able to maintain a commendable silence. I think it was after that encounter that I expressed some sort of regret that I was not able to treat her to the luxury of a bed.

She said: "Chair is best because sitting is best. Ask any lady. You get the full shaft and best clitoris contact. Clitoris knows best."

I said: "That sounds like too much information."

She said: "You can never have too much information. You know perfectly well. Ask Google. And you have said before, one can't have too much sex. *(Pause)* Risky question, sorry, no offence - are you getting any at home?"

I said: "Enough, thank you. No offence. I remain enormously grateful for the attentions of both the good women now in my life, for as long as this can last."

She said: "Does your wife know? About us."

I said: "I really don't know. If she does, she has been wonderfully measured about it. I'm not sure how she would know anyway, unless ....."

She said: "Don't worry about me. Discretion above all else. The last thing I ever want to do is your washing and ironing and having your babies. Or anybody's. Do you have babies? Children?"

I said: "So many questions in one day! No. Mutually agreed. Both too busy to be fair to kids. And I have another problem." (*Apprehensive look from Sara*) "Not that serious! Just that I have a major worry about creating new life without a thought in the world. That life to have to face so many 'slings and arrows' and then - you know – the old bit about 'born in hope; die in despair' as so many of us seem to do. Isn't that partly, or mainly, what we are about in this work? Trying to reduce the despair of the dying?"

She said: "God! OK. I'm sorry I asked! Tell me, can you ever talk without quotes from some bloody book I haven't read?"

I said: "Everybody had Hamlet at school and everybody has read Dickens at some point."

She said: "Let's get to work."

....

She looked at my list of subjects. Very quickly she found a deficit. "Aren't you wanting your thanatologists to assess the results of the scheme? Should they not have some stats upgrade in the syllabus? To include various instruments, not forgetting our own EuroQuoD? They will need to interview families and friends after the event. Like getting patients' opinions of their stay in hospital, the 'patient journey' thing and so on. You should know all about that, Doctor. Except that hospital patients usually go home. Our patients go to the big home in the sky, but we still have to ask the families and friends - 'How was it for you and your loved one?' And where are you going to find all the expertise to cover this list?"

I covered my surprise as best possible at the hint of disrespect from someone whom I took for a believer.

I said: "The only reason I got you over here was to find gaps in my list. (*Big smile with nodding from Sara*). I can't believe I left out the stats thing. The teaching is not a problem. Plenty of folk in the university would bite my hand off to have an excuse to go over to Regents Park on occasion, to teach and eat."

She said: "I know why you left out the stats. It's Freudian. You don't like Geoffrey. Him next door. See? I can be a clever clogs too. Why can't I do the stats and assessment lectures for your Thannies? After all, the EuroQuoD was partly mine. Could help me get a junior lectureship in this place. Better than part-time dogsbody. Then I could sit on

Jeremy Bentham's lap in his glass cage, with full rights. And come on – you got me over here to find a gap in me."

I said: "I am already working on your post in the department. I wasn't going to say anything until I had some firm news. OK. You are more than qualified to do these talks. I'll fix it with the Dean. My 'Thannies'. That's good! You are so earthy today."

She said: " 'Earth to earth. Ashes to ashes. Dust to dust'. Isn't that what we are all about in Thanatology, in the nicest possible way?"

Or words to that effect. We exploited the gap in her as far as I can remember.

....

Still 2022, recalling?

My guards have been holding out on me again re pencils and paper. I had to remind them that my writing was ordained by the Inspector and they might therefore find their jobs on the line.

What happened then? A visit to the Dean of our faculty just before the Christmas break. I delayed purposely until I had certain pieces in place. Boasting the declared backing of the European Commission for Ageing and Population, His Majesty's Treasury, and the new specialty established within the Royal College of Physicians for our great work of humanity, the opportunity for her faculty to be heading up the academic qualifications would be irresistible. It was. She suggested that I submit an outline curriculum in the New Year for her to take to the Vice Chancellor. I handed over an envelope I was carrying. She said I had a bloody presumptuous cheek, but with a delighted broad smile. She read my (*our, thanks Sara*) suggested curriculum and suggested staff list, including Dr Sara. She objected to none of our scheme. She would do what she could to get an Easter present out of the VC and the Senate. My rehabilitation in the university was complete.

....

Recalling 2023

I think this was our last Famous Five meeting at Smith Square. Sam had the life insurers on board on the basis of an agreement that Rainbow Covenant applicants who were policy holders, would either accept a slightly reduced payout on planned termination, or a slightly increased premium until death or termination of the policy. Sam received appropriate praise from me for a job well done but the reception was cool. I suspected there was some disappointment that no invitation to dinner had been extended to date. Oh Deah.

I said we needed another name for when we mature into a Commission. The Treasury minister should be the one to create it, once our work at Smith Square was done. Sparrowman suggested 'The Commission for Holistic End of Life Planning', received with enthusiasm, mostly. 'Holistic' was just the feeling the public would want in the name – kind, gentle, painless, friendly, spiritual, not protracted. All that stuff. All chimed in with our recognition of what constitutes a good death. I questioned the 'HELP' acronym which would inevitably attach itself. I was shouted down. The consensus was that 'The HELP Commission' would resonate with the nation in its own time. The 'Right to Death' people would certainly approve, Sparrowman volunteered. He saw my eyebrows up. He went on to reassure us that the 'Right to Death' crowd were 'OK', not subversive. They came from Dame Helen Wilson's startup movement for legalised assisted suicide on demand. They had never paraded, rioted, nor smashed windows. They were a few middle-class intellectuals who wrote letters to the broadsheets. They had been influential way above their weight during the difficulties with the AD Bill.

Business concluded. I congratulated us on great work for a great humanitarian cause. I declared my next task was to visit the Treasury. It was time to have the Official Secrets clamp on us removed. It no longer made sense. So many folk were of necessity aware of what we were up to. But mainly we needed to have the Commission created, and we would look forward to having the Senator as our Commissioner.

As we left I caught up with Sam in the corridor and apologised for apparent tardiness on the part of Spywife and self, regarding getting together. I said that Spywife felt that it would not be appropriate while Sam and I were still engaged in this work at Smith Square. Possible conflict of confidentiality and all that. I lied. It was a pretty lame excuse even as a lie, but I hoped that it would mollify Sam for a while.

As was our habit, Sara and I walked north together.

She said: "What is apoptosis?" (pronouncing it ay-pop-toe-sis).

I said: "Jesus! Where did that come from?" (ending on a preposition, which I hate).

She said: "What does it matter? I want to know, assuming, that is, that you can tell me anything. One of my ethics tutorial students is a medical student doing a project. I raised the issue of a hypothetical situation where society approved the disposal of the aged. No surprise where that idea came from. He said 'Just like apoptosis!' I couldn't bring myself to ask him what that was in front of the others. And you don't have to bother. I can Google it."

I sighed. I seemed to be causing offence all around me without the slightest intention.

I said: "It is programmed cell death. Evolution, in other words the miracle of biological survival as we know it, requires cells to die after x number of cell divisions, maybe fifty or so. When apoptosis fails and cells fail to die on cue, they become deformed, distorted, dysfunctional. Multiplying rampantly and out of control. Just plain cancerous. There is a programme for cells to die before they become bandits in our bodies. Doesn't always work. We still get cancer. I know some very clever and dedicated people who spend their lives on apoptosis research. Seems like cell division is a hazardous and risky business but we have to have it."

She was quiet for minutes. I wondered whether she had heard any of that sermon of mine.

She said: "That's where this is heading, isn't it?"

I said: "Some people prefer to pronounce it without the second 'p' and they may be right. 'Ptosis' is Greek. Strictly speaking, the 'p' is silent. It means fallen or floppy. In clinical use it refers mostly to floppy eyelids in certain unpleasant clinical situations. 'Apo' simply means 'off'.

She said: "I reckon I have had enough of your smartarse pedantry. Don't think for a moment that I am so dazzled that I can't see that you are fobbing off my question. Aren't you steering us towards human apoptosis?"

I said: "Apoptosis follows the laws of nature, and then only as long as all is chugging along as intended. I have no notion of which laws might apply the same principles to the regulation of human society. Come on!"

She said: "Do you know of the work that was done in our own university on the genetics of Alzheimer's? If that leads to a fix for Alzheimer's, we can all go home and get on with the rest of our lives."

I said: "I know that work very well. Nice man ran that. FRS. Found the gene for faulty amyloid. Couldn't find a way to fix it. If you have the gene for breast cancer you can have your breasts off. You can't have your brain off if you have the gene for dementia. Your fabulous Google went for it but it went nowhere. If it happens one day, it won't be anytime soon."

She said: "What is FRS?"

I said: "Fellow of the Royal Society. Top dog. You don't get topper than that. I can't believe you didn't know that and you have a PhD."

She said: "I did know that. I just hate acronyms. When will you learn?"

I started to make some apology but she waved it away.

"You don't know what you want, really, do you? Do you want a good death for everybody or do you want to control the population numbers?"

"Both. Both. Why not? If enough folk come forward for the first, we achieve the second. 'Win win', remember?"

She turned towards her Tube without offering a hug or a kiss or a backward look. All because I was explaining the etymology of apoptosis and she was on another track, brooding about the evolution of HELP into something beyond my imagining. Such a clever girl. I should have paid attention, but would that have saved me from paying this present price? Inspector?

....

2023 most likely

The posh biscuits and really good coffee were no longer on offer in the office of the new PUS at the Treasury. He was a nice enough young man, entirely without flair or personal attraction, and possibly new enough not to have committed any serious harm. Tall, lean, clean, perfectly suited and shoe-ted, and carefully composed without any hint or display of enthusiasm. I looked for any evidence of collegiate nostalgia on the walls or desk, without success. I was laughably hoping for some of the cosiness of my previous relationship, implicit in a shared past of educational institutions. Access had presented the same initial difficulties as my previous attempt at communication with the new staff. But here I was, with the undivided attention of the new PUS, and for all of thirty minutes. There was some difficulty in defining the purpose of my visit but he caught up soon enough, glancing through my briefing paper and instructions left by his predecessor. Priorities had changed in the interim. Financial survival, threatened by gerontology, had been overtaken by the war against fundamentalist extremism, and the cost of the madly raging storms and floods of extreme weather.

I said: "You will see that everything is in place. Our British/European Commission Working Party in full agreement on all issues; the blessing of the Europe Commissioner for Age and Population; the successful creation of the specialty of Thanatology in the Royal College of Physicians supported by a qualifying diploma provided by my university. And the suggested initial staffing of a Commission for Holistic End of Life Planning. All that is needed is the parliamentary approval for this Commission."

He said: "It won't happen on two counts. I can tell you now that the Members and the Bishops won't touch it; and we have no money to run it."

I said: "The same thing was said about the Assisted Dying Bill and look how well that went through eventually. The country wants it and is ready for it. Look at the latest polls. Everybody wants the chance of what is accepted as a good death at a time of individual choosing and not just when in agony and at death's door. The House and the Bishops in the Lords could be shamed into acceptance by a little adverse publicity showing up the antis as driven by dogmatism into heartless cruelty on behalf of the rest of us. That sort of thing. The Bishops know they are looking at

243

imminent extinction. They may welcome the opportunity to re-establish their relevance while on the cusp of disestablishment."

Onwards! "You might want to get the Right to Death people involved. Not the extremists of course. And the money. Just like folk have to pay a solicitor for drawing up a will or a house sale or any legal service, so people will have to pay for this service. They will if they want it badly enough. And all indicators are that about one percent do. The fee could be structured to cover the full service all the way through to termination. I am sure nothing less would be expected. Cost neutral to Treasury."

He said: "What about the masses who want it but can't pay."

I said: "We could do something like the funeral insurance industry. (*AVBOB!*) Pay in installments over half a lifetime. For those who are really indigent, we could cater for them by building that cost into the fee structure of those who can pay. Robin Hood, just like the whole insurance industry. Won't be masses anyway."

He said, after a very long silence in perfect stillness: "I will put out feelers. Do not expect anything to happen soon. Maybe not in our lifetime."

I said: "Don't forget to keep your predecessor in New York informed of what has been achieved. I think that is something he may be expecting?" Knowing bloody full well he was expecting.

Recalling 2028, more or less

My Dear Inspector. There is not much more to record that will be new to you or which is likely to mitigate my 'crimes' in the eyes of the court. But I shall probably ramble on if only because there is little else to do. There is another purpose: to record some of this history for myself while I slowly lose my grip on memory, it seems. Names, times, and details of past events are slipping away. Especially names. I fear I am becoming my father. I had a HELP agreement, of course, so that I could not become too much my father, but HELP is no longer and cannot help. A further dismal purpose: my ramblings may even cause you some amusement. An intermittent chronic problem is getting hold of pens and pencils. My keepers take some pleasure in keeping me waiting for these items. I am then left to gaze into the middle distance and contemplate my past and future.

Britain got HELP when? 2026? At least three years after we had everything ready to go. God, we are a cautious nation. And then not cautious enough. Look at what has happened.

The HELP Commission was created not long after my visit to the new PUS at the Treasury. Perhaps my Jesus compatriot had suggested, all the way from New York to the new PUS in London that any hope of a knighthood was in jeopardy unless he got the Chancellor to make the Commission happen. So it became the Famous Five Commission to us, and we met at intervals to assess the progress of the HELP Bill through parliament and related matters. We would be joined on various occasions by various experts, Treasury officials, and any who were necessary to the refinement of the Bill and the manner in which the Covenants would be conducted when the time came to honour them.

We had to refine the details for the licensing of premises: dying rooms which resembled small boutique hotels; facilities for families boarding in; counselling and nursing to the end (everything a hospice does, really); the licensing of Thanatologists and support staff; the end signaled by a nod from the Rainbow Covenanter or Thanatologist to pass the tumbler of fruit juice or open the intravenous with the calculated dose of Letheon (secobarbital); family and friends counselled for bereavement; information for the preferred method of disposal.

These meetings allowed me to catch up with Sara but I don't remember many opportunities, if any, for physical conjugation. We were both so busy. By now she was a senior lecturer in our university. She reported once in confidence that one of the Oxford colleges was making recruiting noises at her. She refused to disclose which college. I remember warning her that Oxford was a tank of sharks but that I knew she was well able to fight those sharks. From Oxford she could go anywhere in the world. The aura it gave to a CV, justified or not, was ineradicable. Everybody would be so proud and none more than I.

And so on. I suggested she discuss it all with Sam, to get a woman's perspective on the matter. She declined, saying that she would get enough perspective herself soon enough. It seemed that my life then was increasingly bound about by feisty Oxford women, actual and potential.

....

The Treasury sent me to New York to meet up with my old 'sponsor', the ex-Permanent Under-Secretary become the disenchanted British ambassador to the United Nations, 'for a chat'.

"Take your wife, have a bit of a break. We'll fix it with her Office." When was that? 2028? HELP uptake had gone from my predicted one percent of the British population after six months, to that unbelievable figure of 45 percent of adults over 60, by twelve months. A year later it had swept through Europe and twentythree US states. Canada, Australia, New Zealand not long after that. China! Oh,China! Remember?

The promise of a bespoke decent death when desired, had taken on the provenance of mother's milk – you couldn't argue against it. Why would you? The testimony of so many people so grateful at the prospect of having control over their end, was touching and overwhelming. Poland held out for a bit but eventually relented. The prevalence of end-stage dementia reduced dramatically. You must remember the figures, Inspector! Research funding for dementia and the other late life diseases collapsed because of reduced need. Departments of geriatrics in hospitals and universities were at last able to cope with the numbers needing care because the numbers had so declined. Pension funds on the brink of insolvency were coping once again.

The demand for the Diploma in Thanatology went out of control, while the Diploma in Gerontology withered. Entry requirements had to rise and numbers be curtailed. I was called upon to supervise the introduction of the Diploma course in many universities around the country and around the world. Honours rained down, frequently in languages not understood. Ribbons, medals, medallions, honorary degrees. I was the rock god of good death, but dressed in rumpled linen in the summer and rumpled tweeds in winter. Wherever I appeared, Covenanters would come up to touch me, shake hands, have their picture taken with me, exchange greetings, get my autograph. The most touching experiences were with those who expressed their gratitude for the means to retain control over the circumstances of the end of their lives. Total control, as and when. The absence of anxiety over the 'when' and 'how' of death, where there had been no control previously, improved the quality of their lives beyond imagining. They said. With AD and HELP, we had reached the peak of civilisation. They said they heard it was mostly thanks to me. And so on.

I remember one very earnest elderly lady refuser who questioned anyone's right to these new facilities.

"We have no control over our birth. Why should we expect or even wish for control over our death? Jesus had no control over his birth or his death. Look how violent and painful was his death. We should show respect by accepting whatever lesser suffering we have to bear!" Or words to that effect. I attempted to make the point that both schemes were entirely voluntary but she insisted that the world was lost in sin and the ignorance of Jesus. I refrained from further attempts at persuasion; some people just will not be HELPed.

I was supervising a dozen PhD theses, mainly online, at 37.000 feet in numberless aircraft and in hotel bedrooms. Now there's a word you don't hear much these days. Dozen. Sounds strange even to my ancient ear. I remember my dad describing how he grew up with pounds, shillings, and pence. Twelve pence in a shilling; a dozen. So many goods marketed in dozens. Food especially. Quaint now, to the point of absurdity.

On the other hand, I was failing in my obligations to my undergraduate students. The university came to my rescue by appointing Geoffrey G to take on this burden, with the reward of a Professorship. Geoffrey G, my cheerful condescending office neighbour. Statisticians do have a place in Health Economics, certainly, but I thought at the time that the university was being over generous. Still, needs must.

Spywife was becoming increasingly restive and disgruntled with my extended absences. I remarked during one home visit that we were both saving the best bits of the world in our different ways. Irony was the intention but it was not taken up that way and a great rage was visited upon me. I think our New York trip came in time to rescue a precarious marital situation.

After HELP became established, Sara became 'unavailable' on the few occasions I attempted to renew contact. I heard she had indeed been headhunted by Oxford, much inspired by her place and work on the Commission. And she deserved someone not already spoken for and who could care for her in the appropriate manner. 'Phone calls and emails went unanswered. I wished for a return of old-fashioned conventional postage. Remember that? You couldn't refuse to have a letter put through your mailbox. I would have expected that she couldn't resist the temptation to open an envelope of unidentifiable source. I certainly missed our spontaneous wild sex, perceived as uncomplicated by emotional debt or social commitment. Except - rimmed by a little guilt. I missed the role I had as a mentor of sorts, both professionally and generally, for a clever girl not best educated. Too much approbation of my goodself and associated busy-ness had produced what I have to assume was my perceived neglect of Sara.

Some notoriety was mixed up with that approbation, by the way. I had the occasional infiltrating heckler shout out at conferences. I remember "Satan", "Killer", "Hitler", "Himmler", "Putin". I have to admit that such epithets shook me somewhat. When you feel you are doing so much good for so many, it is desperately disappointing to realise that a few individuals do not fully appreciate that good. The greatest good for the greatest number does not of course include every last soul on earth, by definition.

So, Inspector! Talking of last souls: 55 percent of British over 60 years of age did not take up the Rainbow Covenant. While the 45 percent uptake was brilliantly successful beyond all calculation, the 55 percent refusers did bother me. I got one of the PhD candidates to undertake a project of investigation which could contribute to his degree. He found that most of the refusers had not actively refused but simply preferred to have nothing to do with the concept. They were simply in denial of the inevitable. As if: 'if I don't sign up maybe I won't die'. More interesting: these were very much the same folk who were disinclined to make a will. A terrible fear of tempting fate in the form of fatality. The rest felt they just couldn't be bothered or wouldn't afford the fee, instalments or not.

Rainbow Covenanters were encouraged to write to the Commission to explain what they regarded as the best benefit of the system. This was necessary for the continued justification of HELP. It was touching to discover how many Covenanters valued the anticipation of a good death, well ahead of any horrors of pain, loss of independence, loss of sphincter control. They were grateful to know they were going to die gently of a barbiturate overdose. I had to keep these testimonials in my mind to ward off the dismay induced by hecklers.

"If you're meant to hang, you won't drown." Trad. Irish.

This is not a rhyme.

....

When? Can't remember

"I have always wanted to ask, forgive me. Why didn't you come to my PhD graduation? I looked everywhere for you that day. You know I had a ticket for you. You weren't there hiding away somewhere, were you?" We were walking in the Science Parks. I had come to Oxford ostensibly to attend a Jesus class reunion. With some persistence I managed to track down Sara through the HERC. Health Economics Research Centre. She was now an 'Aspro' – Associate Professor and Senior Researcher, on the back of her HELP assessment and Commission work. And I believe, on the back of some glowing recommendations from me to old university buddies. Sara in all likelihood remained ignorant of this small favour. The network at work. 'Who rules Britain?'

"I bottled out, I have to confess." Showing guilty grimace. "I was embarrassed at the prospect of meeting your parents. I really don't know why except for some feeling of guilt perhaps. Ridiculous in retrospect. I was perfectly in my rights to be there as a member of staff. Dreadful sorry." We walked on in silence. I was surprised that my absence from her graduation should have rankled that much and for so long. She wasn't about to rescue me. I had to revert to the present to rescue myself.

"I am keen to know how you are settling in here. That was the main purpose of my visit."

"Perfectly well, thank you. People are very nice, at least in my department. I don't know why you have such a dark view of Oxford. At my interview there were questions: 'How is David Stern?' etcetera. I don't understand why or how the appointments board made a connection between us." I was graced with a knowing smile at last – so she knew I had a hand in her appointment. "I must admit though, the admin is chaotic beyond belief. Incompetent, arrogant and short-tempered. I am still waiting for my computer login codes. I don't have an office yet and maybe never. I just camp out in my college library. I have digs in Jericho. Bloody expensive but convenient for my base in Green Templeton. And before you ask, I have been able to carry on with the HELP EuroquoD stuff almost uninterrupted. There are rumours. We may be in line for a very large funding grant from the EU. Looks like Brexit never happened."

A happier Sara, at last. This was a good juncture at which to inform her that I could make an early departure from the reunion celebrations that evening, to visit her.

"Thanks, but better not, if you don't mind." Straight. She did not resort to the kind of lame excuse of some prior engagement that I would have used if I had wanted to refuse some unwanted appointment. We strolled back towards the Turl making small talk, mainly to cover my small embarrassment at the rejection of my presumption. I think she spoke about the clever kids working with her. Also, I remember some remark she made to the effect that surprisingly few senior staff were Oxbridge graduates. That gave her some comfort.

I am not good with reunions. Watching friends at intervals ageing, not always very well, sadnesses and tragedies and losses of all kinds, confessed late evening under the influence of varying degrees of pissation. I got enough of that in my day job at HELP (without the pissation). I left early after all, sober and sinless.

....

Recalling 2029?

TEA to JFK. The road trip to our then newish Thames Estuary Airport built on a high embankment, was no less dreary than to any other international hub anywhere in the world. As is so often the case these days, and starting back then, frequent wild storms prevented flight and we were delayed overnight. Spywife was delighted: the high embankment as we all know, is intended to cope with the rising sea, proof positive for her that climate change would get us before human longevity. "It's raining icecaps!"

The copious provision of hotel accommodation on aerodrome sites represents one of the wonders of coping with climate change rather than ridiculously hoping to influence it. The weather presented us with enforced down time; an opportunity to renew acquaintance as of old.   Innocent prisoners, temporarily and wonderfully cleansed of professional deadlines and other commitments. ComCams off. We had an adequate meal and far too much to drink in celebration.   Post prandial sex was inevitable and mutually satisfactory, I believed.   We rewarded ourselves with a room service bottle of sparkles.

In a quiet moment, when I was half expecting some small congratulation, she said: "I know about your young Welsh distraction, you know. But I don't mind, really. I am working on the basis of this being just that, a distraction, not a born-again relationship. Something that boys do because they can."

After a protracted quietness during which I felt all of life's expectations changing forever, I said: "What do you know?"

"Everything. The Service decided years ago that Service 'families and friends' should be subjected to inspection and surveillance. To eliminate security risks. That sort of thing. All sorts of stories have come out of that activity. Some are quite fun. Very few risks have been exposed. They couldn't pin a thing on you or Sara. Quite right. Nothing to worry about. And I just know that your long term commitment is to me."

All this was said without any reassuring terms of endearment. But she never did use those terms anyway. There was nothing I could think of by way of retort or defence except: "Girls can do this too. And if it gives you any satisfaction, my Welsh distraction appears in recent months to have lost the will to distract me. Or middle-age has rendered me less than attractive to a young lady in her prime. I suspect that the Service has kept you informed accordingly."

We were both still quite naked, having no reason not to be, and now more than likely naked to the Service and the world. I undertook a charade of looking for hidden surveillance devices, perfectly inadequately without the tools to expose the usual hidden places. Spywife began to laugh. That laugh and the passage of sufficient time resulted in a second erection, an invitation with her legs apart and arms up in supplication to join her back on the bed. And a second coming for both of us, as I remember.

When we were done, she laughed again and said that the Service had no interest in the two of us together. The Service could not have anticipated that we would be marooned in this airport hotel overnight. The upshot nevertheless was that I would never again be certain of the Service's lack of interest in my activities. I would forever thereafter fuck or masturbate half believing that someone with a camera was looking over my shoulder. Just like I wondered when young, whether God was watching me masturbate. Shades of ComCam to come. Spywife had her revenge of a kind without even intending it. Possibly.

....

An embassy car was waiting for us on arrival at JFK. We were taken to the black concrete and glass stick, with a bandaid down its back that was the home of the UK Permanent Mission to the United Nations. Czech and Slovak architects. Must have found inspiration from the heartless Mies of the spartan

257

Bauhaus. I soon realised I should stop ruminating along these lines: there was something almost Benthamite in box architecture. The greatest space for the greatest saving. And the least imagination. 'Less is more' said Mies. Never mind. We were important people in New York! In an elegant VIP apartment with a well stocked bar. Spywife only then announced, whisky in hand, that she had arranged to meet with some of her US Service buddies while in NY to make best use of her time away from the River. That blew a hole in most of the combined sightseeing I had anticipated after a cosy visit next day with the Ambassador, the Treasury PUS of old acquaintance.

"Welcome to God's own country, young man. Wonderful to have you with us. And the clever Merton girl. We are doubly blessed. You have done well. So well. So many grateful people all over the civilized world. Coffee? Brought the good stuff with me. And the biscuits." He was rounder, balding on top, but no less bluff, no less a whiff of danger somewhere. The 'young man' reference allowed him to not bother (split infinitive!) with trying to remember names. I was not significantly offended. He wanted to know all about my successes and travels and awards and how we pulled off the HELP agenda. I was meticulous in acknowledging the other four of our Famous Five team.

Mention of the long-suffering but devoted Samantha as a Jesus contemporary elicited the remark:

"One up for Jesus. Doing great work, as always!" delivered without the least hint of irony.

When I had run dry, he began to muse about his own situation: "This is a crummy pointless poisonous pathetic piece of nonsense. This job. This snake pit. The mafia should come here for lessons. Bastards back home denied me the Washington job. Must have found me too much in their faces, some of them. Some real arse creeping prick has it. Not for repeating outside of these walls. Probably bugged anyway. Rumour has it I'm for the chop. Retirement looms. Rumour includes bumping me up into the sweaty ermine. If true, I shall see out my days creating seven kinds of shit in the Lords. A girl's got to have fun. Oh, and talking of back home. No rumour. A letter will be waiting for you with instructions to turn up at Buck House sometime soon for the old stainless steel shoulder tap. Congratulations! Called in a few favours, with promises to behave here until leaving. That will be hard work! 'Services to Humanity' or some bullshit like that. Well deserved. But don't tell the missus or anyone else until you open the letter. Scout's honour? Do they still have Scouts?"

He replenished our coffees: "I am embarrassed. I have a small confession. I have booked you to talk to a few people about your great humanitarian mission while you are here. I was simply overrun with rubbish and didn't get round to sending you warning. Everyone agog to hear from

259

you. In one of the committee rooms over at HQ, tomorrow morning. Yes, UN building. Lends lustre and street cred. Good for your CV. Ha ha. Just be relaxed and give them the story. Sorry about the short notice. You will do it, won't you. Great British achievement. Professor Sir David." Statement, not a question. Or words to that effect. PUS embarrassed? Never.

That was some committee room. Seating for a hundred at a rough count. I had an audience of about fifty. The Ambassador informed me in the car going over to the UN that they were a mixed bunch selected from the World Health Organisation, from the medical profession, philosophers, ethicists, national HELP committees including China, and even some health economists, mostly of my acquaintance. The audience that day represented about ten percent of all those who had applied to attend. He warned me to allow time for questions. He assured me I would be amongst friends. No Southern Baptists.

He gave me a flattering introduction. I waved tentatively to a couple of familiar faces. Nobody slept while I spoke although I was the one who felt most like sleeping, not yet recovered from jet lag. The questions were benign and interesting, coming from so many different disciplines and cultures. I was basking in the international respect that was a just reward for years of hard work and inspirational endeavour. The full reversal of the Regents Park humiliation had been achieved, here in the United Nations building in New York.

In retrospect I suppose I should have expected that the pleasure could not last. Just when it seemed that all the questions had been put, a man from the WHO stood to remind me and the audience that HELP was expected to go some way towards solving the population problem as a side effect of its humanitarian aims. Had I come across the recent publication by my British colleague Professor Geoffrey G where a strong statistical case was made for the failure of HELP to effect any useful population control in any country and least of all in China? And that, as Professor G had reported, all the modern economies continued in decline as national debt levels from expensive geriatric diseases continued to rise without interruption?

The sound of his voice faded slightly as the panic rose in my chest and he persisted in more detail from that publication. A distinct risk of a vasovagal faint developed. I was wafted to some place far away as catastrophe unfolded and I was a paralysed bystander watching myself from somewhere outside. A new humiliation was to be visited upon me as a consequence of academic hubris. By a supreme effort of control I managed to remain standing while blood returned to my head and my hearing returned to normal. I had no option but to acknowledge my ignorance of the Geoffrey G article, making some unconvincing lame excuse that I had been 'on the road' a great deal in recent months and that is how I must have missed that publication, adding that I would be most interested to see it for myself, concluding that my own intention all along had been the humanitarian one. That it was for others to manage the population problem. That I was merely a health economist, not a politician. I ended with an appropriately humble smile. The applause, after thanks to me from the Ambassador, was watery thin. My WHO interrogator had achieved more applause for far less effort. His broad smile was directed at me.

"There is always one, isn't there? Smart arse bugger. Still, you made all the right noises. Population control is not your job. Damn right." My shrewd Ambassador of the bluff persona, all heart and sympathy in the car as we were driven back the few blocks to his office. I maintained what was intended as a contemplative silence but was in reality a stunned muteness. That fuckhead, Geoffrey. No hint from him that this was coming. Probably his revenge for not getting the Thanatology Professorship. The Ambassador's staff printed off a copy of the article for me very promptly. My name and publications appeared all through it, my name linked at every reference to the word 'failure' in respect of population control, and much of 'in spite of the laudable humanitarian achievements' etcetera. The Ambassador gave us both a whisky in his office.

"This visit is meant to be fun, you know. I've got you and the missus lined up for the Metropolitan

Museum and Central Park tomorrow. She assured me she would be free from her own obligations, whatever they may have been. Ha ha. And shopping on 5th Avenue if you wish. One of our cars will be at your disposal. Don't fret over this population nonsense. No damage done that can't be repaired, young man. I'll see you tomorrow, here, before our car takes you to the airport." Or words to that effect.

The day off in Manhattan was therapeutic for both of us. That is, Spywife and me, and not just thanks to the shopping. We took ourselves to eat out that night, just we two. Much catching up achieved. A bandage on a developing abscess.

"Your anonymous interrogator. The one who quoted Geoffrey's damaging paper. He was a plant. Trust me. I can smell it. If your audience was as select as your Ambassador boasted, there is no way a troublesome manipulator could have sneaked in. You've been set up, for reasons I cannot understand. Perhaps ex-PUS sees you as lacking sufficient conviction for his radical agenda of god knows what. Extinction of the aged, enforced by law? Be careful. It is just possible you are being set up as the fall guy in all this." She was already talking like her Pentagon cronies. I couldn't take it all in, not when I had just overcome major humiliations, worked ceaselessly internationally, and received so many honours.

"Look out for a bribe to come. Some serious seduction in one of several possible forms, just to bind

263

you closer." Clever, beautiful, clairvoyant Spywife. All in the training.

Next morning, packed and ready for travelling, in the Ambassador's office. Spywife was asked to wait outside with posh coffee and biscuits.

"I've had a call from that pinball wizard from the WHO. He is coming to London in a few months. Wants to meet you and your buddy Professor G, together. He is creating some sort of committee to look at the population problem specifically. Politicians will be involved, for your protection if dirty work is required. Ha ha. He says the UN and WHO are under huge pressure from the G10 and the G25 gangs of nations to come up with some proposals. HELP is not helping. Not getting that gallon out of a pint pot. The usual. Says he has to have you on board because you are the big daddy, the original inspirational figure. I've taken the liberty of passing on your contact details. You will need a good sized venue to accommodate your Commission and reps from all the HELP Commissions in existence. I know and you know how desperate the situation is. We had this conversation a long time ago and far away, and it was bad enough then. I am looking to you to stick with this, if only for my sake. With a bit of luck, I will be back home permanently when you visit Buck House. It will be my pleasure to attend on that occasion and then to have you and the missus to tea in the Lords' dining room. But remember, not a word to the world till the paperwork arrives!"

Or words to that effect. You will have noticed, Dear Inspector, that I have had to try various tricks to get the true impression in writing, of the way he was accustomed to speaking, running words and thoughts together. The fact is that I was seduced, hopelessly and shamefully, both by his personal appeal as well as his personal intercession on behalf of my knighthood. Now twenty years later, to what avail? Dishonour, dispossession, detention, and dismay. And quite likely an ignominious death.

What was I to make of this latest request from the Ambassador? What more could be achieved by more meetings? Whether in London or anywhere else? And having to work with Geoffrey G on this! Another 'd', this time for distasteful. Given enough time, increasing uptake of HELP would deal with the problem of the expensively unhealthy elderly. What is this rush to … what? I had achieved what I wanted – a decent death for any who wanted to sign up to it, and the distinct potential for a gratifying reduction in the expensive bit of the population. Massive achievement, with acknowledged assistance. There was even a sniff of higher honours to come.

It surely could not be the responsibility of a health economist somehow to magic the expensively unhealthy into being inexpensively unhealthy. How well would that go down: "Hey guys, just stop the expensive treatments!"

JFK to TEA. I can't sleep on aircraft even when I am at peace with myself and all is quiet and dark. But the night flight back to London Thames Estuary was dreadful. I was certainly not at peace, churning interminably over recent ridiculous promises made; in the early hours a child cried and could not be pacified; and next to me Spywife snored heroically.

REGRETS
Two in the morning:
Time to regret
farewells not properly made;
unkindnesses too well repaid.
In fretful dreaming a child asleep
had cried
and echoed my mourning
through shames too deep
to forget
and memories too strong
to have died.

This is a rhyme but it is not a nursery rhyme. It has been in my head for years. Must have had some appeal for me when first seen. Applicable now. Where did I find it? Who wrote it? All gone. Can't remember.

....

We landed in Manchester because of storms over the Thames Estuary. We had to sit out the storms in the increasingly malodorous aircraft, parked in the Manchester bad weather park while an unpromising dawn failed to induce any sense of renewed hope. We got to London in the afternoon. Spywife was refreshed and again insistent that the predations of more storms should be seen as confirmation of the superiority of climate change over human longevity as a cause of any apocalypse to come. She refused to shift her position when I pointed out that an asteroid could make fools, and cinders, of us both.

Matthew Mark Luke and John
Bless the bed that I lie on
Blessed guardian angels keep
Me safe from danger while I sleep

Quaint imprecation, second version. Remembered from a good Christian education for a little Jewish boy.

. . . .

Two communications awaited us on our return to London. One was a letter from the Cabinet Office, as promised, offering a low-ranking knighthood and please would I indicate either assent or refusal.

The other was a recorded distress call from recently retired Judge Father of Spywife. The voice of a dignified older man struggling to maintain control. Where are you? Was your flight delayed? Please call as soon as possible. A bit of bad news about your mother. Spywife called back, to receive the news that her Circuit Judge Mother had sentenced a shoplifter to death yesterday and had to be escorted under protest from the court. To be fair to Judge Mother, the accused had only just emerged from jail having served an eighth sentence for similar past offences, and the items lifted were not knickers but top end items of jewellery. There was a time in history when such repeat offending of such choice pickings would indeed have incurred the death sentence. Court officials had reported to Judge Father, with utmost respect, that in fact there had been reports of increasingly erratic behaviour and some bizarre sentencing over the past three months by Judge Mother. And would he be at home to receive her from impending delivery by a Circuit pool car. She was now resting at home. Judge Father was desperate for Spywife to visit as soon as possible, audible from her phone.

"I know how busy you are how was New York is David keeping out of trouble been offered a knighthood bloody hell how come where is mine dammit congratulations anyway Lady (*Spywife*) how soon can you get here I know its late can you come tomorrow?"

Spywife wept: "Oh Jesus the last thing he needs in his retirement is the entertainment of my poor poor demented mother Christ what do we do now you know you've been through this shit oh god I can't face the drive down there can you come with me?" Three appeals to the deities in short order. I dispensed whisky, made a few calls, confirmed my presence on the morrow's journey to the elegant south, and regretted that any pleasure in the enjoyment of her elevation had been denied her by such a cruel development.

"Yes, could be my father all over again. But we need to be measured in our approach. A lot depends on how much physical care she needs at this stage. Your dad is pretty fit still. How old is your mother? Seventyone? No age. Dear god. Everything depends on what we find when we get there. Nothing we can do now. Bed time, I think."

And I was thinking – poor lady, she should have gone at the tipping age of 70.

....

Recalling sometime 2029

It would take more than my steadily failing memory to forget the year in which the honour was conferred. The precise date just will not re-enter my head, however. A ceremony unchanged for decades in circumstances of runaway change in so many other matters, transmits a sense of reassurance not necessarily justified. The ex-Ambassador to the United Nations was there, as promised, as Lord X, having achieved his elevation well before mine. One would have been forgiven for believing that this was his day rather than mine. More of his acquaintances than mine were gathered at Buckingham Palazzo for the whole programme of investitures by King Billy. Lord X was receiving all their congratulations and distributing bonhomie in return. Apart from Spywife, I didn't have even Sara, and certainly no family left to invite. After official photographs and a tea party, we were exclusively his and he was gracious to both of us with much addressing of Spywife as Lady Stern. They knew each other from some dark past, sure as hell, and she giggled at his use of her title as if this was an entirely unnecessary and jokey formality between them.

He had a car waiting to take us to the Lords' diningroom for further refreshments. Spywife was determined to use the Lords' crapper sometime so that she could match me in these experiences. While she was away, Lord X leaned over and asked conspiratorially in a low voice, quite unnecessarily because there was no one anywhere near enough to hear us, as to the progress being made in the arrangements for the WHO-UN Population Conference. Daringly re-named the WHO-UN

Population Control Conference at the persistent demands of the WHO pinball wizard guest. I was delighted to be able to confess with some smugness that apart from provisional dates and venue, I had absolutely no idea. I was not involved in the arrangements. I had not offered my services. I confessed further that I had run out of ideas to do with a subject really peripheral to my ambition for a decent death for all. I became conspiratorial myself and repeated my mantra, with forefinger tapping our table, that HELP was helping and should be given more time for the slowly expanding uptake to do the population job. Lord X pursed his lips and raised his noble head with backward tilt in demonstration of his evident deep disappointment at my betrayal. His sudden incongruous broad smile was explained by his sighting of the return of Spywife. Saved by the belle, you might say, from the anticipated verbal predations of Lord X. He would have expressed some anger, no doubt, at my failure to front the Population Control Conference (PCC) and lead us all to the next great step, whatever that was supposed to be.

In spite of smiles, Lord X had suddenly lost enthusiasm for extending his hospitality any further and with muttered apologies relating to other pressures on his time, we were ushered into the care of an usher, to call us a taxi.

I never understood his fixation with the problem of the ruinous expense of long lives, except on the basis of continuing fixated in his previous

Treasury life. The problem of that expense was surely someone else's problem now. And if the problem was somehow personal for him, why did he not use his recently acquired magnificent status to guide proceedings rather than pick on little me?

"You little shit! You traitor! I rescued you from that Regents Park embarrassment when you were facing the apocalypse. I gave you credit for your ingenious idea, whether or not you considered it a joke. I got you connected to people of influence to allow you to spread your other notions to wide acclaim, even at the UN. I pushed for your 'K'. Then, no sooner have you had the tap than you do a runner. What are we to do with you? I just don't understand you." Or words to that effect. This spluttering castigation was received by 'phone at home on the evening of the Palace ceremony while Spywife and I were sharing a drink and pondering the momentous events of our day. I was surprised more by Lord X's cavalier use of a conventional landline than by the emotional content of his words. Where was the excessive caution of days gone by when he saw fit to take our chat onto the streets around Whitehall? How could he be certain that I was not recording our 'conversation' as a routine precaution in the light of past experience? It must have been a case of caution overwhelmed by rage. It was now my turn to exercise caution. In a break between expostulations I suggested a meeting not far from his new place of work. I suggested we meet at the Burghers of Calais in the park next to his Palace some few days hence. He grunted what I took to be assent and that was the end of it for the evening.

Pussycat pussycat, where have you been?
I've been to London to see the Queen.
Pussycat pussycat, what did you there?
I frightened a mouse from under her chair.

Have I recorded this rhyme somewhere else? I remember faintly. Good for here anyway. I asked Spywife whether she caught the drift of the 'discussion' and the identity of my caller. Yes, and yes.

"You know each other?"

She said: "He started off in the Service. A whiz accountant checking on how our Service budget was being spent. Bribes can get out of hand. That sort of thing. Based in our Berlin office. Really handsome and charming and much older than me, obviously. We met as I was crossing to intern in Russia as a 'student' after Oxford. We had a one-night stand."

She waited, maybe afraid of some adverse reaction on my part. I shrugged and smiled encouragement.

She said: "Made his reputation sniffing out money laundering by foreign states. Promoted into the Treasury. Dog at a bone now, way off his expertise and dangerous, I suspect. Strange. And we haven't had this conversation."

I said: "Not unless we're bugged." And I understood how it was that his German sounded so good.

....

Recalling Christmas 2029

We had agreed to bring Christmas to my parents-in-law, partly to give my father-in-law some small respite and partly to judge how well he was coping with caring for his demented wife in his retirement. As an only child, I had made the mistake of marrying an only child. There were no Spywife siblings to share these filial burdens. Do only children seek out only children with whom to fall in love, without realizing it? Is there some odour or mindmark in us which attracts? Good subject there for a PhD.

There was no hint of anything strange in the first hour or so. Mother-in-law was the charming hostess, working away in the kitchen with Spywife, preparing the Christmas food we had brought. All changed suddenly when she called out that the Lord Chancellor was fucking his daily, and roaring with delight at her revelation, certainly unfounded. Her husband waved a warning to us not to pursue any questions of verification.

"She does this all the time now. Filthy jokes I never knew she knew. We can't go out. We can't have visitors. Then in lucid moments she attacks me for keeping her prisoner in the house. I didn't warn you to stay away, because I was desperate myself for company and hoped you'd be able to take it. I'm sorry. Also for the state of the place. I'm not quite keeping up with the housework on the days when our own help isn't here."

We made reassuring noises. On Christmas day she made to excuse herself from our Christmas dinner because she had to get ready for court. Only after strenuous persuasion was she satisfied that she had been given the day off and was free to enjoy the meal with us. The occasion itself was very pleasant and no outside observer would have detected any problem. With the dessert she asked whether we were satisfied with our lodgings in her house and apologised for the high rent. As we walked to the car on our departure, I asked Mr Justice whether he was coping overall. I could recommend a care home that was acceptably good when my father was beyond our capability. He insisted that all was in order and that much of the time there was some amusement to be derived from Mrs Justice's behaviour. So far. She was mostly still continent, thank you for asking. Neither of them had signed up for HELP and now it was too late. Spywife had a brief weep as we drove away.

"Dear God. Is that going to be me one day?"

"Not necessarily, with a bit of forward planning. HELP is here to help."

....

Recalling Summer 2030

The WHO people decided on the Queen Elizabeth II Conference Centre, attracted by the proximity to Parliament and the capacity for up to five hundred delegates. They were hoping for a good attendance by MPs. Convenience for our lawmakers was an important consideration, apparently. I had offered the Royal College at Regents Park and was privately grateful for the WHO's rejection of this venue. I had a premonition of sorts that something unpleasant may come out of this meeting and I had no wish for a repetition of any notoriety attaching to me and the Royal College. My premonition was inspired, as it turned out, and the inspiration probably came from Sara and her warning so many years ago on the Embankment: "That's where this is heading, isn't it?" I was puzzled by her question at the time but it stayed with me over the intervening years if only because it preceded the partial breach in our relationship. We had been discussing programmed cell death. Apoptosis. Her question was predicting a progression to programmed human death. She had been making

276

the connection. I had not. Clever clever girl, not very well educated.

It seemed everyone involved in the business of death, dying, and living too long was there from across the developed world. Also reps from the various national HELP commissions. And Atul Gawande, become the grey eminence of mortality and still preaching Assisted Living, still not quite getting it that Assisted Dying is for those gone beyond a capacity for Assisted Living. I stayed away from most of the first day's chatter. I left the QE Centre after registering, to meet Lord X at the Burghers of Calais, as arranged. I intended to return for the afternoon plenary session where the guest speaker was none other than Professor Geoffrey G, my corridor mate at the university, bearer of my teaching burden, and published accuser of my failure to devise a workable scheme for reducing the expensive section of the population. I had received a request to give a plenary talk but had declined. I had nothing new to say about population control but I was keen to hear what others were going to say.

Our umbrellas forced us to observe a minimum distance to prevent mutual facial injury. I would have been happy to have been indoors out of the rain no matter who might have been listening in. (*Bugger the preposition*). And we would not have had to raise our voices. I had not done anything to incriminate myself or Lord X for any fathomable reason. I failed to grasp any good reason for maintaining secrecy; HELP was up and running across half the world and I was unaware of anything else in the offing that should require verbal caution. Perhaps my Lord X fancied the veneer of importance conferred on him by this pretence.

Through the racket of the rain on our umbrellas I asked him what it was he wanted of me, and my apparent failure to provide whatever, sufficient to impel him to regard me as some sort of traitor.

"You were the one who appeared on my radar, quite out of nowhere, just at the time the Treasury was developing an institutional panic. No money. Fewer people in work having to support more and more pensioners and many of them needing expensive medical care. Your desperate sarcastic crack at that reporter woman all those years ago had hit upon the only solution that made sense. That can deliver us from this deepening abyss. It was a revelation to me when I saw it on the TV news that evening. The Minister was asking us to come up with ideas. I was head of the Working Party tasked with that. No one outside of our Treasury circle had the faintest notion how serious the problem was. And is. The fact that you had thought and said the unthinkable. And unsayable. Amazing. Whether joking or not, that let me believe that you could deliver. You were the one. It was your published work that pointed to the one conclusion: we live too long, too expensively, and we can't afford it. And now, all these years later when we have Assisted Dying and Holistic bullshit, when we are discussing your solution internationally, you cry off like a virgin all tetchy at the point of her first fuck because for some reason you consider your job done!"

Or words to that effect. I remember with some clarity the impression of pent up fury being expended by that speech, concluded with that great head and mane of hair shaking in apparent disbelief at some great misfortune. I should have been flattered.

"What is 'my solution', as you put it?"

"Off with their heads. You know full well. Hit 70. Oblivion. Go to the big care home in the sky one way or the other. *(Didn't Sara say that?)* All of us. The civilized world cannot sustain us living much beyond that. Even NICE wants it. To save the NHS."

I said: "When you got me started on this, it was about a fantasy scenario, entirely theoretical etcetera. Remember? Now, all changed and heading where? How do you imagine that you could bring that off without civil war. You are mad to believe anyone could make that happen. One nightmare replacing another. Geriatric genocide for real? And how nice of the National Institute for Health and Care Excellence."

He said: "That is where I believed I could rely on you. You have ideas for everything. Look at what you have achieved already. You could find a way to make it happen. If we don't, the random wars that will follow the collapse of all our modern economies will dwarf whatever civil war you were contemplating."

I asked: "You still working for the Treasury? If not, and I assume not, why are you messing with this?"

He said: "My mission is to finish a job I started. The world needs people like me and you to bring it back from the brink."

I said: "Not me. I am a health economist, not a soldier or a legislator. Not very great. Not very good. I deal in information and education. I think and I collect figures. I don't 'do'. And for me the geriatric genocide episode remains my sarcastic joke of bad memory."

"You are joking again? What about Assisted Dying? What about HELP? Those were all 'doing'. Undeniable. Fucking hypocrite. You won't get off that lightly. And I thought as a Jesus man I could depend on another good Jesus man. Fucking traitor."

"You are very grand now, and I respect your fervour. I just wonder whether that combination is a recipe for delusions of grandeur. Forgive me, I don't mean to cause offence, but this is where I need to step away and you need to get makers and doers to carry this bizarre notion forward. Backward. Whatever. You rescued me from the Regents Park difficulty, true enough, but then you led me into an embarrassing trap in New York. I reckon I have paid my debt to you. Now, you must excuse me. I need to get back for the plenary session. My friend Professor G will traduce my reputation, this time in person, because HELP has not produced a sufficient cull of the elderly to satisfy

280

him. Or you. It will be my perverse pleasure to hear it."

Or that is roughly how I remember that conversation. The Burghers of Calais, necks roped ready for hanging, showed no sign of having heard a word.

....

I stood at the back near the door, in the event that any distress I experienced should reach a level which advised easy escape. Geoffrey G's plenary session address was a theatrical masterpiece. It hurts to have to admit that. Still bearded, velvet waistcoated, he introduced himself as a health statistician who admired the remarkable contribution of his friend and academic neighbour, Professor Sir David Stern to the discourse (Jesus! 'discourse'!) on solving the single most urgent problem facing the developed world today. He started by quoting my published work on the potentially apocalyptic consequences of long life. Then he played a clip from the BBC newscast of me recommending geriatric culling as a solution, but the sarcastic element of my delivery seemed lost in the context of where Geoffrey was going with this. He proceeded to quote Assisted Dying and HELP contributions to the cull of the expensive elderly, and revealed with his own convoluted opaque formulae, how these institutions were failing hopelessly to address the problem. He ended by offering his great regret, with softer voice and pretend hesitations to attract greater attention, that the Stern solution of a universally enforced 'End Day' for all at age seventy or soon after, was all that stood between us and catastrophe. The elderly represented a modern plague on modern societies, almost a pandemic. He referred to bits from old Armageddon movies ('The Road'?) depicting blasted landscapes with a few bedraggled survivors to make the point that this is what we faced unless world bodies got a grip on the human capacity for reproduction and ever longer life.

Ring-a-ring o'Rosies
A pocket full of Posies
A-tishoo! A-tishoo!
We all fall down
        - dates from Great Plague of London 1660-something.

        The applause after an apparently stunned hesitation, was thunderous. In my whole career at the podium, I had never achieved such applause. Geoffrey G had attributed all my work without fail. The bastard. The cheek of it: 'the Stern Solution'! And I spotted members of the audience certainly over seventy years of age wildly applauding Geoffrey's recommendation (not mine!) for their own termination.

I left before I could be spotted. Oh where was ~~Sally~~ Sara now that I needed her reassuring huffing against those who misquote me for their own advancement? I see I've written 'Sally' instead of Sara. Two wild girls in my life who merge in my increasingly doddery mind, now merging on paper. I had an idea as to what would happen next, so I began to rehearse in anticipation. The rain had stopped. I used the walk home to continue my rehearsal.

Before I reached the front door, my ComCam was cluttered with messages and as I let myself in I could hear the old landline ringing. I dealt with all these requests for interview by saying I would get back to them. Spywife arrived soon after, thankfully, and I reported on the day's events. I rehearsed my intended responses to her. She suggested a press conference to deal with all requests together. She suggested the ex-EU Commission office of old acquaintance in Smith Square, as semi-neutral territory. The RCP and the university were likely to demonstrate nervousness. Smith Square presented an additional advantage: the BBC was accustomed to parking their Outside Broadcasting vehicles there for concerts across the road in St John's. Perhaps they would park there for me?

The occasion is well recorded, both in the press, TV news, and on ComCam but I wish to provide my own abbreviated account here, as remembered, because I believe there are points which should serve in mitigation of my 'crime', and which I would expect my Inspector to emphasise before the court on my behalf. I started by explaining the purpose of the conference: to correct the perception of intentions falsely attributed to me by my colleague Geoffrey G. There were cameras flashing throughout and standing room only. Gratifying. Except that the high numbers of MPs evident at Geoffrey's plenary session did not feature in my audience. I explained my/our role in the research into the costs of the elderly ill. That we were providers of information, not policy makers. That my colleague remained fixated on the unfortunate incident at Regents Park where my remarks were made in sarcastic frustration at being doorstepped by the BBC. That present company, with a nod to the BBC camera crew, was entirely exonerated. That there was no such thing as a 'Stern solution'. That if modern economies were going under because of the expensive elderly, an alternative approach would be to pay only what was genuinely affordable for the care of the elderly. If that did indeed prove to be quite inadequate and the lives of some of the elderly ill became intolerable, more of those elderly might consider taking refuge in the Holistic End of Life Planning programme. That even this idea was not a suggested policy but a notion to be floated as opposition to 'geriatric genocide'. Care of the elderly remained a serious unsolved problem and to date, policy makers appeared paralysed by it. That was about it.

There were few questions, all peripheral to my main intention of seeking exculpation. What would I recommend for my own parents if they found themselves in the situation I described? I liked that one. I told the truth of how my parents were already dead and how they died and how they would have benefited from a supervised early death, at their behest. No one else's. And so on.

There was little in the way of applause, obviously; this was a press conference, not an occasion for congratulation. Still, I had some encouraging words from various people as the meeting broke up. It seems however that I will never learn. I should not have been surprised at the interpretations offered on the news and in the papers: "Suicide Solution for Old and Sick"; "Stern Solution – let sick oldies kill themselves"; "DR DEATH IS BACK - LOCK UP YOUR GRANS!" And so on.

In the next few days both the university and the Royal College of Physicians suggested that a tactical absence from the premises would be welcomed. Departmental gossip suggested that Geoffrey G expressed his delight at my discomfiture, with some hilarity. The politeness everywhere else was terrifying. At least there was no suggestion of dismissal or orders to fall on my sword. But there I was, at nearly 50, at the top of my game; an international figure in the business of the good death, and a knight. And no workplace other than my study at home. People from HELP Commissions everywhere were sympathetic. Spywife was incredulous. That means supportive, this time.

Sara, bless her, called from Oxford to express her indignation, peppered with the kind of salty language which was her specialty. She could not resist a 'told you so' admonition that this is where it was leading all along. Wait and see. This is just the beginning. Just watch where this will end up. (Privately, I forgave her ending on a preposition).

Did I know, by the way, she asked, that Manchester was advertising a new Chair of Health Economics? They were looking for someone specialising in life/death quality measures to take forward their investigation into the effect of HELP on the lives of surviving families and friends. What did I think? Would I support her application if she went for it? I said yes, of course, to both. But a recommendation from me might be toxic in the light of my recent adverse publicity. She insisted nevertheless. So loyal! I recommended that at interview, assuming she was invited, she was to boast of her share of authorship of EuroQuoD, now the universal test of quality of death, available to families and friends of departed loved ones.

I was flattered that a top university was doing research into HELP. I was confident that HELP would come out well. I was beginning to feel much better and told her so. I included the observed irony that I was on my way down, and maybe out, and she was definitely on the up and up. I wanted to ask whether she had by now acquired 'a good friend' but desisted, realising that she would tell me if she wished, unasked, and the mere half-intention on my part was in extremely bad taste. I asked her whether she had been offered a ComCam. No, why? And why should she ever have one of those ridiculous constant intrusions into her private life? I said it gets us a good seat in the theatre and any restaurant, and an upgrade on any flight. She said she had no use for any of that. Where was my implant? In my bloody head? No no, left forearm, just like in one of those old movies.

....

It was at about this time that a problem arose for the HELP Commission, and which usefully occupied me in my second banishment to the outer darkness. I was grateful for the distraction. Self-HELP Suicide is the best way to describe the problem facing the Commission. Secobarbital suicides outside of HELP oversight were being reported with increasing frequency. Folk were importing the stuff from Mexico, of all places, for do-it-yourself endings of life simply because they did not want to be bothered with too much Thanatology and family fuss. This had all sorts of knock-on effects, not the least of which was dismay in the life insurance industry because these unpredictable events were throwing its actuarial calculations to the winds. The DIY folk were mainly young and unhappy rather than old and expensively ill.

An urgent meeting of our Commission was called. We were informed that the DIY phenomenon was worldwide. I wasn't much concerned about it and said so. I did not consider the numbers to be alarming and anyway, like sex, one could never make suicide unpopular. I really did not see that this was a HELP Commission problem. I was outvoted. Sara could not attend because she was in transition to her new professorial post in Manchester. I could not anticipate how she would have voted but I would have expected her to have views similar to mine. Wasn't she my creature after all? The decision was taken to urge the government to ban all private imports of secobarbital and to encourage British production by our own pharmaceutical industry. As we know, the government did ban and did encourage, and a major factory was established at Pirbright, the 'Farm' in Surrey. Only the Commission, through its officers, could supply the drug. The Commission (the other three present) seemed to have no understanding that there was no longer any such thing as a 'British' pharma. I lost interest long before the meeting broke up but that is how it came to pass that Britain produces 'Letheon' on home soil. Genius name. Must have been thought up by some classics graduate in the marketing department. In retrospect, all that fuss had little effect: the Mexican stuff was much cheaper even after crossing the ocean, and one can get round import restrictions in all sorts of ways, I am told.

....

Recalling more of 2030 and beyond

I made representations to both the Royal College and the university, strenuously emphasising the point that the media had once again misrepresented my pronouncements in the interests of their need for some sensational marketing and in spite of the caveats I offered at the time of my press conference. I was allowed back on the premises of both institutions, warily and with some reluctance, and a normal quiet life was resumed, especially at the university: lectures, tutorials, examinations, research, editorial work for scientific journals. And of course, visiting HELP committees at home and abroad for supervision and appraisal. Nothing to cause any palpitations. I had founded The Journal of Thanatology; shepherding a startup scientific publication is certainly time consuming.

Geoffrey G was conspicuously absent. No sign of Cheerful Geoffrey. News filtered through that he was travelling the country and the world quoting 'departmental' research pointing the way to the need for a population cull in modern economies at about age 70. There were differing opinions as to the enthusiasm for this advice, depending on which member of the department one consulted. And no-one was calling him 'Dr Death'! No paparazzi at his door. No exclusions from professional offices. Why not? Where was the justice in this? He must be enjoying some powerful protection somehow. Geoffrey was heard to spout Jeremy Bentham all over the place, usurping my god in his dystopian cause. Thankfully, there was no report that he was using my name. Somebody must have warned him off. Maybe it was Lord X, because there were further reports of Geoffrey being entertained by Himself at various times between tours. I was grateful for that news. It seemed I had escaped the grasp of a very powerful, imposing and driven man. If Geoffrey was his new favourite, one had to be grateful for a major mercy.

Then there was further news that Geoffrey and Lord X were off to New York for both of them to address a large WHO gathering at the UN. If they were going to repeat the culling gig, they would be blown out of the water by the UN High Commissioner for Human Rights. Surely.

Indeed not! Some local and international HELP people were in attendance and they let me know that the question did come up but questioners were shouted down by many and even by elderly attendees saying 'we must give ourselves up to save our younger families and the next generation' and words to that effect. Stunning. Lord X had done the smooth introduction at his deep resonant best, I was told, making much of how good it was to return to the site of past adventures when British Ambassador. Geoffrey had successfully frightened his audience witless with my/our figures. And again, he had called up the ghost of Bentham to justify his recommendation as the only possible solution. Between the two of them there must have been some element of misleading their audience into the perception that they represented the British Government. Nice.

An African delegate apparently asked how this policy might be relevant in not-so-modern economies. I was told he was reassured by Geoffrey that it was not relevant because it was not necessary. It was not necessary because most not-so-modern economies had achieved steady-state populations thanks to a fine balance between reproduction on the one hand and disease, malnutrition, and local wars on the other. Nice, again. Malthus at work in the Third World. But too true, don't you know? And all that in spite of Dr David Livingstone bringing missionaries and medicine to Africa. I didn't want to hear more and found it difficult to believe what I was hearing anyway.

Not long after that jaunt by Tweedledum and Tweedledee to New York, the UN came up with the

United Nations Population Control Treaty, signed with gratitude (I was told) by a long list of developed countries, and bearing the inspired acronym 'UNPOPCONT'. Another one for Sara's collection.

....

How often has it happened that wishful thinking became fixed as a perceived memory, in countless autobiographies, bar room chatter, reports from a bloody battlefield? I have just been reading over that bit about Spywife being thoroughly modern about my loving relationship with Sara, on our way to New York and the United Nations. No, no. There was a dreadful row with some shouting and much stomping about in that hotel bedroom and bitter accusations of humiliation and even the possibility of a Service career wrecked by the misdemeanours of a wayward husband and the security risk that they represented. The negative emotional tension persisted for some weeks, and well into the time of our visit to Buck House. If you examine the obligatory photograph of that occasion you will note that no one is smiling. Pursed lips on both faces. That was not a scene of maintaining some stiff dignity on a solemn occasion. That was a record of a combination of anger and guilty submission, but who would know unless they were told?

The coincidence of the brain decay of mother-in-law Mrs Justice, and the support I was able to provide, brought Spywife and me a bit closer again. Some subdued tension remained, but we did 'get along'. I did offer to leave home but that elicited an alarmed reaction and a strenuous denial that it would be considered necessary.

So! Two incidents of memory failure in one moment of remembrance that day. One temporary (mine), where perception played internal tricks, and one permanent (mother-in-law) and progressive, where the tricks were external, public, and devastating to several lives as they had been lived.

Memory has to be the single most fascinating brain function of all. That we can have it at all but not much before three years of age. That we can lose it even while all other neurological functions continue as normal. That it reposes in different parts of a slightly disgusting ball of squishy jelly. That it is capable of hosting multiple lateral connections well beyond the capability of the most sophisticated computer. That memory function is split between recording and recall, and recall is the most mysterious and the most unreliable phenomenon. Wishful thinking, dreams, and a variety of mental disorders can create 'memories' capable of confident recall but having no basis in reality. That it is all a massive electrochemical buzz in that jelly ball. That too many long lives are bookended by an absence of memory: infancy at one end and dementia at the other. But that is the crux, Inspector, the pathetic vulnerability, isn't it? Electrochemistry. Not carved in marble or painted on mediaeval stained glass, to last for centuries. Just invisible sparks, wires and juices, but when the electricity fails, the lights go out. And if we live long enough, for so many of us the lights will go out while we continue to breathe, digest, piss and fart, grow hair and nails, and stumble about. We can do all of that, but with the loss of memory we have no personality or person-ness. Imperfectly ambulating shells. Even when we are well, we still need pictures to remind us of people, places, and events because our memories can't hold all that good information. But when the Big Wax takes over, we can no longer make sense of those lovingly preserved pictures. What makes amyloid, and why?

There is certainly an attraction to the sheer dreadful logic of what Geoffrey cheekily called the Stern Solution. That almost certainly explains how it has come about that throughout the world, those modern economies which have subscribed to UNPOPCONT have seen their balance sheets recover as their revenues once again began to cover expenses, including healthcare. Unemployment pretty well disappeared as the population of late retirees disappeared. My contention has always been that HELP would have achieved that, given the chance.

Many of us still remember old folk we once knew, in their nineties, in rude good health and sharp as nails intellectually. Winners in the lottery of genetics. But these impressive people don't exist any longer, sacrificed on the altar of the greatest good for the greatest number. Dear god, Jeremy Bentham, must you be blamed for this madness?

....

Recalling 2032 to 2036, or thereabout

I remain in awe of the cheek of the UN to introduce the Treaty action during Easter weekend 2032, and to trumpet the occasion as the second great salvation action in human history, after the Crucifixion. Other secular Jews of my acquaintance found this offensive.

It never happened. The mutiny, rebellion, revolution, marches, speeches, shouting, arson, looting, and associated public misbehaviours that can accompany public disenchantment. I had been waiting for such reactions to the UNPOPCONT Treaty of 2032, biding my time to be able to indulge in an appropriate sense of smug retribution. 'Twas not to be. The Treaty bought the silence of Treaty populations by providing for families of those due for 'execution' to be awarded a cash payment (£4000 in Britain); the abolition of all pensions beyond the age of 70, just to drive home the point, (always excepting the Exempted); a state-sponsored 'End Day' piss-up with balloons, bunting, and band playing for the family and friends of the 'index' person; an elaborate gaudily framed 'Saviour of the Nation' certificate of commendation for these families, signed by the head of state; a Treaty Officer comes to each party to bring the congratulations of the state; and pervasive publicity based on national financial 'salvation' statistics. Thanks Geoffrey!

In South America the Treaty bosses invoked the ancient pre-Inca history of blood sacrifice to justify the Treaty: then, as now, we must sacrifice some to ensure the survival of the rest. But how greatly we have advanced! No blood, no violence. Just peace.

The publication of horror stories of the suffering of the Previous Days, was (still is?) unrelenting. TV, press, blogs, Tweets, Peeps and Pops – all carried florid stories, probably confected by UNPOPCONT staff, of unbearable pain, deformity, disability, humiliation and poverty suffered by so many individuals forced by longevity to endure beyond 70. Brilliant.

Every Saviour was (still is?) guaranteed a funded funeral of their chosen religion, or none. And burial, in the Old Railway Cemetery of course. And there are bribes for whole nations for their silence while complicit in this slaughter of the slightly aged innnocents. UNPOPCONT introduced a lottery paying the equivalent of a £1 million pounds each week in each Treaty nation to twenty lucky individuals prepared to have their end day at 65. The

'Early Departure Lottery'. Bread and games. And booze and money.

My jokey sarcasm of years ago, offering an unimaginable dystopic solution to overpopulation, had become reality in 2032. Imagination become fact. Death beats life any day, doncherthink? Job done. Quaint.

....

What about the sophisticates in society in all the Treaty states? Surely there would be objections, media protests, distressed editorials? Not everybody can be bought off. Perhaps not but they can be frightened off. Where are the Silicon Valley boys and their 'immortality' projects? Billionaires can't be bought off but they can buy themselves healthcare irrespective of cost. One of the provisions of the Treaty allows for the purchase of a 'Life Certificate' for any individual. Current cost is $5 million or other currency equivalent just for the certificate, and all medical expenses to be covered quite separately by the certificate holders or their family. These expensive elderly are the ones known as 'Lifers'. Unbelievable, but there are enough of them to fund the whole Treaty operation. That's how we have ended up with wealthy Lifers funding programmed death. Nice.

All this is known. Why do I set it down here? As background to what drove my actions once I realised that there was no popular uprising against UNPOPCONT. The sensitive sophisticates were frightened off by legislation enacted almost simultaneously in all Treaty states. Here in Britain it is the blandly named 'Public Administration Disorder and Disinformation Act (2032)'. PADDA for short. I'm not telling you anything you don't know, Inspector, but setting it down in writing does specially illuminate the madness of it all, for me. One may not campaign in any form against the Treaty and its provisions. The penalties are close to those for treason, understandably. Working against the Treaty is seen as compromising the survival of Treaty states. PADDA has its own police, as I have experienced personally. They really are licensed to kill. That is it really. Survival must come before the luxury of democracy and free speech, obviously. Blah blah. Slaughter of the old'uns for the survival of the young 'uns. Must be preferable to having all of us perish through states' bankruptcy, starvation, riotous disorder, civil war, and dark dysfunction spreading across the planet. Blah blah. My contention was always, and remains, that HELP would have done the job, just taking a bit longer. And with HELP, those fortunately well preserved and contented geriatrics who would have chosen to remain alive and within the bosom of their families, could have done so.

UNPOPCONT has become the apoptosis of the human race in modern economies: programmed cell death. Lots and lots of cells. A legislated great extinction.

So! PADDA is what has brought me to this sorry pass. Even before I was arrested, Geoffrey G and Lord X were rumoured to be up for a Nobel prize. Quaint.

Inevitables. Families and spouses short of cash were putting up their loved ones for termination somewhat short of the qualifying age of seventy, and Treaty Officers were content not to scrutinise dates of birth too closely. That reminded me that inevitably you get a lot of whatever you pay for, such as single parent benefit in the 'Previous Days' producing a multiplicity of single parents.

There was an exodus of near biblical proportions of the more adventurous elderly to the third world, not covered by the UNPOPCONT Treaty. Mainly Africa. The Jews started it. They have 'form' as refugees throughout history. That accounts for the relatively prosperous white colonies today in Uganda, Madagascar, South Africa, and Namibia. Even Alaska. Jews were taking their chances with their health in these places where state healthcare is lacking but taking care to bring some doctors and teachers with them.

Then there were the 'Miners', another inevitable – the modern equivalents of the Jews who spent the Nazi years in Europe evading capture by going into hiding 'underground' and perpetually on the move – 'U-boats' and 'Submarines'. But these were not just Jews of course. Anyone over 70 could become a 'miner' if they had the courage, physical fitness, and ingenuity to hide, often 'in plain sight', mostly in cities. It did mean leaving the family home, living in squats or sofa-surfing with brave friends. It helped to dye hair dark and wear clothes hinting at perpetual youth. A forged birth certificate was a help if you were accosted by a PADDA on the street, and if you knew where to get one. One heard of 'miners' through whispered rumours at dinners and parties. And occasionally in the most public way when some were caught and executed by secobarbital after a show trial to extract the maximum educational benefit. And without any End Day brass bands or monetary reward. And no burial, official and free. Just a communal pit reserved for disappeared traitors. Like for the dead of the Black Death extinction so long ago. Quaint.

So, Inspector. How many miners have you caught? Or is that hunt something reserved for lowly PADDAs? I can imagine that is serious fun, very likely with bonuses for numbers of successes? Are there any miners in this building quietly awaiting a show trial? Too quietly, if there are any. I have never had a response to my wall-tapping and pipe-tapping.

Many middle income families with wholly-owned houses destituted themselves by selling everything in order to pay the $5 million for a Life Certificate for an aging family member, even to the extent of ending up homeless. Self-defeating, surely, but how impressive the instinct to cling to any life.

And then came the assassinations of Lifers and Exempteds, especially in the US where sniper rifles are still freely available, I believe, and jealousy must be satisfied. Quaint sport. So here we have these old folk of money and privilege and long life having to live that life barricaded behind high walls and advised never to sit near a window. Exempteds? Yes, like you Inspector. The great, and the good administrators of UNPOPCONT. You must be one of them, Inspector. Who would administer UNPOPCONT and yet be subject to it? Long life; perk of the job?

Who remembers the flap over burials? A Treaty clause provided for a burial and headstone of the family's choice. Stone inscriptions could carry the usual homilies and prayers but families were encouraged to add "Saviour of the Nation" at no extra cost. You do certainly remember that cremation has been banned since 2025 because of the massive energy requirement and carbon pollution. My father's private notion gone international!

The problem at the start then was finding sufficient burial ground. Treaty implementation came without experience in dealing with such unprecedented demand for 'dead' space. Africa had long experience in dealing with such a situation, going back to the 'Previous Days' of the AIDS epidemic. There is always some space if one is diligent in looking for it, hence the disappearance of all our 'brown field' sites at last, and the emergence of beautifully tended cemeteries in place of the abandoned junk yards and neglected flytipping fields of years gone by. The best idea of all was the use of our thousands of miles of rail bed. If we wanted to, we could walk the country from John o'Groats to Land's End and never leave the Old Railway Cemetery. Job done. Desecration and vandalism of graves carries a mandatory death sentence, as we all know, and somehow appropriate to these times of mandatory Treaty deaths. That could explain why the sport of grave desecration is uncommon these days except for that curious development of the 'Death Wish' yob gangs and their cunning schemes for getting away with it. Some of the time. Quaint.

Someone or some people were impelled by the arrival of the Treaty to smash up that poor doll of Jeremy Bentham in the university, that adopted icon and emblem of UNPOPCONT. Glass case, fake body, genuine skull, and all. Somebody like me must have been made terribly angry by UNPOPCONT, but was it really necessary to vandalise that strange effigy? Jeremy did not ask to become the pin-up of UNPOCONT but in the long view of history I suppose it was another inevitable.

It was about then, 2036, that my dismay at the grotesque distortion of our HELP scheme into UNPOPCONT and the Treaty led me into a level of distress which resulted in turn in subversive activity against this dystopia. Details later, perhaps.

UNPOPCONT had funded the introduction of compulsory 'End-Day' seminars for all over-65s. The style of presentation was intentionally modeled on retirement seminars of the Previous Days. The content was very different, obviously. Failure to attend was followed by public humiliation in the media rather than incarceration: much cheaper, just as effective as jail, and all the jails were full anyway. I slipped into one of these lunchtime seminars, fittingly held in a semi-derelict church in east London commandeered for the event, attended by retirees, any and all over 65. I sat at the back behind a pillar, praying to remain undiscovered in the semi-dark. An earnest young man in suit and tie (!) who could have been conducting a tabernacle revivalist meeting in other circumstances, wore a microphone which snaked round one cheek, to help him address no more than 30 forlorn-looking whitehaired men and women, irrespective of skin colour. Body language from behind can be almost as revealing as *en face*. After welcoming noises and an offer of tea and biscuits after, he asked the congregation to join him in prayer.

Then: "Who wants to die? Show of hands? Nobody! Obviously! And who wants to die a horrible death from cancer or dementia or pneumonia? So, nobody! Quite right. But do you know that with every year after age seventy, your chances of developing a fatal disease increases dramatically? I'm not talking some painless rapid release but some drawn out painful and distressing illness. Seventy is the age when health disasters begin to accumulate. We have all the research for that fact."

Yes! My great work and that of my acolytes. What honour, to be quoted at these coaching-for-death meetings around the country! And beyond? I had been peering out from behind my pillar and promptly shrank back, perversely anticipating that quoting my work, unacknowledged, must somehow expose my hiding place.

"So. If someone offered you a free and easy death at seventy to help you avoid these awful deadly illnesses, who would refuse? Show of hands?" Two hands, probably fearlessly preferring to have the Lord take away, irrespective of threats of pain and suffering.
"OK. Let me ask you a different question. Who would be prepared to die to save their country in the same way that members of your families would have been prepared to die, and did die, in twentieth century World Wars? That's better! Unanimous! That is what you would be doing on your End Day – saving the nation from financial ruin, making way for the next generation. These life-ending illnesses after seventy are not just supremely awful in every way but also extremely expensive to manage. Frankly, the country is going bankrupt just trying. The greatest gift

you can offer your younger countrymen and women – and they are your families too, remember, - is to give up your life like our patriotic heroes of the recent past." Or words to that effect.

Applause! In church! Hallelujah! Great stuff. Some more followed, mainly details of the End Day celebrations and final departure. Then questions were invited, while some wandered off to claim their tea and biscuits. Certificates of attendance were handed out. I wandered off myself, heading back to work thinking, yes, well. Actually, what's not to like?

....

So, Inspector. We remain in 2036. The good reason for this remembrance is that this was the year of the second 'flyby' of Apophis, Apophis the Snake, and this asteroid has indeed passed earth at a safe distance of many millions of miles. The first flyby of 2029 was much, much closer and was considered at one time to be good for an Earth collision if it passed into some 'gravitational keyhole'. Beyond my understanding. Evidently it didn't because we are all still here, including my Inspector and my keepers. By the time Apophis returns for a third flyby in 2068, the Treaty will have rendered me and my Inspector extinct anyway. Unless my Inspector is an Exempted. Very likely.

From whence cometh all this interplanetary glumness? In 2036, well before I had to go on the run, and in a spasm of irritation at the persistence for 17 years of the late Dr Harry's dusty asteroid box-file on my desk, I opened it and began a diligent examination of its contents. I was quickly captivated, enthralled, even thrilled. Much of it consisted of Harry's incomprehensible calculations and diagrams to do with the likely journey of 99942 Apophis through Earth's neighbourhood space. What was entirely comprehensible was the frequent appearance of '**2050 !!**' overwritten by hand and heavily underlined as if done in some alarm. The rest of the contents consisted of correspondence with various officers of the 'B612' Foundation in California; copies of his letters to them and their replies. Evidence of Harry's truly old-fashioned life. No ComCam here. Actual physical letters, some even handwritten by Harry. Quaint.

I had to look up the 'B612' Foundation. They are a group of very seriously qualified spaceniks, some ex-astronauts, concerned about Near Earth Objects or NEOs (read 'asteroids') and their potential for causing us a bad day (read 'extinction'). In 2022, (the year Denise died - that I remember, for no good reason) they got NASA to help fund the launch of their Sentinel Space Telescope for spotting delinquents leaving Harry's rock garden and heading our way. The whole point of the Foundation was to raise awareness and early warning of asteroid encroachment so that rockets could be launched to knock these rocks off their track to us. The Foundation literature reminded me that Saint-Exupery's Little Prince fell to Earth from his personal asteroid named B612. Apt. And I could hear again my father reading me the story at some childhood bedtime.

Most of the letters were reassuring and trying not to be condescending – nothing in their calculations even hinted at a near-miss or worse from Apophis in 2050. The return would be in 2068 and nowhere near on a collision course with Earth.

Then there were a couple of letters from a Dr Robert Jones, confessing with some excitement to having reached the same conclusions as Harry but finding himself a lone voice among his colleagues and an object of some derision. Dr Jones described the Apophis orbits as 'chaotic' but his best guess calculations chimed with Harry's exactly. 2050.

Twinkle twinkle little star ………………….

I wrote to Dr Jones at the Foundation. A polite letter by return from a secretary informed me that Dr Jones had taken early retirement and his present whereabouts were not known to the Foundation. I wrote back with copies of some of the letters from Harry's file, asking whether the Sentinel Telescope had given us any more information along the lines suggested in the correspondence. No, none. Thank you for your enquiry.

We have the top astrophysicists in the world in our university. Must be. They say so. I took Harry's box file to the department and asked the secretary there to pass it round, even if just for laughs. A couple of those boys (and one girl) called me back in the ensuing days and weeks, either to say they do far out galactic stuff and couldn't comment on this Near Earth stuff or that there was evidence there of two loons (Harry and Dr Jones), one of them surprisingly highly qualified. There would not be any need for anyone to fire deflecting rockets at Apophis, sorry. Harry's file went into our attic.

Little boy blue come blow your horn
The sheep's in the meadow and the cow's in the corn
But where's the boy who looks after the sheep?
He's under the haystack fast asleep
Will you wake him? No, not I
For if I do he's sure to cry

....

Other troubles occupied my time around 2036, as I remember, to do with aspersions I would cast on UNPOPCONT and the Treaty, in my lectures and tutorials.

'Measures unnecessarily extreme for moderately difficult circumstances'.

'Messianic mass murderers out of control'.

Or words to that effect. It did not take long for these views to come to the notice of the Treaty Office, and my own ComCam would have given me away. I received warnings to desist. Passages from the PADDA (2032) legislation were mailed to me, with the statutory penalties highlighted. I sought advice. Spywife reminded me that I had a responsibility for her career as well as mine. There were whispers in her office already, making her feel vulnerable and embarrassed.

I took a trip to Manchester to consult Professor Sara. She had put on a bit of weight and was taking less care of her hair, the red now flecked with grey. Proper professorial. But she still had the power to deflect my more serious intentions so that I found myself with half an erection for a short while. She had pointedly not invited me 'to tea' at her charming semi in Didsbury. I suggested that we walk along Oxford Road just outside the main University building so that our conversation could be muffled by traffic noise. I pointed to my chip scar.

She said: "You should get rid of that thing", then immediately putting her hands to her mouth in mock fear that listeners may have heard her counselling a major crime on government property. We walked and talked among the traffic anyway.

Her expectation was that the UN/WHO would realise sooner rather than later that it had suffered an unacceptable spasm of zeal and would cancel the

Treaty: the cull had already been successful to the point where budgets were coming into balance in a couple of countries and the trends were encouraging in many others. Many hospital wards were closing for lack of occupancy and geriatrics had become a near-dead profession; a few geriatricians were doing well in private practice, serving the Lifers and Exempteds. I asked her when had she ever heard of legislation being reversed when only recently enacted. I congratulated her on her appointment and on her optimism for a future of personal choice. I pointed out that, for someone in her thirties, seventy seemed a long way off, almost to the point of being never. She corrected me: she was forty and that flattery was inappropriate to our discussion. Sara become Very Serious Sara. But then I had become pretty damn serious myself.

She had resigned from HELP because of the demands on her time in her elevated academic status and because her research into the effectiveness of the scheme required her to have no conflict of interest. She said that the latest figures looked very good, which justified her optimism that the Treaty could not be far from cancellation. Our EuroQuoD measure was revealing high satisfaction rates in the families of our suicides. She was disturbed that so many people were coming to HELP to avoid the perceived humiliation of End Day imposed by the Treaty. She implored me to back off being such a verbal fucking smartarse in public and stay out of very serious trouble. Beloved Sara, forever the passionate foulmouth. I told her I

310

suspected my own motivation had something to do with wanting to disparage Geoffrey G and Lord X.

She said: "Don't be a donkey".

I said: "What do you mean?"

She said: "Donkey Shot. That one, tilting at windmills".

I laughed: "Very clever! I would never have thought that this subject could be funny. But yes, this donkey could end up shot, indeed".

She did not remind me this time that she was the one who had warned me that my endeavours could lead to the nightmare of the Treaty.

I said: "Talking of which, I have a favour to ask. I have brought a package of secobarbital for safekeeping. Would you be prepared to keep it hidden for me?" Sara puzzled and impatient. "I know. Irrational behaviour, but I have had premonitions recently. I may need it sometime when I would otherwise not have access to it."

She said: "You are strange. You could prescribe it for yourself anytime, as if for a HELP client. Why ever would you want it for yourself anyway?" Then evidence on her face of some dreadful realisation. "Or are you planning to get rid of someone else? Things bad at home? Oh no. I'm not getting into that!"

It was my turn to exhibit dismay at her suspicions. I reassured her with some difficulty. She took the package I retrieved from my manbag, with some reluctance.

"God knows where I could hide this!"

"Just make sure He is the only one who does know".

"Very funny, except it isn't. No need to mock. You may yet live to regret your agnosticism."

"Atheism" I corrected her. "I am not a pathetic hedger of bets in anticipation of the day when the trumpet sounds. I will try to remember not to mock, sorry".

"And why pick on me for this nonsense of your parcel?"

"Because I trust you with my strangeness. And other things. Waterproof it in any plastic bag and tie it to a small stone. Dump it in your toilet cistern and forget it. Surveilllance has no interest in you. Even if they did, it would be low-level and they would not be looking in your toilet. Advice from Spywife, not for general consumption." Or words to that effect.

I hadn't come for sex, and it didn't happen. That I remember definitely. Time and events had passed and I had no notion as to what current relationships she might enjoy. And I was too embarrassed to ask. The years of good living had enlarged my waist and all four limbs had diminished: I had become a 'lemon with matchsticks' and would not have presented an attractive physical prospect anyway. She thanked me for my support towards her appointment; having a knight on your side does matter, she reassured me, however tricky his reputation. She loved Manchester, the buzz and the funky feel of the place. Easily as good as Oxford, she said, without the chaotic administration.

I came away wanting to be persuaded by her optimism but failing. Ultimately, my rage would make me my own worst enemy.

....

UNPOPCONT must have read Sara's mind. Not really. The evidence was there for all to see, if they cared. The economic recovery was dramatic in so many countries. Must be thanks to the Treaty. Nothing should be allowed to threaten the continued successful functioning of the Treaty. That must have been the thinking which led to the destruction of HELP. In 2038 the UN/WHO announced the proscribing, banning, End Day of HELP without any consultation with any of us involved in its creation or conduct. Just like that. In one day, thousands of caring and highly trained professionals across the developed world were left unemployed. My Faculty of Thanatology disintegrated. Professor Sara's work on the efficacy of HELP was rendered pointless.

The UN/WHO order included an instruction that all extant vials of Letheon were to be surrendered to the PADDAs and police in all Treaty countries. Unauthorised possession of Letheon would be vigorously prosecuted and severe penalties imposed. I was deluged with panicky calls for help and further information. I was not able to offer either. None of this worked to abate any of my anger.

Geoffrey G and Lord X, the masters of UNPOPCONT, if not quite the universe, had to be the jealous destroyers of HELP. It was certainly my impression, confirmed by Sara, that so many folk were choosing to come to HELP at a time to suit themselves rather than hope to sustain patriotic fervour up to their End Day. It had to be those two buddies of mine, persuading all the Treaty governments that this had to happen; HELP had to go.

....

I continued to express my disaffection with the Treaty in my lectures to students, at conferences everywhere, at HELP Commission meetings where I was assisting with dismantling the service, at dinner parties, at any opportunity where I had some audience, large or small. I heard of others like me, just a few in the Treaty countries, also spreading small discontent. 'Small' because Treaty handouts and propaganda were (and remain) so powerful. The university continued to humour me with uninterrupted employment, perhaps because my various bosses were wary of the financial consequences of suspending me again. They must have presumed that I remained close to the Treasury and its munificence, including that which rained down on the university.

I was returning to my office after delivering one such lecture with interleaved provocative content, when I found a man waiting at my door. Face faintly familiar. He introduced himself and asked if there was somewhere private where we could talk and did I have a moment. His gestures and whispers suggested conspiracy. Irresistible. This was YoungMan1 of about 20 years previously! Amazing! I locked us in my office. He had graduated in history with strong medical modules. Health Economics had been useful along the way. Flattery? But then he had spent his career in prestigious charities working on policy and strategy.

At this stage or thereabout, I suggested we seek an alternative venue. I had to assume that my office had by this time received the attentions of the PADDA surveyors. An electronic infestation of surveillance technology was a pretty safe bet. I ordered coffee for us in the Wellcome Trust canteen; a great buzz of conversation enhanced by echo, provided a useful acoustic environment. I shut down my ComCam after stating clearly that I had to go the toilet, then explaining that it couldn't be shut for long without raising suspicions.

YoungMan1 explained with commendable economy that he had got mixed up with a small gang of miners who had been beneficiaries in one of his charities for the aged. They approached him in distress. Their patriotism did not stretch to sympathy with the UNPOPCONT Treaty. They had no funds to

315

emigrate and start new lives far away. YoungMan1 was sympathetic to their distress. He felt there had to be remote areas in the UK where oldies could hide without having to keep on the move. The submarine life is supremely taxing even for the fit elderly. He had family connections with a village in north Wales, to remain nameless, like YoungMan1 herewith remains nameless. He had succeeded in finding accommodation with families with rooms to let and also harbouring appropriate antipathy to the Treaty. He managed to persuade his charity, faced with extinction thanks to the Treaty, to switch its activities to funding miners in this way. Every face of residents and miners was known to all in the village: a stranger would be spotted immediately, for instance, in the form of a PADDA on the prowl. On the rare occasion when a stranger had been interrogated and been found to be a PADDA, the ambience had become so charged with imminent violence that the PADDA/S had left without further consequence.

He had spread his system throughout north Wales. There was now a vast network involving the valleys and mountains of north Wales, and not a single miner had been caught while they stayed put in their assigned village and didn't use 'phones or the internet.

And that is how mining came to north Wales, he said, smiling for the first time, without a single shovel-full of earth having to be lifted. There may be similar networks operating wherever there are remote areas in the world. Even in England? And Scotland?

And Ireland? How about the Hebrides? Who knows? And in north Wales villages, the arrival of determined and fit elderly had reinvigorated what had been dying communities. Funding continued to be seeded by charities but supplemented by families still in England and elsewhere in Wales. A kind of new beginning, he said, dependent on those approaching their ending. What irony! YoungMan1 bright with enthusiasm.

I glanced at my watch. This was a long stretch on the toilet. My finger to lips. I rose, actually went to the toilet, flushed, and switched on my ComCam to record that event as well as my walk back to our table. I reflected briefly on the possibility that YoungMan1 could be a PADDA plant, and then decided I didn't care. I re-opened the conversation by asking forcefully whether YoungMan1 had any news of any of my old students. I had lost track of Lenny Cohen, but reported what I chose to report on Sara. After some minutes of fake conversation I excused myself again with mutters of something I must have eaten. Using the same ruse for shutting down my ComCam, I returned to ask him why he had sought me out. He shrugged. He didn't really know. He had attended one of my incendiary talks on someone else's recommendation. He just wanted link up with a fellow spirit of old acquaintance. His was a lonely task with attendant dangers. I suspect he was looking for some approbation and I gave him fulsome praise for a remarkable achievement in the cause of humanity, not hu-money-ty. He laughed in recognition of my opening lecture of all those years ago, and he left with my strenuous best wishes.

I returned to the toilets to flush and turn on my ComCam.

....

Treaty people evidently lost patience with the likes of us. Increasingly punitive legislation against Treaty objection was introduced, right up to the charge of treason. Everybody knows. But when was that? Cannot remember. Must have been about 2040. I had visits from anonymous looking men and women in suits, apparently Treaty officers, PADDAs kindly come to warn me off with menaces. They came to the university, to the house, and to the RCP on one occasion. I was holding a meeting there in the hope of finding alternative jobs for some thanatologists cast adrift by the banning of HELP.

I realised I was being effective when the Treaty police came to arrest me on a charge of sedition. Such a compliment! I was in my early sixties and represented such a threat to the orderly conduct of daily life in Britain and beyond? Wonderful! I was interrogated over 24 hours by shifts of officers. Very persistent, even to the point of shouting abuse bordering on racial aspersions. They were obviously trying to figure out the motivation for my disruptive behaviour. I had nothing to hide. I just kept repeating that I felt that UNPOPCONT and the

Treaty were simply unnecessary. I knew I was getting to them when I managed to get in a question to the two at work on me in the early hours.

"Either of you two have family taken away after a pathetic End Day party?" Pursed lips, eyes averted, and shifting bums on seats gave them away. Both of them. They reminded me that they ask the questions and they know what their patriotic duty is, blah blah, but I had my answer. Shortly thereafter they seemed to lose interest and left me to get some sleep. I was released in the morning with the expected threats to my future comfort if I persisted in my treasonous behaviour.

My captors had not considered it necessary to inform Spywife of my arrest. She was losing patience with me anyway and my unexplained but forced absence did nothing to endear me. Our post-Sara partial reconciliation was under threat. Nevertheless, she ran me a bath and sat on the toilet seat to keep me company. She used the opportunity to express her anguish at the distinct possibility that we could both end up jobless, homeless, and living in a cardboard box; that my actions had consequences beyond my own closed world of a Benthamite nightmare. And more words to that effect.

The visible effect of my question to my interrogators served only to spur me on. With a little persistence I could create an international insurrection of my own, sufficient to put an end to this crazy murderous nonsense. So I persisted. My lectures and talks were packed out. Standing ovations, at last. Cheered way beyond anything Geoffrey G achieved. I had assumed a messianic mantle and could not stop preaching against UNPOPCONT. I had become the rock god of anti-UNPOPCONT and a decent death when chosen. Retribution would come unless this new movement could overwhelm the authorities.

So, Inspector. No denial. No exculpation. The evidence is in the public domain. The government, under the compulsion of UNPOPCONT had legislated me into treason. Confession herewith. Haha. As if there was need. I don't expect any leniency but I do expect my Spywife to be released. She played no part in my crusade. If her imprisonment was intended to draw me back to Treaty home, it has been successful.

And Geoffrey was knighted, heading up UNPOPCONT and resident in New York. My own growing celebrity and title gave me some protection, but only for a while.

....

Recalling 2042

I had given an invited talk full of sedition to standing room only and a rousing ovation at the QE II

320

Conference Centre, site of one previous humiliation. By then the QE II was a semi-derelict government building across the way from the Palace of Westminster. No police came to accost me. I was walking through the lobby heading for the doors to leave and having provided the last few autographs, to find Spywife striding up to grab me by the arm. A very forced smile disfigured her still beautifully handsome face. In the street she covered her ComCam and I knew I should instruct mine off.

"You've got to get away there's an arrest warrant in preparation treason this time you know I have access to these things they really want to put you away or worse think of somewhere to go get your passport and some cash go now go go go!"

And she had gone herself.

Jack be nimble Jack be quick
Jack jump over the candlestick

Oh Deah. She had put herself in harm's way by this action. I followed her instructions. I got home quickly, raided our safe for passport and cash from our sad little stash, threw a change of clothes into a rucksack, and took a Dcab to the airport. I needed the speed of the drone and couldn't risk the standard gridlock of Driverless. I bought a ticket to Frankfurt. The first big test was the Border. My ComCam entitled me to the fast queue. Got through in spite of a degree of palpitation which could have given me

321

away. Must have registered on the machine within the limits of Traveller's Tachycardia rather than the racing heartbeat of some guilty criminal secret.

I was ahead. Waiting at the gate was a time of high anxiety; every new arrival in a suit and without a bag could have been the PADDAs come to get me. Even as we taxied out I half expected the aircraft to stop to allow police to board. Got through the Frankfurt Border as if I was here to stay for a bit, but with more anxiety. I bought a pack of old-fashioned razor blades and plasters from a pharmacy in the airport. I made for the toilets where I flushed my ComCam away then cut through the original chip scar in my forearm.

Irony: I had successfully avoided the surgical life up to this point, only to find it necessary to operate on myself, and without anaesthetic. There was blessedly little bleeding and less pain than I expected, the minor benefits of operating through a scar. The chip went down the toilet and a plaster stopped whatever little bleeding there was. I discarded the blades in the bin.

The anxiety continued as I went through the Border again, this time with my ticket for Namibia. The terse man in the Border booth made some remark in good English about my very short stay in Frankfurt, Professor. I shrugged while explaining that I had only to deliver a professional document to an academic colleague before going on to lecture in Windhoek, Sir.

The land of ancient German conquest, Sir. No. I didn't actually vocalise that last bit.

Still ahead. Then came the worst wait – four hours at the gate before the evening departure. I was hyperventilating and having to regain control of my breathing by reminding myself of the great morality of my crusade. Pathetic self-centred self-delusion. Again, I was searching every new arrival at the gate for being too well dressed and bagless: possible Treaty police.

At last, as we accelerated for take-off I was thankful – still ahead. It was only as we left Treaty territory – crossing the wavy line of twinkly lights demarcating the northern Med coast from the black blankness of the sea – that I could relax and look forward to a dawn arrival at Windhoek. After over a century of intercontinental flight, it would still take nearly a whole night. SpaceArc could get me there in two hours, if I was a billionaire.

There was a bit of a fuss when I claimed refugee status at the airport, but Namibian officials were used to dealing with Treaty refugees. I had to wait for the relevant offices in town to open and for the right people to travel to the airport. The Namibians understood perfectly well that the Treaty refugees usually came with substantial financial resources. I didn't, but they gave me temporary residential rights anyway. Who doesn't want an extra doctor? I made sure that my jacket sleeve covered my recent surgery. There was no point in causing unnecessary alarm about my health. I asked about the Treaty refugee colony. There was bound to be one in Windhoek. Everyone knows that there are Treaty refugee colonies in most African cities.

I got myself a coffee in an old-fashioned paper cup and sat down to ponder my next move, appreciative of the risen sun, the warmth, and the palm trees, all remembered from my previous brief visit. I had had a bad first night as a fugitive. I simply cannot sleep in aircraft at the best of times. That night I was capable of only occasional brief dozing full of fearful images and riddled with guilt. Too late, I became appalled at my selfishness of recent months, and then extending back many years to the Sara times. And I should have refused to budge from London. I should have stayed back to deal with the consequences of my mission against UNPOPCONT. Would have been good publicity for the cause. Ah well.

....

I had no idea how I was to make contact with someone who could put me up. Best would be a taxi into town and check into a hotel. A start of sorts. But then a middle-aged couple came striding into the concourse, he white and bearded and impressively tanned; she black, a strikingly handsome face and with intricately braided hair, both obviously looking for someone or something, and seemed to find it when they saw me.

"Morning Sir. Professor. Welcome to Windhoek! You won't remember me. Lenny Cohen. I was one of your HE students in London. Must be twentyfive years ago. This is my wife Jay. We would like to invite you to join us for the day, unless you have other plans?"

My stunned reaction must have been apparent. Even after a sleepless night and the tiring element of anxiety added, there must have been a big question in my face.

"We knew you were headed here. We can explain later. Is this all you have with you?" The sun was temporarily blinding as we walked to their dusty utility. A small pleasure - to see old-fashioned self-drive vehicles again. He kept up a cheerful reminiscence of student days in London while I struggled to confirm for myself that this was all real and not a dream. He remembered a Welsh fellow student called Sara who seemed to impress me and who went on to major in HE. Wasn't she a professor now somewhere in England?

We arrived at a luxury thatched lodge on the outskirts of Windhoek. They wouldn't let me carry my rucksack. There were no check-in formalities.

They drove me to a rondavel suite overlooking some hills. They must have sensed my exhaustion because I had been very quiet. I was encouraged to get some rest and to walk back to the main building in the evening when it suited me. We would have an evening meal together. I didn't have the strength to bother with washing and must have passed out on the incongruously luxurious bed.

I woke in thick darkness and completely disorientated. I showered off the sweat of anxiety and the first dust of the southern hemisphere. I walked up to the main building covered by a black shroud pierced by billions of microscopic diamonds. I was guided by footpath lighting to the racket of crickets and the distant howls of hyenas. Africa is so intense and extreme; nothing soft here.

At dinner I said: "I had no intention of imposing on your hospitality. I had no idea you had left England. I had to make a decision in a great hurry. I had to choose a non-Treaty destination which did not require a visa, beyond the clutches of UNPOPCONT and its PADDA goons. Also, I have fond memories of a brief visit here many years ago on sabbatical."

Lenny offered a more extensive introduction to wife Jay. Turns out she is a public health physician, British trained, from humble beginnings. 'Jay' is short for Jahohora, a legendary Herero heroine of the 1907 genocide of the Hereros by the German occupation. Turns out also that the two of them own the lodge.

He said: "Sidavid, we are delighted to have you. Our first knight. We will find work for you, never fear. We are part of a multinational colony of UNPOPCONT expats. We operate as a loose collective because of what we have in common. We live all over Namibia; we are not ghetto-ised. But we are blessed with a variety of useful skills including locals who are sympathetic. For example, one of our IT fundis has hacked into your ComCam centre. ComCam hasn't a clue. That is how we knew you were headed here. They were looking for you somewhere on the outskirts of Frankfurt, chattering away all the while, apparently at a sewage treatment plant, and still chattering on ComCam when they finally questioned the ticket sellers in the airport."

"Fundis?" I asked. He explained: southern African slang for teachers or experts, probably from Zulu but in widespread use. "And we don't barbecue. We 'braai'. Afrikaans. Don't worry. You'll get into it soon enough."

"PADDA goons?" he asked. I described the essence of the 2032 Public Administration Disorder and Disinformation Act and the associated enforcement personnel. It had apparently passed them by in spite of the hack into ComCam. Lenny and Jay laughed. He explained: "Here, a padda is a frog. Pronounced 'pudda'. Afrikaans. Not flattering for a human. 'FROGS'. Good name for your goons."

I remarked on the fact that many other diners were oriental in appearance, unexpected in a south west African desert country. Lenny explained that they were Chinese uranium miners, some of them second generation, management really. They speak good English, Afrikaans, and Herero. The actual miners were confined to company camps. I asked my hosts whether they had discussed the subject of UNPOPCONT with any of the Chinese.

"Oh yes. They love it. Anything better than the hated one-child policy abandoned nearly 30 years ago. Some of these guys are just old enough to remember. Better to go at 70 after a good life with brothers and sisters rather than no siblings at all, they say. They still sing the one-child policy anthem: 'Fewer lives are better lives', just in a different context. True believers. Not just propaganda".

I said: "No surprise. The HELP programme never really took off in China. They don't like having to make end of life planning for themselves. Simply a cultural difference. They prefer having such decisions forced on them by authority. Such a pity. Makes UNPOPCONT look good."

Jay said: "Sidavid, honestly, looking back at the figures, do you really believe that HELP would have done the job of controlling populations even in the western countries? Lenny doesn't want UNPOPCONT, which is why he is here, but that doesn't detract from the fact that UNPOPCONT is making a great difference to international solvency. It sounds ridiculous to have to agree with the Chinese that fewer lives are indeed better lives?"

I was silent, in reflection. I am sure I sighed: "You could be right. I just could not accept the genocide of the geriatrics. I was doing this for the likes of my own father, not for everyone reaching their seventieth birthday. To some extent it was personal."

After another silence, getting to grips with the enormity of my admission, and Lenny calling for another bottle of wine, I said: "Where is Malthus now? What we need is a massive check to population which comes from nature and not from man. So, not war. Not UNPOPCONT. Not famine, even if that comes from nature. Just too awful. Maybe disease? A major extinction, like the 1918 'flu pandemic? Fifty million gone in months, maybe a hundred million, nowhere on the planet exempt. Mainly young men in the best of health. Potential babymakers. Brilliant. The First World War itself killed fewer than 20 million, soldiers and civilians. The 'flu killed more than the Black Death, proportionately. At one time we all thought AIDS would do it. That virus is a genius, as you must know. It is transmitted by man's greatest need after hunger, and that is sex; it populates and destroys the very white cells supposed to protect us from invasion; and it mutates, a constantly moving target when you try to medicate against it. Didn't do it. Even Ebola didn't do it. No one even talks about AIDS now, unless some isolated unlikely acquaintance has been diagnosed."

329

Jay said: "If you think the 'flu did such a great job, why are we having this discussion a century and a bit later?"

I shot out: "We need a 'flu pandemic every one hundred years. But how do you arrange that? And we can produce vaccines quite quickly now, so it won't happen except in tiny outbreaks."

Jay said: "So UNPOPCONT is what works best? Let's face it, genocide or not, it is the only scheme proven to work, so far. It is in fact that great extinction you are looking for. You may not like it and I wouldn't want it, but hey, I don't have to bother. We live in a third world desert paradise. All I have to bother about is the safe disposal of the nation's shit and other such uplifting matters."

Lenny said: "Sidavid, with respect, it is surely not your burden to save the world from itself."

I said: "Strange, yes. I was persuaded, flattered, early on that it was indeed my burden. I have spent a major portion of my career believing that. Time to quit, do you think?"

Lenny said: "We are a bit anxious that you would want to take up campaigning from here. We wouldn't want your FROGS flying in to abduct you back to the UK. By the way, Sidavid, if you're interested in the 'flu story in Namibia, you should visit Aus one day. Something interesting in the cemetery. For another time perhaps", waving the subject away.

I said: "Please, no more Sir-ing."

Or words to that effect.

....

"First world health economics won't help us here. Health economics of any kind, especially the academic kind, will not make you a living, assuming you are intending to stay long enough to need to make a living."

It was a few days after my arrival in Namibia. Lenny and I were discussing my prospects in that country, short and long. I was concerned as to how I was going to pay for my stay. There was certainly no possibility of extracting any savings from Britain, as my Inspector can confirm, and Lady Spywife would probably need whatever there was, for herself. I said I couldn't go back any time soon, so I would be looking long term. We were sharing breakfast. The fizzing elation of a narrow but successful escape had dissipated. The needs of daily life encroached, in an environment so alien to a London professional as to suggest another planet, not just another continent. Despite the previous brief visit. And I was increasingly distressed by nagging guilt. I should have ignored the dramatic instructions from Spywife and stayed to carry on the fight against UNPOPCONT by whatever means, even in captivity or in hiding. Become a miner myself perhaps.

"You have other skills that could get you employment. You are a geriatrician by training. We don't have one of those here yet but we do have an increasing population of aged as Namibia has prospered. And of course we have the influx of the not-so-young ex-pats easing into old age. You are a general physician in the first instance, so you could double up in that way. We still have some TB, occasional malaria and yellow fever, resistant gonorrhea, occasional heatstroke, and whatever the tourists bring us. There is no osteoporosis except related to alcohol excess. There is a war going on between gangs of poachers. They shoot each other in between shooting rhino and elephant. The Chinese insist they have cured themselves of their ivory obsession but no one believes that. A major cause of accidental death is warthogs running into the road in front of oncoming traffic. And you could teach at our medical school. Most of us have two jobs, sometimes three. My sociology degree serves no purpose here, but I did enjoy your lectures. More like performances. Should have been a lesson to others. Jay and I grow tomatoes for local consumption and export. The Israelis are here so we use their irrigation system. 'The desert blooms', just like in Israel. You are welcome to pick and pack, but that won't be gainful employment except in the sense of enjoyment and the satisfaction of contributing to the finances of the Collective. By the way, the Israelis have their own expat rabbi, just in case you feel the need of one."

I thanked Lenny for what was too much information for one session, for one displaced person, and that I remained a Jewish heathen quite comfortably. It was Jay who was not satisfied.

"I would have thought. Someone like you with your heightened social conscience and caring would claim some guiding god or at least some feeling of spirituality. I have a belief but I don't shout about it. It comforts me and that is good enough, don't you think?"

I said: "I have no belief and don't shout about it, and don't begrudge anyone their beliefs. I just don't feel the need for that kind of comfort. I have been intrigued in the past by all this talk of spirituality – please, no offence – but what does it mean? Or is it some substitute for conventional religious adherence: like 'I don't go to church but I am very spiritual'. That sort of thing?" I then played the Father Christmas parallel for her (see above) like I was to do for my Inspector: do you believe in Father Christmas? No. Did you once? Yes, she did! And so on.

"Wait till you come close to your end. You will come crawling back to faith!" Wagging finger but broad smile. I smiled to indicate no offence taken at her confident prediction.

I said: "What if the end comes too quickly for that luxury of contemplation?" She waved her hand in front of my face as if to shut me up, wanting me to enjoy my drink in my new home.

And so, Inspector, I found myself with two jobs, in nature entirely in contrast to each other. I became, at last, the kind of 'proper doctor' my London students of old wished to apply to clinical practice. In the hospital and the medical school there seemed to be an insistence on the 'Sir' and nothing would deter my colleagues and students; on the farm, first names only. The pleasure of getting hands dirty, and the unaccustomed but invigorating physicality of the farm job, came as a revelation. The hospital job required some homework, to get an update on all medical subjects but especially geriatrics. I looked for opportunities to apply a lifetime of experience and knowledge of health economics, and could not find any. Was the whole of my previous professional life pointless navel gazing? Esoteric and abstruse stuff, until I let myself get involved with the problem of overpopulation. Well, it did bring honours and titles and a consuming interest. Indeed, eventually a consumption too far.

The lodge bar was the Collective's social hub. Very international, sociable, occasionally intellectual, and characterised by intense networking. All necessary skills and knowledge could be discovered here. And some unnecessary skills and knowledge, but fascinating just the same. I met the man who had hacked ComCam. He would bring us snippets of news from time to time. He had to exercise caution in what he divulged in case it could somehow get back to

ComCam and he would be shut out. And have to start hacking all over again. Those who had seen his equipment spoke in terms of awed wonderment.

Friday night was the big night. Some folk would travel vast distances to attend. You did not have to be in the Collective to join in. Government officers, businessmen, travel agents, lawyers, farmers, uranium miners, tourists, were all made welcome. It was evident that a lot of business was transacted at the bar.

One evening the IT Man (Bles Bezuidenhout – a name remembered!) came up to me to impart the unsurprising news that the United Kingdom government had revoked my British passport and citizenship. Bles? Afrikaans for bald. And he was. Shiny bald and thickset so that there was a continuous sloping line from skull to shoulders. A bullet head, the antithesis of the standard perception of an IT geek. By way of compensation he carried a flowing beard of proportions befitting any Orthodox theologian or rabbi or imam. Or of the dark arts of IT. He said they were openly discussing me by name and my destination of flight. I was stateless. With a knighthood! I knew that latter honour had been in the gift of the King and could not be revoked without his indulgence.

I had to apply formally for permanent residence. Namibia was inclined to be happy with that and went the extra mile (kilometer, here) offering me a passport with citizenship. I was queue-jumping without realising it at the time and without the need for a ComCam to do so. Lenny was helping me with the paperwork. He asked whether I had heard from my wife.

"No. She probably doesn't know how to reach me directly."

"Do you not want to get her out here to Namibia?"

"Yes, I suppose so but she probably wouldn't want to come here. There is unlikely to be any call here for the work she does."

"What work is that?"

"Can't say. Never mind."

"You should investigate. There might be something for her here. You can't be on your own here forever. Or maybe that is what you want? Sorry, didn't mean to pry."

He was perfectly correct. I had been swept up in my new life and had been waiting for something to transpire that would prompt me to get her out here without news of that intention getting to the Treaty authorities. I couldn't communicate electronically. That would be detected immediately. I would write to an acquaintance in Germany and ask them to post on my letter to Spywife. Wasn't it wonderful that the old postal service had been brought back thanks to popular demand? It would be my means of persuading Spywife to contemplate and plan her own escape. PADDA must surely suspect that she had something to do with my own sudden departure. I wrote to one of our previous HELP thanatologists in Berlin, asking him to use someone who could not possibly be on PADDA's radar. It remained a possibility of course, that all her mail, whether paper based or electronic, was being vetted by Treaty PADDAs. I would have to take the risk.

On another occasion Bles told a few of us gathered around a Friday night lodge barbecue ('braai') with beers, that the UK government had started euthanasing the mentally disabled who were a financial burden on the health system, including all expensive brain injured, depressed, manic, and schizophrenic people of any age. There was a fuss about some prominent female professor in Manchester. Despite the usual security, the media had gained access to a story describing the Treaty euthanasia of her younger brother with severe paranoid schizophrenia, and her vociferous objections couched in heavily consonanted curses. A memory from the distant past came roaring into my head, a mad attack of remembrance. Sara describing a scene from the disparaged 'Mrs Dalloway', a man in a wheelchair in the park exhibiting symptoms of a psychotic attack and Sara saying she knew that Virgina Woolf was describing paranoid schizophrenia and that she, Sara, knew what she was talking about. It just had to be her brother that Bles was reporting to us. Here was some of the twentieth century repeating itself.

But then the truth is that every century repeats itself somewhere in the world. The default behaviour of mankind. Nice. Quaint.

....

See Saw Margery Daw
Johnnie shall have a new master
He shall have but a penny a day
Because he can't work any faster

During my next tomato packing duty I saw Lenny come into the shed: part of his 'ward round' of the day. I called him over while continuing to pack. He made some jocular reference to my untutored packing skills and associated slowness. Pupil become master. I asked whether he remembered the Welsh lass, Sara, in his tutorial group in London all those years ago. He must have. He had asked after her some weeks previously.

"Ah yes. Teacher's pet. Sorry, no offence. Freckled redhead. Clever girl with strong opinions. Ended up in Oxford, didn't she?" He gave no sign of having any awareness of our intimacies beyond the formal of teacher and student.

"Yes, and now a professor in Manchester, a valued colleague, and co-founder of HELP." I brought him up to date with the information I had had from Bles Bezuidenhout, almost certainly relating to Sara and her 'late' younger brother. I said I nursed a notion of responsibility for her safety and well-being, and was there some way of finding gainful employment for a female health economist of middle age, in Namibia? Not unless she retrained in something useful to Namibia, was his first response, not unexpected. After an apology for the negative implications of his advice, Lenny asked after any other skills she might have. I remembered her ability in maths and stats, particularly useful in the validation of our European Quality of Death (EuroquoD) index. Lenny lightened up – there was a nationwide shortage of those skills, with vacant teaching posts in the university in Windhoek but not necessarily at professorial level. It was up to me to have a word with the Vice Chancellor. And so it came to pass. All Sara had to do was get herself out here to Namibia. Again, I sent more messages via ex-HELP colleagues in Germany.

Coming back to the tomatoes. I was served a whole raw tomato with my lunch yesterday. Obviously there was no part of the vine with it. Why would there be? But the mere presence of a real raw tomato did remind me of the aroma of fresh tomato vines in Namibia. I was happy then to work in that shed, just to have that in my Jewish nose. I indulged the fancy briefly that this was one of my tomatoes, having faithfully followed me all the way back to England.

....

Still 2042, I think

Aus. 'Out' in German. And it is certainly 'out'. A heat hole on the edge of the Namib desert. The Aus cemetery was even further out. In amongst all the others, there were two rows of uniform military headstones together, dated within two weeks of each other, 1918, all German soldiers. In 1918 all German soldiers in what had been German South West Africa, were prisoners of the South Africans fighting on the British side. Then there was a row of South African soldiers' graves, all together, a mix of English and Afrikaans names, all dated within two weeks of each other, October 1918, and days only before the German soldiers' stones. What happened here? Lenny Cohen had said I would find something of interest. What I had found was the definition of 'pandemic' carved in gravestones. The Germans would have been prisoners of war. The South Africans would have been their keepers. One or more South Africans must have arrived from home after leave or freshly recruited, and already infected with that 'flu virus. They went first, after infecting their fellows and then their prisoners. Entirely my construction of the likely sequence of events but the only entirely logical one, surely. Evidence of one of the mass extinctions of the twentieth century even in this remote hot outpost near the edge of a desert a whole continent away from the main action of the war. What with Paschendaele and the Somme, German South West Africa would not have attracted much attention from historians nor the wider public.

My accommodation for the night was a bungalow beyond the outskirts of town, in the veld among massive rocky outcrops. Indeed, the back wall of my bedroom was bare rockface. I sat on the verandah, all lights off, with a glass of my travelling whisky, unable to take my gaze from the hypnotic blaze of the Milky Way, as never seen before. In the dense darkness, as aways to the accompaniment of crickets, I felt I was looking into the uttermost ends of the universe. Could one of those uncountable twinkles be Harry's Apophis on its way to create an extinction sufficient to solve all our puny problems forever?

The only means of achieving sleep in that heat was to lie under a wet towel with the ceiling fan on max.

"Twinkle twinkle little star"?

....

What we are missing, Inspector, is a natural mass extinction for the twentyfirst century. Natural, so that no one can be blamed for it. The UNPOPCONT Treaty is unnatural, man made, and

341

ultimately blameworthy. Perhaps my fate here in your custody is appropriate to that bit of blame which could attach to me. There is still hope, Inspector, for a mass extinction, even quite soon if some folk are to be believed. Apophis, the Snake. Where are you?

What I am missing, Inspector, is some non-authoritarian company and some view of the outside world. No point even in asking, I am sure. The missing flake of paint on the window allows me enough of a view to confirm what I certainly know – the changing of the seasons appropriate to six months of solitary, so far.

....

I was on a tour of peripheral hospitals in my role as a consultant physician in the employ of the government of Namibia. I was to look out for trends in patterns of infectious disease, apart from dispensing medical wisdom towards saving lives. How refreshing, even in the heat, to be working towards saving lives again, instead of ending them.

But no word from Spywife. I was beginning to develop a belated panicky anxiety as to how this was going to play out.

....

"Ohgodno. Here comes Cassie. Poegaai already and he hasn't even started drinking", said someone at the bar loud enough for some to hear above the din, and raising some laughter.

"Poegaai?" I asked, feeling left out of the joke.

"Pissed" explained Jay. "Doc Cassie is our local depressive, forecasting doom and treating himself with alcohol. Cassie is his nickname. For Cassandra. For tiresomely predicting doom. No one is sure of his real name but it could be Cassidy. If he finds you, a fresh face, that's your evening gone. He's from Cape Town. Was on the staff of the observatory there. He was fired because of his drinking and his obsession with asteroids. He washed up here where he is tolerated and where he found work on the farms. He's harmless but you had better hide."

It was a Friday night at the lodge. The bar and lounge were well patronised. The wild-haired dishevelled man in sweat stained khakis, with wrinkled face and baggy bloodshot eyes was ordering a drink at the bar. We were safe. But not for long. Swivelling his head while waiting for his order, his uncertain eyes acquired a definite certainty when their gaze found me. There was purpose in his tottering gait as he made his way over to our table. I had been describing my inspection tour findings to a deputy minister of health, and Jay and Lenny. They greeted Doc Cassie with reserved politeness and started shifting their chairs as they added excuses on leaving. I couldn't find the courage to leave, and my curiosity had been stoked by an old memory of obsession with asteroids.

"These people." With an expansive wave of the arm not holding his brandy and Coke. "No-one believes me. They mock me but they are all going to die. We are all going to die. Soon man. Hi man. I'm Cassie. Who are you?"

And that was indeed the evening gone, in the course of which I discovered a fascinating, highly intelligent broken man taking me into his confidence. Apophis was coming to get us and the whole planet. In 2050. He had made all the calculations again and again, to the neglect of his general work at the observatory. Sure, they represented just one possibility but didn't any possibility require action?

"It's an enemy aircraft. We could shoot it down. You know what I mean. Deflect it with rockets and all that."

He had contacted his 'B612' American colleagues running the Sentinel Space Telescope. They had acknowledged the possibility of a strike by Apophis but even they were half-hearted in their support. His independent action had irritated his employer and he was asked to leave. All the while of the telling, he would put his sad face close to mine in the way that drunks do, the better to fix me in his gaze. I took the risk, ordered another brandy and Coke for him, and told him of Harry and his 'rock garden' and his notes of all those years ago. I said nothing about my own fruitless correspondence with 'B612'.

He was galvanised. "Yes man. Look." He grabbed an exposed pen from my shirt pocket and started writing on a paper napkin with shaking hand. Scribble scribble. All maths and trajectories of which I could have no understanding but which resembled something of what I could remember from Harry's notes. Addled or not, he must have seen the recognition in my face.

"You see?! Not just me, man!" Triumphantly. Standing suddenly but swaying and turning about, he shouted to all who could hear: "Hey, you lot. This man believes me" pointing to me. "He knows. 2050. The Snake is coming! Too late for rockets. We're fucked man, we're fucked." Or words to that effect.

I was not sure that I believed him and the glances back suggested that many of those who heard Cassie's announcement were embarrassed for my sake. I was not embarrassed but intrigued. Half a world away from the late Harry the amateur, and half a lifetime later, a once-professional astrophysicist had made the same finding. A paper napkin on the table before me registered the trigonometry of our extinction, hieroglyphics of destruction inscribed without hesitation despite an uncontrollable tremor. Was I just possibly looking at the kind of 'natural' massive extinction I had been brooding about, but perhaps more massive than I would wish? Not another 'flu epidemic, but a total celestial calamity? That prospect would eradicate any sense of satisfaction experienced by the Treaty people and UNPOPCONT. And Sir Geoffrey G. And the ghost of Lord X. And you, Inspector?

Time for bed. Cassie had retaken his seat to avoid a fall. I was a bit staggery myself, I discovered, but mellow, mellow. I thanked Doc Cassie for his time and trouble. As I left I had an impression of leaving a sad man with his head in his hands, possibly weeping.

Diddle diddle dumpling
My son John
Went to bed with his trousers on
One shoe off and one shoe on
Diddle diddle dumpling
My son John

....

My prison room has a Bible! I have a feeling I have mentioned this previously. The wonderfully 'correct' King James version of my youth. Your influence, Inspector? Like the Gideon bibles in hotel bedrooms of a bygone age. There is a cheerful piece in Revelations to support the celestial predictions of Harry and Cassie, and Dr Jones of 'B612'.

"And the third angel sounded, (trumpet, that is) and there fell a great star from heaven, burning as it were a lamp, and it fell upon the third part of the rivers and upon the fountains of waters ...... ". Revelations 8 of St John the Divine, Verse 10 (and the rest). So there you have it – Harry, Cassie, Dr Robert Jones, and St John the Divine. Could the third angel have known something way back then? St John even had his own name for the great burning star falling from heaven: Wormwood! There it is, right in front of me, Verse 11. Also, poison in 'Hamlet'. Maybe poison in our heaven too.

Right up your street, Inspector. Quaint.

By the way, who has actually read Revelations apart from fundamentalists and priests? Have you, Inspector, of true faith? Nowhere have I read any remarks on the completely bizarre hallucinatory nature of its contents. Revelations must have been written by someone really high on something approximating LSD or mescaline of the Previous Days. And unrestricted access to writing materials! Lucky John.

So! For my own amusement, my reconstruction reveals the exiled St John of Patmos alone in a cave, stoned out of his skull from some herb he has discovered on the island, writing like a demon possessed, and all of it bonkers. Except perhaps for the bits predicting celestial Armageddon? Such fun.

....

Some weeks after the Doc Cassie episode

Some Friday evening. Lenny, Jay, and I are in the lodge bar. Jay is evidently not satisfied with my cavalier attitude to Faith. She sees me as some sort of Faith delinquent. I don't mind because she is always good company and lovely to look at. And I was not quite sober. And not lovely to look at because I had started to grow a beard. Jay pointed and laughed, but her amusement did not last.

"How do you attach meaning to your life without some sort of belief that you were put on this earth for a purpose?"

"There is no meaning to our lives, surely? What do you mean by 'meaning'? What do you mean by 'purpose'? We are here because we're here. We're here because two people fucked, and bingo! Here we are, without meaning or purpose, just here. And then we are gone, sooner or later. Everybody dies. So what?"

Marmalade, papa laid
That's how I was made

More fruit of an expensive education. Not Mother Goose.

She shook her head. I was able to use crude language because I was among friends and because I needed to make a crude point. (No pun). And I was cheerfully half-pissed.

"So how can you carry on with your life without a purpose?"

"Easy. I just keep breathing in and out. I go to bed at night and am amazed every morning when I wake up to find I am still here. Especially at my age. Who cares except perhaps some family and some friends? But we are fortunate that we can feel good about ourselves because of some little good we can do for others. Doctors, nurses, farmers, scientists, engineers, carers, plain bloody hard labourers, soldiers who stand on the wall, and others. That's a feeling, not a meaning, not a purpose."

Lenny was nodding gently, saying nothing, but Jay caught him at it.

"Are all Jews like you two? Godless, breathing in and out?"

"No no! Just we two, fortunately for mankind." I couldn't help the tease. "I tell you what. You need to ask cockroaches about the meaning of life. I read somewhere that somehow they were one of the few creatures to survive the last great extinction. That one where an asteroid fell on Mexico and all the dinosaurs died. The cockroaches survived, don't we know! They must know something about the meaning of life."

"OK. That's enough. This round is on me" Jay said, rising. I saw Doc Cassie tottering in. I nodded in his direction.

"If he and some others are right, we've got another one coming, another asteroid. There won't be much 'meaning' or 'purpose' flying around after that. Except for the cockroaches."

Or words to that effect.

Blessed guardian angels keep
Me safe from danger while I sleep

....

Recalling 2043 (must have been; not that long ago)

Lenny, Jay, and a large group of local well-wishers held a first anniversary party for me in the lodge lounge. They were there from the university and the department of health, and the many new friends I had made on planet Namibia. The Israelis who had tried to teach me a bit of Hebrew were there, perhaps to celebrate my failure. Even the Chinese were there. The uranium miners were grateful for the enhanced Health and Safety (don't laugh, Inspector) inspection programme I had persuaded the government to introduce, funded by the Chinese. A couple of the Chinese bosses showed up at the behest of the department of health, if only to demonstrate that they harboured no resentment. Even if they did. Harbour resentment, that is.

It was a jolly event initially. The Chinese were the first to succumb to advanced inebriation. I was their best friend. I must come to China. They would find me a nice woman. I shouldn't be alone at my age. And so on. I was still perfectly sober, I believe, but burst into tears, suddenly and intensively missing Spywife. I managed to cover up and hide myself in the toilet until I looked presentable again. What took so long to feel this way? You may wonder, Inspector. I wonder myself. In mitigation I could plead that even while I was so busy creating a new life for myself, I was constantly brooding about the means whereby I might safely extract Spywife from the certain surveillance of your Treaty PADDAs, to Namibia. I consulted many of my Namibian friends and some political *prominentes*. We even had a scheme worked out whereby Spywife would simply walk into the Namibian embassy in London and claim asylum. But how would we tell her? And there was every chance that she would end up a prisoner of the PADDAs, in the embassy, before she could be moved out of the country. And Namibia, while not a Treaty country, was on good terms with China, the number one Treaty country in terms of volume; there may have been some unwelcome sharing of information there. And we must not be so arrogant as to assume that Spywife would have wanted to join me in Namibia. She may have been sufficiently disenchanted with me as to be grateful for the separation. Confession relevant here: whenever I happened to fantasise about sex, those fantasies involved Sara of a bygone era, rather than Spywife. And I did not spend every night alone, it is true; I had reason to be grateful for occasional company and even sex with equally grateful unattached women, thankfully without unrealistic expectations on their part. At my age then, and no less now, impending erectile dysfunction imposed its own limits on performance. A veil over that.

And what possible employment would a middle-aged British spy find in Namibia?

Many 'Ands' there, as you can see Inspector, and nothing accomplished. But in reality, Spywife was seldom very far from my thoughts.

....

Still 2043.. plus

"I need a Welsh speaker. I need to get a message to Prof Sara. I need a greater degree of security for this message. I am hoping that the Treaty PADDAs are as ignorant of Welsh as the Germans were at the Normandy invasion of 1944. Or so my father told me from his reading of history."

I had accosted Lenny in the tomato shed. Sara needed to do something for me before she came out to Namibia, and supposing she was planning to come out.

"That's a lot of needing and hoping. And I have no idea what you are talking about. Welsh and German and 1944?"

I told Lenny what I had been told in late childhood: that in the confusion of the June allied invasion almost a century ago, wireless operators were in chaos with their codes having to be changed frequently. Someone suggested employing Welsh speakers talking Welsh into open mics. The Germans hadn't a clue, and since which time wireless operators were called 'Taffies', whether Welsh or not. I was hoping the English and all Euro PADDAs remained equally ignorant.

Lenny shrugged. "We have an expat farmer in the collective. Euan Pritchard. He breeds Damaras in the northwest. I have no information as to his Welsh language skills. He comes down once a month to sell his sheep and to shop. He comes alone. His wife died in the yellow fever epidemic from Angola. We'll get him next trip down."

We met in the bar of the livestock market on the edge of town. Lenny kindly made the introductions. Our man was lanky, deeply tanned, all sinew and suspicion. Euan had been Welsh-fluent on arrival ten years previously. Relief. He became friendly after a beer and small talk about sheep prices. I showed him the script of the message I intended for Sara. In it I repeated the offer of the sabbatical opportunity that remained for her 'in Africa'. Then I asked that she kindly make a journey to London to deliver the parcel she was holding for me, to my London address, possibly in combination with her 'sabbatical' to Africa. Euan smiled and read out my letter after he had transcribed it into Welsh with what sounded like untroubled fluency.

"How's that? Not bad after ten years? OK. How do I get this to your colleague?" It was only then that I realised that I could be compromising Sara instead of ensuring her safety away from that section of the northern hemisphere. My inherent selfishness must have overcome my apprehensions. I asked whether Euan would be prepared to use an old-fashioned landline number. I was not to be named but described as an old friend from her undergraduate university. Euan wanted to know whether Sara was Welsh language competent, failing which this exercise would be pointless, apart from being dangerous. I reassured him on that score without revealing that Sara had proved what sounded like Welsh fluency to my satisfaction on several occasions, either *in extremis* of passion, or anger.

I suggested to Lenny that we test the scheme on Bles. Bles was sceptical.

"Hey man, they have three 'doughnuts' now in that Chelten Ham place. What is it called? GCHQ or something? Don't you believe they don't have Welsh speakers in there listening. Jy sal jou gat sien, ou beesblaas!" (You will see your arse, ie come to grief, old oxbladder). I made the decision to take the risk. It worked. Sara arrived on the 6th of June 2044. That I remember because there was a bit of fuss in the Namibian media to do with the centenary of the D-Day Normandy invasion. Only a bit of a fuss because it doesn't mean much to folk living in Namibia except perhaps the descendants of leftover Germans, and they wouldn't want much reminding, one supposes. There were no living veterans of course but old interviews from previous anniversaries were repeated on TV. Lenny and Jay kindly brought me to the airport to meet our most recent refugee. She didn't recognise me at first, because of the beard, I suppose.

Sara looked haggard on arrival, slightly travel stained, smudged spectacles, pale, more than slight weight loss from what I remember of my Manchester visit, slightly wrinkled, slightly disorientated by her hurriedly very changed circumstances - geographic, social, and professional. My lover, as was, but unlikely to be again. This was not the time for such considerations nor enquiries as to her success in making a parcel delivery in London. Just by looking at her you would not have any inkling that her brother had been murdered recently by the Treaty. She brightened during the reunion with her London classmate of old. Lenny put her up in the lodge with instructions to rest and join us in the bar lounge in the evening, if and when she felt ready. The routine of generosity lavished on waifs and strays, again.

....

"She was very kind once she made the connection and because I arrived on her doorstep – your doorstep, without warning. I was not allowed to refuse tea and a light lunch. I told her what was in the parcel and that she should hide it in a clever place you never know when you might need the stuff for yourself or others she said she knew about hiding things and was grateful to hear that you were able to contact someone in the UK and she was thinking she should join you but what would she do in such a strange place and leaving all her friends behind and so on I couldn't help feeling she was studying me to find out what you saw in me but nothing was said she called me 'Professor' at all times so kind but so formal she drove me to the short-haul at Heathrow for my air taxi to TEA nothing I could do to put her off."

Dinner was over. Lenny and Jay had given Sara the standard briefing for new arrivals, and left us to catch up. We had drinks and Sara was debriefing on her recent movements unprompted but in a kind of rush. I did prompt her to talk about what happened to her brother but she shook her head. She was more interested in the gecko she found in her room and how cute it looked and did I know the proper Latin name for it and something about its physiology. I had to declare ignorance on all counts. I knew what she was doing and let her do it. We could come back to her brother another time, anytime.

I said: "How do you explain the obsession of the Treaty police with private possession of Letheon?

You would think UNPOPCONT would celebrate every suicide. One less to age expensively."

She said: "They fret about the stats. Suicides introduce an unexpected variable into the actuarial mix and spoil the anticipated certainties of the insurance industry and the pensions people just when things were stabilising and profits growing. Isn't that just the most fucked up irony? They want to kill you at 70 but you cost the insurance more money if you kill yourself earlier. And why otherwise would you want your own Letheon? It's all about control. I'm sure the insurers are helping to fund the running of UNPOPCONT but I have no proof so I can't publish. Rumours are rampant that there will be new legislation to return to the days when suicide disqualified your life insurance policy. There is a further irony you may not have heard about out here. Letheon or unbranded secobarbital is everywhere. It is being smuggled in by the ton, easily available on the dark web if you can navigate it, probably from Mexican labs. For all the folk who are doing DIY Last Days at their convenience just like we used to do for others under HELP. UNPOPCONT is suppressing the figures but I have sources. Can't publish of course. So in a perverse way, HELP is alive and well and only pensions are loving it."

Her words, or a semblance thereof.

Two months in Namibia had been healing for Sara. She was good company again, alone and with

357

others. Sex (with me) didn't come into it. I didn't ask. She didn't offer. Just as well. I was sufficiently, if only intermittently catered for at my age. She had the beginnings of a tan. She was teaching maths and statistics in the university. She had even done a bit of travelling. She was still in mourning for the loss of Wales in her life, and even the loss of things English, as one would have gathered from her conversation. She was still in mourning for the loss of her brother. She knew that we knew that something had happened to him. I felt that she was strong enough again to discuss it.

Lenny had put her with the tomato packers in the tomato marquee. We were packing together one day.

"Your brother. What happened?"

"The only notice families had was an announcement in the media that UNPOPCONT had decreed that the chronically mentally ill constituted an unacceptable burden 'on the public purse'. Next thing, I received a note to the effect that he had been 'disposed of by appropriate means, with regret'. 'With regret'! Fuck it! Fuck them! 'With regret'. They just took him from his independent-living house. No questions asked. It is going on countrywide, Europwide, USA, Japan, China, everywhere where UNPOPCONT rules." Silence. We packed. There was nothing to say.

Then: "Perhaps it was for the best. For him. He was very unhappy most of the time. The medication was less and less effective. He had no friends. No boys or girls, men or women. No sex. Deluded and hallucinating. Voices and visions. Paranoia over all. I expect you know enough about all of that. Still, he was there. He was all my family, all that was left. Our parents long gone; I don't know if you knew. Went thankfully before the masquerade of that Last Day shit."

She had stopped packing and gave me a long sideways look, I suspect to check my reaction. I did wonder if she felt that somehow I was responsible for having started something which had run out of control and killed her brother. I don't regret not having the courage to ask. Eventually she said:

"It was like a centenary rehash of the 1940s but it has nothing to do with genetic purity this time. It is just about the money." Sara must have improved on her knowledge of early 20th century history since our time together in Berlin.

We carried on packing until the end of our shift.

On another occasion (where? lounge bar?), I asked her for news of our HELP commission colleagues. She had kept in touch with Sam while trying to wrap up her HELP research once HELP was banned. Sam had come to Manchester on legal business for her firm and stayed overnight with Sara. Sara smiled at some aspect of the memory. I waited.

"She was fine until we had a couple of drinks in the evening. She became quite angry. She started on about how you had fucked up her life. She didn't use those words, of course. She said she was mad about you way back at Oxford. She said something about both of you being rowers and both Jesus. You hardly noticed her and then you fell for her friend. She said she never quite got over that. Career success and a doting husband nevertheless. She ended in tears. It took a good few drinks more to settle her."

Or words to that effect. I was stunned by this revelation. The implications were momentous. If I had known at the time, would we have been together? Married? And all the rest? How different would our lives have been? In the end how much would it have mattered? In the end we are all dead.

Spywife, Sam's friend, must have had some notion all along and that possibly explains her lack of enthusiasm for my suggestion of a foursome dinner on renewing acquaintance with Sam. All those years ago.

I should have experienced some retrospective flattery; girls, women, had never come after me apart from Sara. Now there was a disappointed talented woman out there, a lifetime later, probably retired, blaming me for the life she feels she should have led but lost, because I failed to notice her silent devotion. I regretted intensely having enquired after the past.

There was nothing to say. For many moments the responsibility I assumed onto myself for a life perceived unfulfilled, was crushing. At the same time there was an element of disbelief; I had never remotely considered myself attractive to women. Except to Sara, and that beyond my understanding.

I said: "I was never anything much to look at. And even less now. I know that. What on earth did you see in me when you were a student and we played Russian roulette with sex in my office, and beyond?"

She said: "Your style. The way you spoke in lectures and tutorials. A little bit of theatre every time. And your voice. I found it very sexy. I don't understand why more women didn't. Or did they and you're not telling me?"

Once again, Inspector, I indulge myself with this account of these memories because they may be lost to me forever if I didn't record them here.

So. I had two women of the law in my life; sadly neglected Sam, and some lady Judge hearing my case and reading these confessional notes. Ah well.

....

Recalling later 2044

"Soutie! Jou vrou sit in die tronk. Your wife is in jail, man. Those FROGS have got her!"

361

Dear Inspector, that information, conveyed in a considerate whisper by Bles some weeks later, again in the lodge lounge bar, again changed everything. Bles had 'listened' in to Treaty chatter again. Spywife was in custody of some sort. The chatterers named the prisoner as my wife, using my name, the escaped traitor David Stern. Identity undoubted for Bles. Bles detected a distinct element of satisfaction expressed at this clever move, he informed me further. She was suspected of conspiracy to aiding a Treaty refugee; and Lack of Conviction in her own work.

What took them so long to make that discovery? Did you have any inkling, Inspector, that the Treaty communications were hackable? A demonstration of Treaty determination combined with incompetence. A demonstration also that I must return to London to provide whatever support I could, whatever the consequences for me. Perhaps that was the Treaty hope and intention? How could they possibly know that I was privy to their porous security?

Ladybird ladybird fly away home
Your house is on fire; your children are gone

'Soutie'? Actually a short form of 'Soutpiel', salty penis. A slightly perjorative term in Afrikaner culture for an Englishman in southern Africa, straddling the continents with his penis dipping into the salt water of the oceans between.

I had been discovering the wonderful colour in the Afrikaans language; idiomatic in a manner just not available in English. Pity. It is my pleasure, in your custody Inspector, to offer you this useless information.

....

Recalling 2045

My departure from Windhoek was delayed by a day because of the usual storms over Africa and Europe. It was raining icecaps they said. Spywife used to say that. She is likely to be proved right again: climate change will end it for all of us with rising seas overwhelming a baked earth. Except possibly for Apophis? And hasn't UNPOPCONT been magnificently successful in dealing with the Malthusian end-of-the-world nightmare of overpopulation? Job well done, Inspector. Climate change and wayward sky rocks to be dealt with next. No big deal after overpopulation, surely?

I was sorry to be leaving Namibia. I had begun to create a good enough new life for myself with old friends and new, and doing some real clinical good at last. But at the same time suffering guilt for the abandonment of Spywife, even on her orders. With Spywife a prisoner of the PADDAs, I simply could not stay away longer, whatever the

363

consequences of my return. Leaving my aspirational medical students was a major wrench. Earnest friends Jay and Lenny attempted dissuasion. There were even some tears (Sara). Oh Deah; more guilt. Bles Bezuidenhout was encouraging, again: "Jy sal jou gat sien, Soutie! Daai paddas moet gaan kak." ('Those frogs should go shit themselves'). The paradise years were over.

The turbulent air over Africa had caused some concern from the start. Nobody slept. Then we were in the centre of yet another climate change storm. Lightning that night was incessant and terrifying. The violence of conflicting air currents so afflicted our new thousand passenger metal tube that lockers sprang open, oxygen masks fell down unbidden, screams and cries here and there gave voice to distress, and then the unmistakable stench of vomit, urine and faeces offered further evidence of distress. We were not allowed out of our seats, obviously. There were times during our shuddering dance to the rhythm of the lightning, when I would not have been surprised to hear the captain announce that some essential component had detached itself from the aircraft. With obvious consequences. I was proud of the fact that I managed to retain control of all my sphincters even if at times it was a close run thing. It helped to keep imagining arriving back in England in the Spring, in that soft beauty so different from Namibia.

Oh, to be in England
Now that April's there
And whoever wakes in England
Will smell vomit in the air

With apologies to the memory of Robert Browning

You will know of course, Inspector, that I gained a new sense of my importance in the Treaty world on arrival at Thames Estuary. The crew had achieved a safe landing much applauded by the passengers. The aircraft stopped some distance from the terminal; the captain apologised for some slight further delay; a fleet of official-looking cars raced up and parked all around the aircraft; a shiver of alarm spread through the passengers – there must be a terrorist among us; stairs were pushed up; uniformed PADDAs ran in and up to my row, leaning across my fellow travellers to handcuff me where I sat in my window seat; these travellers were ushered out of their seats; I was hoiked out of mine. Quite without need. It was not the case that I had any available route of escape. But I was the 'terrorist'. Passengers leaned away from me and my extraction party as we progressed down the aisle to the door. Perhaps some even suspected me of being responsible for the turbulence? In a way I was grateful to be forced to leave those poor wretches to their stench.

365

We sat in the official PADDA cars without moving while the aircraft with its malodorous traumatised cargo moved on to its gate at the terminal. I had issued repeated and vociferous protests to the effect that the actions of my captors were illegal: I was a Namibian citizen; this could become an international incident and a case for the International Court in the Hague. Stony silence. Except one PADDA even giggled. Eventually a Dcab landed in the spot vacated by the aircraft. As we glided over London and on somewhere into the countryside, it was obvious that all roads were once again in gridlock. I remained handcuffed, this time to the drone structure itself. I felt flattered that the possibility of my escape from a thousand feet up should cause so much apprehension. At least I didn't have to pay for the drone this time. I was the guest of UNPOPCONT. Nice.

Thus the ignominious end to my white knight escapade to rescue Spywife. If your reports to me are truthful, Inspector, my return has probably reduced the degree of oppression exercised on her; there is nothing more for her to reveal. I am here, and at the mercy of the Treaty.

"We went fishing, with your wife's custody as bait. Great bait! We reckoned that the news of her stay with us would reach you one way or another. We were taking a chance on the state of your affection. And here's our fish. It could be a good while before we know your fate." My Inspector makes no comment on my healthy Namibian tan, but then he had never seen me without one.

Ding Dong Bell
Pussy's in the well
Who put her in?
Little Johnny Flynn
Who pulled her out?
Little Tommy Stout

Except that Tommy/I didn't quite. Not nice.

. . . .

One of my four evangelists delivered a document in a very official envelope, sealed and stamped with a Justice Department logo. I have been sentenced at last. I have lived with the verdict of guilty of treason for so many weeks now. I had made my peace with the prospect of a death sentence. That is the traditional expectation for that verdict, isn't it? But my judge came up with something ingenious and counterintuitive and cunning. I am sentenced to life. Not imprisonment. Just life as it always was, with all its traditional freedoms: home, family, mobility, facilities. Here comes the 'But…". No state support of any kind. No employment, no pension, no medical care under any circumstances, and no 70th birthday End-Day Party. I am now 67. If I make 70, I will be allowed to live on until death by natural causes, just like the Lifers and the Exempteds but without any medical care of any kind irrespective of suffering. She (the judge) flattered me by describing my incendiary threat to the established international order and UNPOPCONT. I had engaged in subversive activity which could have led to untold social disorder, chaos, and the financial collapse of many nations. The disgrace so much the greater in the light of my previous great reputation.

On the other hand, the judge was grateful on behalf of the Treaty, that through my prison journal I had alerted the authorities to the fact that ComCam was hackable. ComCam security has been improved appropriately.

My punishment must serve to demonstrate to all, the consequences of disrupting the current and enduring and democratic arrangements whereby life expectancy is limited for all, for the sake of saving the planet and ourselves, for the better but shorter life we have. I was to be taught a lesson furthermore for showing disrespect to the memory of Malthus, Bentham and the others. I was to endure the rest of my life as if I was alive in the Previous Days, with the world in penury, crippled by the financial cost of caring for the diseases of the aged. If I was to end up demented, cancerous, starving, and homeless, then that would serve as an appropriate lesson as to what would await most of the world but for UNPOPCONT.

Not the expected death sentence for treason but a life sentence of quite possibly the very unpleasant kind I had campaigned against. Let the sentence fit the crime. And on and on. Clichéd reference about being careful of what we wish for, and so on, completely missing the point of my misbehaviour.

No news of my release date. Inspector X will come in triumph for a final winding up visit, I have been told. Perhaps he will reveal his identity, but that would not serve any particular purpose except to satisfy natural curiosity. He will collect my last notes for the court archive as part of the total case notes. The writing has helped fill some of the endless days. *Tick tock.* To be buried somewhere in a basement box file. No matter. Purpose served. Or not. My Inspector X had said that my notes could assist the court in dealing with my plea in mitigation. I will never know what effect my notes had.

Hickory dickory dock
The mouse ran up the clock
The clock struck one
The mouse ran down
Hickory dickory dock

Tick tock through the endless days

"So! Professor! Clever sentencing, don't you think? Cunning judge. Personally, I would have had you done away with, as is current practice for treason.

I got the impression Judge was leaning heavily to leniency. Got the impression she was fond of you in some strange way. One time I was in her office when she had been reading some of your notes and she was in bits. Must have been tears of anger, I imagine. Women are definitely too emotional for this job, really. For most jobs that men do." Quiet moment while he arranges his files. The judge cried over my notes? What is going on here? My Inspector must be winding me up.

He still wears his lapel ComCam, perhaps in case I attack him. Help will come running without a word from him. Maybe he wears it to taunt me as to what I once had myself. A ComCam brings many privileges with it. And the possibility of a sniper's bullet. Our Inspector is an example to us all for his bravery.

"I shall miss you and our chats. I learned a lot. Mainly horseshit but briefly entertaining. You may have had good intentions, but I doubt that I will ever quite understand how you of all people could betray everything that works for our continued survival. You, of all people. You helped make it work! Strange, really. Whatever made you think that HELP could do the job of UNPOPCONT? Orders have gone out to all Treaty states that you are to be refused medical care of any kind, anywhere. In any event, your passport remains with us, permanently." His arms raised in a gesture of feigned helplessness.

"Anyway. That's it. I have established that there is no need for confiscation of your scribbles after all. Much academic garbage but essentially harmless. Not very complimentary, to me especially. Certainly not flattering for UNPOPCONT. Partly your creation! Amazing. Ultimately, just pathetic. Pathetic sad sex confessions. Pathetic pedantry. And you are a real pain-in-the-arse pedant, with the moral compass of a randy rabbit and sanctimonious with it." Thus, a compliment at last from the Inspector. A treasured small pleasure in my disgrace. He extracts my pile of writing and passes it to me, letting go at arm's length as if the pile was toxic. Have I described this event already somewhere? Can't remember.

"Don't even think of putting this about, in any form whatsoever. You'll just find yourself back inside here, forever. Incorporated in your terms of release. And your ComCam licence has been revoked, permanently. No surprise. A nice touch I thought, is the fine for damage to government property – your chip discarded in Germany. Serves you bloody right. So! Any last comments, questions etcetera? Professor? Sorry, Sir Professor".

He just couldn't resist the temptation to be offensive. Quaint.

What now follows is what I have written for myself. I have passed beyond the boundary of any professional interest the Inspector may have had in me.

I said: "You asked about regrets recently. My only regret is allowing my bloated ego to lead me into the nightmare of UNPOPCONT as it now operates. And which led me into the tender care of low level operatives like you. Expensively trained apes. I never wanted to do away with UNPOPCONT. I just wanted it to work differently. And where is my wife?"

The Inspector reminds me with the theatrical forebearance of having issued a multitude of previous reminders, that there is no such thing as a 'differently' and that vast trials of 'differently' had all failed the numbers test. He implied the perceived helplessness of HELP. As on so many occasions in the past, I ask him his name. As expected, he declines my invitation.

"Don't be ridiculous! Official Secrets Act and all that. People who have the courage to do our job are vulnerable to all kinds of attack. You should know that; your wife certainly does."

My eyebrows question this unexpected reference.

"I've known your wife for years. She was one of my bosses when we were both in Surveillance. She was retired early if I remember, for Lack of Conviction. Looks like you both have a problem in the conviction department. Too bad. She was good, by the way! Taught me most of what I had to know in that job. You will get nothing out of her. 'Official

Secrets' works for life. That you obviously didn't know of our professional association proves that point, doesn't it?"

"She retired because she reached compulsory retirement age!" I half-shouted back. He suggested I extract the truth from her, now that we are about to be re-united. Retirement age rules were suspended for the Department of Internal Security. She was fired; I had better believe it. His arrogant air hints that he could be one of the Exempted as he certainly could not have afforded the asking price to be a Lifer. There is no way of confirming this possibility, and the knowledge would not do me any good. He was waiting, gazing away from me as if trying to decide whether to leave or stay. Then from nowhere:

"You never had children. Could you have had children and decided not to?"

"Excuse me. That is surely none of your business whatever my perceived misdemeanours!" I was emboldened by a court judgment delivered and presumably unalterable; I no longer had any incentive for excessive politeness. He was quiet for a bit, and then:

"We couldn't have children. I think you are a very selfish person. I think that explains your criminality, your rudeness and your lack of respect for your betters. There are souls out there waiting to be given human form but you wouldn't do it. And your posh wife, I suppose. My wife was desperate for a baby but it couldn't happen. She found consolation in food. I do become curious about other people who are childless. And jealous, I must confess, of those who have children without seeming effort."

It was as if the jailer-prisoner relationship had broken and in this last harmless conversation I had become his confessor. I was astonished and alarmed. I had no training for this role except as for HELP requirements. It remained the case that our lack of progeny was a matter for ourselves.

I was embarrassed by the silence: "It has always been a curious thing for me, this yearning in many young women. And men for that matter. For a baby. Why just a baby? I have never heard anyone desperate for a raging sixteen years old acne-ridden young man shouting abuse at his parents, stealing their money and wrecking their furniture. Too many people want a human pet and are disappointed when it grows into an ungrateful adult insisting repeatedly that it did not ask to be born. And how many parents in mindless procreation anticipate the despair which will come to dog the lives of so many of their offspring, for so many different reasons? And pertinent to this discussion, are you convinced that the End Day hype is so successful as to save all candidates from some of that despair? Better to get a dog, I think. Dogs make better pets than do children. And if you persist to insist, remember that many people believe that animals have souls."

"Some speech! You have been alone too long. If more people thought like you, we wouldn't have a population problem and you wouldn't be my prisoner. On the other hand we may have been overrun by dogs." Surprising big sigh, as if canine overpopulation would then have been his problem.

I said: "You were the one who asked, poking right into a subject of no concern to you. If you get a dog, I will consider my speech successful. You would perhaps do me the kindness of keeping me informed?"

Or words to that effect. I feared I had said too much without providing any consolation. He sat in silence for a long while, nodding slowly, as I remember. It occurred to me that he may have been dealing with some regrets of his own.

Hush a bye baby, on the tree top
When the wind blows the cradle will rock
When the bow breaks the cradle will fall
Down will come baby, cradle and all

I said: "There is a short poem about regrets in this stuff I've been writing. I thought it was rather good. Have you any way of finding out who wrote it? As a favour."

He said: "I saw it. Didn't mean anything to me. I can't be doing with that stuff. Poetry is for ponces. People not coming out with what they want to say but making a mystery out of it all so that you are meant not to understand quite what the hell is going on."

I decided my Inspector did not much like poetry. Or me. I wondered what he thought of the rhymes. He never said. Yes and no? I now regret that I never asked.

He sighed again and gathered himself stooped-erect with slow deliberation. Inspector X is at the door. Here came the question on leaving. Classical interrogation technique, I think.

"Where have you stashed the Letheon? I am directed to retrieve any quantity you still have. Same terms of release. If you are found to be hiding Letheon … back in here, for good." Bony index finger jabbing towards the floor. Normal relations resumed. My turn to remind him that Surveillance surely must have done a professional job on my house, garden, university office, car, extending to homes of friends and distant family. No Letheon?

Hard look from the Inspector, with nodding. Nodding not with assent but as a warning that they were on to me. And he was gone.

Fee Fi Fo Fum
I smell the blood of an Englishman
Be he alive or be he dead
I will grind his bones to make my bread

High calcium diet. Nice.

....

Notes for myself. Still had to nag for paper and pen.

After that episode (how long after?) my keepers opened my door one afternoon and called out "Visitor!" Jolly Professor Sir Geoffrey G, still athletic and exuding good fortune. Still with the waistcoat, now mauve. ComCam in the waistcoat for all to see. Still with the goatee, now grey-flecked. Clearly an academic eminence.

"How *are* you, David? It's so good to see you after such a long time." (Sniffing the air) "Bit muggy in here, isn't it?"

"I am meant not to know where I am, so no windows. Ventilation is not always appropriate to the season or the occasion. For some reason a bad smell is suddenly overwhelming, as you came in the door. The ventilation can't cope, it is that bad. You noticed?"

"Now, now. No reason to be catty. I asked to see you, to congratulate you. Came all the way from New York. Had to jump through a dozen hoops to get this visit fixed. Life beats death, don't you agree? You know. I'm referring to your sentence!" An American voice, also gloating, quoting something similar, floated back into my awareness all the way from Berlin and so many years ago.

"If that is the case Geoffrey, if 'life beats death', why are you killing on command at 70?"

"Because you told us to, old chap! Remember? And how right you were. Our saviour of

377

the civilized world. That's what you are, no less. Come on! That's also why I'm here to congratulate you. I would have thought you would receive me with better grace."

"I'm sorry Geoffrey. This has been sprung on me and I have not had time to rehearse my grace. I fail to see why I should act your Tuesday's Child. Now why don't you just fuck off and go figure some stats that work for humanity rather than against."

He looked disappointed rather than offended but I shut him up long enough to get in a question:

"Where am I? This place, where is it? Whatever transport you took, you must have known roughly where you were going?"

"Not at all, old chap. I took nothing. I was brought. Driverless with smoky windows. Condition of agreeing to let me visit. No one up front to ask. And who is Tuesday's child? You are strange."

"Where is my wife? What has happened to her?"

"Not a clue, old chap. All I know is that she is in safe custody somewhere, for her own protection. Apparently necessary after the widespread provocation you caused. Before that, I paid a visit, just to see she was OK. You know. Shouldn't have left her on her own. You know. Cracking good looker, middle-aged and gagging for it. Someone had to help her out. Turns out it was me. Turns out we have a lot in common. One thing led to another. Sort of just happened. Sorted out the climate change problem together. Couldn't keep her out of PADDA's grip though. Not that influential. No hard feelings? Actually, I was doing you both a favour. Good while it lasted, I have to admit. Gorgeous creature even in middle age, and randy as hell. Finest fuck, ever. Can't beat that." Actually? Gorgeous? Yes, Spywife is gorgeous, and a killer even if from a distance, but you don't know that, you prick. Lucky Geoffrey.

The whole point of a revelation is that it should overwhelm, whether for minutes or a lifetime, otherwise it is not a revelation, merely information. I was overwhelmed. It was Geoffrey's turn to shut me up while I undertook a mental rampage through incredulity and guilt and just desserts and envy. Envious of the probability, if I was to believe his boast, that Geoffrey suffered no erectile dysfunction. And trying to imagine the physicality of a close association of Lady Spywife with a Geoffrey I considered as repellent as my Inspector. My imagination failed me. Finally, why should I believe the master of unreliable numbers? Finally, I chose to.

He said: "Talking of humanity, by the way; the fact that humanity continues in existence at all is entirely thanks to UNPOPCONT and the Treaty. Solved the organ donation problem too, you must know. Just remember that, the extent to which the Treaty gives new life to thousands. Why didn't you take credit for a massive achievement? Why did you go down that crazy side road with that sorry excuse of a scheme. What? HELP or something? You are such a puzzle David. Like that fellow tilting at windmills. Professorship gone. Now knighthood withdrawn. Did you even know? Everything gone. One good thing though. Life not gone. Lucky you! Release must surely come soon and you will have time enough to contemplate the error of your ways."

"That was not the 'humanity' to which I was referring" I said, carefully avoiding ending on a preposition, I'm sure.

"I know. I had a point to make and have made it. I leave you more in sorrow than in anger, but with my best wishes, old chap." Sanctimonious traitorous arsehole. Exactly how my Inspector regards me. Except that Geoffrey was probably not a pedant. And he hadn't finished.

"By the way. My network informs me that your judge was an old girlfriend from your privileged Oxford days. And after. How did you work that one? The old upper class network of your own, hey? Who rules Britain? Now we know. And Professor Sir David Stern gets to live, to fight another day!"

Another revelation. For the second time in half an hour some ground beneath me seemed to liquefy and my surroundings became unsteady. And then gradually solidified again while I could do nothing but maintain silence and some semblance of composure. Sam? Sam! Sam who must have been made judge and applied specially to take my case. Sam who managed to keep me alive and dressed up her verdict in language sufficient to disguise any hint of favouritism. Sam, who loved me all these years and I didn't know until Sara's report. Oh god.

He shuffled as if to go. I found my tongue. "Geoffrey. What do you know about asteroids? Especially asteroids on steroids?" He raised his eyebrows and shook his head to indicate that he did not consider there was any hope for me. He knocked on the door and waved as my keepers let him out. I was left to contemplate on the circumstances of a previous reference to Don Quixote. Sara.

Monday's child is fair of face
Tuesday's child is full of grace

....

Knighthood gone? Well, to hell with it. The honours system is a beserk anomaly in a modern democracy. I am a hypocrite; I certainly did not think like that when I was being honoured perfectly deservedly. On contemplation, a hypocrite twice, being a Fowler Fascist but only when it suits me.

Wednesday's child is full of woe

A few days after Geoffrey's visit, one of my keeper evangelists (Matthew, the Sword?) took a risk and brought his tablet with the news of the day. There smiling at me from the screen was a half-screen archive picture of Geoffrey, attached to his obituary. The keepers would have remembered Geoffrey's visit, my only visitor ever, apart from my Inspector. Geoffrey had been 'yet another victim of a sniper, not yet apprehended'. Seems there has been a rash of assassinations, not just of Lifers and the Exempted but of wearers of the ComCam. Of such jealousy are revolutions made. The obit was glowingly laudatory of his lifetime achievements but omitted any reference to his entertainments of Spywife. I reflected somewhat without charity that shooting was too good for him. Lucky Geoffrey.

It did occur to me that Geoffrey's demise came disturbingly soon after his visit to me. Is it possible that Spywife called in a favour? She could do that from 'custody', something less than actual prison. Certainly. She would surely have had 'phone privileges now that I am safely in PADDA hands. One call is all it takes. Spywife the mantis? Spywife the black widow spider? Wonderful thought. Did Spywife destroy Geoffrey after sex? Perhaps he went to visit her 'in custody' after seeing me. Perhaps to boast that he had seen me and confessed his conquest. Perhaps as a spy, she saw that as a fatal flaw in Geoffrey – too cocky to keep the secret of very much cock.

Fantasy? No matter. The fantasy sustains me in this place. I had one more nightmare recently: lost again and naked again, I wandered by mistake into

382

that animal auctioneering pit. Geoffrey G and Spywife were engaged in noisy and mutually satisfactory sex in a variety of increasingly athletic positions before a crowd cheering them on and placing bets as to how long they could carry on. The performers were naked of course except Geoffrey, in his mauve waistcoat. There was music, a trumpet 'voluntary' to provide rhythm for their fucking. The presiding auctioneer was Sam, Samantha the Jesus rower, the lawyer of our Famous Five, judge and jury for my treasons, who loved little me and I never knew; now also naked but without any embarrassment. She was using her gavel to beat time with the trumpets to the rhythm of copulation. Some in the crowd noted my intrusion and shouted out their discovery. Mocking jeers and pointing at me, distracted them from the enduring performance in the centre of the pit. Sam became enraged at my disruption of proceedings, shouting obscenities at me in between remarking repeatedly how it served me right. She waved to the genderless trumpeters in a high gallery. There were seven of them, dressed as white angels with huge wings. I didn't count them in my dream – I just knew somehow that there were seven. The third angel stopped playing, opened his/her fist to show me the stone held there before casting the stone at me. In its flight across the pit, the stone grew massively, catching fire on its flight in my direction, until it obliterated the scene and overwhelmed me. I did wake with a jolt this time, my reflex response to being struck by this huge fireball. Apophis had arrived.

As usual, it was some minutes before I was quite certain that it had indeed been a dream. A blessing; at least no roaring oven.

....

Everybody dies, some sooner than others. Some none too soon. My keepers whispered to me that people are abandoning their ComCams in great numbers and in great haste. Including our Inspector, don'cherknow? In spite of he almost certainly being an Exempted! Perk of his highness in the job. So! Not much point then in the heightened security for ComCam at GCHQ.

Ho hum. Piggy's bum.

....

2047

And there is little or nothing more to record than already stated in this account, which is just as well; my jolly keepers say they are struggling to find more paper and pens for me. Spywife was not to go on trial – merely sentenced to medically unsupported life and to be released with me 'sometime soon'. I remain apprehensive ahead of our reunion. She may not want that. I want it very much.

....

My keepers, my evangelists, have been teasing me. Quaint. Yesterday, when I complained that I hadn't had breakfast, they asked since when was I entitled to two breakfasts? They insisted I had had breakfast. They did bring my breakfast eventually. I hope this kind of behaviour doesn't form a pattern. If it happens again, I shall have to lodge an official complaint. Not that breakfast is such a big deal in this place but it does help to give shape to the day: a beginning, with lunch at the middle and supper sort of at the end. *Tick tock.* With my release date impending, none of this awkwardness will matter. All will be well.

....

Isn't that interesting? There was a moment, indeed many moments this morning when I simply could not remember my wife's name. Was that because I have coyly referred to her as 'Spywife' for far too long and possibly quite unnecessarily? I now have her name again. Sally! Sally. Now that I have written it I should not forget it. *Sally go round the*

385

stars. I do so look forward to our reunion, however imperfect. All is well.

....

Annals of Thanatology   31 May 2049

Reprinted below is a letter written by the late Professor Sir David Stern addressed to a member of staff in the Department for Population Control, with a request for publication on his death. This document has had no alteration by Annals' editors, and honours a request from the author, a revered past Editor-in-Chief, Founder of this Journal and founder of Thanatology as a necessary profession for its time. We, the Editors, have retained his earned titles.

The prison journal to which the author refers is to be found on the Black Web under his own name, accessible to those with particular IT skills, and then accessible to all who may have an interest.

As stated in our editorial, it is very likely that this will be the final edition of our Journal. The collapse of the profession has rendered continuing publication irrelevant.

Editor-in-Chief.

....

To the Department of Population Control and Inspector 'No-Name',

You are reading this because my wife and I are successfully and safely dead. Some kind person will have found this letter near our bodies and has passed it on to you as instructed on the envelope. A copy has been sent on to a prestigious professional journal, in the company of my prison writings. With good fortune, the editors will have the courage to publish it, on the Black Web if necessary, not as a benefit to science (there is none of that to be found here) but to reveal my final thoughts and motivations; my effort at exculpation. The editors are not implicated in any crime or conspiracy. My sentence failed to proscribe any post mortem publication.

I hope that my prison journal may achieve some limited circulation among those interested in these esoterics.

There is no doubt that my memory was beginning to fail while I was incarcerated and we were having our enjoyable discussions on the origins of my moral failure. In the two years since my release and sentenced 'to life', my memory failures became alarming and embarrassing, especially to my wife (of your long acquaintance, Inspector).

Here is my last acronym for the warehousing of memory: AIAO. All In, All Out. You won't find it in any warehousing magazine, but that would have been my fate. It was not much fun for my wife to find me in various states of undress, and frequently lost within yards of our home. This is a good day for me, hence this letter, supervised and probably much edited by your same long-suffering ex-colleague. It is addressed to you but intended for that larger audience, my colleagues and friends, whom I could not reach once imprisoned and sentenced to silence thereafter.

I questioned my wife about your mutual previous professional association. She recalled, among other things, that your limp was widely accepted as the consequence of a severe fracture of some lower limb bone, imperfectly healed, and in turn the result of a hasty and courageous escape from an upstairs interrogation room when a prisoner of the North Koreans. She assured me it was the result of a hasty and courageous exit from an upstairs room of assignation in Brighton, a secret she felt no longer obliged to keep once I was free.

So! (just to make you feel comfortable, Inspector). It was never my hope or intention that assisted dying should become compulsory dying, however much sense that would make in terms of health economics. I fear I did too good a job of publicising the figures demonstrating the cost of life beyond 70. These became an obsession for certain misanthropic politicians, local and international, paradise idealogues, fundamentalist soldiers in the Benthamite barmy army. Poor Jeremy, my Jeremy! He was fortunate to enjoy a decent death at 84, working until shortly before dying.

Assisted Dying guidelines became protocols and in turn legislation for compulsory dying and the murderous 'End Days'. The monster that is UNPOPCONT is an unfortunate example of the way in which the hallowed UN (rarely) goes too far, but is too frequently paralysed when there is an urgent need for intervention of some other kind. A small final pleasure for me is to perceive the progressive unravelling of the Treaty as Letheon traffickers profit to help folk help themselves and snipers threaten Lifers, Exempteds, and any sporters of ComCams. Miners and emigration will finish it off. Definitely, but too late for me to witness.

My 'culpability' was within professional bounds only and never political. Wags will say that everything is political. So it would seem, as we have come to this sorry pass. It just goes to show what a dangerous business is health economics. Up to the start of UNPOPCONT, the uptake of assisted dying through HELP and the Ante-mortem Contract was increasing impressively, contrary to the malevolent preachings of one ambitious colleague, no longer with us. All voluntary, for anyone who wanted it. Most did indeed want to avoid the bad things that happen after 70; all wanted a decent death. That alone was reducing national health and pension costs in Europe, Scandinavia, even China, and the US, in a very satisfactory manner, as I explained in my statement put before the Court. My final request is that you should remember me when UNPOPCONT is disbanded and compulsory dying is consigned to history. That will happen; my firm conviction. I hope that will not leave the Inspector bereft of his post-retirement career and its pointlessness.

My wife entertained me one day during our restricted recent existence, with an account of the end of Lord X: how he rose repeatedly in the Lords shouting and pointing to one or other colleague, all Exempteds, insisting they be executed for Lack of Conviction, until he was finally banned when the joke palled, and confined to one of the residential retreats for the Exempteds. There he died, very recently, shouting to the end for more executions. Everybody dies.

Now, celestial events beyond all control may deliver you and UNPOPCONT from the threat of redundancy. Remember Harry, the amateur astronomer and asteroid obsessive in my prison memoir? And Dr Robert Jones of 'B612'? And sad Doc Cassie in Namibia? 'Apo' something (somewhere between

Apoptosis and Apotheosis) is now considered by many more astronomers to be on its way, and those who could have arranged to have it deflected years ago, didn't believe it. I believe it, in my ignorance, and have no wish to wait till 2050 to see if Harry and Robert Jones and Cassie were right. If they were, everybody will die. Sooner rather than later.

I could predict with greater certainty, an undignified and uncomfortable lingering end for me (if Harry and Co were wrong) such as suffered by my unfortunate father and goodness knows how many millions more. I am rapidly running out of brain and we have nearly exhausted our savings. My wife is emphatic that she does not relish the prospect of nursing a no-brain adult child in circumstances of humiliating poverty. I had the foresight to have retained a supply of Letheon for myself and wife, exactly as you suspected. It was hidden in the cistern of our antiquated toilet. It was in the plastic bulb. Clever wife cut it open and resealed it. Your PADDAs need more training, Inspector?

So you might say that the Letheon, with a little stretch of the imagination, was to be found in a chamber pot, or at least very much substituting for one. My valued student and later colleague, Professor Sara, is safely away and doing good work in what we used to call the Third World. Latest news from Namibia is that she is helping a Welsh expat raise Damara sheep in the north of the country.

So. We have had a tender time together for two years, Sally and I, making do with the little we have and ignoring past indiscretions. Some friends have remained loyal and supportive even to the extent of frequent invitations to dinner and occasional donations of medications for our occasional ailments. Others not so, fearful of contamination by association, quite understandably. I was terrified on release, as to how my wife might receive me, or not. My anti-Treaty campaign had ruined her career, cost her the 'Lady' designation, and the loss of most of her friends. She stood very still as I approached, all tentative and fearful. Her hair was all grey but elegantly groomed. A case of 'white overnight' from distress? Or from the passage of time? She had gone from slightly podgy as I remembered from when last seen, to something less, not quite scrawny. Still stunningly beautiful, an older version of the Vision that slew me nearly a lifetime ago in Christ Church Meadow. The sign for me of good portent was the fact that she was watching me all the time, not looking away in disgust or distaste. After some hesitation, she opened her arms. There was a lot of hugging and kissing. And tears, all mine, I have to confess. This time, no Sam.

And what of Sam, Judge Samantha, who loved me and I never knew it until reported by Sara? Clever enough to save our lives while pretending to pass a creatively cruel sentence fit for Treaty traitors. Retired soon after our trial, and gone. Our residual friends were not able to trace her on our behalf – we had not the means ourselves. She had performed the greatest good for only two people and then vanished. Jeremy Bentham may not have approved. I don't give a shit. I am past caring about all that stuff.

It is our wish to be buried together on a section of the Railway Cemetery halfway between London and Bristol. We have paid for this burial with the last of our funds. No ceremony but also no common criminals' pit. We are aware that no inflammatory epitaphs are allowed which may give succour to like-minded Treaty rebels. We have chosen anonymous standing stones, one for each, our own fraction of a Stonehenge.

So! (for the last time). You are reading this because I have achieved my intention and that which was always my hope for others: Sally and I had a decent death when it suited us.

Final irony: we two deserve 'Saviour' certificates, and 'Saviour' crests on our standing stones. We will have ended our lives before the 70 years deadline, and before becoming a burden on the national purse. We will have cost the health service not a brass razoo.

Everybody dies. These days, too often too soon. So it goes.

Sally go round the stars
Sally go round the moon
Sally go round the chamber pot
On a Saturday afternoon

Twinkle twinkle little star ?............

David Stern 2048

Printed in Great Britain
by Amazon

36027528R00231